KHELBEN

*Dwell not on your past, child. Gain the knowledge
to serve us over centuries.
Unto you we impart three truths, seven secrets,
nine soulnames, and thirteen omens.*

The thief's attention returned overhead when Kemarn
began casting a spell. From his robes, he drew a red, fist-
sized globe, which glowed for a moment then blinked from
existence. The tower's young defenders yelled. A red haze
grew around the shattered gate and the two figures there.
Raegar shuddered at the writhing mists filled with teeth,
eyes, and grasping claws—a nishruu. The halfling used his
wand quickly, but its purplish ray melted into the nishruu's
growing scarlet mists, its claws and teeth happily pulling
the magic apart and into itself. The eater-of-magic engulfed
Khelben and his apprentice, swiftly wrenching magic and
life from them. The stunned archmage grunted, and his
young aide screamed in pain under the assault, as the monster ripped magic from their minds and bodies.

IMMORTAL?

FORGOTTEN REALMS®

THE WIZARDS

FORGOTTEN REALMS®

THE
WIZARDS

BLACKSTAFF

steven e. schend

The Wizards
BLACKSTAFF

Published by Wizards of the Coast, Inc. FORGOTTEN REALMS, WIZARDS OF THE COAST, and their respective logos are trademarks of Wizards of the Coast, Inc., in the U.S.A. and other countries.

Printed in the U.S.A.

Cover art by Duane O. Myers
First Printing: July 2006
Library of Congress Catalog Card Number: 2005935518

9 8 7 6 5 4 3 2

ISBN-10: 0-7869-4016-6
ISBN-13: 978-0-7869-4016-5
620-95544740-001-EN

U.S., CANADA,
ASIA, PACIFIC, & LATIN AMERICA
Wizards of the Coast, Inc.
P.O. Box 707
Renton, WA 98057-0707
+1-800-324-6496

EUROPEAN HEADQUARTERS
Hasbro UK Ltd
Caswell Way
Newport, Gwent NP9 0YH
GREAT BRITAIN
Save this address for your records.

Visit our web site at www.wizards.com

TO MY PARENTS, RICHARD AND LINDA,

for making me the author they always knew I'd be,
even when I didn't believe it myself.

ACKNOWLEDGMENTS

As it is in the Realms, no one person or work stands
alone without dozens of connections to other people and
other stories.

Many thanks go out to those who helped pave the
path to this novel. The foundations are built on the
works of L. Frank Baum, Edgar Rice Burroughs,
Robert E. Howard, Stan Lee, and Jack Kirby. I'd not
have finished this book without the moral support of
Eric Boyd, George Krashos, Bryon Wischstadt, and
"the guys in the Shire."

Still, my greatest appreciation is saved for my editors,
Phil Athans and Peter Archer
(thanks for your keen editorial eyes and hands on this,
as well as taking the gamble on my first novel),
and my mentors, Jeff Grubb and Ed Greenwood
(thanks for bringing me into the Realms and sharing
your knowledge and your friendship).

PROLOGUE

Feast of the Moon, the Year of True Names
(464 DR)

"Get back here, you malevolent windbag!"

The wizard was dark in demeanor, garb, and action. He snarled out an incantation, and his arms erupted with orange energy.

His colossal spell-arms seized the creature by its tail and yanked it hard away from its prey—a wide-eyed elf child. The mage then whipped his arms downward as if he were swinging a hammer. The green creature in his spell's grasp smacked against an outcrop of rock, popping many eyes along its length with each impact. The wizard could tell the phaerimm was in pain and angry by the high-pitched wind whistling around it, and he repeated his actions to disrupt any spells it tried to cast. He felt the creature collapse and stop its struggles, its body broken with bones jutting out through its sickly green skin.

The man kept his focus on his spell but yelled to be heard over the wind, "Child, come here!"

The small elf girl only shook with terror, unaware she was safe for the moment.

He visualized his hands wringing the creature out like a dishrag, and a harsh whistle on the winds were the phaerimm's final screams.

Phaerimm, to him, were the ugliest creatures ever to hover over the lands of Faerûn, their strange conical forms ending around an ovoid head filled with barbed teeth and surrounded by four angular arms. Their tails ended in a poisonous barb, and they flew at all times unless prevented from doing so. The ugly creatures were usually imprisoned beneath the desert they formed with their malicious spells. Apparently, some had either found their way free or came from elsewhere, hoping to free more of their own.

The black-clad wizard grabbed the amulet around his neck. He ran toward the tiny child, but spoke low into the amulet. "Take this child to her mother and protect them both. Follow the elf woman's directions, if in doubt."

A short distance away, a massive figure made of steel and wood turned its head with a shriek of straining metal and began running. Its massive limbs and body seemed to ignore the problems of running in sand as it thundered forward. By the time the shield guardian had reached them, the wizard had scooped up the shivering child whose eyes saw nothing but her fears. He ignored the dimpled chin and steel-blue eyes they shared.

With one free hand, the mage cast a short spell and whispered to her, "Your fears are over, little girl. Find your courage, and know that our father and I will keep these monsters at bay. Now, let my servant bear you home, tiny Phaerl."

The girl blinked at the sound of her name, and her face filled with color again.

She asked, *"Osu?"* The young girl reached in relief to touch his full beard but reared back as she noticed his rounded ear. *"Ru n'tel'quess! N'osu!"*

"Aye, *d'nys*, I am no elf, but we share fathers, you and I." His waist-length black hair whipping around them both like a creature alive, the human mage untangled his amulet's chain and looped it around her small neck twice to ensure it would remain in place. "I hope to get to know you soon, but he and I need to stop these phaerimm. Now, this *aegiskeryn* will carry you and keep your family safe. Get home, and we shall follow when we can!" Despite the child's clinging to his robes, he placed her in the cradling arm of his shield guardian and yelled, "Go!"

The twelve-foot-tall construct stood, and the child gasped to find herself seven feet in the air and swiftly moving away.

The wizard turned and surveyed the battlefield once more, sweeping his long hair from his face yet again and cursing the blowing sand. The phaerimm he had slammed against the rocks remained there, dead. Despite the blowing dust, the setting sun illuminated the surroundings well. Another phaerimm lay dead on the field. A short distance to the east, three more phaerimm hovered around or near a humanoid that stood atop a low sand dune. The man held an axe in one hand, his other hand glowing with arcane energy. At his side, a dire wolf shimmered into existence between him and his foes.

"He uses Mother's axe," the human wizard muttered.

Nightmarish portents had led the man up from the lush forests to the south. His trust in his goddess led him into the wastes of the Sword of Anauroch. His dreams the past three nights were of teeth, green magic, and his father's aged face. The wizard had planned for battle. What he had not planned for was finding Arun leading a family of elves across the wastes to some western destination. The wizard faced many challenges, but he was not ready to face his father, the man who looked, pointed ears aside, like his twin brother.

What name his half-elf father bore then, the dark-clad human knew not. He only knew that it was definitely Arun Maerdrym of Myth Drannor—the Lupinaxe confirmed that. The wizard had only seen his father nine times since his seventh birthday, and each time together they had less to say to each other. He wondered if they would ever get another chance to speak, as the phaerimm engaged Arun and his dire wolf. The black-maned wizard winced as one phaerimm blasted Arun with boulders of steaming ice. He heard the half-elf mage scream in pain, and that moved the younger man into battle.

Slightly to the west, a cluster of figures fled into the wastes. The wizard put himself in harm's way to buy Arun's new wife and children time to escape with his shield guardian. He tightened his grip on his intricately carved gray ash staff and laughed mirthlessly. It looked as if Arun had yet to notice who he was, other than to acknowledge a much-needed helping hand.

One of the three phaerimm floated toward him, its flight unhindered by the whipping winds. The wizard swept his arm in a wide arc, umber crackles trailing his sleeve. The dune rose and became a wave of sand that engulfed the phaerimm. While the magic animating the sand ended on contact with the phaerimm's aura, the weight of it still buried the creative. The mage then engulfed the mound with balls of fire and bolts of lightning from his staff, turning the sand to raw, heavy glass. Despite its glass cage, the creature cast a wave of ice daggers . . . toward the empty air where the man had stood.

The wizard popped back from his subdimensional jaunt right next to the other man. "Hello, Father," he said flatly to the man at his side, as he unleashed a barrage of magical bolts at their foe. The ocean-colored bursts melted against the phaerimm's magical resistance. The taller man threw his axe at the creature, its head emitting a wolf's howl as the blade sliced into its target. A breath after contact, the axe disappeared before the phaerimm could grab it, reappearing in its master's hand.

"Calarel saw a reunion written in the stars today," the man said and grunted as he threw the axe again. "What are you doing here, son?"

The human wizard answered him by sweeping his staff behind Arun's knees as he threw himself backward as well. Both men fell down the descending slope of a sand dune, as a slash of razors whipped through the space where they previously stood. The half-elf screamed as he rolled. Both men coughed as sand threatened to flood their mouths, eyes, and noses.

Rolling backward to a kneeling position, Arun's son asked, "Any spells left?"

Arun rolled to his right, coughing up sand as he crouched and cradled his left arm. "Very few that will do much good, like walls for temporary shelters. Most of my spells sped us across the desert and protected us from the elements. Besides, it takes longer to cast with only one hand." Arun turned, revealing his blood-covered left forearm, its bones obviously broken.

"Use Petrylloc's Gambit!" the human yelled.

The half-elf looked confused, but he started casting after his son began his own spell. The largest phaerimm loomed over the top of the sand dune. Its toothy maw and strange elongated arms lashed out at them, trying physical attacks for a change over its spells.

The human wizard watched his spell take effect, the outline of an iron wall appearing beside and behind the creature. The massive wall fell onto the monster's midsection with a wet crunch, the phaerimm screaming its airy whistle. Arun, for his part, cast a spell on his axe, picked it up, and threw the weapon into the throat of the phaerimm as it screamed. He dived to one side and covered his head. A breath later, the phaerimm exploded, fire shooting out of its mouth then rupturing its entire form.

The human asked, "Why didn't you cast your wall spell to fall on it?"

"Because I had no idea what you said, son," Arun sighed as his soot- and gore-stained axe returned to his hand in a shimmer of magic. "You forget—not everyone had your teachers. You need to—watch out!"

Arun's son turned, too late. The phaerimm he assumed

was trapped in glass had floated silently behind them, and all the wizard's spell mantles failed. The phaerimm's barb gored through his defenses, lodging its poisonous stinger into his lower back. Within a breath, he felt his entire body go numb and float up off the sands. He bobbed helplessly in the air as the phaerimm grabbed his torso and his left arm, then yanked hard. The man screamed as his shoulder ripped out of place. He didn't feel bones snap, but his left arm hung limp and useless.

Arun picked up his son's fallen staff, and howled a command word: *"Arkatid!"* The phaerimm disappeared for a moment beneath a blast of white. When the effect ended, an icy sheen coated the phaerimm. Arun barked out: *"Suralam!"* and a massive energy axe head formed on the staff. He swung this down, and the axe leeched into the phaerimm's form and utterly disintegrated its body.

"Thank the gods you still have the Duskstaff of Sarael, son!" Arun reached up and grabbed his son's belt to pull him closer. He said, *"Ruthais,"* and a sphere of translucent energy appeared around them. The two men floated within the sphere as it rolled down the eastern side of the dune and away from the last phaerimm. Both Arun and his son were happy to draw the phaerimm even farther away from the fleeing elves. "Why didn't you use the wrack-blade before?"

The man was still floating in mid-air, but he was starting to move his head and his unbroken arm. ". . . too few charges . . . too many foes . . ." His eyes widened with fear as he looked over his father's shoulder.

Outside their shimmering sphere stood a man in a heavy black leather cloak, every inch of his skin hidden from the sun's touch. The man noticed them as their globe settled into the soft sand no more than ten paces away from him. His spells still smoked in the sands beside him, and headless bodies littered the ground surrounding the crater, an oily smoke flowing from them into the pit. The black-cloaked one locked eyes with the floating mage, and his smile flashed his fangs.

Both Arun and son whispered, "Palron Kaeth," and they paled with fury, pain, and fear.

From the crater the man had just blasted rose three more phaerimm, all much larger than those they had previously fought.

"How fortuitous," the vampire laughed, his voice sounding tinny to them through the sphere, "that the son and the father should be sacrifices to my plans just as their precious mother and wife was decades ago. Your blood ought to allow us to shatter the Sharnwall completely . . . assuming I don't get too thirsty. Still, I suppose I could feed on your pitiful relations, eh, *Gohlkiir of Cormanthor?* Or should I continue culling the ranks of your Harpers in Twilight?" His hand gestured toward the headless bodies behind him.

"We shall ever stand against you and your corrupt Prefects, Kaeth!" Arun howled at him.

The vampire laughed and mocked, "At least your son learned composure from his mother. You could learn something from his reserved nature, Arun."

The setting sun no longer between the dunes, the vampire threw back his hood, exposing his bald head and black sigils tattooed on his cheek and neck. He turned to the phaerimm rising from the pit and spoke the strange whispering winds of the creatures' speech. The last survivor floated down into the steep dell, and the four phaerimm took positions surrounding the sphere.

Arun gripped his staff tightly and leveled its head toward Palron Kaeth, but his son put his hand on his shoulder. "No, Father." He touched the staff, said: *"Erarla,"* and the sphere darkened to black, preventing either set of foes a view of the other. Inside the sphere, runes along the staff glowed blue, providing the pair some light. The Nameless One asked, "Any teleports left in you, Father? I'm out."

"No. Use the staff to get yourself to safety. Inform our friends of the threat."

"No, Father. We're down to one option and you know it. There's only one way to make him pay for murdering

Mother and those Harpers . . . and it should prevent these other problems from spreading as well. Unfortunately, each of us lacks the two arms to do it."

Both men looked into each other's eyes and nodded. The human finally settled back down onto the sphere as his system fought back against the phaerimm poison.

"No matter what you believed these fifty years, I am proud of you, my son." Arun handed his son the Duskstaff as spells began to crack, splash, and thunder at the outer surface of the sphere. "I only wish we could have found your name in this lifetime."

The human wizard nodded, blinking away tears and setting a grim resolve on his face. He whispered, "Sweet Lady of Mysteries, let this not be in vain."

He seated the staff hard against the sphere's bottom, hooking one foot around it to brace it. He leaned against it, pulling as hard as he could with his uninjured arm to snap it over his back and shoulders.

Arun grabbed the Lupinaxe, the blade worked to resemble the profile of a snarling wolf's head. He smiled grimly as he hefted it, saying only, "For Arielimnda and the Harpers in Twilight, my son."

Arun swung the axe at the staff's bending point as his nameless son replied, "Indeed."

Neither man heard the furious explosion that destroyed them instants before turning the surrounding desert dell into a glassy crater.

❧ ❧ ❧ ❧ ❧

Awaken, Son of Arun. Know that you are Chosen.
Mother? Is that you?
In a way, child, though not of your first body.
Where am I?
Between life and death. Are you prepared to serve me?
Who are you?
Our mysteries have touched you. Our name you revere. Your prayers are answered.

Surrounding white, no sense of self, only the voice, soft

yet awesome, a whisper to drown out the thunder of a beating heart.

Your blood's sacrifices are powerful and they go not unnoted. Know that you are Chosen.

Floating, suspended, no pain, no sense of touch, but feeling stronger with each loud heartbeat.

Your tasks are many, so shall be your gifts.

Blue and silver whirls around, surrounding, filling every sense beyond their limits, feeling a tingling that cannot be ignored, shut out, or denied, a tingling that grows to burning.

Our fires do not consume but convert. Accept them. Let the silver become you and you become silver.

The man remembers the silver-white hair of his *u'osu*, the disapproving stare of an otherwise-noble elf's disdain.

Dwell not on your past, child. Gain the knowledge to serve us over centuries. Unto you we impart three truths, seven secrets, nine soulnames, and thirteen omens.

The pain subsided as the fires brought with them flashes of insight, and an old memory. "Stare into the firelight, Nameless One, and you shall see truths you hide from your own mind."

Mentor spoke our will that day. You shall aid the Weave Ourself. You are crucial to us, e'er moreso than these twelve-score you see.

The man saw faces of strangers . . . a white-bearded wizard with a red streak of hair at his lower lip . . . a dark-skinned man with a dead right eye and a gold brand on his right temple . . . a toothless old woman awash in the filth of the gutters despite her rich robes . . . a black-haired man straining against chains, his elf lover tortured before him by a shorter man in a mask . . . a bald man with a green gem glinting where his left eye should be . . . and so many more. He struggled, wondering where all this came from.

Hear me, dutiful one. We are the Weave. We are the Mysteries. We are Mystra. Know that you are Chosen.

The man smiled and let the fires kindle and grow from cinders of hints to flames of awareness.

CHAPTER ONE

28 Uktar, the Year of Lightning Storms
(1374 DR)

"Hush, now . . . not a sound," she whispered.

The woman brushed a ginger-colored curl from her eyes, tucking it behind her slightly pointed ear. The only noises were the rustle of deadfall where a doe walked cautiously through the clearing and the tiny protesting groans of the bowstring as the woman readied an arrow.

Crashing noises startled both the doe and the hunter and both froze in horror.

"Tsarra, come see!" The boy's yell preceded him as he trammeled through the underbrush toward them. At the same time, the woman's bow sang and a whistle in the air was all that remained of her arrow. The doe leaped away from the clamor—too late. She fell dead, a white-fletched shaft piercing her heart.

"Tarik!" Another boy kneeled at the woman's side, but his face matched his flaming red hair. He jumped up and grabbed the far-shorter boy by the heavy cloak. "You nearly lost us our deer, fool!"

"Let him go, Lhoris. Close your eyes and breathe your bad humor out." The woman stood and placed a hand on his shoulder to calm his temper."Try to remember what an excitable boy you were at ten, before Danthra and I remind you of your first days in Blackstaff Tower," she added with a wink. Lhoris exhaled loudly, but held onto the smaller boy. She looked at him and asked, "Now, what is all the noise for, Tarik? At the very least, I need to teach you how to move more quietly in a forest, little Myratman."

The Tethyrian boy shrugged himself from Lhoris's grip, sticking his tongue out at the older boy. He looked up at Tsarra and beamed. "Chaid found it! Or it found him. Come see!" He pulled on her cloak, attempting to drag her in the direction from which he'd come.

Tsarra smiled, trying to remember how long it had been since she'd been so impulsive. She looked over at the fifteen-year-old Lhoris, who stomped and kicked at the fallen orange leaves. She worried about the young man from Fireshear and what lay at the root of his bitterness and anger. Until he was ready to talk, she could do little beyond hold her curiosity in check. Tsarra guided his talents in both sorcery and wizardry away from spells his moods could fuel too explosively.

"Lhoris, why don't you take that rope, set up a noose over that big branch, and get the deer ready for dressing, please? We'll be back in shortly. I think Tarik deserves the *fun* of doing that." Tsarra was glad to hear Lhoris snort in response. As she let Tarik drag her away, she added, "And no magic to haul that deer up, boy. You need to build a little muscle, before you become a living skeleton."

Tsarra allowed Tarik to pull her along to the next clearing a little to the south. The boy was happily intent on showing her the source of his excitement. He chattered as he forced his way through the underbrush, not making any attempts to slow down and look where he stepped.

"Chaid just sat there all night and this morning, just

like you taught him, but I got bored and Danthra was showing me herbs and how you chew on one leaf to stop a headache—boy she ate a lot of those!—and use another one to stop blood from flowing quick and there was this really fascinating seedcone, but that turned out to be a beetle of some kind I couldn't catch and Chaid started laughing and—"

Tsarra asked, "Warm enough, Tarik?" By the gods, the boy never paused for breath!

The Tethyrian nodded, and forged on with his report on what he had found in the forest. The child came from much warmer climes, and was spendng his first winter north of Zazesspur. Accordingly, he wore heavy wool robes and a cloak, even though Tsarra made do with her hunting leathers and a light travel cape. Tarik and his brother Chaid al Farid al Fuqani were both dusky-skinned Tethyrians with jet-black hair, and both were years yet from their first beards. While Tarik wore his straight hair in a small ponytail, Chaid's curls rivaled Tsarra's, though shorter. The only other difference between the twins were their eyes—Tarik's were a deep cobalt blue, while Chaid's eyes were a startling bronze color with flecks of the same cobalt blue.

Tsarra and Tarik finally broke through a bramble and into an open clearing. Tarik ran straightaway to his brother, who sat cross-legged at the center of the clearing, his back to them. Tsarra noticed Danthra the Dreamer picking burrs off of her woolen dress.

"I told you to wear something more appropriate for camping and hunting, Dreamer," she teased. Tsarra loved hunting in the Pellamcopse, the small woods east-northeast of the Northgate, but it had more than its share of briars.

"I would have been fine if Tarik didn't barrel through everything rather than move around it." Danthra was a railthin, delicate creature with long night-dark hair as straight as an arrow, a wan complexion, and a beaming smile that overpowered any who saw it. "I always regret joining you on these jaunts, even if it is a nice change of pace."

"How are you feeling this morning?" Tsarra asked in a

low voice as she kneeled by her friend, so as not to be overheard by the students. "No more visions I hope? Can you tell me what you saw that shook us both from sound sleep?"

"The images are mostly the same—three lightning bolts of blue, purple, and black; Khelben's sigil; a green glowing gem; and a Blackstaff shattering amid the full moon and a field of purple stars." Danthra whispered. "You were there too, screaming."

"As were you, last night," Tsarra said. "Weird stuff too. You said, 'An old secret and the Blackstaff shatters and seeds duties of old anew are sown by lightning and sorrow,' then passed out again."

"I'm just glad you heard it. I never remember that stuff."

Tsarra arched an eyebrow and shrugged. "Well, it makes no sense to me, but we'll tell Khelben when we get back."

Danthra said, "But Tsarra, aren't you—"

Tsarra put a finger to the young woman's lips and shook her head. "Your visions come true, and I've learned it's best not to worry about what you can't control. So let it go. You've nothing to apologize for. In fact, I should thank you for coming. What was I thinking, bringing six apprentices out on an overnight hunt?" She got up, crossing her eyes, which made her friend laugh.

"You were thinking you can train some of them to be rangers, like your father taught you? Give up, Tsarra. The only two of us with any skills outside of our books are Trehgan and the new girl," Danthra said, and she jumped as a brace of scarlet-feathered tarrants fell at her feet. Both women looked up to hear a low, mellow voice reply, *"One four times your elder should not be called 'girl,' human."*

Perched easily across a pair of stout tree limbs, Tsarra's newest student looked down at them. The copper skinned elf girl was not quite an adolescent, but she was already older than all of Tsarra's other students combined. Walaxyrvaan of the Wealdath's Elmanesse tribe apparently came north with a referral from Arilyn Moonblade and the master's nephew, Lord Danilo Thann. She had helped guard the caravan along the way north and had also tried—to no avail—to quell the exuberance of the al Fuqani brothers who traveled with her. Walaxyrvaan's name translated into "Lynx of Approaching Dusk," and she preferred to be called Lynx.

"Don't take offense, Lynx," Tsarra said. "And what a marvelous catch. Did you and Trehgan find any more?"

"The barbarian's got a brace of grouse as well. Not as good as your deer, but it's a light morning. He's not a bad hunter for a human, I'll give him that. Surprisingly quiet too, given how massive his feet are," she said in Elvish. *"Traya, meanwhile, would be useless on a hunt, even if she could do more than moon after Lhoris."*

"In Common, Lynx. Don't be rude. Where are they, anyway?"

"After his loud swearing loused our chances of catching some partridge, we found the angry one where you left him. Lhoris lacks the strength to haul up the doe. Trehgan's helping him, and Ginara has at least made herself useful picking late berries. Did the *ivaebhin* find what he was looking for?" Lynx did an effortless handstand as she talked, walking onto one tree limb and launching herself to land in a silent crouch at Tsarra's and Danthra's feet. Tsarra was amused that the elf girl referred to the quieter Fuqani brother as "boy filled with brightness."

"I'm about to find out." The three women walked toward the two boys as the sun came out from beneath the clouds, lighting up the forest glade in gold and scarlet splendor among the leaves. "Tarik, I'll need you to go with Danthra and Lynx. She and Trehgan will teach you how to dress the deer."

The ten-year-old stood up and perched his fists on his hips in defiance. "No. I won't do it. Our father didn't send us here to hunt deer in strange woods—that's *servant's* work."

"Be that as it may, my haughty little Tethyrian," Tsarra said, quickly winning the staring contest the boy had tried to start, "you are a servant of the Blackstaff and of me until you learn magic that proves otherwise. It is our will that you learn how to gut a deer this morning. Besides, if we don't fill the larder of Blackstaff Tower before winter comes, we'll be out here in chest-deep snows hunting rabbits. You'll be out here regardless, as you need to learn how to walk more quietly."

The boy stomped off in a huff, swiftly pursued by Lynx who playfully tossed a handful of leaves into the boy's face, encouraging him to chase her.

Danthra rolled her eyes and said, "Well, hurry along and don't leave all the worst work to us. We still need to break camp and return to the city before it gets much later."

"Aye. See you soon, Dreamer." Tsarra said, and she moved over toward the giggling boy who rolled in the fallen leaves, a fast-moving, sleek creature scampering around and atop him. As Tsarra neared them, the creature squeaked and fled inside Chaid's wide sleeve. That provoked a "Whoop!" from the boy, and Tsarra smiled as a bulge moved around beneath the wool, seeking a safe place to hide on his new friend.

"Chaid, it's wonderful to see you've found your familiar."

The boy looked up at her and beamed. Just as heavily garbed as his brother, Chaid was the opposite of his twin in most ways. Quiet and contemplative, he only spoke when necessary, perhaps because he rarely got a word in edgewise around Tarik. Chaid's remarkable bronze eyes stared at her—and a weasel's head popped from Chaid's shirt directly beneath his chin. Tsarra gasped—the weasel's fur matched Chaid's eyes perfectly.

"He's so happy to meet me, and you too. I think he likes your smell. Can I call him Brakar? That's the queen's coin of Darromar!" Chaid asked, coaxing the weasel out to snuggle in his arms.

"I don't know, Chaid. He's not a pet. You should only use a name he prefers to be called, in case he already has a name. If he doesn't provide one or ask for one, don't call him anything. After all, my tressym has yet to tell me his name after ten years of bonding, but he and I get along fine. Lady Laeral has taken to calling him Nameless for the sake of convenience, so if you need to talk to him, he doesn't seem to mind being called that."

Chaid brought the weasel up to his eyes and spoke to him. "Do you already have a name?" Even Tsarra needed no explanation when the weasel shook its head. "Would you like a name, so we can be friends?" Chaid asked, and the weasel chattered and bobbed his entire body. "Then I shall call you Brakar. I'm so glad to meet you, friend."

Chaid's eyes were rimmed with tears as Brakar jumped up onto Tsarra and began sniffing her.

Chaid said, "He likes the name, I think. It's like he's never had a name so it's a present to him. I'm feeling excited, but there's something more."

Tsarra said, "You're feeling his emotions too, through the link you now share. As time goes on and you learn more magic, that bond witll grow stronger. He's another living being, like you, that responded to a call by the Weave and nature to bond. That bond teaches each of you more with an expanded perspective on magic and life both."

"Well, I learned one thing already, teacher," Chaid said, smirking.

"What's that?"

"Tarik is jealous that I have something he doesn't and he wants a familiar too, now."

"Well, we can try another day."

"Tarik can't sit still for even one bell, let alone one day, listening to the call of the ritual."

"Well, on that note, let's go see how the others are faring at prepping our catches for transport back to the city. The sun's now fully above the horizon. We've got to hurry back."

CHAPTER TWO

28 Uktar, the Year of Lightning Storms
(1374 DR)

"Oh my . . ."

They had just turned onto Seaseye March, and Tsarra looked to see at what Danthra had gasped. She saw a man ducking his head and much of his shirtless torso into a rain barrel. He quickly whipped his body from the water, small ice shards obvious on the disturbed surface, and he growled as he shook his long hair and shoulders, spraying the area with water.

He was trim and muscular with a small tattoo Tsarra couldn't identify on his left shoulder. He ran his fingers through his hair, squeezing more water from it, and smiled a dazzling smile as he noticed Tsarra, Danthra, and Traya watching him. He winked, and Tsarra blushed. He was directly along their path, so they could hardly avoid him. As explanation, he shrugged and explained,

"Cheaper than a festhall or bath house."

"Isn't that cold?" Traya whispered. Danthra's and Tsarra's eyes both widened—Traya was often too shy to speak at all, let alone to strangers.

"No worse than on Auril's Blesstide." He winked at the girl.

Tsarra smiled, imagining the fit young man running naked through Waterdeep's streets the morning of the first frost to plunge into the ocean. *He's alluring, I'll grant him that,* Tsarra thought. The man pulled his hair back into a tight ponytail and stared at Tsarra. To her surprise, she didn't mind.

Tsarra only shook her head from her daydream when her familiar—one of the very few winged cats in Waterdeep—zoomed past her, yowling, "*Mistressfriend wantneed horseheadmale matebehappyfriend?*"

Even though she knew no one else understood him, she snarled back at him before addressing her students, "All right, all of you. Boys, help Trehgan with the deer."

In response, Tarik cupped his hands and cackled as a scarlet disk hovered in the air before him. "I can carry it myself with this!"

Trehgan, the wild-haired and strongly built man who had been carrying the carcass across his shoulders, shrugged it up and over, dropping it onto Tarik's floating disk.

Trehgan stretched his shoulders with a groan and griped, "Wish you'd thought of that a few miles ago, midget . . ." He playfully tousled the boy's hair to defuse any tempers.

Lhoris and Lynx bore the two braces of birds over their shoulders, and Traya carried a basket heaped with a wide variety of herbs. Chaid remained fascinated with his weasel familiar as it darted from one shoulder to another or perched on his head, excited at its first view of the City of Splendors.

The group, having just come up from the beaches, entered the city through the Westgate. They bypassed the northern gates and used the path to walk the sand and mud flats, their passage only slowed by the occasional fishing boat or a call from a guard on the wall above them. Tsarra always came back into the city that way to avoid a lot of hindering traffic. They were late, so they had to hurry back to the tower to not miss mornfeast. In the hustle and bustle of the morning crowds, by the time they had reached Julthoon Street, they'd forgotten the man in the alley.

That was too close, Raegar old son.

The man wiped off the last of the water and pulled his red shirt over his head. Raegar watched the eight apprentices of Blackstaff Tower turn off of Seaseye March. His impromptu act appeared to have worked, at least on the two older apprentices. Still, the suspicious looks the elf girl had given him and the large barbarian with them showed him he'd wandered too close. None of them noticed him following the night before as they headed off to Pellamcopse, nor did he think they'd heard him as he left them to return to the city before dawn.

For the past few tendays, he had watched the tower and its denizens. He'd avoided being noticed at all . . . until that morning. He expected the group to take Westwall Street around to Julthoon, but they cut down Seaseye, where he skulked with no place in which to hide. The impromptu morning ablutions in the rain barrel were the only thing Raegar could think of to make himself fit in there and not stand out as an obvious spy.

Raegar knew his looks could be a distraction, but he had a larger problem. They didn't know his name, but neither Danthra nor Tsarra Chaadren would forget him soon. And that made his job all the more troublesome.

As Tsarra, Danthra, and their six charges made their way down Calamastyr Lane, a number of acquaintances cried out to them from their windows or shops.

"Good hunting this morning, Tsarra!"

"Willing to sell a haunch? Or spare a bird or three?"

"Looks like the Blackstaff eats well tonight!"

The eight made their way through streets crowded with merchants and stalls. Their pace slowed due to the crush of people and their necessary wariness of pickpockets, until they reached Elvarren's Lane. From there, it was a quicker jog back to the dark stone walls surrounding their home. All of them touched their left palms onto the slim gate in the wall's northmost face. Their touches allowed them through the apprentice's gate, rather than using the main entrance on the Swords Street side of the walls. They all waved to their fellow apprentices who either walked the top of the walls or stood atop the tower high above on guard duty.

As they rounded the courtyard to enter the tower's main door, Tsarra gave her students their assignments. "Lynx, Lhoris, Tarik, and Trehgan, take the carcasses into the kitchens and begin the butchering. The rest of you can either help them and learn a useful skill or help the others with mornfeast. Tell the others that I'll be busy this morning, but I think I'll have time after highsun to speak with each of you on the progress of your studies. Then we'll all prepare a venison feast for everyone on our last night of kitchen duties. After tonight, we have no extra duties for a tenday, so—" Her next words were drowned out by the cheers of the brothers al Fuqani and Lhoris.

Danthra clapped a hand on her shoulder. "Let them be. All of us enjoy that shift when we only have our studies to attend to, instead of kitchen or guard duties. You and I should get ready for meeting with the Blackstaff soon. We have the ritual and that other matter to discuss." Danthra smiled, but her eyes were haunted and nervous.

Tsarra gripped her friend's trembling hand and asked, "What was the original reason for our meeting him today? Maresta is your teacher, so why me again?"

Danthra and Tsarra were the last to step into the tower, the junior apprentices racing in ahead of them. "I need you there to supervise as a senior apprentice, since Maresta's still abed with that bad cold. Besides, I'm trying a new spell, and I want you to be among the first to see it. Also, Master Arunsun wants a third party to choose the magical item to investigate, so be sure to bring one. Besides, why wouldn't I want my best friend there for support when under the Blackstaff's scrutiny?"

"Well, we'll both stand up better under Khelben's scrutiny after we clean up and change clothes. See you soon. Lower, not upper study, right?" Tsarra said and smiled when Danthra nodded.

The Dreamer turned and said, *"Tahakim,"* as she stepped on the lower step of the tower's central stairs. The young woman vanished, to no one's surprise.

Even after fifteen years as a resident, Blackstaff Tower continued to amaze Tsarra. From the outside, it looked to be a simple three-story stone tower, which is all it was—physically. Anyone trained at the tower soon learned that there were at least a dozen more sub-levels reachable only by magic. All areas linked to the central stairs, and they required magical passwords to shift a walker on the stairs to that level. While every student asked where exactly the sub-levels were, none of the senior apprentices, Master Blackstaff, or Mistress Laeral, would say more than, "That secret must be earned, youngling."

Tsarra spent more than a year trying to figure it out, and she guessed that the windows were no more than illusions projecting what was going on outside the tower. She could never determine if the added levels were in separate dimensions or just far away in other towers elsewhere in the Realms. It was nigh impossible to alter the outside or inside walls of the tower.

There were four command words Tsarra used most often while walking the stairs. *"Summath"* teleported her to one of the dormitory levels, the one assigned as her chambers and those of four other female students; *"Aradsol"* took her anywhere on the stairs to the roof; *"Vhuarm"* sent her down to the cellar where tunnels linked it to Piergeiron's palace and other places across the city; and *"Traeloth"* deposited her into the main entry chamber of the tower's ground floor. The three core levels of the tower could be reached simply by walking up or down the stairs.

Tsarra said, *"Summath,"* and her step took her to a landing off the stairwell. The teleports were always so smooth that someone not paying attention would scarcely believe they had shifted from the main tower. She moved around to her door and opened it, pulling her bow and quiver off as she shouldered the door open. She put her weapons on the bed across from the door, unbuckling her sword belt and laying it on the bed as well. She quickly unbuckled her leathers and stepped over toward her wardrobe.

She pulled out a shallow but wide ceramic basin from under the wardrobe, its bottom holding a mosaic of Sune. Tsarra shivered, thinking of the man's cold ablutions earlier. She was glad she'd made friends at the Firehair's temple, trading minor items for others easily made by her own hand. She grabbed her large pitcher from the windowsill and stood in the basin as she poured the water. The water, shockingly cold as it hit her feet, rose in a shimmering wave, warming as it rose and fell again, as comfortable as a summer shower. Tsarra stood in the basin, letting the water rain down on her two or three times before she felt clean. As she stepped off the basin, the water fell and steamed away.

Tsarra toweled her long hair but dried herself in the morning sunbeams and air. She stood before her wardrobe a while before choosing a simple shift of gray wool. She approached the bed and took up the bow and arrows, placing them carefully back in their places on hooks next to the wardrobe. Finally, she drew the scimitar from its sheath, and its silver sheen caught the morning light to dazzling effect. Mhaornathil—the only thing she'd inherited from her mother other than her elf blood—was a Rilifane-blessed scimitar that could cut ghosts as easily as flesh. Tsarra loved the blade almost as much as she hated undead, the bane of her existence since her father died by undead hands fifteen years before. Still, Tsarra knew she couldn't use the scimitar for the test. Danthra already knew a lot about the blade, and it wouldn't be a fair test of the spell. She snapped the weapon back into its sheath and hung it and the sword belt on their pegs above her headboard.

Tsarra approached her window to stand in the sunlight a moment and breathe in the fresh morning air. Within five breaths, she sensed her familiar coming, even though he didn't loop around the tower and land on the windowsill for a handful of moments. She loved the muffled rustle of his wings as he landed, as well as his purred greeting.

In its language, she said, *"Good hunt to you too, mighty one."*

Jet black in hue, the tressym stuck his head out, gesturing for a head scratch, his ravenlike wings ruffling slightly over his back. Tsarra obliged him, letting him rub his head solidly on her palm. She stopped a moment, staring into his mismatched eyes—one of deep blue, the other green—and smiled.

"Of course you're a good companion and a very good hunter," she said.

When the creature tensed to hop onto her shoulder, she held him back, smoothing his feathers and chucking him under the chin. In Common, rather than the purrs of tressymspeak, she said, "Not a chance until the smell of those chipmunks you ate fades from your breath. Now, go take a nap. I've got to work with Danthra for a while. Oh, and remember to leave Chaid's familiar alone until he gets used to you."

Nameless let out a trilling purr, and she said, "I don't care if he looks and smells like prey. He's not food, any more than you are." His trilling retort made Tsarra laugh as the tressym flapped his wings and headed out the nearest window, en route to the sunny top of the tower. Tsarra chuckled as she finished combing her hair with her fingers. Satisfied her auburn curls were under control with a white ribbon tying them back, she exited her room and descended the stairs. When leaving from the dormitories, the lack of a command word deposited the descender on stairs at the second level of the tower.

Alcoves and tiny shelves lit by permanent fey lights lined the walls along both sides of the winding staircase, revealing random books and knickknacks. Tsarra remembered her first tendays in Blackstaff Tower, as she spent her free time staring at all the magical items and artifacts seemingly left out unprotected. By the end of the first tenday, she'd learned that none of the items could be removed from the alcoves without command words, and the things changed so often one might never see the same twice within the same tenday. After her first year, Tsarra knew she had seen more than two hundred magical tomes and at least as many unknown items and artifacts littering the walls of the tower. She stopped counting and just accepted that Khelben Arunsun had more magical items within the tower than all the rest of the City of Splendors held within its walls.

In the short walk from her second-floor room down to the ground floor, she saw a pyramid of fifteen tiny silver frogs, the glistening black leather cover of *The Fanged Tome of Lykanthus Szar* with its four dragons' teeth clasps, a gnoll's skull carved from or transformed into green marble with eyes of scarlet flames, the golden crystal called Alaundo's Loop—forever turning in on itself in a twisted curl and hiding eternity in its depths—on a pillow of white velvet, a floating square blue-wax candle burning from each corner, and a clockwork cat whose buff rag tongue lent a shine to its mechanical paw as it cleaned itself with only the mildest of ticking sounds. She turned to her other side and started scanning those niches for objects she had never seen before, spotting a miniature throne with a small wax figure seated on it, a round book with a ring binding and solid silver covers, its runes identifying it as *The Annals Adamarus*, and a goblet made of glacial ice and set with rubies, its contents steaming hot.

"Choose one, Tsarra."

Tsarra started, and shook her head in frustration. Despite her better-than-average hearing, the half-elf had not heard the mage come down the stairs behind her. He stepped from the gloom of the upper stairs, reminding Tsarra why so many feared her master. He stood only a bit more than six feet in height, and his build was strong, but hardly threatening. His robes proclaimed him a wizard, and he carried his trademark staff of blackened wood at his side. His hair fell just past his shoulders, its jet blackness interrupted only by a silver-white wedge on the chin of his full beard. While normal and fully human in many ways, the Blackstaff cultivated an aura of power and mystery. There were very few he couldn't intimidate with a simple stare. For the moment, that stare was leveled at her.

He said, "I haven't got all—what is it, love?"

The look on his face changed instantly, and his eyes focused on something past her. Tsarra smiled as she tried to ignore Khelben's conversation with what appeared to be the wall. The Blackstaff and his wife Laeral shared a bond and could hear each other's words when they spoke the other's name. Khelben seemed distracted, but his voice never rose above a whisper.

Tsarra returned her attentions to the niches and their magical items. As the items before her shimmered away and others materialized in their places, she spotted a fascinating object—a golden belt of chain mail loops made of either gold or some amalgam. Ornate golden scales shaped like swords, shields, and oak leaves covered the surface of the belt. Set atop the shield scales, small, sea-green, opaque gems glittered, sixteen in all. The buckle was breathtaking in its workmanship—it was an ice eagle's head in profile, a larger sea-green gem as its eye. Tsarra had never been a great student of magic items, but the belt absorbed her attention. She reached for it, whispering the command word to release it . . . and failed.

As a senior apprentice, Tsarra was privy to many of the command words to access certain places and things within Blackstaff Tower, so she said the command again, louder, only to have a force field remain around the belt and niche.

She sighed loudly and said, "Sorry to interrupt you, Lord

Arunsun, but I cannot get the niche to release its burden to me for this test."

Khelben did not even turn toward her as he began vaulting the steps.

"Adkarlom." The niches all briefly flashed and Tsarra's hand closed around the cold metal belt. Khelben dashed upstairs and spoke as he spun from sight. "Wait for me in the lower library. I'll be there . . . soon."

Tsarra was stunned. In sixteen years at the tower, she had never seen Khelben run for any reason. While she'd heard the rare snort or chuckle, she'd also never heard Khelben laugh, which he seemed to be doing from up the stairs.

"Something weird is going on, Danthra," Tsarra said as she entered the library. "Did you hear that? Khelben laughing!"

Danthra blanched, her porcelain skin paling even more than normal. Tsarra placed the belt on the table, and put her arm around her friend in support. Danthra hugged her fiercely, almost squeezing the air from her. After a few moments, she relaxed, and Tsarra held her shoulders as she asked, "Gods . . . What's the matter, Dreamer? You can't be *that* nervous about this spell."

"It's not that . . . it's that vision . . . I didn't know it before, but Khelben's laugh was in my vision too."

"You're kidding me! Well, tell me—"

"Ladies, good morning. Let us proceed." Khelben walked briskly into the room, his face cloaked in its usual stone-seriousness.

Tsarra saw what had gone unnoticed in the dark stairwell. Instead of his normal dark robes, Khelben wore modern-cut robes of deep crimson wool. His trademark black staff that he often carried with him was not the usual trim staff shod in silver on the ends. Instead, he bore a gnarled and blackened piece of wood that seemed more a small sapling blasted from the ground. As Khelben closed the door, Tsarra also noticed that blue sparks danced among the cluster of roots at the staff's top. He also had a broad smile on his face, and his steel-blue eyes danced with delight.

Khelben turned, noticed his apprentices' stares, and within a heartbeat, his face returned to its normal impassive countenance.

"Why is it so surprising that I am not wearing my usual dour robes? I have of late been at the Tchazzam villa for mornfeast," he said in a low monotone. "Now, I believe the Dreamer has a spell to show us. Tsarra, please place the item before her so she may begin." Khelben spoke quickly, leaving them little room to respond or question. "Center yourself, Danthra, and educate us as to the parameters of your spell."

"Uh, Master," Danthra interrupted. "I had a vision this morning that concerned you."

"Indeed? Fascinating. You can tell me all about it after you've performed this spell, yes?"

Danthra looked at Tsarra with a weak smile. Tsarra gave her an encouraging grin. Danthra always got nervous around the Blackstaff, even after spending the past nine years in his home and under his tutelage. He was the one to name her the Dreamer, after her unpredictable and debilitating visions. Each vision could incapacitate Danthra for moments or whole days, but all of them proved prophetic.

Tsarra laid out the belt, smoothing its links and getting slight tingles from the green gems. With her back to Khelben, Tsarra winked at Danthra to set her more at ease, and the girl smiled weakly back. Tsarra took up a parchment and quill to record the spell test and all things said during it.

Danthra released a long breath then stood and placed her hands on the table without touching the belt. "The spell has no name as yet, but it's an extension of the divination theories behind basic detection and identification spells. It can divine anyone who crafted the item or anyone who used it for extended periods of time. Most often, it deals with concrete factors about an item, not ephemeral legends or historical information. With concentration and time, this spell should allow its caster to learn as much about the physical and magical properties of any item she encounters."

"What is the spell's range?" Khelben asked, his fingers steepled before his lips.

"Less than an armspan, sir. I limited it, as this is a spell for study, not combat."

Khelben nodded his approval then rose. He seemed lost in thought but waved his hand for her to move along. Oblivious to how he was distracting her, the archmage moved behind Tsarra and placed his gnarled staff against the outer wall, leaning it against one of the bookshelves.

As he returned to his seat, he explained, "Best I get any other magical items from your sight, lest they disrupt the casting. Please continue, but go slowly so our sorcerous friend—" Khelben gestured toward Tsarra—"may record the nuances of the casting."

Danthra coughed nervously, took a drink of water, and resumed. "The older an item is, the longer the casting can take to divine all its properties, but unlike the common identify spell, this can root out all of an item's abilities with enough time. If an item is made of many different materials, that may slow the effects as well, since the magic will take the caster through all the information on all components. Again, depending on the time spent casting and concentrating, this spell could potentially show you where an item's metal was shaped, forged, or perhaps even where the ore was mined for it."

Khelben interrupted her. "Intriguing, young lady, and certainly research of some merit. Be warned that the item before you could take days to reveal all its secrets, but it should suit for this test. Begin your casting, for theory can only get you so much of my praise."

Danthra nodded and breathed deeply to center herself. She took a handful of incense—"This is purified olibanus resin"—and dropped it into a small brazier at the table's center, its sweet smoke wreathing her and the table's contents. She traced mystical movements in the air within the incense smoke and around the belt. Danthra drew one finger in a perimeter around the belt and brazier, and the smoke stayed within that boundary thereafter. She then picked up a small pouch and said "This is powdered ivory and pearl mixed together." She poured the powder into her palm, intoned her incantations, and dusted the item with the powder in her hand. The dust undulated within the incense smoke before settling in a light layer upon the item. After a number of incantations, the dust glowed a variety of colors, all reflected in the smoke and the eyes of the entranced caster.

Danthra's voice dropped an octave due to deep concentration and relaxation. "The belt is made of platinum, steel, gold, and beljurels, all of different ages and constructed at different times. This item's primary purpose is defense both physical and mystical. It augments physical armor with magical defenses but cannot aid other mystical defenses. It can add lightning's touch to one weapon wielded by its wearer." With each revelation and comment, the dust and the smoke sparkled and one color among the many dissipated.

Still deep in her spell trance, Danthra's brow creased in confusion then surprise, and she smiled. "This belt has held other dweomers and other powers . . . other names. The dominant magic is no more than three centuries old, and the stones were enchanted centuries before that . . . cut even longer centuries ago."

Tsarra's nose itched due to the incense, and she scratched while Danthra paused in her monologue. While the cloying sweet smoke prevailed, Tsarra caught another scent—the smell of air after a lightning strike. Tsarra's thoughts were interrupted as Danthra began again, her words coming at a swifter pace.

"Zelphar Arunsun changed this belt. He added the buckle, repaired its scale. . . ."

Tsarra looked over at Khelben, but their master reacted not at all to the name of his long-dead father.

Danthra continued, "A half-elf warrior wore this belt last, eleven decades ago. His name was Dakath of Nesmé, and he died wearing it. His squire brought it to Blackstaff

Tower and delivered it unto Zelphar. . . . His family knew it as the Shield Belt of Storms. . . . A dark wizard crafted the weapon scales with a dwarf centuries before."

Danthra touched nine of the individual scales across the belt as she spoke. "Ryttal Ghalmrin forged the metals, and Theod Darkwhisper laid in the enchantment of weapons . . . they twisted an older magic to bond their work to the belt. . . . Seven warriors wore it in lands cold across many years."

Tsarra stretched her cramped hand and refreshed the ink on the quill. Danthra remained in her spell trance, concentrating for long moments. Khelben looked at Tsarra, glanced down at the parchment, and looked back toward Danthra without a word. The sharp smell of lightning's wake remained with Tsarra. She noticed the belt was sparkling even more brightly, shooting off sparks that bounced off the spell boundary hemming in the incense smoke.

"Must be part of the spell," Tsarra mused, as she reached for another sheet of parchment.

Danthra flinched and her brow knotted again in frustration. "The belt was filled with darkness . . . spiders crawling . . . drow held this for some time . . . muted the light it once held . . . this belt was made for elves in sunshine. . . . It was the—*ow!*"

Danthra's concentration broke when a stream of sparks and crackles came from the belt, striking her and arcing past her to Khelben's gnarled staff. Tsarra noticed that it too crackled with blue energy. She put her quill down, staring in wonder at Danthra and the two items.

Danthra looked up, shaken from her spell trance. "Master?"

Everything seemed to move in slow motion as Khelben lunged from his chair toward the table and yelled, "Down, both of you!"

Tsarra saw brilliant blue crackles coalesce around the belt and the staff. She felt paralyzed as the energy engulfed them all.

She and her chair were both launched from the floor. She

saw fear and confusion in Danthra's eyes, but only anger in the glare of their mentor. The wall behind them exploded inward. Tsarra felt as if she were sinking in a whirlpool then suddenly jerked skyward, and she heard lightning filling the air above a soul-rending scream.

Energy crackled all around them, making their bodies jerk spasmodically before it bolted upward, lightning stabbing the crystalline sky. Wracked with pain, Tsarra lay where she fell, staring through the ragged hole in the tower and outer courtyard wall. In the middle of Swords Street, Tsarra saw the young man she met earlier that morning. He was down, clutching a short sword, smoke and blue sparks surrounding it. The only details she could make out were his dark, close-trimmed beard, ponytail, red shirt, and three golden diamond designs set into the blade of his sword. Her sight darkened around those diamonds, the three glints of gold playing with blue lightning as she lost consciousness.

CHAPTER THREE

28 Uktar, the Year of Lightning Storms
(1374 DR)

The rogue had walked by Blackstaff Tower nine times in the past four days. His encounter earlier with Tsarra and her apprentices was only his second time being seen by denizens of the tower, both times of his design. Raegar looked for hidden doors in its courtyard walls, though to any watching he appeared only to wander among the wagons and carts scattered around the streets. In late autumn, the guilds, Guard, and Watch turned blind eyes to the many foreign vendors who spread carts beyond the Market, anxious to unload the last of their wares before leaving the city and returning to their homes for the coming winter. A bundle of southern traders crowded Marlar's Lane and Tharleon Street, providing Raegar with ample distractions. As he dickered with an Amnian weaver over the price of a traveler's cloak, he felt a tingle on his hip where his sword rested—the new short sword Damlath had given him only a few tendays ago.

Raegar broke off negotiations with the trader and moved in his planned path across the street and close to the wall surrounding Khelben's tower. He expected to walk across the front, then turn at the southeast corner to urinate in the midden behind Jhrual's Dance, the festhall adjacent to the tower. But the sword's tingling increased with each step. Raegar wanted to stop before it got worse, but a noble's carriage barreled down Swords Street, forcing him and other pedestrians to the roadsides. Raegar's right hip brushed up against the outer gate of Blackstaff Tower's curtain wall. The gate's intricate ironwork—its bars shaped into a mixture of wands, staves, and vines of metal—unleashed an explosion of magic on contact. The sword shattered its own scabbard with a blast of lightning that did the same to the gate and part of the wall. Raegar bent down to pick up the fallen sword but hesitated as the sword stood up, balanced on its pommel, and crackled with energy. At the same time, bolts of lightning blew away the wall at the base of the tower. Those bolts zeroed in on the sword, unifying and launching skyward from it as a massive lightning strike. The energy and booming thunder threw Raegar and his weapon into the street.

Ears still ringing, Raegar quickly grabbed the fallen blade as thunder echoed down the street. He stared at the three gold diamonds emblazoned into the blade, wondering what might have happened if he'd held onto the sword.

"So much for subtlety," he muttered.

All around him, people yelled and pointed at him or stared upward at the path the lightning took. Others still stared at the uncharacteristic holes in the defenses of Blackstaff Tower. Raegar also looked through the hole in the wall, straining to see what secrets he could glean from this distance. All he saw through the settling dust was an injured woman in a gray woolen dress lying on the floor, staring at him with deep hazel eyes—Tsarra Chaadren, the half-elf who had caught his eye earlier. Until she fell unconscious, Raegar froze in place, kneeling as the magic and dust swirled around him. Once he shook his head clear, he slipped the short sword into the torch loop on his belt and got to his feet.

The thief looked across Swords Street, and his stomach sank. He stared directly into the face of the Blackstaff as the archmage staggered from the smoking crater in his tower. Break into Blackstaff Tower and plunder its secrets? Raegar thought. Good idea, if done discreetly. Face its master? Better idea to leave quickly.

Raegar used the magical ring on his left hand to wrap the street in a shroud of fog. As always, the ring allowed him to see through it, and he slipped backward to the edge of the cloud and behind the Tavern of the Flagon Dragon. Whispering thanks to Tymora, he watched Khelben and realized the archmage was too stunned to notice much, let alone note him and his part in the chaos. Raegar heard someone yelling across the alley.

He had rented rooms for the past two months at Sapphire House, an expensive rooming house across Swords Street from Blackstaff Tower. The speaker was a neighbor— Kemarn, a professed scribe buying materials for a wizards' consortium outside of Nesmé. He showed his true colors boldly, as he hissed, "The tower is breached, men, and the Blackstaff is wounded! Take them both! That sword shall be mine!"

Kemarn pointed at the tower, but his attentions were on the fog.

Raegar had met many wizards before and found most to be arrogant, over-reaching, and convinced beyond all reason of the rightness of their causes. He stayed cautious, as he knew he was a target. Even if he didn't know his sword's capabilities, the thief knew that anything that could make a hole in Blackstaff Tower was something every power-mad fool in the North would want.

Raegar thickened the fog, filling Swords Street with it to keep from being found too soon. Panicked vendors abandoned their carts, and even the natives backed away from the fog and the troubles that once again enveloped their city's archmage. Raegar climbed up the side of the tavern and hid among the roof eaves to watch and wait.

Let's see how this plays out before I get an explanation from Damlath, he thought.

The Blackstaff slumped against the shattered gate, his robes scorched and smoldering. Kemarn cast an intricate spell from his third floor balcony above the fog cloud. Raegar watched four jet-black wolves leap from the mists in the wizard's hands, growing as they descended until they were much larger than normal wolves. The massive beasts loped across the street, undeterred by the fog, and surrounded the wounded Blackstaff

Sudden movement from above drew Raegar's attention to two young men flying down from the tower's roof. He pulled himself a little closer under the eaves as the older one shouted, "Duty patrol to the wall! Tower under attack!" The younger one's hands twisted in casting, and the fog cloud dissipated. He spotted Kemarn across the way and pointed a wand directly at him. A green ray struck the balcony, but the wizard no longer stood upon it.

Raegar smiled ruefully as he heard the roof above him creak. Kemarn had blinked to the back slope of the tavern's roof, just out of sight of the tower's defenders. Raegar pulled a small mirror from his belt pouch and held it carefully to watch what the wizard did without revealing his presence there.

His grin increased as he overheard Kemarn mutter, "Where did that man and his sword go?"

On the tower wall, the apprentices skillfully dispatched two of the fiendish wolves.

I don't know what those wands are, Raegar thought, but I want one.

The other wolves bowled Khelben over, biting and clawing at his robes and outstretched arms. Raegar found himself almost feeling sorry for the archmage, who seemed incapable of defending himself at the moment. From his vantage point, Raegar could also see a few figures moving among the tower's shadows. Even without the fog, he knew they would not be seen by the two apprentices, who were distracted by the danger threatening their master. Raegar followed their progress along the northern wall away from the gate and the battle there to slip into the northwestern shadows. Raegar smiled as more apprentices—two young women and a halfling male—appeared atop the wall with wands at the ready. In seconds, they used their wands to dispel the summoned wolves. The halfling leaped off the wall to land by the Blackstaff in a defensive crouch.

Blackstaff Tower's students are well trained to respond to trouble, Raegar thought. Too bad their master seems incapable of living up to his reputation today.

The thief's attention returned overhead when Kemarn began casting a spell. From his robes, he drew a red, fist-sized globe, which glowed for a moment then blinked out of existence. The tower's young defenders yelled. A red haze grew around the shattered gate and the two figures there. Raegar shuddered at the writhing mists filled with teeth, eyes, and grasping claws—a nishruu. The halfling used his wand quickly, but its purplish ray melted into the nishruu's growing scarlet mists, its claws and teeth happily pulling the magic apart and into itself. The eater-of-magic engulfed Khelben and his apprentice, swiftly wrenching magic and life from them. The stunned archmage grunted, and his young aide screamed in pain under the assault, as the monster ripped magic from their minds and bodies.

The elder boy shouted orders easily heard from Raegar's vantage point.

"Triam, be sure that no one's trying to breach the walls from other sides. Send up a signal if there is. Jalarra, Sarshel, destroy that thing before it gets into the tower! Pikar, do what you can from there!"

The trio blasted the creature beneath them. The nishruu drank up the magic, its floating mouths smacking disembodied lips with sounds that reminded Raegar of gutting and cleaning a hog. The nishruu growled as the halfling slashed with two glowing daggers. The blades reduced some maws and hands to mist, only to have them reform in other places.

The nishruu moved over the fallen wizards and drifted toward the tower, which was a vastly more powerful source of magic than any wielders in or around it. Khelben had collapsed, but Pikar still slashed away at the creature's tendrils and teeth, yelling in anger and pain, "Keep it from the tower!"

In swift response, Sarshel gestured, and a mist rose at the breach in the tower itself. By the time the nishruu reached it, the opening was sealed by a wall of solid ice.

Two more apprentices joined the others atop the wall in the blink of an eye—gold elves both.

"Foolish humans—don't feed that thing magic! That's all it eats!" The female's voice dripped with disdain toward the others.

"Watch and learn, *n'tel'quess*. This rod of absorption should kill it, Maeralya," the male said proudly, "and the master will know which students of his deserve his praise."

Raegar had tailed a number of wandering apprentices of the Tower over the past tenday. He had seen that haughty gold elf before—Fhaornik. The elf threw the magical rod into the nishruu, and it appeared to burst one of its floating eyes as it entered with a muddy splash . . . and the mist continued forward, stretching thinly as if torn between feeding more on Khelben's internal magic or the powerful forces in the stones of the tower.

Fhaornik sputtered, "But—that's supposed to kill it on contact!" His face bronzed in fury and embarrassment.

At the same time, Triam yelled from behind the tower, "Elkord! Back here! Someone's climbed the wall!"

The tall Tethyrian shouted back, "I'm coming!" He turned to the four standing near him and snapped, "Sarshel, get to the library and find out what kills this thing. Jalarra, go find Laeral. You two," he barked at the two elves, "slow it down or get Khelben and Pikar from it!"

Elkord flew over the courtyard and around the tower to

help his young student. Fhaornik and Maeralya both readied quarterstaves aglow with magical auras and leaped into the red mists. Raegar heard them both muttering angrily in Elvish, but while he didn't understand the language, he knew they resented being shown up by human and halfling alike. The two women both said something too low for Raegar to hear, and they teleported off of the wall.

Pikar Salibuck was a very young halfling, and he fascinated Raegar the most. While spying on the apprentices, Raegar heard that Pikar's father had lost his life working for the Blackstaff. Pikar was among the rarest of hin to be able to touch the Weave, and Khelben took him in as recompense for his father's sacrifice. Raegar watched as the strong halfling grabbed the Blackstaff under his arms and dragged him toward the sundered gate as quickly as his short legs allowed.

The smoky tendrils of the nishruu stretched to reach them, but it relinquished its grip to wrap its mists around the tower. As Pikar pulled the unconscious archmage toward the street, argent flames flashed around Khelben and blazed through the tower. Pikar fell back, screaming, and Khelben's form spasmed as the fires seared away bits of the nishruu and destroyed the ice wall that sealed the tower as well.

"Intriguing. Absolutely intriguing, don't you think, thief?" Kemarn knelt behind the peak of the roof, watching the fray across the street, but Raegar knew he spoke to him. "I don't know what that last effect was, but I trust the creature and my agents can fend for themselves a bit. I for one have learned enough today. The students use preset trigger words to move from the walls into the tower, yes? They probably use many such preset magic to quickly move throughout the tower. What else did you learn while watching them and the tower this past tenday, skulking one? I heard the Sapphire House barmaid last night and another two nights ago in the Flagon Dragon call you Raegar Stoneblade."

Raegar grimaced and wondered how Kemarn had

detected his presence. "What gave me away?" he asked.

Kemarn replied, "Your familiar face kept wandering past my own reconnaissance people, so we started to watch you as well. You've shown no obvious connections to the usual interested parties who might harass the Blackstaff. You inadvertently helped us figure out the best ways to follow the wizard's apprentices while they wander the city, skulking for news to bring their master. As for how I found you just now, you're not as good as you assume, and all of your magic comes from items. Now, I can roast you in your little perch beneath the eaves or we can negotiate. Give me that sword—the one that punctured the tower's defenses—and I'll let you live. Refuse and you suffer the wrath of Kemarn Darkthrush of Nesmé."

Raegar, smirking at the wizard's overconfidence, used his enchanted boots to cling to the wall like a spider. "Here's all you'll get of the sword, Kemarn," he said, and he shoved the short sword with all his strength through the eaves and the roof above him.

Kemarn shouted in surprise as Raegar's sword stabbed through the roof and gashed his shin. The wooden shingles erupted beneath him and clattered down the steep roof, taking the cursing wizard with them. Raegar heard Kemarn's painful landing in the dusty street below as he pulled his sword free from the damaged roof.

The rogue sprinted across the Flagon Dragon's outer wall, leaped over Marlar's Lane, and ran up Sapphire House's walls. Once he scaled the inn's five-stories-tall roof, he dropped onto the empty rooftop terrace adjoining it. Raegar raced across the veranda of the opulent four-story townhouse of the Delzimmer clan. He vaulted down into the rooftop gardens of Sablehearth, the Irlingstar mansion adjoining it to the north. Both were vacant for the coming winter, but he couldn't hide there without drawing attention. Raegar knew he had to get out of sight before either Kemarn or the Watch caught him.

"Raegar, old son, you've got to get a few more answers before this continues," he muttered to himself while he ran.

"Stick to your rules, man, as you broke two of them today. 'Never get into a game if you don't know all the players,' and 'Make sure you know what you're carrying.' Damlath's plan will have to wait until he coughs up some answers. . . ."

The thief dropped the final eight feet onto the corduroy surface of Zelphar's Walk and headed east to lose himself among the Market's throngs on Bazaar Street.

CHAPTER FOUR

28 Uktar, the Year of Lightning Storms
(1374 DR)

blindingpainoverwhelmingsensesfloatingdrifting
  falling
  soaring
  the brilliant gold-white sunrise over the towers
of Deshkant
  swelling pride of accomplishment in the
building
  scent of marble dust and brimstone as a demon
tears away at the base of Phalam's Tor
  anger boiling up and quenched immediately in
cold resolve
  Laeral's face contorted in a grimace of hatred
and evil laughter as blackened horns erupt blood-
ily from her forehead and temples
  horror and despair flooding
  scent of jasmine upon silk sheets still warm
from her body

*running through the underbrush, leaves and twigs snap-
ping and lashing at my face and arms and exposed body,
the spring of untrammeled deadfall beneath my feet, the
pleasure of the hunt and the chase alive in me*

*her slim hand reaches in earnest toward me, the glisten-
ing magic closing the portal around me and wrenching me
from her saving grasp*

confidence and determination to return

*feeling the tingling and the subtle warmth of the silver fire
crackling along arms and fingers, interlacing together with
the fires from Dlaertha, Vethril, and Myroune, all ablaze to
hem in the otherwise fire-immune demons of* Manth'ehl'nar
Ascalhorn

happiness at love felt through the fires

*Laeral's face shines with tears, her emerald eyes a
stormy sea of happiness and apprehension, determination
and fear*

bliss and peace, a smile soul-deep overtakes me

*I feel her touch and that of the wind, tickling the light
hair only recently grown and rarely exposed to the sun, and
I ache for more*

*curiosity and lust mixed, a teenager's crucible of confu-
sion and fear*

"I know a storm is coming, Master. I can smell the rain
on the wind as it wafts up from south of the Vowstone."

"Tsarra?"

*whirling mist and a flood of faces, stopping at almond
eyes of hazel offset by a green gem with tattoos around it,
confusion of long-standing clearing*

*Shock of recognition—that's my face, but older! Why do
I have tattoos on my face?*

*Pains soul-deep release under the warmth of the silver
fire, bones mend, and man and goddess laugh together*

"You shall serve us well, son of Arun. Try not to discern
all the secrets our fires place in you. Know simply that they
are things of import to us."

*Voice of bells in morning cloaked in fog, the laughter of
children, and the excitement of a wild mare . . . .*

"She's lost in my memories. Tsarra! Focus on my voice, girl."

I know that voice. Black beard, steel-blue eyes. Voice that could command gods. He sounds worried.

Focus and concern, worry and decision, lightning clashes of emotions and drives

Lancing light stabbing behind . . . through . . . beneath . . . into eyes, mind, soul

A child dances through a puddle, laughing at the spray and smiling at the rainbow overhead, then the violet drips off the bow's bottom and floods over the street. Hands reach from the slough and teeth grow in the puddles.

Surprise and shock, then a stray thought of gems

"Concentrate, girl. Use your mind, Tsarra. Come back to us."

I know him. Master Arunsun. Help me, master!

A delicate elf's face, ragged with mummification and a veil of webs, a purple gem glistening on the bridge of her nose . . .

decay mixed with dust and the sharp tang of recent spellwork

"Tsarra, they're only memories. Ignore them and join us."

the whisper of time's touch, the tug of the spider's cloak, the chill of time gone by and death interred

Lightning bolts flashing—one, two, three; wait for the crashing—deafening to me

The sewer's darkness suddenly swells, an eyeless face pushing itself through the grate, and its teeth are not hampered as its head reforms and lunges . . .

Pain brings focus and terror as its teeth gnaw through my arm, gnashing, grinding, and my arm falls away, its protection gone and the teeth geyser toward my eyes . . .

"Child, awaken!"

Her scream launched her upright, the two archmages around her rearing back in surprise. Her dress clung to her sweat-covered body, and Tsarra could do nothing but gasp for air, her lungs fighting to breathe. Khelben and Laeral helped her lie back down onto the bed, their faces filled with concern. Above them, Nameless settled back down onto the wide headboard above her, his green and blue eyes wide with surprise and his tail and wings twitching nervously. She felt as well as heard his low growl reverberating through the wooden headboard and silently willed him to calm himself.

"Nameless has been reluctant to let us near you, dear. I've never known a familiar to be quite so protective." Laeral dabbed Tsarra's brow with a cold cloth, and smiled at her.

A malevolent cackle—"Do you still wish to bed me, Blackstaff? Do you wish to know this Laeral whose petty morals lie in ashes?" Blood ran freely across hate-twisted features as the horns continued to push their way out through her skin.

Tsarra's eyes widened, and she recoiled from Laeral's touch. She didn't even realize she'd begun a spell until Khelben grabbed both her hands and held them still.

"Enough, Tsarra! Close your eyes and breathe." Khelben's stern whisper thundered through her aching head. "Get back into yourself so we may both shoulder our burdens." His voice sounded heavy as he placed her hands back in her lap and rose along with Laeral to the far side of the room.

Tsarra closed her eyes. Her sides were taut with fear, and it took time before she relaxed and her breath came easily. The feel of her own room and bed and the comforting scents helped, though how she got there she didn't know. It was highsun when the ritual began, but the night sky hung black outside her window.

How long was I unconscious? she wondered.

Flapping wings whipped by her head, and a weight landed on her lap. He uttered a series of meows and yowls, which Tsarra understood as, *"Happynow mistresssafe. Longnapgood? Washsickscent you must. Scratchtweenwingsnow."*

He rubbed his scent markers against her palm and nestled into her lap. Tsarra happily obliged him by scratching him just between his wings at the shoulders. Across the room, she could hear Khelben and Laeral talking, though they kept their voices low. Tsarra lets the tressym's deep purr help her relax, but she suddenly tensed and her eyes snapped open.

"Danthra—is she all right?"

Lord and Lady Arunsun looked at her with sad eyes, and Tsarra's heart sank. She wanted to mourn her friend, but it felt as if the Dreamer was there on the bed, embracing her. Tsarra ran her hands through her sweat-slick hair to pull it back from her face, and for a moment she felt Danthra's hands on her shoulders.

"What in—?" She looked at her teachers with fear and confusion, and they seemed worried as they moved closer.

Laeral said, "We found you unconscious, and the study had been partially destroyed. The lightning bolts that exploded through the room took out a large section of the wall. Khelben, stubborn fool that he can be, wandered out and into a battle despite leaving his brain behind." Her teasing tone didn't cover up Laeral's obvious concern over her husband. She looked to him and laid a gentle hand on his cheek, then she turned her eyes back to Tsarra. "Nothing was left of Danthra, Tsarra. At least physically. You feel her, don't you?"

Laeral reached over to touch her reassuringly, but Tsarra recoiled from her. The Lady Archmage of Waterdeep sighed after a moment and looked at her husband, who dropped his eyes. She got up and walked away, her hand trailing briefly on Khelben's shoulder as she passed from the room.

Tsarra had to fight herself. While she had known and loved Laeral Silverhand-Arunsun for more than a dozen years, she kept getting flashes of fear and revulsion when she looked at her.

Tsarra managed to ask her master, "What's going on?"

Khelben cleared his throat, looking pointedly at her. "Danthra's body was destroyed, Tsarra, though it had nothing to do with her spell. The magic that did this was far more potent—powerful enough to catch me off-guard. As to why you feel her presence, she's not entirely dead—she's in you *and* me *and* that." Tsarra followed Khelben's eyes to the bedside table where the metal belt she had been investigating lay. Khelben continued, "When her body died, her soul splintered among us, and we must find a way to save her without harming her, or us, in the process."

Tsarra gawped and closed her mouth as she assessed what had happened. She put her hand up to her head and felt something small, cool, and foreign stuck to her forehead. She tried to pull it away, and pain lanced through her skull. Nameless leaped into the air and away from the bed, his howls of pain communicating their mutual discomfort. She even noticed Khelben wince slightly at the same time.

"Leave it be, my dear." Khelben said, "It's what keeps us both sane."

Khelben brought her a small hand mirror, and Tsarra looked at herself. Aside from the haggard look and the disheveled and damp hair, Tsarra looked the same—but something new glinted on her forehead. Centered just above her eyes was an intricate tattoo on her skin with a small green gem affixed at its center.

"What is it?" she asked.

"It's all that keeps our minds and souls separate right now, Tsarra." Khelben sighed. "I adapted an elven *kiira n'vaehlar* on which I had been working. Luckily for both of us, it was nearly complete, but not entirely. When I awoke, I found myself thinking your thoughts and experiencing your past. While I have experience with mind sharing, I had to protect you from what's in *my* head. The touch of Mystra can be devastating to those not Chosen by her. That gem keeps your soul intact and allows us some measure of privacy from each other's thoughts. It's not perfect, given the time I had to enspell it, and the tattoos were necessary to stabilize the magic. They, like the gem, are now yours. Permanently."

Tsarra fell back against the headboard, her eyes wide. She looked at Khelben in disbelief then laughed nervously as she tried to assimilate the news. "Permanently? I'm a simple observer in a new spell trial, and I end up with my best friend's soul and the Blackstaff's memories in my head. Got any other surprises for me beyond facial tattoos?"

The Blackstaff glared at Tsarra. "Don't take this lightly, apprentice. Magic now binds us on numerous levels, and the powers I contain can do you even more harm than those you've already felt today. Just after the lightning strikes, the Tower came under attack, I'm told, by an over-reaching mage and his agents. Pikar Salibuck sustained serious injuries this afternoon trying to drag me to safety from a nishruu. The power I bear flared up to aid me when he dragged me too far from you, and the magic that binds us incapacitated both of us for a time. The fires are among my greatest powers, but I dare not use them without risking your life. Mystra's fire could sever the links, but not without destroying you, your familiar, and what remains of Danthra in the process. Until we can afford the time to separate our souls, you and I will remain bound by magic and must remain within eight armspans of each other at all times. For good or ill, apprentice, we are each other's company until Mystra deems our task fulfilled."

"How is Pikar? Is anyone else hurt?" Tsarra asked. "Were the invaders caught?"

"No one else suffered injuries, and Pikar is fine now as well. Yes, four intruders are the newest guests of Castle Waterdeep's cells, awaiting a magister's pleasure come morning. Their ringleader, however, escaped." Khelben frowned. "I did not see him, but to summon fiendish wolves and nishruu requires some power. None of those captured had magical ability—merely mercenaries told to loot what they could grab. The sixth figure, however, interests me the most. He wore red and bore a short sword—"

"With golden diamonds on the blade?" Tsarra asked. "I saw him just before I fell unconscious. He didn't seem to be attacking, though, Master. He looked as surprised as you—er, all of us." Tsarra blushed and looked away from the startled archmage.

"You saw him?" Khelben asked. "Oh, of course. Your

mother's keen eyes. Well, his sword interests me more than the man himself, and we'll have to glean more on that later, when you're able." Khelben gave the briefest of smirks as he said, "Some congratulations are due you, Tsarra. Apparently, your youngest students stopped the nishruu. While Elkord and his students captured the invaders, your two young brothers from Myratma knew of nishruu—from bedtime stories, of all things. They used floating disks to dump salt appropriated from a nearby vendor onto the creature to dissipate it. "

Tsarra laughed at that but winced as Nameless launched himself off her lap. She didn't have to ask why, as she felt what he did—and his nose smelled food moments before her own caught the scent. As he flew by, the tressym bit a hunk of venison off the platter Laeral brought into the room. Nameless settled onto an exposed beam overhead and began tearing away at his prize.

Laeral said, "Your charges in the kitchens worry about you and had this ready for you to test for taste. If it's suitable, all of us should join the students for dinner. That is, of course, if you're done telling her what she needs know, darling." Laeral handed the fork to Tsarra, who tried then devoured the heavily spiced deer meat.

Khelben took Laeral's hand as she set the tray down between him and Tsarra. "You know more of me by choice than Tsarra may learn by accident, my love. You alone know my soul." Khelben kissed his wife lightly before he turned again to Tsarra. "Tsarra, the next few days will be rough on both of us, but I insist you not share what you see with anyone without my express permission. You may learn more about me than any living being knows, aside from Laeral. Likewise, the magic unleashed this afternoon is older than this city, and it will be our task to contain it properly. We have until the Feast of the Moon to resolve this. I dare not focus beyond that, as more is at stake beyond our four lives."

Khelben's steel-blue eyes bored into hers, and Tsarra felt the seriousness of the moment. She also heard Khelben's voice in her head say, *Understand?*

"Was that this link?" She touched the green jewel.

"Yes." Khelben replied. "The gem normally just stores memory and magic, but as a *kiira n'vaelahr*, it also allows mental communication between you and me. The gem also helps stabilize the fragments of Danthra's soul so we might help her survive." Khelben gestured toward the tressym overhead. "I can even feel your connection to him, and a familiar's bond is not something I've felt in ages."

Tsarra asked. "If this is so dangerous, why aren't you wearing one? And what is so important that we can't tend to Danthra first?"

"I only had the one *kiira*, which you need more than I do. Mystra's fire protects me from the confusion and the damage the link can do," Khelben said, as he got up. "Danthra is safe, if uncomfortable, for the time being. Waterdeep may not be. Still, the dangers will hold at bay until dinner is completed, since you deemed the main course acceptable. We shall dine then make a few visits this evening."

"I'm feeling much better, Master, thank you." Tsarra said, and she got out of bed. She looked down at her sweat-soaked dress and asked, "Um, Master Khelben, I'd like to change from this and into something cleaner."

Khelben sighed and said, "Help her, Laeral, would you?" He idly speared one piece of venison with a knife and turned his back to stand in the doorway of the room. "Oh, be sure to wear the belt for now, but beneath your cloak. You're to bear the majority of Danthra's spirit through it."

"Not very patient, is he?" Tsarra whispered to Laeral as they opened the wardrobe. She smiled, happy that her normal comfortable feelings for Laeral were back, instead of the fear and revulsion.

"Not when he gets caught unawares, no. That's why he always plans—to avoid surprises like the one we had today." Laeral grinned at Tsarra, "My dear, in your first years here, you wished you could get more personal time with the Blackstaff. As more than one faith on Faerûn will tell you, 'tis best be careful what ye wish for. You're going to learn exactly what my love endures nearly every day for the Realms. Should you survive it, you're going to fully understand what makes him both irascible and honorable at the same time."

"It is regrettable," Khelben said, licking one last shred of venison off his fingers as they walked, "that you and your charges are finishing your kitchen duties. Aeraralee's class hardly shows any magic . . . of the culinary type, at least. I'd forgotten how much I enjoyed Tethyrian-spiced venison. Spices are nothing without cooks who know how best to use them."

Tsarra said, "I'll be sure to tell Ginara and the twins their contributions were appreciated."

She had barely had time to grab her scimitar, quiver, and bow as requested before Khelben hustled them downstairs again after dinner. Tsarra rarely saw Khelben when he was actually content, wholly enjoying a satisfying meal.

Khelben said, "I shall have to thank Gamalon for dropping those spices off here with our new apprentices before he headed north to Longsaddle. I expect him and his retinue back just before the Feast of the Moon. Gamalon plans to challenge the 'Tethyr Curse' by wintering here in Waterdeep . . . and surviving."

"So will we be receiving guest lectures during the winter months from Tethyr's court sage?" Tsarra asked, fully knowing the answer already, "or at least history lessons on the evils that befall Tethyr's nobles within the City of Splendors?"

"Indeed." Khelben said as they reached the bottom of the stairs.

Khelben crossed the entry chamber of the tower to stand before a looming wardrobe. He reached up with his staff to tap a rune on the left-hand door thrice. Tsarra noticed the staff was a different one than he bore earlier—still as night-dark as any carried by the Archmage of Waterdeep, but it was shod on both ends with brass and had very tiny and subtle carvings on the staff she could barely see.

Khelben opened the wardrobe door and said in a low voice, "I can access most every closet in my tower, depending on how I open this wardrobe, and we'll need a few things for our night's travels." He pulled out two cloaks, one of which he handed back to her, and she felt the tell-tale shiver of magic in its weave. "Illusion cloaks of a very old design, very handy for not being followed. A different illusion envelops you for each viewer or even when someone loses track of you. Easiest way across the city that doesn't involve teleporting."

He rummaged through a small chest, pulled out another drawer, and slammed it in frustration. He whispered something, as if having a brief conversation, then slammed the wardrobe shut. He turned and motioned for her to don the cloak as he did his.

Laeral came into view moments later, magically descending the stairs of the tower from somewhere else. "Honestly, my love. Betimes you've the patience of a quickling. Here are your things, and let it be known that *someone* left them in his workshop rather than their intended locations, which is why *someone* can hardly snipe at his lady wife over the matter." She handed one ring to Tsarra and placed two others in Khelben's hand. She also looped a small necklace over his head, holding it a moment and looking in his eyes. Tsarra thought she looked worried as she whispered something to Khelben, and she pressed close and embraced him.

Khelben stiffened, and Tsarra knew he disliked such displays in front of students.

"Tsarra, put the ring on and do what you can to keep him from trouble, dear." Laeral smiled then gave Khelben one last kiss. "Be sure not to keep your aide here in the dark, as she's as much invested in this adventure as you are, my love."

Tsarra did as she was bade, placing the silver ring on her left index finger. It had three bands intertwined around a dull green stone. She noticed that the two rings Khelben donned were entirely different. "In that light, will either of you tell me what this ring does?" Tsarra asked.

The sigh from within Khelben's hood spoke volumes.

"Why can't you discern such just from the item's construction, apprentice? It's to protect you from any more errant lightning bolts. Now, we must be off. Do like this, and the cloak's magic does the rest."

He snapped the cloak around his shoulders and suddenly looked like an average Waterdhavian merchant in a dull wool cape rather than the city's preeminent archwizard.

Tsarra pulled the cloak around her and while she couldn't see what her overall appearance was, her leather armor and the bulge of her back-slung quiver were gone and replaced with elaborate mage's robes.

"How will we recognize each other?" she asked.

When Khelben grunted, Laeral rested one hand on his shoulder. "Peace, dearest. An honest question deserves more than impatience. Look at Khelben's cloak clasp, Tsarra—that will remain in some way, no matter what guise the cloak throws on him." The Lady of Blackstaff Tower stepped toward the door and opened it, allowing in a moist draft of chilled autumn air. "Safe journey, you two, and call if you need us."

CHAPTER FIVE

28 Uktar, the Year of Lightning Storms
(1374 DR)

The pair stepped out into the night, and Tsarra noticed the courtyard looked normal despite the damage from earlier.

The tower repairs itself, as does the wall and gate, and Laeral helped it along.

Tsarra shook her head and whispered at Khelben, "Why didn't you just say that? That makes my head ache."

"Because I didn't wish to be overheard by anyone," he whispered in reply. "The Tower exposed too many secrets today, even if no one managed to profit from that breach. I'll not suffer another such exposure for the next century."

Tsarra nodded but replied, "Do you realize you speak differently when you're outside the tower? It took me two years to realize that you put on a far more formal and forbidding face when you're out in public than the one you show your students."

"Indeed?"

Khelben didn't say anything more as they exited the courtyard. The repaired gates glistened with night mist and opened as they approached, closing behind them with no gestures or castings at all. Khelben turned and headed north on Swords Street at a fast clip. Tsarra followed quickly, walking at his side within a pace or two.

She preferred the woods to the City of Splendors, but she did enjoy the city at night. It was slightly quieter, at least away from the inns and taprooms, and she could hear herself breathe—a task impossible in the daytime hustle and bustle. She drank in the darkness and the cool mists cloaking the rooftops and alleyways. Here and there, she spotted lantern-bearers guiding noble parties to and from their destinations. On the winds she heard far-away criers hawking tidbits of news into the night. "Last inbound caravans due at highsun! Four die in harbor accident! Lady Tian Simgulphin to marry, come spring!" Tsarra took a mental note to ask one of Maresta's apprentices about the news, as they were on rumor details that ride.

For the next two bells, Khelben led Tsarra on a maddening chase, crisscrossing the city in a seemingly pointless and meandering path. He stopped a number of times, casting minor spells or dropping small parcels into odd places, such as a drainpipe in Tarlaek's Court and the mouth of a lion statue on the walls of the Maernos estate. They didn't take a direct path until they had skirted the City of the Dead and turned up the Coffinmarch to follow it across the High Road into Buckle Alley.

Khelben ducked into a modest establishment, its sign proclaiming it to be the Griffon's Grog tavern. The wizard's hand signal suggested Tsarra wait a moment before following him into the building, so she stared at the sign a moment. The sign, covered partially in mold and in need of fresh paint, showed a carved griffon volant, its upper claws gripping a foaming mug.

After a short interval, Tsarra entered the smoky taproom,

the inhabitants of which paid her less heed than the mugs in front of them. A reedy-voiced bard—Tsarra recognized him as one of many students who passed near Blackstaff Tower from the New Olamn bards' college—sang acapella while quickly fixing his broken lute string. No other noise rose above the murmur of conspiracies.

Tsarra found Khelben talking at the far end of the bar with the owner, a fat, peg-legged man with only a thumb and forefinger on the right hand scratching his face. The two men nodded, concluding their business. When Khelben turned to motion to Tsarra, his cloak rendered him as an older Calishite gentleman, rings aplenty on the hand with which he waved her on. The pair ducked behind a hanging tapestry, and Tsarra's nose wrinkled at the acrid smell of a badly tended privy. Khelben tapped on the wall twice in two spots, and the wall pivoted, allowing them access to the back alley.

Without any further explanation, Khelben continued southward on a twisting path among middens and old courts. Tsarra knew the city well, but even she found some alleys into which she'd never looked, let alone stepped.

Stop worrying so, Tsarra. We're only taking Traslim's Cut to avoid notice of our entering the Elfstone. Khelben's communication to her was the first beyond hand signals in the past hour.

Within moments, they found themselves at a back entrance to a well-kept building. Tsarra sensed his arrival before she heard his wings, and put her elbow out at an angle to allow Nameless a place to land other than her shoulders.

Tsarra had never set foot inside the Elfstone Tavern, since her mother insisted she avoid it. She always told Tsarra she would not be welcomed, not only for being a half-elf but for being her daughter. Tsarra guessed her mother held an old grudge against its proprietress or vice versa. Since Khelben brooked no argument on the matter, she crossed the threshold and found herself, despite all warnings, feeling strangely at home. They doffed their hoods as they entered, revealing their identities to those inside the tavern.

The back entrance they used off Traslim's Cut led directly into the central taproom. The only thing between floor and the roof thirty feet overhead were living branches and a few floating tables with elves among them. To Tsarra's amazement, the nondescript but well-kept building allowed living trees to thrive inside, a few dotting the floor in various places. Four large oak trees dominated the great room at its corners, growing up from beneath the floor, their canopies spreading across the space. On either side of the greatroom, ceilings lowered and boxed in both ends of the building to provide upper-story rooms for either privacy or a night's lodgings. Despite the usual smells of tavern cooking and many people in close quarters, the tavern reminded Tsarra of the light woods northeast of the city. Torches on the walls and among the chandeliers glowed with silver-white flames to complement the moonlight streaming through the skylights in the roof.

A small bar directly across from their entrance served many of the guests in the greatroom, but Khelben's grip on her elbow moved her to the right side of the room with its main taps. Khelben seemed not to notice or care that all conversation stopped when he entered. Tsarra still found it unnerving—the only people not stymied by his entrance were the elf harpist in the room's center and the staff. The Blackstaff moved them to the far side of that bar, away from the main entrance to the tavern, and he stood without explanation or apology. Scanning the crowd, he either nodded silently to various elves who met his gaze or dipped the top of his staff to them in salute. After a moment, they were joined by an elf woman with a blue-green faerie dragon as comfortable on her shoulders as Nameless was on Tsarra's. Her skin shone pale copper, as did her hair that reached nearly to the floor, and her color was offset by a simple dress dyed red. Her eyes widened when they fell on Tsarra, but she offered no explanation as she turned to Khelben.

"You have a great deal of nerve, Khelben Arunsun, arriving here unheralded." The woman's address was no less sharp than her stare.

CHAPTER SIX

*28 Uktar, the Year of Lightning Storms
(1374 DR)*

"The time between your visits is long, even as we measure it, Lord Blackstaff," she said in Elvish. "Seeking a return to a measure of your youth, perhaps? Or are you showing this young one what facets of her heritage she neglects? I could show her how to wear her hair in elven style to accentuate her features." She smiled warmly at Tsarra, who remained unsure if she'd been insulted or praised.

"That is hardly our pressing concern at present, milady Ilbaereth. We must speak in private, Yaereene." Khelben said in the common tongue, his tone allowing no disagreement.

"Pyrith," the elf woman said to the faerie dragon on her shoulder, "watch the room for us. We shall return anon."

The blue-green dragon, only slightly larger than Nameless, hopped off her perch and flapped over to settle onto a large bough in the center of the taproom, whistling a reply only Yaereene understood. As she motioned them to a door behind the bar, she spoke to a nearby maid. *"Nuovis, bring us a bottle of maerlathen, three glasses, and some of the spiced silverfin on fresh biscuits, please."*

Yaereene smiled as she led them back through a service corridor to her private rooms. *"Pyrith doesn't like the smell of the pipe smoke hanging about you, milord Blackstaff. She insists you should not smoke pipeweed grown from a midden."*

"Indeed." Khelben said blankly. A few days earlier, Tsarra would not have recognized the slight tone shift that revealed Khelben's amusement, given how stolid his public persona appeared.

As a female cat rubbed up against Tsarra's ankle in the passage, Nameless tensed to jump down and pursue it. Tsarra grabbed one of his paws, mentally apologizing for interfering with his love life. The familiar growled openly at her but quickly settled down.

They arrived at a small sitting room in the back, its furniture mostly lounging chairs and chaises. Yaereene said, *"We shan't be disturbed here, as no staff uses this chamber for Reverie until late tonight. Its magical defenses also prevent any attacks or eavesdropping, as is your usual concern, milord. Now, will you continue to be discourteous, or will you introduce me to the young half-elf on your heels? Her familiar is certainly a handsome one."* She chuckled and reached to touch the tressym.

Nameless hissed loudly and flew up to the exposed beam overhead, his back was up.

"My apologies, milady. He's had a rough day, and he's not very sociable right now." Tsarra said, careful to speak in Elvish in deference to her hostess. *"I am—"*

"Her name," Khelben intoned in Common, a touch of irritation in his voice, "as you well know, Yaereene, is Tsarra Chaadren, and she is Malruthiia's daughter, as she appears. We don't have time to dredge up the past, save for this, Tsarra. Yaereene Ilbaereth is your mother's elder half-sister, and the family had a falling out with your mother well past a century ago, over what I choose not to know. Thus, your shared sylvan elf heritage brings you back together for this crisis."

"Don't belittle matters you choose to ignore, Blackstaff," Yaereene snapped back at him, "and don't insult my hospitality by being rude. Surely you remember some manners from your elven upbringing, even if you prefer folk to assume you're a far younger namesake. Even my half-human niece shows better etiquette."

Elven upbringing? But sir—? Tsarra asked mentally.

Khelben didn't even look at her, his glower saved for Yaereene.

"Scant few know more than a smattering of truths about me, dear lady. Do not be so blithe with entrusted secrets." Khelben said, his whisper angry enough to stun those listening.

Tsarra could feel his ire through the link they shared, and it seemed to spread to Nameless, who began hissing up above them and darting around, looking for something to hunt.

"Can we all please just calm down?" Tsarra pleaded. Her head swam from Khelben's revelation. She reclined on the nearest divan, trying not to smile as she luxuriated in its overstuffed comforts. "I am pleased to meet you, Lady Ilbaereth, but now isn't the time for family matters. We have other issues at hand, even if milord Arunsun has not told me of them either, correct?"

The seats were all arranged around a low table, and Khelben settled into one so all three of them could see each other while talking. They remained silent, questions lingering in the air. The only sounds were those of a moon elf maid bringing them wine and food and the tressym's scratching and marking of the roof beams. Nameless only halted his vandalism when Tsarra tossed him a shred of silverfin.

Khelben cleared his throat and said, "True enough. My apologies to you both. Like the tressym, the past day sits unwell with me. I hope you too can later learn more of each other, for your family's sake, as reunion and healing old wounds was my reason for coming here."

"I was not aware you and I had wounds between us, Blackstaff," Yaereene said.

"We do not, personally, but the debts and wounds run older than us both. I call to account the blood debts of House Maerdrym, as I need the help of the elves on matters that affect us all."

As Khelben spoke, he withdrew a heavy metal badge from his cloak and held it in his left palm, his right hand casting over the object. The metal badge multiplied in his hand, and with a flick of his fingers, Khelben floated one into Yaereene's lap and eight others landed in an arc on the table between them. Tsarra saw that all the badges carried a seal of four roses entwined around three staves—the mark of the elven House Maerdrym.

Yaereene flipped the badge over in her fingers. "I am hardly the elder or heir of my House, Blackstaff. Why bring this to me?"

"I have neither the patience nor the time to politic with your uncle in Neverwinter Woods, nor could Malchor Harpell deliver these in my stead. Besides, it was long between meetings for us, as you said."

"Even so, I find it odd. If rumors are true, you have a gate to the Fair Isle in your tower, Lord Arunsun. Why not ask these favors of Queen Amlauril?"

"Evermeet cannot know of our work here until done is done. This matter must be handled discreetly outside the notice of its irresponsibly political noble Houses."

"No doubt they think as highly of your approaches to matters of import, Blackstaff."

Khelben shrugged off the veiled barb and leveled his stare at Yaereene. "Your own family's debt came in the Year of the Dusty Shelf, when my parents rescued Ryul Ilbaereth and his followers from ignominy and death on the shores of Lake Eredruie. I trust I need not reveal to Tsarra the secrets that bind our names and honor?"

Yaereene's face paled and she gripped her gown in a fierce fist, then she relaxed and cast her eyes down. "No, Lord Blackstaff. I am at your beckons, last Maerdrym. How may my House serve yours?"

Khelben kneeled by her and put his hands over hers, the elf's eyes widening at the supplicating gesture. "I need you to assemble a company—yourself included—and travel to *Manth'ehl'nar Malavar* before Selûne is full in the sky in three nights. Relay these same biddings to the Houses on the other badges, an easy task as highly placed scions of all of them frequent your establishment and the City of Splendors. Request their utter discretion and that each family send one or two wizards bearing each of their family's long-dead or long-dormant moonblades."

Tsarra gasped, and Yaereene stood up sharply. "You dare much, archmage, and even more to ask the People to move with such haste. I'll need more than oaths and honor debts to a nigh-dead House to goad them to action *and* to part with fabled House heirlooms."

"None in twenty elven generations have wielded those blades among those Houses. They simply hold them as holy relics, as if they mean more than failure." Khelben sighed then swept his hair back from his face. "Tell them those heirlooms shall soon bless them with use and honor in the coming days. A great time is upon us, lady, for the People's redemption. We do not do this work for any mortal partisans. What we dare requires elves and others to work in accord to undo the damage of millennia past. I make the request in the names of Sehanine Moonbow and Corellon Larethian. You know the vows they made when Ivossar's House strayed from the path of true *tel'quessir*. Hold the badge to your heart if you truly doubt me."

Yaereene's face remained impassive, but she placed the gold badge over her heart, and immediately she whispered, "*Faer'tel'miir?*" Khelben nodded solemnly and tears flowed over the elf woman's porcelain features. She replied, "Very well, *akhelben*. It shall be done. We shall be honored to share this burden with thee, *ol ahnvae Sehanine*."

Setting the badge down on the table, Yaereene stood. Tsarra saw the disk also had the Ilbaereth seal on the other side—a pegasus rearing over six wands, a sun surrounding all from behind. From her studies of elven Houses, she recognized that the mark combined elements of the seals of Houses Ealoeth and Ildacer, suggesting a long-ago marriage created the Ilbaereth line. Tsarra bowed to her aunt as Khelben also rose. Yaereene took Tsarra by the shoulders. A growl resonated from above, but she ignored the tressym warning the elf away from his mistress.

"A'su'nys, you are half-blood, and our family regrettably tolerates that less than some. Still, you walk beside an honored elf-friend. That alone tells me more than you know. I and others would know more of you in times to come. Malruthiia is sorely missed and I would know her daughter, regardless of my family's views on the matter."

Tsarra tried to respond but only managed to nod after her throat swelled up. Tears flowed on both women's faces, and they embraced briefly. As Yaereene dipped her forehead toward Tsarra's in familiarity, Tsarra drew back and cleared her throat, startling Yaereene.

"No disrespect intended, *osi'nys,*" said the appreatice. "I wished you no harm from touching this." Tsarra pulled her hair back from her forehead to reveal the gem and tattoos there.

Yaereene inhaled sharply. "The Blackstaff provides his apprentices with *kiira* as well? You must be special indeed, niece. I look forward to learning more about you soon. Even so, when next we meet, politics demand we not acknowledge each other openly. Do not be offended but rather realize that elven ways differ from those of your father."

Tsarra nodded in response, guessing that the moments of closeness were only for private times, not public display.

"We thank you for your aid, Lady Ilbaereth," Khelben said. "May our next meeting be even more harmonious."

He drew his cloak back around his shoulders and donned the hood. They exited the Elfstone's front door out onto the Street of the Sword. They turned south to Waterdeep Way and headed north again. Tsarra wondered why they went through so much trouble to cover their tracks. Anyone looking to follow the Blackstaff would hardly look at a much-scarred half-orc in a muddied wool cape and a female gnome in red leathers and a bright pink silk cape.

Master? Tsarra sent as they dodged two pair-carts, their four drunken noble passengers racing them full tilt around the corner from Selduth Street and down the Street of Silver. *What was that meeting all about? And are there any other family members you're going to spring on me?*

Nay, Tsarra. No more hidden family. Now pick up your pace. We're running from time even with three days to work.

Khelben hurried his pace, and even with her half-elf's grace, Tsarra had a hard time keeping up with him.

Can you at least tell me with whom we're meeting and why you're in such a hurry? The person's not going to die before we get there, is he?

Doubtful, lass. Khelben replied. *She has been dead now for nearly seven score years.*

CHAPTER SEVEN

28 Uktar, the Year of Lightning Storms
(1374 DR)

"Haulaurake, Damlath! Don't hand me that 'You knew everything you needed to know' garbage!" Raegar whispered at his companion. "That sword summoned lightning powerful enough to blast a hole through Blackstaff Tower! You didn't think a power like that was worth mentioning?"

The two men turned off Swords Street and into Melody Mount Walk, the tunnel that led to the New Olamn barding college on the city's western cliffs.

"Talk to me, Damlath!"

"Quiet. I'm concentrating." Damlath said, dismissing his companion.

The mage willed his flying carpet to hover closer to Raegar's horse. He'd brought the item back from the city of Llorbauth with him and had ever since refused to use horses for travel. The mare, recently purchased from Fetlock Court, shivered and shied away nervously until Raegar held her in check with leg and reins. Raegar seethed as he stared at his friend.

What happened to him? he asked himself. Ever since he returned from Erlkazar in Mirtul, he's been dismissive and almost as mysterious as those we've stolen secrets from.

Despite their differences as rogue and wizard, the two men had worked together for three years. The Holy Church of Oghma united them in purpose—both men worked furtively to break the hold some wizards had on secrets and to spread those same secrets by the will of the god of knowledge. Raegar had enjoyed the past few years, working with both the Font of Knowledge, Oghma's grand temple in Waterdeep's Castle Ward, and the dark-skinned wizard. Still, things had changed and their missions had grown more dangerous with each passing month.

Damlath had originally come from the south, a small country called Erlkazar on the shores of the Deepwash east of Tethyr. The wizard was a pious devotee of Oghma from the Lore Halls in the city of Llorbauth. He ventured to Silverymoon twenty-four years ago with his wizardly master to work with Sandrew the Wise. When Sandrew began building the Font of Knowledge in Waterdeep, Damlath helped in the temple's building. Damlath had an acerbic personality that few warmed to, but Raegar enjoyed the edge in his humor, and they worked well together.

The younger Raegar had grown up in Waterdeep's South Ward as the son of a stone carver and a sailmaker. His parents died during the undead assault on Waterdeep in the Time of Troubles, and Raegar had been on his own since then. Surviving as a street thief and later a stone carver, Raegar grew bitter at the mages who infested the City of Splendors. He saw disaster after disaster brought down upon them by wizards who rarely bothered to explain to the people what had happened or why. His abilities as a thief—necessities when fighting to stay alive—came back into play as he began filching some scrolls and books from the homes of wizards and selling them. He did that infrequently enough that people never suspected the stone crafter who carved new gargoyles outside their windows was the culprit. When Raegar found work helping to finish the construction of the Font of Knowledge, he befriended some of the priests there. For the first time he found a voice that spoke to his heart in Oghma's teachings. They also confirmed that his mission in life was to honor Oghma in taking secrets from the hands of those who would abuse them and spread the knowledge. For six years, Raegar worked unofficially for Loremaster Gustyl "the Curious," a gnome priest whose knowledge of wizards of the North astounded the young man. The only wizards Raegar could not spy upon, by Gustyl's insistence, were Maaril the Dragonmage and any wizards directly associated with the Wands clan or Blackstaff Tower. Recently, those rules had changed, and that made Raegar nervous.

Three years ago, Gustyl died suddenly, and his responsibilities fell to his assistant Phanar Manthar, a devout priest and disowned lesser son of a Waterdhavian noble House. Phanar introduced Raegar to Damlath, insisting they all work together. Long used to working alone, neither man liked the idea, but together their surveillance and dispatching of Surkhas of Leilon kept the Arcane Brotherhood from claiming the High House of Thalivar and its secrets. By the end of that adventure, the two were fast friends, though Damlath was more than twice Raegar's age. The two were known devout lay members of Oghma's temple, though very few outside of the upper clergy knew the tasks they undertook in the Binder's name.

Raegar's musing ended when Damlath cleared his throat and began muttering some incantations. Raegar's grip tightened on the reins. Damlath didn't tell him what he was casting, something that happened more often of late.

When the wizard finished, he said, without turning back to Raegar, "Come along, boy. Must remain a few steps ahead of the Blackstaff. Stay close."

"What are you talking about?" Raegar asked.

He urged his horse forward, staying within a stride of

the hovering mage who sat cross-legged on his magical carpet. Raegar's thoughts kept him from paying attention to the tunnel, its interior length lit by infrequent torches, until the tunnel disappeared entirely. Pain lanced through Raegar's head, and he slammed his eyes shut.

When he opened them, Raegar saw he'd pulled his horse up short on a muddy track only partially paved with ruined stones. He and the mare stood just past an archway, the wall fallen to rubble on either side of it. Blue and purple sparkles hung in the air around them.

"Blast you, Damlath! Never do that without warning me!" Raegar's head throbbed, and immediately he regretted yelling.

"Don't just stand there. Some magic lingers about, and we don't need to find out its meaning. We need to make haste to get to the inn before it's too late." Damlath sped away. Raegar could barely spot him by the moonlight breaking through the trees.

Too late for what? he wondered, as he urged the mare forward. Still spooked, the horse was only too happy to break into a canter. Raegar groaned then gritted his teeth against the headache and rode swiftly to catch up to the mage despite his increasing speed.

As the wary horse settled in next to Damlath, Raegar said, "Wizard, you've told me next to nothing in the last tenday. For someone dedicated to sharing knowledge, you're not doing very well, friend." He smiled, trying to break his partner's reserve with the joke.

Damlath looked at him and scowled. "I liked you better when you chose to be silent for most of a mission."

Raegar raised his eyebrows but let the insult pass. "Where across the Nine Hells have you taken us? And what's the rush? You wasted all afternoon and evening at the Font of Knowledge and insisted I meet you at Fetlock Court instead of the library."

Damlath's explanation was monotonal, as if he could hardly be bothered to explain himself. "Time in research is never wasted. We seek to not miss a particular traveler on the road. We've just left the ruins of Rassalantar's Keep, the portal between it and Waterdeep sat unused for more than a century. I doubt even the Blackstaff knows of its existence. We're approaching the hamlet of Rassalantar, and we have business at the Sleeping Dragon. After that, we can rest at a manor east of the village overnight. A friend of mine owns Stagsmere and insists someone check on it before winter. If we get separated, it's nine miles east of Rassalantar's pond. Just follow the creek, rather than the road, and turn off when you see the Stagstone. The manor's a mile to the northeast with a trail that's a bit overgrown."

As Damlath fell silent, they broke from the trees and onto a muddy trail between two farms. The nearly full moon and the Tears of Selûne behind it lit a downward slope and the tiny little cluster of buildings and farms around a pond. Raegar enjoyed the crystal clear night sky and all the stars not easily visible from inside Waterdeep's walls. He'd been through Rassalantar before, but not in a while. Raegar wondered how many others knew of that portal that saved them nearly two days of hard travel.

A short while later, Raegar slowed his horse to a trot when they crossed a small wooden bridge over the eastern edge of the pond. He dismounted, loosened the saddle's girth, and walked the mare cool before leaving her to drink and rest. Meanwhile, Damlath only had to step off his carpet, roll it up, and slide it inside his cloak's magical pockets.

Damlath said in a loud whisper, "We're to meet someone who wishes to remain anonymous. You keep an eye out and distract anyone who takes any notice of my meeting."

Raegar nodded, and left his mare to graze. The two men moved toward the inn's door. Damlath's eyes seemed blank and lifeless, and Raegar wondered why someone nicknamed the Laughing Mage no longer laughed. In accord to their usual methods, Raegar turned off and walked around the inn, both to examine points where he could make a quick exit and to avoid any surprises from additional guards. He noted useful egresses such as wide windows on every level.

He also noticed chimneys on both the eastern and western walls, the former chimney wafting cooking smells aloft. Complete with the usual stables and privies, the Sleeping Dragon Inn seemed comfortably normal, despite a local legend that a gold dragon hid among the barmaids to defend the inn and its patrons.

Raegar finished his circuit and retrieved his horse. He walked the mare over to the rail across the road from the inn and lashed her reins to it. Raegar crossed the road again and approached the door, but yells behind it and approaching fast suggested he step back. The door slammed open in his direction, followed immediately by a howling drunk and the barkeep shoving him outward and into the mud.

"Guard or no Guard, Anthan, ye're an ugly drunkard and ye're disturbing me inn. This ain't no Dock Ward dive, after all. Now go sleep it off and ye can fix things with me in the morning."

The man was older and hardly rose to Raegar's shoulder, but the muscle on his exposed arms and the stern look on his face made Raegar think twice about what tactics he'd try in the inn that night.

The innkeeper turned to reenter and noticed Raegar standing aside in the shadow. He smiled, nodded, and gestured his newest patron toward the open door.

Raegar returned the smile and said, "Well, I suppose there's an open seat within for me, then."

"To be sure, lad, to be sure." The man chuckled and offered a hand in friendship. "Welcome to the Sleeping Dragon. Ye can call me Spider, if all ye bring to my place is a smile and some coins. Ye've seen what happens to those what cause trouble, eh?"

"I'll be on my best behavior, then, Spider. My stomach and seat demand I stop for a moment and a meal." Raegar chatted amicably with the innkeeper as he entered the inn. "Oh, where are my manners? I am Terrol, late of Waterdeep, and I am a courier on way to Longsaddle one last time for my masters before Auril spreads her snowy tresses over the North."

When he stepped past the threshold, the rogue took in the entire room in a glance before crossing to the bar. The door entered the taproom in its southeast corner to not dilute the heat from the fireplace dominating the western wall at the far side of the room. The bar ran half the length of the northern wall, and men sat hunched over their beer on the high stools there. The rogue noted with surprise the slim mirror that spanned the length of the wall behind the bar—a rare luxury even for Waterdeep, let alone a tiny backwater such as this. Still, it made his job easier to watch Damlath and his companions without being noticed. Immediately on Raegar's right was an archway leading into the kitchen, and Raegar became famished once he smelled what cooked therein. The rest of the eastern wall held cloak pegs and crates, barrels, and various packs beneath the stairs that led to the rooms on the next level up.

Raegar turned to Spider as the man slipped behind the bar, and asked, "Could I trouble you for a bowl of that boar stew I smell and a tankard of your best?"

Sitting at the end of the bar to keep the entire room in sight, Raegar placed a few coins on the counter. Spider disappeared into the kitchen with the coins. Very few patrons took note of his entrance, so apparently the previous upset was not remarkable. Raegar returned to scanning the place.

The center of the room held a handful of round tables with chairs and the southern wall was lined with nine long tables with benches. The inn wasn't busy, the tables still having ample room for more patrons, and Raegar finally spotted Damlath at one of two round tables sequestered into the corner between the bar's end and the hearth. He sat with a couple and all three kept their hoods drawn.

Why do mages think keeping cloak hoods up indoors will do anything but draw more attention to them? Raegar thought.

Despite that error, Damlath's companions did a good job of avoiding attention, their clothing well-worn and dirty to defray interest from thieves or eavesdroppers. To the casual eye, they seemed nothing more than late-season travelers heading home from or to Waterdeep before winter. From his viewpoint, Raegar could only see the profile and left arm of the brown-cloaked companion, and he squinted to be sure he saw correctly. Between her half-hidden features and the shape and length of her hand, Raegar guessed she was a female elf with dark blond hair. The blue-garbed man to her right was good at subterfuge. He stabbed his left hand onto the table as if to punctuate a point. To any other than a trained thief, the wand in the sleeve beneath that hand was unnoticeable. Raegar's eyes widened as he noticed a light blue glow and sparkles around the wand, which were quickly covered as the man brought his arm to rest back on the table. All Raegar knew of the man was that he carried a mage's wand, wore expensive rings, and his pristine hands didn't look like they'd been subjected to work beyond magecraft.

What surprised him more was the tingling he felt on his back—where he'd strapped the Diamondblade. It had been tingling and glowing like a blue ember all day, but the sparks seemed to be growing in intensity. Luckily, while he could feel his sword reacting to something again, no one else could see the sparks beneath his heavy cloak. Raegar realized he'd been used. Damlath's plan did nothing more than draw trouble to him like a moth to the flame.

CHAPTER EIGHT

28 Uktar, the Year of Lightning Storms
(1374 DR)

"I am going to kill that mage. . . ."

Twice in one day, Raegar had been made a stalking horse to test out certain magic—while not a wizard, Raegar understood that the sword reacted to something else nearby, and he guessed it was that wand. Worse yet, since Raegar hadn't been informed that this might happen, he'd chosen a disguise that would not allow him to easily explain away any magic. In fact, his chosen role even prevented him from slipping away and getting the sword off of him before something else happened.

Spider's heavy steps belied his short stature but were a testament to his strength. Raegar turned to him, his face hardly betraying any worry he felt, as Spider approached with a large tankard.

"This won't do. Ye've got to take a table for proper room to eat."

Spider led him to the small round table with chairs for three and obviously recently vacated by one or two patrons. "Now, try this, young sir Terrol, and it'll warm ye to yer boots." The innkeeper slammed the mug down while a lissome green-eyed barmaid slid a steaming bowl of stew and a warm handloaf of dark bread toward him as well.

Raegar drank the lukewarm porter and raised his eyebrows. The porter was slightly nutty with a pleasant bite in its aftertaste. "Excellent, goodsir Spider. What do you call this hearty brew?" Raegar kept his tone light and in keeping with his disguise—he had combed his beard and oiled his hair, and he wore his richer leathers and a well-made cloak in his guise as a well-to-do courier, the House Lanngolyn badge as his cloak clasp. The barmaid brushed up against him suggestively, and Raegar mentally noted that she was after his attentions more than his coin purse.

"Ryssa, let the man alone a moment to eat, for Tyr's sake!" Spider chastised his young barmaid, who pouted then moved along with a pewter pitcher to refill wine glasses around the room. Spider wiped down the bar, and said, "That be me own brew—Sleeping Dragon Dark—from the local barley and oats. Won't get that in Waterdeep, no sir. Well, enjoy, and be sure to tell the Lords Lanngolyn of our hospitality, sir."

Raegar nodded and tucked into his bowl of stew, careful not to meet the eyes of a few whose attentions fell on his rich cloak or the words of the innkeeper. Inside, he argued with himself: Curse that wizard. He still hasn't explained about the blade or this morning's incident, and it feels like he's set up this encounter as another test. It'd almost be better if I just left, but that would draw attention if I go too abruptly. It'd be justice though, to leave Damlath out on a limb unknowingly as he's done to me twice now.

Raegar fumed inside but his face and body language were the measure of calm and contentment as he finished the stew and idly sipped at his drink. He began taking in the company around him. Most of those seated at the bar were local laborers, the mud of the fields still on their boots and clothes. One long table and its nearest round table were dominated by fighting men, their tabards and armor noting them as the local Guard contingent that the Lords of Waterdeep kept patrolling on the roads north to and from Amphail. Still, if trouble came up, those eleven men could be a problem. Two tables away sat a small party of six—traders from the looks of it, all tired from days on the trade road and praying to make it to Waterdeep before season's end. Other locals took up only two other tables, but the farthest two long tables and the round tables closest to the fireplace were suspiciously empty. Raegar winked at Ryssa when she passed back by him, and she resisted only a token amount when he swept her into his lap.

After a playful kiss to dismiss suspicion, Raegar whispered to her. "Why are the best seats in the house empty? Seems odd, especially with winter's chill starting to creep in."

The raven-haired woman's eyes widened then lowered. She turned in his lap slowly, and playfully took a swig from his tankard. Raegar guessed she might have been a thief at one time as well, given how smoothly she blended her passing whispers with her actions. "Spider's expecting a group of travelers here some time tonight, coming back from Longsaddle on the Long Road—a count and his party, all from Tethyr, I'm told. They stayed here about five tendays back on their way north, and a scout arrived at dusk to ask that rooms be readied for their arrival. Now, did *you* need a room readied, sir?" By that time, she had risen from his lap and straightened her dress, her eyes always locked on his. Ryssa's clear desire made Raegar even more irritated with Damlath's plans.

"Alas, no. I'm to be east of here by highmoon, no matter what. As much as I might wish it, I must away after my meal to Stagsmere." Raegar tried to rekindle hope for both of them. "Mayhaps my errand there will be short, so I might return, should there still be a room for me."

Ryssa's eyes confirmed as much but she said, "Wait a breath—Stagsmere? "Why'd you want to go there? That place has been abandoned for years. Only things out there now are rabbits and ghosts."

"Not my place to question my duties, I'm afraid. I've already said too much, but for your discretions, fair Ryssa."

Raegar placed three silvers into her fingers as he reached out and put his hands over hers on the tankard. The girl smiled as she slipped the coins into her pocket.

Raegar stood up and made his plans clear to Damlath by sighing loudly and exclaiming, "Innkeeper! That was the finest meal to be had in the North outside of Sea Ward! I thank you and your good serving girl for it."

He moved toward the bar, noticing that all eyes were on him, including Damlath's. As he made a show of counting out coin for the meal, he watched in the mirror as Damlath and his companion shook both hands together. Disguised by this motion, the blue-garbed mage slipped the sparkling wand into Damlath's sleeve while he in turn slid a scroll into the man's other sleeve. Once that transaction was complete, all three stood and made to leave as well.

Raegar paid Spider a bit more than required, if only to keep his memory sharp on his generous identity as Terrol, servant of House Lanngolyn. He then bowed to him and Ryssa, and headed for the door . . . only to find it blocked by a large party of dark-skinned armed guards. The foremost guard—clean-shaven but with shoulder length black hair and richly appointed clothes only marred by the grime of the road—smiled at the innkeeper, who greeted him with, "Welcome, Captain. Honored greetings to ye and their excellencies!"

The captain said, more to the party behind them than to Spider, "Your Excellency, our tables are ready."

The captain and some of his guards moved past Raegar and headed directly toward the fire, creating a perimeter of guards around their tables. Raegar watched them pass and noticed how Damlath's companions pulled their hoods a little closer and shied away from them.

The guards all wore livery in enamel badges—a green

field with a golden emblem of wheat stalks wrapped by a scroll and a blue ring. While Raegar wasn't a short man, half of the guards loomed taller over him than he did over Spider. Raegar had seen the badge before in Waterdeep when his surveillance of Blackstaff Tower began. He knew them as the retinue of Lord Gamalon Idogyr, Count of Spellshire and Sage of the Royal Court of Tethyr.

Raegar stepped back toward the stairs to allow them access and realized there was no room at the threshold for six guards, four servants, the entering noblepersons, and himself. Fitting his servant's guise, Raegar backed up the stairs to clear the way for the party's entrance. He also realized that the tingling on his back was growing ever stronger, a fact made all the more disturbing when he looked out the door of the inn.

On the porch, a man and a woman stood facing each other, their excellencies Lord and Lady Idogyr. The lady smiled at her husband, and Raegar strained to hear her over the hubbub generated by their party's arrival. He caught only the tail end.

"—don't be such a show-off, making your eye glow with blue sparks for a grand entrance."

She turned away, and when the count faced the doorway, Raegar's blood froze while tingles ran across his back from the sword. Gamalon, his bald head wrinkled in confusion, had a green gem where his left eye should have been, and the blue sparks spitting from it were easily spotted against his dark skin and salt-and-peppered beard.

Raegar remembered the morning's destruction and glanced briefly toward Damlath, who seemed just as surprised as Gamalon. When their eyes locked, Raegar nodded and looked directly at the window on Damlath's left hand. He also made a quick hand signal, long practiced by them, to tell him to toss the item in that direction. He didn't want everyone in the inn getting blasted by lightning, but Damlath stood, ignoring or misreading the signals.

Raegar shot him a glare and thought, Guess it's every man for himself.

Raegar backed the rest of the way up the stairs, fumbling with the buckle behind his back that held the blade and scabbard in place and muttering as he went, "Blessed Tymora, free me from Beshaba's bad luck!"

His attentions shifted between the buckle and the building glow that presaged arcs of lightning between the count's gem and the sword. Raegar groaned as the buckle caught on one of the other clasps for his armor. The scabbard and sword swung below his right arm, the leather smoldering and charring. Upstairs, he saw a short hallway with doors to seven rooms and windows overlooking the entry, the top of the stairs, and the end of the hallway flanking the chimney. Raegar heard a blade clear its scabbard as one of the count's guards mounted the stairs after him, having noticed his interest in their party.

Raegar's mind raced as he tried to judge the best option in a bad situation. He yanked hard on the scabbard to free it just as a small bolt of lightning arced up the stairs to his sword through the guard, dropping him instantly. Knowing even more destruction was to come, Raegar threw the blade as hard as he could out the window over the entrance, praying that the lightning bolts would spare most of the people inside. Just as the sword cleared the window's frame, the blue sparks coalesced again into two arcs—one leading straight down at Gamalon's Eye and the other angling to the left, reaching for the wand Damlath had just acquired. The sizzle and flash of three full lightning bolts blasted through wood and stone, and the bolts gathered together to send a fourth blast skyward. Raegar watched the lightning dance across a clear sky, the massive bolt jerking across the horizon and heading toward the southeast.

Below him, the screams of the patrons nearly overwhelmed the groaning noise of the building as the lightning-blasted front began to collapse. Raegar felt the upper floor start to strain and break. He launched himself into a tucking roll backward through the window behind him. He went off the back roof and landed easily on the ground below, landing like a cat on all fours. His plummeting arrival startled a stable boy who was leading two rearing horses toward the stables.

Raegar had a sudden idea and yelled, "Quickly, boy! Go fetch more of the Guard from their garrison. There's some evil magic unleashed inside!" Raegar, for his part, ran around the inn to retrieve his sword then flee as fast as he could to reach his horse.

Around the eastern corner, he found chaos. The front porch and a large area of the upper floor lay crumbled and smoldering. Much of the front wall was gone, and numerous people lay dead or unconscious. Others ran screaming from the ruined inn, while two guards remained next to their fallen count. Raegar didn't see Gamalon's wife or half the guards, but piles of ash and bone showed him their fate. A pair of young lovers, their rendezvous interrupted, tumbled from their bed by the removal of the front wall, clung screaming and dangling over the remnants of the floor above. Raegar used the distraction to dash past the guards and join the panicked throng heading over the bridge and away from the inn.

He ducked by his horse, which was still lashed to a rail and trying to flee in terror from the lightning strike. Raegar held its reins and soothed it with a quiet voice, all the while looking toward the wreckage of the inn's front, scanning for his sword. He saw the count's guard captain had a sword out on Damlath, who stood his ground behind a glimmering spell shield. Damlath's mysterious companions were nowhere to be seen, and Raegar didn't feel particularly obliged to help the wizard at present. The flickering firelight lit up the area, and Raegar finally spotted a glint of metal. He saw the short sword lying in the grass, another scabbard burned away entirely around it. Raegar crawled to the sword, keeping himself hidden among the shadows as he heard more guards thundering down the road on horseback from their garrison on one of the nearby farms to the west.

The golden diamonds in the hilt of the short sword glistened beneath the moonlit sky. The ground beneath it was an inky black and oily, as if a patch of tar had bubbled up beneath the sword. The rogue gripped the pommel, but the ground held it fast. As Raegar fought to pull the sword free, two four-clawed hands formed from the tarlike patch and wrapped around the sword. An eye opened on the back of one of the hands, and a mouth on the other.

"Wakessssss ussssssss. Callsssss usssss," it hissed at the thief.

The tar patch grew beneath the sword, encroaching on where Raegar knelt. He grabbed the sword again and yanked it free from the growing horror, which screamed as he twisted the blade's edge to cut into the blackness. The scream seemed to echo across the ground and grow louder in two other places around the inn. The sound was instantly drowned out by another crash of lightning, and Raegar looked up, knowing it wasn't coming from his sword.

Damlath had fired a volley of lightning bolts across the wrecked inn to knock away the count's guards. Raegar wondered why he attacked and didn't just leave, but he was shocked to see the wizard close on the now-unguarded and unconscious Gamalon. Raegar watched in horror as his friend reached down and ripped the sparking gem from the man's eye socket. Darnlath held the gem high, his face triumphant and joyful. He cast a spell as new guards came up the road and surrounded him, and massive hailstones and mists of intense cold engulfed men and horses alike.

"Vengeance!" the captain screamed and swung his sword with both hands at Damlath, but the attack bounced off his spell shield.

Behind them in the ruined taproom, a growing mass of purple energy formed, and a massive black form lunged through a vortex, its surface bristling with teeth, claws, and eyes. Damlath turned to look at it then teleported away before anyone else could react.

Raegar had watched this scene as he unlashed the mare and mounted the saddle. He felt sick to his stomach and leaned over the mare's shoulder to vomit. That's when he noticed the blackness on the ground was thickening and growing toward him, the claws forming strange arms with three hands each. Among those claws, purple sparkles danced and the mouths continued hissing, "Give usssss . . . Oursssss . . ."

Raegar flinched from the creature and thought, Got to get away before that grows bigger. I'll get answers and more chances to be sick later.

He finally allowed the mare her head, and she bolted down the eastern road, her terror giving them the speed to leave whatever horrors they'd unleashed in their dust. All Raegar couldn't outrun that night were his nagging doubts about his much-changed partner.

CHAPTER NINE

28 Uktar, the Year of Lightning Storms
(1374 DR)

Khelben's words struck Tsarra like a physical blow, and she stopped in her tracks. Her face flushed as she restrained herself from shouting: *How dare you ask that of me, master or not?* Tsarra's ears rang, a side effect she attributed to using the *kiira*.

Khelben's current guise was a fat man in Wands livery, and his abrupt spin on his heels would have seemed comical at any other time. *This is not the time to indulge in childish fears.* Tsarra could feel his irritation with the sending.

Childish? If you've already been through my memories, you know exactly *why I hate undead. Hate, not fear.*

Those around them saw only the fat little guard and his charge—a well-dressed noblewoman in a stunning aquamarine gown—standing and glaring at each other in the middle of Calamastyr Lane.

Fear is the true source of hate, Tsarra. Regardless of what happened in the past, you need to meet Syndra at this time. It's crucial for your development and all that is to pass these next days.

You always do that. Do you know how much we hate it?

Do what? Make appropriate decisions when called for?

Oh, snideness too. No—make decisions for everyone around you and automatically assume they're both right and set in stone as if by godly fiat!

The constant ringing made it almost impossible for Tsarra to hear anything else. Khelben approached her and grabbed her by the arm.

Nameless flew from the darkness across the way, his snarl evident even from two stories up, and he flew directly into Khelben. The feline lashed his wings behind his body and into Khelben's hood while he sank his claws and teeth into the arm that held his mistress. With his free hand Khelben grabbed the tressym by the scruff and held him so his exasperated yowls and agitated wings were all that disturbed the peace. As Tsarra shrugged herself loose of Khelben's grip, she noticed the tressym had drawn blood and rent the archmage's sleeve. She wondered why her familiar wasn't calming despite her mental urging to do so or why she could hardly feel him in her head. She also wondered about the heavy smell of violets filling her nose, so thick she felt unsteady on her feet.

Khelben whispered, "You forget yourself, child, and with whom you're dealing."

"I'm . . ." Tsarra felt her rage drain from her so quickly she began to fall. All she could manage was a weak whisper before she collapsed on the cobbles. "Khelben, help me."

Midusmmer, the Year of the Lone Candle (1238 DR)

The dark-garbed man flew into the courtyard of a four-story stone tower nestled at the foot of Mount Waterdeep, violets covering every inch of the courtyard wall. The local watch patrol looked up, and all saluted the city's archmage, but Khelben the Elder waved them off, using their own hand signals to keep them from joining him. Despite their duty, none of them wished to argue with the centuries-old wizard. The watch civilar returned a hand signal to Khelben, his eyes directed above and behind the wizard.

Khelben looked up to see four overzealous apprentices flying overhead, and he scowled. He waved thanks to the watch and sketched a furious spell in his other hand. The archmage's whisper traveled upwind to the senior of his apprentices hovering above.

"Tandar, Mystra herself won't save you, should you or any others interfere here today. Were I in need of assistance, I would have asked when I left your class moments ago. Remain and watch from there, if you must, but never follow me again unless you have irrefutable reason."

Khelben cut off the spell without listening to the young Chondathan's response. The teacher in him was proud of his students showing initiative and drive, but he shuddered as he remembered the funerals of seven apprentices in the past ten years.

"No more, especially today of all days," he growled. At least he didn't have to keep Cassandra distracted, given how busy she and the Lady Simtul were with the wedding plans for that evening.

Khelben glanced at the tower, realizing it had been more than two dozen years since he'd darkened its door, despite it only being a short walk from Arunsun Tower. It was an oddity, even for Waterdeep: one of the very few examples of Shoon-style architecture north of Amn. The tower sat on an octagonal stone base two stories tall, its solid stone walls smooth save for random sigils carved about its surface, two arrow-slit windows per side, and the door on the northeastern facet. The door was flanked by two smaller minarets attached to the base on the adjacent east and north facets. Most believed the minarets generated great defensive or offensive magic against intruders. In truth, they were decorative from the outside and concealed rooms for a privy and ablutions inside, but Khelben knew the benefit of leaving others' fears and fables about wizards unanswered. The top two stories blended in better with Waterdeep, the darker local stones and bricks finishing off the tower's body. Atop the construction was the most indicative mark of Shoon architecture—the pyramid that marked the dwelling as a noble's house. Fashioning the pyramid from crystal marked her home as that of a worker of magic.

In his left hand, a crumpled parchment summoned him to the tower over a matter of urgency. It was signed with the mark of the sorceress Syndra Wands, and its teleporting directly to his hand suggested either knowledge or power that allowed it through the defenses of his home. The blood on the parchment bore enough hints of trouble to drag Khelben from his lecture on the ethics of charms. His right hand held a new weapon, a duskwood rod set with a row of diamonds and sheathed at head and foot in brightsteel. He didn't understand why his dreams had been haunted by that image or why Mystra herself insisted on both the weapon's creation months ago and his use of it that day. He understood he had been warned of the day's events, but familiarity and the unsure nature of dreams kept him from realizing it until moments before.

Committed to his role in these events, Khelben walked calmly through the street gate and strode through Syndra's herb garden path to the door. Just as in his dreams, he found a field of magical silence around the door and its flanking minarets, which he dispelled. Unlike the dreams, however, the door hung askew by one hinge and was pockmarked with dents that still dripped acid.

Whoever was behind the vandalism could strike quickly and silently. There was no other way to cause that kind of damage without alerting neighbors or the watch. Casting spells in quick succession, Khelben negated any additional standing spells within ten paces of the door, sent magic around to reveal any hidden or invisible creatures, and let slip another whisper on the winds to see if the mistress of the Eightower could respond.

"Granddaughter?" he asked the empty air as he stepped across the threshhold. Though he and his daughter's daughter had not spoken in years, a twinge of familial worry crept in to distract him.

The entry chamber, which Khelben knew was always immaculate—like its mistress—shamed itself with disarray and chaos. Someone had obviously come through on a rampage, counting on the magical silence to keep unwanted attention away. Khelben sniffed the air and several of the spell-blast points on the wall, raising his eyebrows in surprise.

"No sulfur or charring from a flamestruck blast point. Curious."

The archmage slowly moved through the four rooms on the ground floor, all with tapestries, rugs, and furniture thrown about by someone looking for something without success. He stalked through the silent tower and up the central stairs, stopping only to note blast marks where spells scored the stone steps and walls. He knew Syndra's fire spells left the scent of cedar smoke, a unique touch indicative of her sorcery. The other blast points and places where Khelben detected magic were either wet or cold to the touch, if not both. His eyes narrowed and his fist clenched.

"I know you now, traitorous whelp."

Casting spells on his person, Khelben stepped sideways into the stone pillar that supported the stairwell. Merged with the tower, he cast his senses around, checking for any sign of movement or damage within the tower. Sensing a cold spot despite the pulsing warmth of the magic atop the tower, he willed himself upward and into the wall directly before that location. He had a few moments with the spell to survey the land safely within the wall before committing himself to battle.

The walls of the room leaned inward, meeting fifteen feet overhead and revealing that the top floor of the tower was the pyramid itself. The walls and floor glimmered with magic, their translucence allowing some small glimpses of the darkening skies outside. Khelben saw draped before him, half on the stairs and half on the floor, the bloodied body of his granddaughter Syndra Wands. Her simple dress suggested she had been asleep when attacked, and its folds were stiff with frost and ice. Her skin was a dull gray, her legs had been shattered, and she had fallen on one arm, which had also shattered on impact. Her body was frozen solid, shown by the minimal presence of liquid blood pooling on the floor.

Even though Khelben knew the identity of Syndra's attacker, his former apprentice's appearance took him aback. The man wore cornflower blue robes elegantly stitched with cloth-of-gold and arrayed with his family crest and personal mark—three icicles hanging from the bottom edge of a pyramid. The bronze circlet around his brow gleamed with active power, its sickly olive glow casting a jaundiced veil around his eyes. He held his forearms crossed over his chest, a classic defensive pose favored by old-time Shoon spellcasters as well as a way to show off magical items. Two ring gems gleamed at Khelben—one sapphire, the other diamond—and the arcane energies they stored pulsed around the younger man. In all, his form and accoutrements exuded power, but his eyes betrayed desperation and a beggar's yearning.

"I can sense you near, Sunderspell. Come out from hiding and fight!" The man remained seated, his face and voice laced with anticipation.

Khelben spoke, his voice a grating monotone from the stone face carved into the end of the banister facing his foe. "You are drunk with power, boy. A wise man does not beg a reckoning from his betters."

"My betters? I unlocked secrets that have eluded you for centuries!" The man cackled, his eyes locked on the stone face. "I found and claimed the ancient legacies of the Necroqysars of Shoon! You're merely afraid to test your mettle against me."

"Trinkets and toys do not a wizard make, boy." Khelben

said as he willed his spell to an end and stepped from the stone. "Nor does reading someone's memoirs or spellbooks make you their equal."

"Interesting. Muaryn's Maedarwalk, isn't it?" The man's face broke into a grim smile. "Our second meeting in as many years, but this time, I shall leave the victor. I already have what I needed from her," he gloated as he pulled back his right sleeve. He exposed a silver bracer decorated with what looked like holly leaves and berries carved from silver and gold metals entwining its surface. The red and white berries were inset rubies and moonstones, and all shimmered with power.

"Issylmyth's Bracer should never be worn by the likes of you." Khelben said, his voice a harsh whisper as he knelt by his granddaughter and closed her eyes. "You have slain blood of my blood, and you shall answer for it." Khelben rested the rod on Syndra's corpse, its head bloody from her thawing wounds.

"Don't call me boy! I will make you say my name, old man, and give me the respect I deserve."

The man lashed his arms forward, his rings adding magical power to his casting. Blue-white claws of energy reached toward Khelben, growing larger as they approached him.

Khelben stared into his foe's eyes while he dispelled the magical attack. "One cannot command respect nor can one expect it from a vainglorious appellation. One earns respect with deeds and mettle."

"Deeds and mettle, spell-shatterer?" The wizard scoffed. "Your own granddaughter lies there dead. My deeds say enough."

"Indeed," Khelben snapped. "From the moment of her birth, I knew of Syndra's sad fate but knew neither the cause nor the instigator until moments ago. It saddens me that your petty vanities and overinflated sense of worth brought you to this, little Rakesk."

Khelben paced around the glowing chamber, keeping distant from both the glowing walls and his foe at its center. His detection spell continued, and he tried to glean as much information as he could about the wizard's defensive shields.

"You never mentioned you were an oracle, Khelben. You always were a miser with your secrets. That's why I had to journey to Shoonach to grasp the power that was my due! Once I've slain you as well and claimed your tower, I shall reign over Waterdeep!"

"Boast less, cast more, fool." Khelben snapped, as he unleashed tight streams of purple flames from each of his fingertips and arced them to stab at his foe from all sides.

The vain wizard smiled smugly as the flames flattened and died against a pyramidal shaped spell-shield. The glow of the crystalline ceiling repeated the kaleidoscopic colors in its own energies overhead.

Khelben allowed himself a tight-lipped smile. "At least your shields are worthy of respect. Tell me, does the room dictate their form or your will?"

"My will is not lacking, Sunderspell, though the room aids me. One secret Syndra didn't know about these pyramids is their ability to hone and focus magical fields. I doubt even you could shatter my defenses now, Arunsun! They only break when I ask them, thus!"

The four sides of the spell pyramid around Rakesk tipped upward then launched themselves at Khelben. The archmage managed to dispel two of the whirling planes, but the latter two stabbed into his right thigh and his lower back, their energies leeching into him after drawing blood. Khelben screamed and fell backward, his body spasming from the spell's fluctuating energies.

"Overconfidence must run in your bloodline, Arunsun. I felled Syndra with that same spell. A pity, as it's hardly one of my signatures, like this."

The man stood and raised his hands high. Khelben strained to counterspell the magic but failed. He couldn't overcome the last effects of the previous spell. Rakesk completed his casting, and smiled coldly as a pillar of blue fire engulfed Khelben in icy flames. Khelben screamed anew, cursing himself for his weakness.

Behind Khelben and Rakesk both, the duskwood rod and its gems glowed and shimmered. Unnoticed by the gloating wizard, the rod twitched and slowly rose from the bloodied corpse. Trailing an opalescent mist, it swung silently, almost hesitatingly, in the air. After two swings, the rod looped back and brought itself down in a powerful blow to Rakesk's head. The impact forced the bronze circlet into the man's scalp and face as it bent down over his left eye, scoring his left cheek and right temple as the circlet tipped on his brow. Rakesk screamed in pain and anger, his sight temporarily blocked by blood flowing over his eyes. As he turned to face his unseen attacker, the rod swung again, and the bones in Rakesk's right wrist and arm crunched audibly. The diamond ring on that hand fell, and the impact knocked loose Issylmyth's Bracer.

Khelben propped himself up on one elbow and chuckled as Rakesk howled in pain and recoiled from the hovering rod.

"That's a very singular weapon, boy. Its usual trick is to revisit pains on its victims both physically and magically. It repeats the pain of the worst hurts in your body or mind while also dealing its own hurts. Makes it very useful against overbearing warriors. Still, its greatest talent is to allow the spirits of the recently slain one last chance to avenge themselves upon their killers." While Khelben spoke, the glow around the rod had steadily increased and outlined the slim figure of a human woman, the fury on her face belying the peacefulness of her own corpse at her feet.

"Thank you for this chance, grandfather." The ghostly mists mouthed the words but the voice rang out from the rod itself. "Unfortunate you didn't know how far your former pupil had fallen before he killed me."

"Apologies with deepest sorrows, *a'a'sum,*" Khelben said, a lone tear burning down his hoar-frosted cheek. "We all play our roles as our Lady bids us. Now play yours in rightful vengeance."

CHAPTER TEN

29 Uktar, the Year of Lightning Storms
(1374 DR)

Tsarra's eyes snapped open as she awoke. She sat up and shook her head to clear the glittering fog in front of her eyes, to no avail. In sympathy with the vision she had just endured, her right thigh and lower back ached painfully. The noises of combat did focus her concentration. She heard loud snarling—the tressym—and shouts—Khelben's voice immediately in front of her, and at least four others around her. She also heard a horrifying sound she couldn't identify—a raspy hiss coupled with a high keening tone like a rabbit's scream. She didn't know what he was fighting, but she could feel the tressym angrily battling to *"protect mistressfriend like young."*

Khelben yelled, "Get back, fool! Enough have died already tonight."

The unknown person replied, "I can help you, Master!"

"Not against that you can't. Just do what you can to keep the inn from collapsing atop us."

Khelben's voice intoned in Tsarra's head, but without the ringing in her ears she had before: *Good. You're awake. Stay down until I say.*

I'm blind, Khelben! Tsarra tried to control her panic, but she started shaking even as she sent.

His response was cold, but she could sense his concern as well. *Explanations later. Don't distract me now.*

She could hear him beginning a spell, wherever he was, so she took several deep breaths to calm her racing heart. That exercise cleared her vision slightly, and she could see vague outlines.

Tsarra reached out and felt the wood floor and what she guessed was an overturned table or a fallen door against which she was lying. She felt an odd tingling around her middle again and realized she could see a glow—blue sparks wreathed her body, centered on the golden belt she wore beneath her armor. She remembered being surprised when she first donned it, and it seemed to merge with her skin. Looking around at the detritus around them, she realized the sparks provided some protection.

Khelben's spellcasting ended with a sound that reminded Tsarra of shattering glass and a shield bouncing downhill. Whatever it was, she didn't recognize it, but it stilled the odd roaring by the large creature that fought Khelben.

Tsarra pushed herself up on her elbows and realized she wasn't alone—someone lay next to her against the wall, breathing unevenly. Tsarra blinked a few times in rapid succession and cleared her eyesight. She looked and found a dark skinned bald man whose face, neck, and chest were heavily blistered and bleeding, his left eye blasted away. She flashed back to the day she found her father dead in the Ardeep Forest with similar wounds.

Tsarra pushed herself away from the horrific sight, gasping for air and hitting the foot of the stairs at the same time. She heard Khelben in her head again.

He's alive, unlike your father. See to it he stays that way, and don't draw attention to yourself. The sharn is looking for you and that belt. Don't send in return—I need to concentrate.

Tsarra had read about sharn but like most folk, had never seen one. Still, she resisted looking out from behind the table and focused on the task at hand. She undid a pouch on the back of her leather belt. Retrieving some yarrow and acacia leaves, she chewed them and used the moistened poultice to treat the worst burns on the man's face. Along with a silent prayer to Fenmaril Mestarine, Tsarra thanked her mother for the skills she taught her in woodland herbs and their healing applications. If nothing else, the man's breathing steadied and relaxed. Tsarra's eyes fell on his hand and its ring, which bore the crest of Spellshire. This was Khelben's friend the count, Gamalon Idogyr, and something had stolen the gem he used as his left eye!

Tsarra noticed a purple glow growing in the underside of the table that quickly became a spiral of winking lights. She reached inside herself and cast one of her most common spells to detect magic, though she perceived it by scent rather than sight. The growing spell carried the scent of apples, which she associated with translocational spells for some reason, but the scent was musty and stagnant, as if cast by something old or dead. It didn't smell like any spells she'd sensed from allies, so she assumed the worst.

Tsarra brought a different spell to bear quickly. With a quiet murmured casting, she summoned to her mind's eye an invisible dagger of magic around her right hand. She quickly slashed away the magical connections between the purple glow and the Weave, dispelling the magic. The magic ended, but to Tsarra it felt different than other spells she'd disrupted in the past.

Suddenly, two swarms of purple sparkles erupted around her, all swirling in faster patterns. Tsarra dispelled one of them but then turned to stare into an eyeless face. Its skin glistened an oily black, and its mouth moved as if it had no jaw beneath its sharp teeth. Saliva sprayed from its mouth as it roared at her, the sound reminding her of both a mountain lynx and a wounded hare at the same time.

"Khelben! It's found us!" Tsarra yelled, falling onto her back to avoid the lunge the floating head made at her and to protect the fallen Count Idogyr.

She hooked her thumbs together and summoned up rage and magic. Red and orange flames shot out in a fan from her hands. The sharn's head retreated through its purple portal, the energy still swirling around in mid-air. Before Tsarra could even think of dispelling the portal, a slimy black arm with three smaller arms attached to it thrust through at freakish speed, and its collective twelve fingers all lashed at her. Tsarra kicked at the nearest hand as she sent out another fan of flames. The sharn's translucent black skin crackled and burst like a frog in a campfire. Still, the arm kept reaching for her, and some of its hands began casting a spell. His loud snarl preceding him, Nameless slammed into those upper hands, clawing and biting at them before any power was summoned.

Tsarra breathed easier and worked to dispel the purple portal. She could hear the sounds of battle in the background as well as Khelben's deep monotonic spellcasting. The sharn arm stretched toward her, though some of its hands attacked the familiar. Tsarra slashed away in her mind's eye, severing the magic's ties to the Weave, and the portal snuffed itself out, only to be followed by a tremendous scream. The creature's massive arm lay on the floor before Tsarra, severed when the portal snapped shut on it.

Tsarra stood up, her presence no longer a secret, and surveyed the scene. She stood not on Waterdeep's streets but inside a wrecked tavern, its thatched roof almost entirely blown away and its edges smoldering. She saw at least eight bodies. Khelben stood a few paces away, his back to her. The Blackstaff was the only person within the room, the rest standing on the periphery where the tavern's front wall used to be. Five local laborers or tavern patrons, and a dozen men in guards' livery, fought to shore up the creaking second floor with a fallen support beam, before it collapsed upon them.

Tables and chairs were tossed every which way, as were some unconscious or dead patrons. Among the wreckage the sharn's bulk hovered just above the floor and its skin stretched, as if other creatures pulsed inside its greasy amorphous flesh. Despite Tsarra's luck, the sharn produced a second arm from its form to replace the severed one. It kept one arm busy stretching to grab up fallen weapons while the other worked to cast spells. Eyes appeared and disappeared everywhere on its body, though a few always remained trained on anything that moved. Once it spotted Tsarra, the spellcasting hands twisted toward her with a sick wet crunch.

Khelben was doing some rather long and intricate casting, his attentions wholly focused on the sharn, so Tsarra worked the counterspell against whatever the creature was casting. She smiled, as she had never cast it so quickly before. Once she'd stopped the sharn's spell, Khelben completed his own, and Tsarra she felt it permeate the room and thicken the magic all around. The air crystallized slightly, and she sniffed the telltale smell of burnt rosehips and sulfur. She guessed that Khelben did something to affect teleporters in the area. She hadn't mastered any transmutation spells, but at least she knew their signs.

"That should prevent any additional headaches for the moment." Khelben chuckled, and Tsarra realized he was enjoying himself.

Amazing he's lived this long, she thought as she threw off her cloak with one hand and pulled her bow off her back with the other.

Indeed. Khelben's sending startled her. *I'm glad you're not one of those who gets ill from long-range teleports. The sharn is devilishly tough to affect without magical weapons.*

And that's why I've been turning my studies toward arcane archery. Tsarra pulled back on the bowstring and let an arrow fly, willing some of her sorcerous energies into the missile. It struck one of the eyes in the sharn's central mass, but the creature morphed a mouth around the arrow and bit it to pieces.

"A fine shot, but you'll run out of arrows before it runs out of patience, my dear," Khelben said. "Get Gamalon away from harm before you dive in to attack, Tsarra, but don't wander too far. Mind the danger of us straying too far apart. I'll take care of this." With that, Khelben turned his attentions to the sharn and began another long and complicated casting.

Tsarra still had many questions, but she stored them for later. She returned to Gamalon's side and found his lone eye open and looking at her.

"Where is Mynda? Where is my wife?"

His voice was raspy, and he was in obvious pain. He tried to move to a sitting position, but his strength failed him and he fell unconscious again with a faltering groan.

Tsarra looked at the count and tears welled in her eyes. While Gamalon looked no older than his early fifties, his head wounds and body damage left him in no shape to cast spells or even move easily. Tsarra cast a spell she often used to bear the fruits of her hunts home, interlacing her fingers together into a cup to materialize a russet-tinged floating disk beneath the stunned mage. She willed the disk to move slowly out onto the lawn, pushing it a slight distance ahead of her.

The familiar flew a loop around her and its snarls and purrs told her a little more. *"Firemarkedoldmage and house got hit by skylanceburningbright, like you and darkmage and sunnybrighteyesgone. We fight shiftshapemanysmelling thing, yes?"*

Tsarra was glad the familiar was all right, but she shook her head. "No, we won't. You stay with him, and keep him safe. Let me know if anything other than his guards try to get near him."

"Wantfight, protect mistressfriend. Not afraid."

The tressym's loud yowls surprised the nearby men almost as much as when Tsarra meowed her response:

"Staysafehere until weknowfoeweakness." With that, she settled the disc and the count onto the grass, the tressym landing nearby with an angry rustle of his wings. Tsarra picked up her bow and turned to see where she could help Khelben.

The sharn howled, "Thievess! Sssscentssss mark you . . . Take what is oursssss!" and threw an axe and a long sword in Tsarra's direction.

"No!" Khelben yelled and leaped in front of the weapons, his arms glowing as if armored by magic.

The long sword glanced harmlessly off his left forearm and fell to the side. The axe, however, hit his right hand with a wet smack, and the Blackstaff grunted in pain.

"So messy. He'll never cast that crushing grasp now, will he?" a woman's voice sneered from empty air across the inn from Tsarra. "Needs both hands, given the way you humans cast it."

"No, my dear, he can't. Imagine—us lending a hand to the Blackstaff. Such a strange day," a man's voice erupted from the same area over by the fireplace, and a form took shape as the man's arms waved in intricate spellcasting, dispelling his invisibility.

The lightly bearded man stood taller than Khelben by perhaps a handspan with long black hair pulled into a pony-tail trailing halfway down his back. His face was tanned, but that was the only healthy thing about him. His form was scrawny rather than lean. Rings glittered at least two per hand, and a heavy gold pendant hung on his chest atop his amber-colored tunic, richly embroidered but fraying at the cuffs and sleeves. His leather breeches were well made but looked as if they'd been worn overlong.

With great speed, the sharn launched a chunk of ruined table at the man, but other arcane words filled the air. A blast of flames engulfed the wooden implement and the arms that held it. The trailing end of the fires led to the recently visible hands of an elf woman. She stood about Tsarra's height and wore traveling clothes of dark blue and gray leathers and linens—not protective so much as practical. Her snow-blond hair, bound in multiple places by silver ties, nearly reached the floor and seemed white or gold, depending on how the light hit it.

Tsarra's surprise at the arrival of two other wizards ended when Khelben shouted at her, "Stand away, girl!"

He turned around and spoke to the other two wizards, and the three of them created a triangle around the sharn. The man's casting finally ended, and a hazy shimmer settled around the sharn, slowing down its movement to closer to normal speeds for a creature its size.

Khelben said, "Petrylloc's Gambit, now!" and started casting.

The other two, after a moment, took to casting similar spells—or at least they sounded similar to Tsarra's ears. She kept her bow ready but began a spell, happy she knew how to cast without movement. In her mind, she summoned magic and the sounds of a hummingbird's wing and the twang of a bow. Four glowing green energy pulses leaped from her hands into four open mouths on the sharn. When the sharn howled, its speech slowed so it sounded like a wounded bear with a human voice. Tsarra and the assembled guards had their bows drawn, and the wizards were all occupied with their collective spellcasting. The sharn sprayed all of them with magical bolts. While the spell didn't disrupt the wizards' castings, Tsarra and eight others let arrows fly. Six of them hit the sharn, but only Tsarra's ensorcelled arrow appeared to do any damage. Despite that, the volley kept the creature suitably occupied.

Tsarra saw twinkles of white and gray collect first into a wall of ice and followed by two walls of stone. All three perched precariously on the remnants of the upper floor just above the sharn. Their weight immediately crumpled the floor on which they rested, and all three fell atop the sharn. The creature's speed still belied its bulk, and it managed to dodge the first wall, but the second wall pinned it in place. The third wall dropped on it, the ice broke into three large pieces, and the sharn died beneath it with a lowing cry and the sound of something heavy slapping onto thick mud.

"Honestly, Blackstaff. Couldn't you be more direct in battle instead of spouting obscure references?" The man kept his eyes on Khelben but extended his hand to his lady, who placed her hand on his as they moved toward Khelben.

The Blackstaff replied, "If you hadn't known it, I'd have been even more disappointed in you and your teachers than I have been in times past."

Khelben kept his attentions focused at all times on the man and woman, though he grimaced while he pulled the axe free from his hand. His hands returned to his sides, and he left the wound alone. Tsarra flinched but stared with fascination as Khelben's hand bled a bit, leaving a puddle of blood at his feet. Within moments, the wound closed, flickers of silver flame bubbling and burning at its edges.

Tsarra left Gamalon and her familiar behind her on the ground as she moved to Khelben's side. She slung her bow over her shoulder and placed her other hand pointedly on the pommel of her scimitar. Silently, Khelben sent to Tsarra a request to *keep an eye on them a moment, please.*

The wizard turned his back on the wizardly pair and approached the guard captain. "Captain Grellig, we shall have to track and capture those responsible for this on the morrow. Tonight, I'm afraid there's naught left for you and your men to do but prepare graves for the unfortunates. Major Jharna, I shall need your assistance."

The major approached and muttered, "I don't like the smell of this, Lord Arunsun. It's the curse for certain."

Khelben said, "Healthy skepticism is good, Major, but superstitions carry their own powers whether we like it or not. Pray, do not speak of curses until your lord is safe. Your troops can return to the city with Grellig's Guard contingent in two days, but I need you to act more quickly for me." Khelben pulled a ring from his belt pouch. "Use this, and it will take you and Count Idogyr directly to my tower, where he can get help. Tell Laeral to prepare Nine Silvers for the Legacy's rise. Give her that ring, repair to his excellency's rented villa, and refrain speaking of this to anyone outside my tower, please."

"Right away, sir." Major Jharna walked over to the nine Tethyrian guards and servants who surrounded their count. He put the ring on his right hand, grasped Gamalon's left hand, and twisted the ring's gem to teleport away. Khelben returned to Tsarra's side and faced their impromptu allies.

It bothered Tsarra that she didn't know who she faced. Something about the elf woman reminded her of a vague half-memory from her youth in Ardeep. Perhaps Tsarra had gazed too intently at her, because the elf woman stared back. There was haughtiness and regal bearing in her face, followed by some amusement and flickers of shock and disappointment.

"You give *kiira* to half-breeds, Blackstaff? Either you like risking their sanity or you simply wish to insult *tel'quessir*. To add further insult, she's not even a true wizard!"

Khelben spread his right arm in Tsarra's path as she surged forward, his palm still bearing a smoldering, angry wound. *She wants you to take her bait to see what you'll do. Don't give her the satisfaction.*

"Is our truce at an end so soon, Blackstaff? You surely don't intend to leave us to the mercies of an insulted child? However shall we prevail against such a foe?" The man's smile reminded Tsarra of an overbold weasel.

Speaking in Elvish, Khelben said, *"Neither. Your business here is with me and my pupil, who deserves only the blessings and none of the burdens of such elven gifts. Tonight has proven more troublesome than expected. I thank you for your help, but hold from insulting each other in the interests of our tasks at hand."*

"My Elvish is a tad rusty, but I understood enough. Our agreement stands as discussed, despite the altered circumstances, provided you intend to honor it. You have our word to meet two days' hence at Malavar's Grasp."

To Tsarra, it seemed the man either had the greatest confidence in the Realms or he was a fool to talk down to Khelben.

Actually neither, Tsarra, Khelben sent to her. *Our helpmates here are formerly of the Zhentarim outpost of Darkhold, the mages Ashemmi and Sememmon.*

CHAPTER ELEVEN

29 Uktar, the Year of Lightning Storms
(1374 DR)

It took Raegar nearly an hour to work his way up the path to Stagsmere. The night was murky, clouds having covered up the moon. Because of that, he'd missed the moss-covered and ruined Stagstone the first time he passed it, taking it to be the corner of a fallen stone cottage. Raegar scraped off enough moss to identify the sculpture as a stag's head, once he realized its antlers had long since worn away from weather or vandals. He turned his horse north up a long-unused trail that required him to dismount in places to slash away heavy undergrowth.

The moon broke through the clouds as Raegar approached the manor. Like its marker stone, Stagsmere had seen better days. The central manor stood three stories tall, off of which sprang two two-story wings on east and west. The entire front corner and much of that part of the western wing's second story had collapsed into a pile of rubble. Raegar couldn't gauge the color of stone in the moonlight, but it was lighter overall, with dark stone forming surrounding porches, jutting balconies, and random details and decorations. On the battlements atop the roof's edge, Raegar noted that a stone stag reared at each corner save the fallen one. The manor house was grand, and its architecture reminded Raegar of some of the older buildings in North Ward, especially the Brossfeather villa off Simmikan Court. He'd have to check that stone shield over the main door, but he suspected he might find the same Brossfeather coat of arms there as well.

Raegar, long used to the sounds of a city at night, listened intently to the clamor around him. Even with winter coming on, many animals croaked, cried, trilled, or howled on the night air, and the rogue could hear other creatures scuttling away in the tall grass, reeds, and underbrush around him. Still, he was glad not to worry about how much noise the mare made in her approach. As he came within a hail's distance of the manor house, he heard shrill, unearthly screams and the sounds of spells in play. While the bulk of Stagsmere remained dark, lights crackled and flashed blue and gold in the eastern wing of the manor around the back.

Raegar urged the mare into a gallop along a gravel path leading around the building. The ground was unsteady on the long untended path, slowing his horse. Raegar drew the Diamondblade with his left hand and was glad to see it wasn't sparking for a change. For that, at least, he let out a sigh of relief as he readied himself for another battle. From the scabbard on his right leg, he pulled his second short sword, a nonmagical one but still a weapon, and he wanted every weapon he had ready. He listened as Damlath shouted out his spells and heard the roar of flames or the crackle of lightning bolts. What Raegar realized he didn't hear was Damlath's laughter—the wizard always cackled with glee between his spells, and Raegar hadn't heard him do that for tendays.

"Raegar, how did you manage not to notice that until now?" he asked himself. He gripped the pommels of his short swords all the tighter. He had to be careful or he might have more than one foe to fight right away instead of a time more to his liking.

The gravel path widened around the backside of the manor, allowing space for carriages and three-horse-wide teams. He didn't need that much room and urged his horse up the steps of the porch that spanned the back of the entire manor. Lights and noise erupted through the long-shattered floor to ceiling windows where the eastern wing met the central house. Raegar leaped off the horse, landing noiselessly, and lashed her reins to the stone railing on the porch. He slipped into the shadows among the window breaks to assess the situation before leaping into it.

Raegar looked into what was once a proud dining hall, but its splendor was long since ruined. Loads of animal scat was piled in various places in corners and along the walls, together with the detritus of leaves and dirt and other natural debris blown through the missing windows. A few rags clung to the walls and window rods, the tatters silently framing the scene within. A long table that might have once seated twenty lay splintered and askew at the long room's center, its chairs reduced to kindling. The cabinets that once lined the walls opposite Raegar to hold china and glassware still retained a few small panels of glass, but most of them had been shattered, their contents long ago looted. Blast marks along the walls and floors and the smoldering remnants of a large cabinet provided mute evidence of a spell battle only moments old.

The acrid reek of various spells and smoke drifting from the room was bearable but told Raegar that Damlath—or whatever he fought—had unleashed many more combat spells than usual. He knew the wizard memorized very few offensive spells unless he planned to be in an unavoidable fight. Usually, his repertoire consisted of many investigative spells and methods by which the pair of them stayed hidden from any potential opponents. But that day, Damlath—or whoever posed as him—seemed spoiling for a fight. Raegar looked through the broken windows and realized the battle had ventured beyond the dining room. The rogue stepped sideways and slipped inside easily, making his way to the nearest door through which he could see crackling golden energy.

He looked into an entry chamber with grand marble staircases rising over Raegar's head to the upper floors on both sides of the room. The chandelier had fallen long ago onto the hard marble floor, its metal construction twisted and broken in places but still holding a few now-dry oil lamps. Damlath stood within the massive round chandelier's center, weaving a blue-green sphere of energies upward into the domed room's center. Raegar had to move forward and through the small hallway formed by the stairs overhead to see Damlath's target.

What hovered in the room's center reflected the energy off its oily black hide, the eyes thick on its front closing to shield themselves from the bright lights. Its two massive limbs stretched apart, and the blue-green energy coruscating across its form collected around the ends of those limbs. At its base, where Raegar expected legs, he saw only a tail, as if the creature was a torso atop a teardrop shape. The creature's three heads all roared in pain and anger, its jaws distended and moving sideways or tipping the head fully back. Raegar shuddered and was glad he didn't have to fight the creature, whatever it was. Its skin moved and shifted, fingers, eyes, and mouths constantly forming and disappearing, keeping the aquamarine energy arcing across its form at all times.

The battle paused, and Raegar listened rather than leaping in to aid a no longer trusted ally.

"Now, creature, tell me why you bother me," Damlath asked. "There is no mention of guardians within Rhaelnar's Legacy."

"We know of no Rhaelnar . . . Guardiansssss ussssss . . ." the creature hissed. "Lightning and sssstormsssss awaken ussss . . . Awaken from Sssslumber Willing . . . and remember . . ."

"Remember what? I know you to be sharn, creatures of power and mystery. I have no qualms about killing you if your answers prove pitiful." Damlath closed his right hand, and the aquamarine globes pulled slowly together, wreathing the sharn's form in greenish arcs of energy. All its heads roared, as did at least half the mouths along its arms and trunk.

"Look, little creature," said the sharn, "into our mind, if you dare."

Damlath laughed, but it was hollow and angry, unlike the joyful mirth Raegar liked to hear. "Don't mistake me for a fool of short years, sharn. I know enough to not risk my sanity delving into your heads."

"The Awakening isss upon usss . . . You quicken sssoulsss without knowing what you do . . . The remnantsss ssspark and affect our mindsss . . . remind usss of oursssselvesss . . . The powersss that ssstir usss fragment our mind into many . . . bring pain memory . . ."

Raegar watched the sharn intently, its voice growing melancholy. Raegar also noticed random faces pushing forth from the sharn's skin as it spoke, though the speech still came from its massive unfeatured heads atop its torso.

Damlath shook his arms in anger at the creature and said, "I could care not a whit for your minds, save what they hold. The remnants—tell me more about them! I have many of them but not all. Tell me more about them, that I may claim more than one Nether Scroll."

Raegar's brow knitted. Damlath had never expressed any interest before in the ancient lore of Netheril, let alone tracking down the sources of their ancient magic. In fact, Raegar knew Damlath loved history but willfully ignored the North's wizardly history over that of the southern Lands of Intrigue.

The exchange confirmed to Raegar that the man posing as Damlath was an imposter. The rogue looked around to see if the wizard—whoever he was—had set up a camp or at least had laid down any of the artifacts they had been collecting. He didn't see any, but a light purple glow of sparkles began forming well behind the wizard.

A black-skinned pair of four-clawed hands slid from the cluster of purple sparks and began to trace mystic symbols in the air. Small mouths at the center of the palms whispered arcane words. A beam of orange light shone from the pair of hands and enveloped the southern mage, whose form shimmered and shattered. The illusory Damlath fell away and Raegar saw his true form.

The wizard wore olive-green robes trimmed with gold runes, a hood drawn up around his face, even though Damlath's face had previously appeared exposed. The wizard turned and spotted both Raegar and the sharn's additional hands and began to laugh. The rogue gasped as he saw the wizard's hands were skeletal, as was most of his head. All that remained of his face was a shred of grayish-black skin across his forehead and down the right side of his face. Red energies glinted within dark eyesockets, suggesting eyes where no physical orbs remained. Around his torso and over his olive robes, the lich wore a harness made of black leather and a large round silver plate covered in runes.

Raegar had fought undead wizards and sorcerers before, and he knew that this lich had been impersonating Damlath, but for how long?

"Ah, Raegar. So now you know, little thief. Inconvenient. You've been a useful pawn even more unwitting than that dullard at the temple," the lich said, its jaws moving without lips and pantomiming magically produced speech. "Still, before this creature strips me of more than base illusions. . . ."

The lich that was Damlath gestured quickly, and ice-blue bolts rocketed into the free sharn hands. Raegar was close enough to note the rapid drop in temperature and the ice and frost that clung to the once-moist black hide. The purple sparks winked out as the hands receded through them, and Raegar saw some frost appear on the sharn behind the lich, even though Damlath hadn't cast on it directly.

"Impressive, sharn. Your ability to bypass a spell designed to inhibit spellcasters is intriguing. I will learn that secret from you as well, but not before you tell me more of the remnants."

"You merely ssserve to awaken, not to claim any treasssure, little lich. We hide enigmasss far older than you, and thossse who pry never benefit from it." The sharn seemed to smile, its eyeless heads all turning toward the lich and baring their teeth.

Raegar stepped forward, brandishing both his swords before him in a defensive cross. He knew he didn't have the power to stop either creature, but he hoped to keep the lich's attention on him to perhaps allow the sharn to attack again. Raegar felt cold as he realized his friend had either become undead or was dead and had been replaced.

"Are you Damlath and damned," he asked, "or are you the bastard that killed him?"

Once Raegar stepped fully into the chamber and toward the lich, the Diamondblade spat a shower of blue sparks, as did a ring on the lich's left hand. Raegar stopped dead in his tracks, and the lich stepped back and behind the fallen chandelier, putting the hovering sharn between them. The sparks ceased.

"Your friend Damlath died swearing oaths too, rather than having useful spells with which to fight for his life. If it's any consolation, he died with the Binder's name on his lips."

Raegar froze as the death of his friend became reality. The only weapon he had that might affect this creature was one he had given him—the Diamondblade. Since it was obvious the short sword was important to the lich, Raegar made a split-second decision and dived toward the doorway. He heard one syllable in the lich's raspy voice and sensed the magic hit him. Though he remained facing the doorway, unmoving, Raegar felt as if he had been slammed hard against the wall. He stood stunned and trapped in his own body.

"Ah, ah, ah," the lich mocked. "No, bring that closer, young Raegar. You've been such a useful tool these past few months. Show the sharn what we have here."

The undead wizard gestured again, its skeletal fingers beckoning, and Raegar felt the Diamondblade twist in and rip from his grasp, even though the effort turned his stunned form around toward the sharn. The moment the blade crossed into the larger center of the room, it both reflected some moonlight from the skylight up above and mirrored sparks along with the ring on the lich's hand.

The lich floated the sword directly into the sharn, point-first, and it unleashed a shriek reminding Raegar of a sword crashing against a shield. The blue sparks joined the other magic and danced across the sharn's form. The sharn's own movements pulled the greenish energy globes closer, and their energies also spilled across its liquid form, invoking a mournful moan that sounded like five or six wounded people and animals at once. Raegar flexed his muscles in hopes of shaking off the magic and fleeing into the wilderness rather than face these two creatures. He managed two slow steps before the lich's magic placed a heavy wall of ice over his exit.

"No, boy. I still have tasks for you, and secrets to cull from this creature as well. Sometimes, though, it's sensible to make it clear you have your audience's attentions."

The lich pulled the sparking ring off its hand while he spoke, setting it on the floor where he stood. He gestured with one hand toward a doorway hidden from Raegar's sight, beckoning something or someone forward. The lich moved around and set the sparking Diamondblade on the floor as well.

Raegar held back when he saw the sparks building, but stepped around in hope of discovering another exit beyond the front door behind the lich. He spotted the skeleton lurching forward, a small green gem alive with more sparks resting on a dusty, threadbare pillow.

Once the skeleton stepped fully into the chamber, lightning bolts arced among the sword, gem, and ring, and the sharn screamed as bolts slammed through its form. The lightning bolts formed a triangle, and the energies came together into one massive bolt that exploded upward.

Neither the sharn nor the stone and glass ceiling stopped the bolt from smashing out into the night air. What little moonlight there had been disappeared as clouds quickly formed, allowing the lightning a path across the horizon.

"Well," the lich said, "I might have gained more from it, but at least I know it can be killed, despite some rumors about the sharn. Hmph." He opened his cloak and reached into the lining with his skeletal hand, pulling a small metal skullcap from its magical pocket. The lich placed the skullcap on his head and turned to stare fully at Raegar. "Now, little man, let's set your orders in place. I've another task for you. . . ."

Raegar's mind swam with fear and revulsion as he gritted his teeth.

"I'll never work for you, you bastard!" Raegar yelled, hoping to keep the lich's attention on his face, not his foot that edged beneath the ring of the chandelier.

As the lich's hand rose to cast a spell, the rogue kicked upward, tossing a large shard of the metal chandelier toward his face. At the same time, Raegar grabbed daggers from his belt and threw them at the lich's chest. All three missiles bounced harmlessly off a shielding spell, and the lich completed his spellcasting gestures.

"Futile defiance," sneered the lich. "Your will is mine, Raegar Stoneblade, orphan, thief, and holy seeker of Oghma. I allowed you autonomy so long as it aided my disguise, but speed now determines my course. Be still while your master sets your tasks in mind."

The crimson glints within the lich's eye sockets flared, and Raegar screamed as the lich's magic invaded his thoughts, freezing his mind with every passing heartbeat. The last thing Raegar heard as he lost consciousness was the lich in his mind saying, *Yes, a handy scapegoat was the last piece I needed. The Blackstaff will doubtless untangle the truth, but not until far too late . . . especially if you cannot protest or reveal any truths. . . .*

CHAPTER TWELVE

*29 Uktar, the Year of Lightning Storms
(1374 DR)*

Ashemmi smiled then spoke in Common. "Her face alone speaks volumes, *evae'n*. The Blackstaff has finally identified us for his precious apprentice."

"Khelben? How can we possibly ally with *them?*" Tsarra gripped Maornathil's pommel with white knuckles, staring at her mentor in shocked disbelief. Khelben remained silent.

Nameless shared Tsarra's emotions, and his back bristled with anger. He landed on a table near Tsarra, loudly hissing at the couple and making himself as threatening as possible, wings fully flared open.

"Khelben?" Tsarra asked, not wanting to meet the mocking eyes of Sememmon or Ashemmi. "What is going on here? How do we know this situation here isn't his—"

Sememmon laughed. "Honestly, girl, if you believe every rumor you've heard about me, you'd best be prepared to swallow every falsehood the masses bandy about regarding your glowering tutor here."

"At least she's not one of those who thinks all elves must hide their passions and bottle their emotions." Ashemmi said, staring Tsarra in the eyes. "The most useful thing a wizard can learn from another's familiar is their true emotional state. Even the most intelligent animals tend to reflect how their masters feel."

"That's enough, all of you," Khelben snapped. "This is neither the time nor place for this discussion. We shall all meet again two nights hence at the agreed-upon site. You gave him the item I made you?"

Sememmon nodded and said, "Yes, the wand now lies in his grasp. Enamored of Shoon artifacts, that one is, and he wears one of them openly—the Duel-Ring of Ghuraxx, if I'm not mistaken, and I'm not. Given how few Northerners bother with knowledge of the south, he stands out like soot on snow. I could not penetrate his disguise, but it is painfully obvious he cloaks himself in illusion. With patience, one can easily notice such things, don't you think, little half-elf?"

Tsarra answered Sememmon's affected smile with a glower, punctuated by the deep growl and lashing tail of Nameless, who flexed his full claws as a warning. Sememmon only rolled his eyes upward and sighed.

"This Damlath stinks of undeath, not that any of you—save perhaps the tressym—could smell it," Ashemmi added. "Either he's a necromancer seeking more power or he's undead himself and passing as a live human."

Undead? Khelben? Tsarra sent, her temper rising again. *You owe me—*

Patience! Your temper is fraying the edges of my own, apprentice. Explanations are due once we are alone. Now be still.

Khelben's sending startled Tsarra by its forcefulness, but his face did not betray the least shift in emotion or attention off the two former Darkholden.

"That fact has been known to me for a time," Khelben said. "Now, we must all be off before more questions than answers arise from our presence here."

Sememmon sketched a bow, and Ashemmi nodded at both Khelben and Tsarra. The wizards' hands cast spells, and the pair of them disappeared. The air imploded behind them with a slight whoosh of air and a soft thump.

Khelben looked around, shaking his head sadly. His eye caught Tsarra looking at him harshly, and he said, "My dear, that temper will force a quick death of you, should you not tame it. I know you have many questions, but like many things in a wizard's or sorcerer's life, they must wait until their proper time in the casting."

He stepped outside of the ruined inn and onto the grass and Tsarra followed. Nameless, however, busied himself with some fallen plates of food.

❧ ❧ ❧ ❧ ❧

The trio arrived in the entry chamber of Blackstaff Tower, startling a few younger apprentices who bowed and ran up the stairs. Khelben shed his cloak and placed it in the wardrobe. He and Tsarra kept silent, sending between themselves while Tsarra doffed her cloak as well.

Now what did we learn from our questioning of Spider and Ryssa?

That eyewitnesses are poor judges as to what happens in a spell duel? Tsarra offered.

True, but hardly helpful. Spider saw a wizard in a cloak and leathern cape cast a massive lightning spell upon the count that punched a hole through the front wall simply to reach him. Does that sound like a normal spell?

While they conversed mentally, Khelben, Tsarra, and Nameless mounted the main stairs of the tower. Tsarra watched Khelben for cues, but he said no command words and touched no stones. Thus, they remained in the physical tower and merely walked to the guest level.

No—it sounds like what happened to us, Tsarra sent. *That might explain why Ryssa believed the count attacked some courier with lightning just for being in their way.*

Perhaps her judgment was biased toward the younger man, a malady common among tavern girls. Still, the majority of the inn's destruction came when the bolts came together and arced skyward, just as happened here. At least I could help with the reconstruction efforts.

Do you always travel with rubies the size of a small child's fist, master? Tsarra let a wry grin spread across her face, dashed by Khelben's unchanging mien.

Only when I expect collateral damage—thus, far too often. Still, Mystra blessed us with at least one person in Rassalantar who could learn the magic to mend the inn before too long.

How—why were we in Rassalantar, Master? That's more than two days of riding north of the city! The last thing I remember was turning onto Selduth Street toward Turn-back Court.

It appears that Danthra's unpredictable visions are still active, and you succumbed to one of them, Khelben replied. *Apparently, you lock onto a related memory of mine and it overwhelms you for a time. While you walked through my past, we were summoned by contingency magic I granted Gamalon. When he went off to Tethyr, I gave him an item a few years ago and an oath to answer its call. Strange how Mystra works, isn't it? The boy survives the entire Reclamation Wars, but fate calls on me now when we are well embroiled in other problems. I could not ignore the ring's summons, nor could I leave you insensate in your visions on the street. Thus, you and I traveled to the Sleeping Dragon Inn, met your first sharn, and returned here.*

What do the sharn have to do with this? Or the lightning bolts? Is this realizing one of Alaudo's prophecies to match the year's name?

"Later for those answers," Khelben said, as they approached one of the guest chamber doors. "We must look in on a wounded friend and kinsman."

"Can't he wait until you give me some answers? I thought we were in a hurry!" Tsarra grabbed her mentor by the shoulder and held him back from touching the door. Once she felt her anger rising, she knew she couldn't stop her next words. "You can't keep me in the dark here, Khelben. My life is tied to this as well, just like the injured man in there. I feel like I've died twice in less than a full day with no real answers from you. Tell me what's going on. What happened last night? Answer me!"

Khelben glared at her. To her credit, Tsarra squared her shoulders and did not budge, unlike other recipients of what many believed was a spell called "the Blackstaff's Baleful Glower." The moment stretched for eternity until Khelben exhaled softly, his eyes and face relaxing.

"'Tend to one's wounded, for one never knows from whence the next attack comes.' Forgive me, girl. I forget we too are wounded as much as his excellency in there." He looked up and away and said, "Laeral, see to Gamalon. We're in my library." Khelben's eyes wandered a moment as Laeral apparently responded, but Tsarra did not hear the reply. The archmage's eyes darted back to Tsarra. "Now, come along, if you would have your answers. Just remember that you asked for this information, and know that the burden to carry it may prove heavier than you realize."

Khelben walked up the stairs of the tower with Tsarra in step behind him. He reached back and touched her shoulder with his right hand, and his left hand traced a pattern on the mortar of the stone stairwell.

"*Yuhiurlemn,*" he whispered.

Tsarra felt the familiar *whoosh* in her stomach as they accessed a level of the tower she had never visited. They continued a few steps upward, and Tsarra smiled.

Khelben removed his hand as he said, "You've never seen my true library, have you? You're only my eighth apprentice to see this chamber. Truth be told, I think Elminster visits this place more often than I get the chance to do so."

Unlike the usual levels of the tower, the library remained one open room all the way around with no intervening walls, the only interruption of the floor being the stairwell. Against the wall opposite their landing was a massive fireplace, the logs blazing instantly at the snap of Khelben's fingers. Four overstuffed chairs arced in front of the fire, each with its own footstool, side table, and a softly glowing globe that hovered overhead. When Tsarra and Khelben stepped onto the granite floor, two globes increased in brightness and floated over to hover a few feet above their left shoulders. The tressym angrily took flight and batted at the globe to keep it away from his mistress, but it remained tantalizingly out of his reach.

Everywhere else she looked, Tsarra saw floor-to-ceiling bookshelves lining the walls, with shelves intermittently jutting out perpendicular to the walls between two other bookshelves to allow more shelf space. On the ends of those shelves were glass cabinets holding curios, glowing objects, crystals, and other items. She realized she'd caught her breath, and as she inhaled again, the scent of light dust and the tiniest hint of mildew proved comforting to her. Even though she was a half-elf, she had never seen an elven library other than what few books and records her mother kept. She wondered if the fabled Lost Library of Cormanthyr looked something like Khelben's.

At rough count, Tsarra guessed there were at least fifty bookshelves and more than a dozen cabinets of priceless books and artifacts within the chamber. She saw books chained to the shelves, two full shelves of massive tomes bound in white dragon hide that chilled her even from a distance, and a set of books with wings on the covers, thwarted from flight by the light chains that anchored them to their shelf. Tsarra's eyes followed the fluttering books then spotted what might be Khelben's library guardians— golden statues standing in niches near the ceiling, looking like elf archers, dwarf crossbowmen, or even one golden bugbear shouldering a massive axe. She wondered about the magic used to animate the statues.

Khelben walked around to the left of the stairwell, tapping the globe slightly to increase its light. Tsarra followed at a distance, her eyes distracted by seven huge spindles of crystal levitating inside the glass cabinets and large incunabula lying on open shelves. The writing looked only vaguely familiar. Behind the stairwell and opposite the fireplace was a long row of work tables covered in large disheveled piles of manuscripts, scrolls, and massive tomes.

"The events of the past day took me by surprise, not so much unexpected as they were unraveling in an uncontrolled manner. My dreams have also been occupied of late with portents from Mystra, though in my haste, I have misinterpreted some of them." Khelben spoke with his back to Tsarra as he rooted among the piles, seeking various sheaves of parchment and books. "Ah! Of course. There it is."

Khelben pulled a slim green leather folio from one of the piles and held the book out to Tsarra. She found an empty spot on the table and set the book down, opening to its title page.

"'*Rhaelnar's Guide to Legacies Lost, Volume the First, of which there are to be Volumes Four*,'" she read aloud. "'A gift to our most esteemed Warlord Laroun to commemorate the completion of the great Castle of Waterdeep and to honor a new legacy founded on this eighth day of Ches in the Year of the Bent Coin.'" She looked up and asked, "Why haven't I heard of this book before?"

"It's a rare tome, and I have the pleasure of owning both volumes—'tis the most complete set outside of the Vault of the Sages. Rhaelnar died before ever completing the third volume, let alone the fourth. I have the notebook of his incomplete third volume as well."

"What did you do? Steal it from the castle's library when you were a lord?" Tsarra asked.

Her only answer was an upraised eyebrow immediately obscured by a flash of flame from one finger as Khelben lit a pipe. He gestured, the finger still ablaze, for her to continue reading aloud.

"'This be the accounting of lands and lords, lights and loves, luminaries and legacies, all lost to the sands of time. Herein I shall unveil many mysteries lost from histories, though not in the order of the stars or by geography. Nay, of these matters I shall speak in the orders that my patrons demand them. Thus, *Volume the First* contains the heritages known and lost from those human realms of Jhaamdath and the Shoon Imperium.'"

Tsarra turned the page, shaking her head. "This fellow is more long-winded than Kappiyan Fluyrmaster."

"Pray, continue silently and spare yourself needless tortures. He belabors endlessly on the trinkets and trysts of many a noblewoman before he gets to anything of substance. The information you need is at the mark," Khelben said, his nose buried in three other tomes that floated in the air before him.

Tsarra touched the small face painted onto the silk strip jutting out above the pages toward the end of the book. The face puffed its cheeks and blew, making the pages rustle briskly until the book opened at the marked place. She smiled at the panting, caricatured face then began reading "The Screed of the Scroll."

CHAPTER THIRTEEN

29 Uktar, the Year of Lightning Storms
(1374 DR)

Tsarra stood, stretching her back and shoulders after sitting too long over the book. "Khelben, this is the worst doggerel you've ever subjected me to in sixteen years of study. Did he write this way to punish people?"

Khelben coughed and closed the last dusty tome before his eyes. He kept his back to her, so she couldn't read his face. He levitated the books back to their resting places on various shelves before he answered, "Rhaelnar's ears may not have been good for poetry, nor obfuscation really. Still, from what we've already discovered and discussed today, what leaps to mind? What might Rhaelnar's Legacy be?"

Tsarra didn't have to reread the poems. Her ability to instantly recall what she read allowed her to recite from memory. " 'Gilded lore of Netheril's pride,' is fairly obvious. He's talking about finding one or more of the Nether Scrolls. Even Volo could see that one!"

Khelben snorted loudly. "No, I'm afraid Master Geddarm yet postulates that Rhaelnar's Legacy is some form of magical potion, the poem an elaborately disguised recipe."

Khelben and Tsarra blinked at each other a moment then burst out laughing.

"Never underestimate the power of misdirection, Tsarra. You know this from hunting, if you want to distract a predator. True as well when tracking prey through written words," Khelben said. "Now, can you identify any of the items of the Legacy from the poems? We've already found a few of them, though regrettably we don't hold them all."

Tsarra repeated the eighteen stanzas in her head, shuddering at the awful rhymes but focusing on what they said. "That man I saw outside the tower! He had one of them, obviously. Wait—do you have a copy of *Selchant's Catalogue of Swords Enchanted* here? I want to check a hunch."

"Fourth row of Shelf G, red leather binding—the only one without singe marks on it."

Tsarra hadn't noticed before but each massive set of bookshelves was marked by an Elvish letter, and the G sigil glowed faintly to show her where to look.

After a few moments of page flipping, Tsarra grinned. "I knew it! He's carrying Rhoban's Diamond Blade, isn't he? That's the first 'dream' in the sixth stanza!"

"Indeed. Congratulations on your deduction. So few of my students bother to learn the Vilhon Reach histories, let alone its prehistories in the Twelve Cities of Swords," Khelben said. "Not one of the twelve ruling blades, you know, but certainly a blade of distinction. One wonders if its current bearer is as noble as Rhoban himself."

Tsarra put the catalog aside and looked again on Rhaelnar's book. " 'Dream next of the forceful hand that wrested hope for a waveswept, deepwater land?' I'd guess the seventh stanza refers to Raurlor's Ring, here in Waterdeep?"

"Indeed." Khelben muttered, searching through the piles on the table for something.

"The tenth stanza refers to a glistening girdle, so I'll just take a wild stab in the dark and suggest it's this belt I've worn for two days now."

Khelben nodded, his brow knitted in concentration as he blew smoke shapes. She'd seen him do that with Elminster, whose facility with it created elaborate murals of smoke with moving figures. Khelben only managed to create a smoky image of the belt she wore.

"I don't suppose you could tell me what it is? My knowledge of elven artifacts is lacking, despite my blood."

Khelben shook his head and said, "Another time, we'll look into it together and you can prove to me you can do research. Now, what of Rhaelnar's Legacy? What else do we know?"

Tsarra continued, thinking aloud, "The next stanza that makes any sense to me—'Sleep again to see your goal apparent. In the laughter of the lyre can one find the Legacy penned.'—is an awful stretch for a rhyme. The context of the earlier stanzas, though, hints that we're looking for a golden scroll. 'Laughter of the lyre?' Are we looking for music written on gold? That's not a topic I know much about."

"Neither do I, and I've had more time than you to learn. That item, I believe, is close at hand, but we must wait until late tonight to retrieve it, lest we disturb too many pious brethren. Continue," Khelben said, still searching for a parchment.

"What is it? You know where it is?" Tsarra asked.

"I know where *all* of these sundries are, Tsarra. I would hardly be the archmage of Waterdeep if I did not. The question remains how much you have gleaned of all this."

Tsarra felt her pulse jump in anger, and her exasperation seemed to infect her familiar. The tressym, having grown bored with chasing the glowglobe, alighted upon a pile of tomes, which quickly collapsed beneath him, and he tumbled off the table. Correcting his fall and taking to the air again, the tressym flew up atop one of the nearby bookshelves and settled in, as if he'd planned that all along. Tsarra felt his surprise and embarrassment but her horror at his disturbing Khelben's research overshadowed that until she saw his eyes never left her face.

Khelben steepled his fingers and said, "Tsarra, as your teacher, I need to test your understanding of the situations and my edification as to how well you will do without my tutelage. After all, you need to graduate beyond Blackstaff Tower, and it seems this current emergent situation presents itself as your final examination."

"You're forcing me to leave the Tower? Because I'm losing my patience over too many unanswered questions?" The tressym's growl and lashing tail audible from across the chamber underscored Tsarra's irritation.

"Calm down, Tsarra, lest you slip into another vision. Your temper sets off those visions, doesn't it? Whenever you lose your focus on the immediate, Dantha's gift for visions taps into my memories. Whereas I already remember my experiences and dismiss the memory, Dantha's visions force-feed you the whole experience from the briefest flashes of my recall."

"So what I saw—that battle in the Eightower . . ."

"Yes, that was a memory. In fact, that was the place we were to visit last night, before your vision and our side trip to Rassalantar changed our path."

"But I've met Tandar, the so-called Green Wizard of Sea Ward, and he's over a century old! How could you know him as a young man?"

"After all you've learned here, do you truly still believe me to be the son of Lhestyn and Zelphar?" Khelben's eyes went wide with surprise. "You're smarter than that, even if I do keep up that pretense at all times for the emotional comfort of the common folk. Zelphar was *my* son."

"So you're really Khelben the Elder?"

"Among other names I have worn, yes."

"Why tell me your secret now?"

"Because you already suspect it, and thanks to this mishap of bound souls and that gem, will always know it. Even if I manage to save Danthra's soul after dealing with Rhaelnar's Legacy, I suspect my memories will remain with you in that *kiira* forevermore. Still, our conversation wanders onto paths best trod later. Do you have any other deductions on the poem?"

"Hang the poem, Khelben! Give me a moment to understand all this."

"Time is the luxury in scarce supply now, my dear. The only time I have had to plan and think was when we were first laid low yesterday. While you remained unconscious, I worked on the *kiira* and tattooed your forehead to accept the gem's altered magic. Laeral contacted many agents to whom I've entrusted some secrets and other tasks. Some of them safeguard many of these Legacy artifacts. Those people in turn contacted their agents. We have already spoken with other key players in this drama, and we'll contact more soon."

"But you still haven't told me what's going on. How do you know what to do?"

"My plans have been in place for centuries. Those who needed to know anything ahead of time did so, either by my hand or Mystra's."

"Mystra's hand?"

"I've had portents sent in my dreams from the goddess in past months. They share a chronic imagery of threes, lightning bolts, and the city's seal. These dreams recurred frequently enough that I knew the message came from her. I simply had to eliminate any other possible explanations or options before I knew the Legacy was the key."

"So that's why you've been attending nobles' parties for the past year! I thought that was out of character for you, since I remembered you only attended those functions you couldn't avoid, such as Thann family gatherings or functions at the palace."

"I certainly don't enjoy them, no. Even family parties are endurable only for brief moments. Unfortunately, now the lords Agundar, Cragsmere, Ilitul, Ilzimmer, Jhansczil, and Gauntyl all believe me a close personal friend for my attentions." Khelben shook his head sadly and ran his hands through his hair, shaking off frustration.

"So Mystra doesn't tell you everything as you need the information?"

"She would hardly be the Lady of Mysteries, were that so. Even this new Mystra understands that. No, she only leaves me with hints and reminders of previous omens, including some I haven't seen since the day I was Chosen. Your face—tattoos and *kiira* and all—was one of those."

"You knew all this would happen? You've known this was coming for sixteen years?"

"I've known something would happen for fourscore decades, Tsarra. I only knew, after we first met and I recognized you, what you were called. I've known for ages that you would have an important role to play for Mystra and her Weave. Beyond that, I don't know your fate in this venture."

"But you seem to know everything about Rhaelnar's Legacy."

Khelben snorted. "That's because I made that all up. Only those fools who believe in it think they can find the Nether Scrolls by chasing down its clues. It is a logic-trap to hide a greater secret and to draw out those who might try and usurp power not rightfully theirs."

"What?"

Behind them, Nameless took to the air again, a low growl that spread around the room as he flew and darted among the bookshelves to shake off the emotions he felt from his mistress. In response to her shout, the tall crystal spindles began to spin and hum an unearthly harmony.

"Don't shout, Tsarra. It upsets your familiar and can disturb my Uvaerenni lore-crystals. Again, calm yourself or you'll slip into another vision."

For a few moments, the only sounds in the chamber were the dying hum of the crystals, Tsarra's breathing, and Khelben's footsteps as he paced from shelf to shelf. When he touched their spines, the books pulled themselves off the shelves and their covers flapped merrily to fly across the room and pile themselves upon the table. Khelben returned to the table and looked at Tsarra.

"You recall the troubles with the phaerimm two summers ago? All of these events have been imminent since then."

"Don't change the subject, Master. What do the phaerimm have to do with this?" Tsarra asked. "They haven't attacked us or anyone else within hundreds of miles of Waterdeep, at least that we know of."

Khelben waved one arm to the side, and hands grew from the table's wood, both on its surface and along its legs, to grab fallen items. The hands reorganized the morass of books into neat piles until the area was cleared. He placed out one scroll and three large tomes in that area and gestured Tsarra forward.

"You're neither ignorant nor stupid, Tsarra. I expected you'd have worked it out yourself already if we'd had a chance." Khelben's irritation came through his tone. "Very well. Simplest lore first. Against whom did the phaerimm battle most?"

"Netheril and its archwizards. So this *is* about the Nether Scrolls? But you said—"

"Patience. Did they have any other prominent foes?"

Tsarra smacked a hand down on the table. "The sharn! Gods, I feel stupider than an otyugh." Her face went red from embarrassment.

"Don't berate yourself," Khelben continued. "This situation has more conundrums and enigmas within it than most wizards see in a lifetime. You demanded this knowledge, and we're building it up from its most basic. Now, what is different about the Realms now compared to the past millennia?"

Tsarra's anger flared again, but she kept her response civil. She hated condescension, but she knew Khelben meant to put her back in the place of the student. Still, two could play that game, and Tsarra recited Khelben's lecture of the last month back to him: "'Netherese walk the Realms again, and their myopic and self-serving use of powerful magic threatens all of us. They bring a darker magic not of Mystra with them that may have unforeseen effects upon the Weave. The Sharnwall that once hemmed in the phaerimm beneath Anauroch is no more. These two events above all others must be studied seriously, as I suspect they bring greater effects than are yet known. However, they are not to be feared—Fear keeps you from seeing what you need to see to counter a spell or divert a disaster. Respect your foes, understand all you can about each event, and never let your emotions keep you from learning all you can. Your lives may depend on it some day.'"

Khelben smirked at her and said, "Word for word. Good. Your eidetic memory's intact. You had me worried for a while, my dear. Now, you've studied lore on Netheril in the past and you've had more experience than many with the sharn—at least more than most who still draw breath. Where's the connection? You've got most of what facts you need, so put it together."

Khelben's face took on an eager yearning, one Tsarra used to see on her father's face when they were hunting game for a feast.

Tsarrra paced around the table, since she thought better while moving and she wanted to get out from under his stare. Khelben watched her, rifling through the tomes without looking at them.

Tsarra started to consider aloud, "For some reason, the sharn attack us when we get Legacy artifacts together and the lightning strikes. They have some unknown link to both phaerimm and Netheril." Thinking back on her research and an unfinished scroll on her desk, she remembered something. "Wait a moment—you had me studying any other possible methods of survival Netherese archwizards might have used to see if there are others out there. In Camarlenn of Hunabar's *Musings on Magic Past,* he spoke of a theory that the sharn fought the phaerimm because they were transformed Netherese."

"That is what that source says, yes." Khelben said, with a nod. "Pray, continue."

"I can't. I tried to find sources he referenced, but our students' library and those of five sages in the city didn't have any of the relevant writings. I did find out that Malek

Aldhanek—the mage-historian Camarlenn studied—was the court wizard of the first Laeral, the ruler of Illuskan and the first Witch-Queen of the North. He died—oh, Horned Lady, no!"

Tsarra interrupted herself as she heard and felt her ears fill with the roaring that heralded one of Danthra's visions. Tsarra fought against it, but the vision proved too strong. She dropped to the floor just as she lost consciousness. Again, she smelled things before the vision took hold: dust, mildew, the tang of new leather, and the smell of unwashed men in close-quarters.

CHAPTER FOURTEEN

2 Ches, the Year of the Laughing Swan
(816 DR)

"Jhaurn, where is Lord Bladestroll right now?" Malek thundered at his aide as the wizard exited the tower's secret stairwell into the inner room of his sanctum. Jhaurn had been dozing by the fire, and his master's entrance startled him right from his chair.

"Um, sorry, milord. Who were you looking for?" Jhaurn tried to compose himself and straighten his jerkin as he stood, not meeting the angry glare coming from Lord Aldhanek.

Malek glowered at Jhaurn. "Lord Rutyk Bladestroll. Baron of the Easting Marches. Tall man with a strange creature on his face he calls a beard."

Jhaurn snorted then said, "I believe Lord Bladestroll is with our Lady Witch-Queen for a morning repast before departing to the Duke Zelhund's estates to the south. He should be with her now, as she hardly sleeps in, much like yourself, milord."

A small bell on the fireplace mantel chimed three times.

"Go through the passage, Jhaurn, and fetch Arms-Master Phommor and as many guards as can be mustered to the audience chamber. Tell him a coup is in progress and to protect Laeral," Malek said, smoothing his long black hair back after shrugging off his filthy cloak.

"But Master, what about—?"

"Go, boy, with one last lesson. Trusted advisors must also be slain when attempting to kill queens, but queens are always more important. We shall meet at the Griffon Throne. Now go!"

Jhaurn hesitated only one last heartbeat and filled the archway to their chamber with sticky webs before he turned and opened the secret bookshelf door. "For a moment's more preparation time, Master." With that, he darted into the darkness, and Malek closed the door behind him.

No noise from the outer room betrayed the assassins' presence, but Malek knew magic he did not share with any, even his queen. Numerous spells lay within the tile floors of both chambers. He left the door less protected to avoid suspicion. Above the archway's keystone hung a mirror. It showed Malek the shape of the outer room and four intruders marked as glowing dots on its surface—a pair flanking each side of the doorway. A small flame jetted into the center of the webs and consumed them quickly.

Malek concentrated and uttered some incantations. The first sounds of battle were the assassins' yelps of surprise as the stone wall and floor reached out to grab at them and hold them fast.

Malek smiled and thought, Finally getting some use from my guardian enchantments.

He stepped through the archway, clapping to activate the magical shields his rings provided. As expected, a sword clattered harmlessly off his defenses.

He entered the larger front room, finding three black-garbed men held fast by large stone tentacles, though only two of them had their arms pinned.

"Have the Black Blades fallen so far as to not expect magical defenses in a wizard's chambers? Now, tell me who hired you, or I'll ask the wall to squeeze."

From behind him came a sound of rustling fabric. Malek whirled around into a crouch, lightning scattering off his fingertips. The magical bolts crackled around him, striking and destroying the three darts coming from behind him. He faced his fourth attacker, and Malek smiled grimly.

"I should have known it would be you, Varret."

"Southern scum of an outlander, you slight me even now? No wonder I chose to slay you instead of that hussy upstairs. I will have you address me properly before you die." The less-than-honorable Lord Varret Tryshaln, Count of the Xornmoor Riding, glared and grimaced at him, his pale skin flushed red enough to match his unkempt and thinning hair. Dressed down from his usual foppish manner, Varret wore a brown robe and cloak with a hood. He gestured and hooked his thumbs together, sending an arc of flame directly at Malek.

The flames illuminated the edges of his magical shields, and the fire agate on Malek's left ring began to glow ominously. While the flames licked dangerously close, Malek gestured with his left hand, and the flames leaped into the ring.

"Now, Lord Tryshaln, I've given you all the respect you've earned, but imagined slight is no impetus for treason. Put down your arms. Her Majesty's mercy is far warmer than mine, I pray, and I have no wish to fight your family over your death."

"The only deaths today shall be yours and the Witch-Queen's, Tethyrian!" Varret's face contorted with fury as he barked out an incantation that Malek had not encountered before. His curiosity slowed his counterspell, and he threw himself to one side to avoid the fiery dragon's jaws that lunged from Varret's cupped hands. The fire construct bit Malek's lower torso and legs, and he screamed as the fire burned him. His clothes caught on fire, though the leathers fared far better than his linen shirt.

Despite the pain, Malek managed to thrust his left fist into the fire construct and scream, *"Alakedarth!"* The fires pulled into the ring's gem, leaving only a shimmer in the air as the magic dissipated.

"I'll add that ring to my wardrobe as Stornanter's new Court Wizard, Aldhanek," Varret promised as he moved closer and loomed over the prone Malek, his hands moving in intricate circles and his mouth muttering a new incantation.

Still too pained to stand up, Malek grabbed the edge of the rug and yanked hard, tripping up Varret and ending his spell.

"My turn, fool." Malek whispered, and he cast quickly.

One of his simplest and newer spells, the magic touched the Weave of magic and the weave of Varret's clothing. The robes, cloak, and hood writhed and constricted on the wizard's body, making it hard for him to move or cast. Malek used the moments the spell bought him to pull the carpet the rest of the way from under Varret. As he rose, he kicked the mage in the stomach, knocking the wind from him and stopping his counterspell against the weaveweird. Just as Malek suspected, Varret planned defenses only against magic, leaving himself open to more mundane attacks.

Malek snapped out the small carpet with one hand, and the square Calishite rug remained level and floating on the air two feet above the floor. His other hand worked another spell over Lord Tryshaln. Malek didn't seem to notice Varret finally gaining against his seemingly possessed clothes. Malek and Varret completed their spells one atop the other. A translucent sea-green dome appeared over Varret just as he unleashed a fireball, which, to his misfortune, remained inside the dome. Malek looked at the charred and damaged noble and his three accomplices still pinned to the walls and shook his head. He turned his back on all of them, hopped atop his small floating carpet, and with a few gestures and the *pop* of imploding air, he teleported away.

Malek reappeared in the audience chamber of Port

Llast's Griffon Palace to a scene of utter chaos. He had safely teleported into the upper dome of the chamber unnoticed above the archers' perches. Blades clashed with blades, and spells flared in every corner. Malek immediately identified the main traitors—the Lords Elsmyth, Rushfire, Argentouch, and Bladestroll—and their retinues of guards and mercenaries. More than a dozen royal guards and almost as many traitors lay dead and bleeding on the stone floor. The Griffon Throne of the Witch-Queen was dark with blood, and Laeral, Witch-Queen of the North, lay sprawled alongside it, her short silver curls matted with blood. Barons Bladestroll and Rushfire bent over Laeral, stripping her of protective or life-sustaining magical items.

Malek spun some magic around himself, suddenly adding three identical images of himself. The four Maleks swooped down into the fray, keeping a tight formation, though each Malek seemed to do things slightly differently, standing, kneeling, or sitting on the carpet as he flew.

One Malek strafed the main knot of attackers with arcane bolts, and another dispelled the wall of flame that blocked the entry. The remaining pair swooped toward the throne and the downed queen. A pair of massive magical rams' heads materialized in front of them and knocked both traitors away from Laeral and into the walls.

As one duplicate wove an occultrap around the stunned mages, Malek leaped off his carpet and threw his body on top of Laeral to protect her from any further attacks. Malek's heart pounded as he rolled her over to find two daggers buried hilt deep in her stomach and heart. Her dark emerald eyes were glazed over, and she was barely breathing.

He struggled to save Laeral, but he had no more teleports memorized for the day. He let his awareness slip through his illusionary selves, seeing that the other wizards had taken the bait and concentrated all their spells on his images. Every spell just got absorbed either by the figure or its magical shields, causing them to glow.

"You're too late, Aldhanek! We've killed her and taken

her throne. Long live King Elsmyth!" Lord Argentouch boasted as he fired a barrage of magical purple missiles at the Malek closest to the door.

Malek only partially heard the boasts and the opposing spells. He willed the spell to its completion, so he could buy time for another more important working.

"Hang on, my queen," he said, but Laeral could only blink and her breath bubbled in her throat. She failed to see the tears streaming down Malek's face. "Stay with me, my lady. I swore to protect you, no matter the cost."

Three glowing Maleks floated or walked to within arm's reach of the four wizard-nobles turned traitors and raised their arms as if to cast a spell. Both the masters and their servants saw the threats and fired spells and arrows or other weapons at the glowing figures. With deafening roars, the images exploded, unleashing all their absorbed magic onto their targets through eyebeams, open wounds, or blasts from their hands.

With no time to check on his foes, the court wizard placed one hand on the throne and invoked its powers. A crystalline griffon stood where the throne had been, its massive form and wings providing some cover for the two wizards at her feet. With that action completed, Malek opened himself up to another working—one far more powerful, more intricate, and more personal. Malek's fingers and eyes danced with silver licks of flame, and he incinerated the two daggers in Laeral's body. She screamed as the daggers dissolved, and she slumped in Malek's arms.

"Laeral! *Laeral!*"

Malek heard someone barking orders and the *twang* of bowstrings behind him, but all that seemed miles away. His world was only the bloodied face in front of him, blurry through his own tears. Malek cradled Laeral's head in one palm and whispered to her, the silver flames in his eyes growing and flames creeping from his other hand into her wounds.

"I loved you from the moment I first saw your face—three centuries before you were even born. I am yours, forever and always, through as many lifetimes as we may share. Ignore the poison, love. Ignore the pain. I have a gift to share that can save you if you let it. If your will is not enough to revive you, take my love as well!"

Malek kissed her deeply, forcing power down her throat and suffusing her with magical silver flame.

Let the silver fires spark within you, my love, and realize you are more than mortal. No more may I say, for you must learn your own destiny before we can be united again. Malek's voice spoke within Laeral, mystically coaxing her back to life. *You shall know me always. My truename, for you to guard in your heart, is Wrytham, and all I am I freely share with you. Know I shall always be a true servant of your mother and your soul's mate. Now, heal in body and mind, until you are ready to remember and understand.*

Malek felt Laeral's heart start beating stronger and she began breathing again, without breaking the embrace the two shared. The silver fires receded as Malek let Laeral back down onto the marble floor. Both of them lay naked on the floor, the fiery magic that saved the Witch-Queen's life having burned away their clothes. Moving slowly, as if in a dream, Laeral tenderly touched the hand-wide angry scar that crossed Malek's chest from his left armpit down to his right hip.

"Malek? What are—?"

Malek smiled at her, and opened his mouth but his response was lost in the griffon's roar. They looked up to see the crystal griffon rearing up and over them to attack the smouldering and badly burned form of Lord Essmyth, armed with a short sword shining with azure energy.

Malek turned around toward their attacker, putting himself between the threat and Laeral. The last thing he saw was the blue short sword's point and the raw grimace of the traitor lord.

As he fell backward, Malek Aldhanek heard Laeral scream, *"No!"*

He didn't feel his head hit the floor.

CHAPTER FIFTEEN

29 Uktar, the Year of Lightning Storms
(1374 DR)

Tsarra woke sharply, her eyes snapping open and seeing directly into Khelben's staring back at her. For a moment, Malek Aldhanek's clean-shaven and olive-eyed visage hung in the air as a translucent mask over Khelben's.

"You're peeling back far more memories and secrets of mine than I ever expected, Tsarra. I'm just glad neither one of us truly had to remember what it feels like to be stabbed in the eye." Khelben said, as he helped her sit up. Sometime during the vision, he'd moved Tsarra to one of the easy chairs in the library.

Tsarra found the questions flooding even faster than usual, and she struggled to keep still, as her head throbbed with pain, especially around her left eye. "You're even older than anyone believes, Master, aren't you? Even Khelben the Elder wasn't around for Stornanter. And Lady Arunsun is the same Laeral, the first Witch-Queen of the North?"

"I was only Malek Aldhanek for ten years from the Year of the Warrior's Rest to that of the Laughing Swan. In that time, I helped build Stornanter, restore Illusk, and write a few books people still try to comprehend fifty-six decades later. The identity was in fact significant only because it allowed me to meet my soul mate and establish many of the conundrums surrounding us now. You've now seen one of the most important moments of my long life, apprentice. Now tell milady she's as beautiful now as she was five centuries agone." Khelben waved his hand, and Tsarra noticed Laeral approaching with a steaming mug that smelled of cinnamon and cloves. Aside from a change from shorter to longer hair, Laeral looked the same as in the vision.

"How did you survive? And why didn't you heal yourself, Lady Laeral?" Tsarra demanded, her response as tied to the vision's emotions as to her own curiosity.

Laeral slid onto the arm of the chair next to Tsarra's, leaving the seat for Khelben who sat down with her. "At the time, I was not yet aware of who I truly was. My time to be Chosen was a few decades later, though that was my last day ever in that audience chamber. I've not set foot near Port Llast in five centuries because of all that." She shifted her attention to Khelben for a moment. "Did I ever tell you how long it took us to drop that smoldering traitor after he killed you? Honestly, the man was more stubborn as a corpse than he was in life!" Laeral chuckled, but her white-knuckled grip on Khelben's hand told Tsarra other things. She saw the tension and pain it brought up again.

Khelben looked at Laeral then shifted his eyes to Tsarra, then back to Laeral. "My only concern at the time was that you wouldn't bury me too deep. I'd used a lot of silver fire to keep you alive, so all I could do was keep myself from abandoning my body. The tougher part was feeling my body healing but having to lie there without breathing for four days while my body lay in state. It was a nice funeral, love, did I ever tell you that?" Khelben winked at Laeral, then turned to Tsarra. "My lady here was the most inconsolable woman I'd ever seen at a funeral until I met the widow at Lord Raventree's funeral about forty years back. Laeral did have a nice crypt built for me—unfortunately very solid, and tough to break from from the inside, I must say. Especially when one is buried *without his spellbook.*"

"I was *curious!*" Laeral shrugged, then giggled. "I was going to put it with you . . . eventually."

Despite her shock at it all and the headache, Tsarra joined the two of them in laughing. "Dug yourself from many graves, Master?"

"Once before and since," Khelben replied. "After that third trial, I disposed of my identities away from sight and spread rumors of their passings. It's also easier to build an empty crypt and hide things therein for later. Tsarra, this vision only knocked you out for a few hours, but it's a lot to digest. And it has been some time since you've had a chance to sleep. We'll continue later this morning, as it's nearly dawn. For now, let us return to the main tower, shall we, ladies?" Khelben held out a hand to each woman and led them up toward the stairwell.

"But what about Aldhanek's theories? That the sharn were Netherese transformed to fight the phaerimm?" Tsarra asked. She held her elbow out for the tressym, who flew down from the rafters.

Khelben smiled. "One of my better attempts at misdirection, my dear. I made it up and wrote seven other books under three other names that expanded those theories until the idea itself was accepted as fact. Safer that way than to allow people to stumble upon the whole truth of things before the world is ready for them."

"So you deliberately mislead people into accepting false-hoods? You write up lies to cover the truth?" Tsarra found herself getting angry all over again. "How can you live with the deceit?"

Laeral put a hand on Tsarra's shoulder and smiled. "Child, those who truly seek the truth are rarely misled by these . . . hurdles, shall we say? Only those who greedily seek power—like our current foe, apparently—accept these short answers and are hoodwinked. Besides, we follow both the dictates of our intellects and the directions of the Lady of Mysteries. The machinations demanded of us sometimes rival those of Shar's servants, but we do this willingly, knowing that we eventually expand people's understanding of magic."

"But—" Tsarra protested, but Khelben held up his hand to silence her.

"All right, Tsarra. Enough protesting. Time to directly learn one of my greatest secrets—one that may become a task of yours as well in the future. What do most common folk whisper when they guess what I am up to in my Tower? Other than the usual 'taking over the world' paranoia or 'conspiring with the Zhentarim' that has become popular the past few years?"

"Most still wonder if you've truly abandoned both the lords and the Harpers. Oh, and the Watchful Order assumes you're producing major magical items for Piergeiron and the Guard without their due taxation or supervision."

Laeral said, "It's astounding how fussy the guild of mages can be when they've nothing better to worry about."

"Of course. Neither Laeral nor I need sleep unless we choose to—or are injured or ill. What occupies many a night—Stop smiling, Laeral, I'm not sharing *those* revelations—is writing. I enscribe as our Lady bids me or as my own heart deems. Even if what is written doesn't follow history, who is to say it doesn't hold a kernel of truth? Sometimes I work on my memoirs, and sometimes I write things to delude those seeking the easier paths to power. One of the reasons why the Darkholden stand with us is Sememmon proved more cunning about some things than did his former master. He saw through a thick web of intrigues and as a result, we struck a bargain, Sememmon and I."

"Ah, I was wondering if they'd shown themselves or not," Laeral said. "You won't believe how angry Malchor is about having to work with them. Still, these are all worries and thoughts to be wrestled with a freshly rested brain. Let us get you to bed, dear." Laeral slipped one arm through Tsarra's and led her toward the stairs.

"Well, I can't possibly sleep now! I'm fine," Tsarra protested. "All of this changes so much."

Khelben took up her other arm, nudging Nameless to the floor, and said, "You've had a hard enough day, my dear. I have endured your temper more than enough as well. That anger comes from exhaustion more than true outrage." He waved one arm, and the lights in the library dimmed. "Best sleep on this, and we'll discuss any further objections you have in the morning. I shall spend the night aiding Gamalon. Given our need for proximity, you'll have to sleep in one of the guest chambers. Besides, you need to be refreshed to properly wish Lord Wands the happiest of birthdays when we visit him tomorrow."

"As long as he won't be offended by my wearing full armor and weaponry," Tsarra said. "If our foe is undead, as the evidence suggests, I don't intend to be caught without protection and a means of fighting back."

"I wouldn't dream of suggesting otherwise, my dear," Khelben replied.

As the three of them moved toward the stairs, Tsarra's eyes found a cabinet she'd not noticed earlier. Through its glass doors shone a flickering white light, only noticeable in the diminished light around them. The staff appeared to be blackened wood sealed along major cracks with silver metal. At the top, an axe blade, carved like a howling wolf's mouth in profile, seemed fused to the staff. Silver metal also filled in a multitude of runes carved into the staff along its length.

"I've never seen this blackstaff, Master."

"That only leaves this chamber in the most dire of emergencies."

"Why? It looks like it's got powerful magic in it."

"It does, but that power comes with costs and is not for idle use. In fact, it's the true blackstaff that ties my strength to the tower here."

"When was the last time you used it?"

"Not since the day I truly entered Mystra's service. Now, enough of things past. With some luck, you'll never know the burden of touching that staff. Let us go."

"It's a good thing we know you love us, dear, or we'd be irritated by your half-answers and dismissals," Laeral teased him as they stepped around to the landing.

"I've no doubt he loves you with every fiber of his being, lady." Tsarra whispered to Laeral.

"I know," Laeral smiled, "so it's a wonder it's taken us over five hundred years to have our first child together."

Tsarra gawped a moment and hugged Laeral fiercely.

"Laeral!" Khelben snapped, but his face softened. "I thought that would be our secret a while. Have you told anyone else?"

"Only Sylune and Alustriel. I couldn't help it. Happy news is so rare among us, I had to share."

Khelben sighed and nudged the two women ahead of him. "I just hope our enemies don't get wind of a child of two Chosen before we're ready for them."

"Isn't he sweet? Worried about them already. . . ."

"Them?" Khelben asked, his eyes wide.

"Dear," Laeral caressed Khelben's face as they all descended the stairs, "do you honestly think I don't know when I'm carrying twins? I may not have borne as many children as Alustriel, but please. Besides, I'm glad you've no need to brag, but you've twice in the past bred twins. It seems you've done so again."

CHAPTER SIXTEEN

29 Uktar, the Year of Lightning Storms
(1374 DR)

Tsarra, disoriented by her dreams and the unfamiliar bed, ran her fingers through her hair, massaging her scalp. She could tell from the angle of the sun through the window she had slept far later than usual. Her pillow and face were moist with tears. Remnants of her dream returned, a frustrating kaleidoscope of Malek, thrusting sword points, lunging and roaring mummified faces, chains, and the spirit of Danthra moving through it all with a look of tremulous fear on her face. Tsarra had tried to comfort her, but her friend remained out of reach. The final dream image terrified her—a sharn suddenly erupted between her and Malek Aldhanek and engulfed Danthra, her face screaming at Tsarra from beneath the black, oily skin.

Tsarra shifted slightly to extricate her feet from

beneath Nameless. The tressym bit her toes through the blanket, complaining that she was disturbing his sleep.

"Ow! Blast you! Long time we were up anyway."

The tressym narrowed its eyes at her and she felt rather than heard his response: *"Been a-hunt. Tasty mouse. Played with the happylittlemanPikal up top. Sleep now. Mistress-friend tired too. Sleepgood . . . unless food?"* He yawned, arching his back and stretching claws, tail, and wings all at once.

"I have to eat too, but we need to go with Khelben to the Wands villa," Tsarra said, getting out of bed with a loud yawn.

As she suspected, the tressym perked up when she mentioned the Wands villa and began to groom himself with vigor. Tsarra smiled, remembering the lovely white tressym Lady Olanhar Wands had as her own familiar. She also remembered the arrival of five black and gray tressym cubs months after their last visit to a Wands gala early last year.

"Promise me you'll behave with some restraint while we're there?" she asked the familiar. His only response, as if on cue, was to cough up a large hairball onto the woolen blanket.

Tsarra stretched her body in the sunbeam then paused to look at the belt she'd been wearing all night. It had seemed odd to leave it on, since she preferred sleeping unclad. Still, the belt was warm from her body, and its green gems glinted in the sunshine. She ran her fingers over the metal, its texture and lightness far finer than any her fingers had ever touched before. It felt like the belt lightened and became part of her skin the longer she wore it. Tsarra made a mental note to do some study of elven artifacts when she had the time. All she knew at that moment was that it was an ancient artifact of the elves and it had something to do with their current dilemma.

She looked around for her clothes, which she had dumped on the floor before collapsing abed. She found her leathers piled neatly on a side table across the room.

A scrap of parchment on them said, "Meet Khelben next door after you rise. I had your students clean your armor and better waterproof it. L."

Tsarra dressed quickly in the clean, supple leathers. As she buckled on her sword belt and grabbed her quiver and bow, Nameless growled deeply. She turned to see him standing on the bed's footboard, his claws digging into the woodwork and every hair on his body tensed and up. The emotions hit hard, as a wave of anger suddenly washed over her, carrying with it frustration, impatience, and sadness. The emotional eddy swirled around her and her familiar for seconds, both of them not knowing what caused it until a voice came into their heads.

Khelben sent, *Apologies. My concentration slipped a moment. Things are tense with the count.* Tsarra happened to notice in the mirror that her *kiira* glowed slightly when that power was used. *Now that you're awake, come meet our guest, since none of us can breakfast without tending to him first.*

Tsarra nodded. *I'll be right there, Master.*

Tsarra, you're a colleague now, given how many of my secrets you now hold, the Blackstaff sent. *I think you can drop the formality imposed on younger charges. Khelben will do. Leave Nameless out of our interview, as Gamalon seems to have a feline allergy.*

Tsarra ran a reassuring hand over the tressym's body, smoothing out his fur. He began a light purr then sneezed, and forced his head under her palm once to mark it. *"Not staying inside. Sunnywarm morningflyabout, chase more food. Goto happymateplace to play?"*

"Not yet, friend, or at least not me." Tsarra replied. "I have to stay with Khelben, but we'll meet you at the Wands villa soon enough. Enjoy your flight, and let me know if you find any trouble."

"No preythoughtfear, mistressfriend. Flyfast and strong-claw. I nofear. I fightwell."

The tressym leaped off the bed onto a table and launched himself out the window, his wings taking him aloft over the City of Splendors. Tsarra felt how happy he was to have a sunny morning, a sentiment she shared. Winter would soon bottle the city in with clouds and cold for months. She slung her bow and quiver over her shoulder and exited the guest chamber. A few steps to her right brought her to a closed door.

Khelben enchanted every door in Blackstaff Tower to prevent the room's noises from traveling. The only way for occupants to know someone knocked was to use the metal knocker set at the door's center—Khelben's elaborate wizard mark set in brass over a plate of the same. Tsarra rapped once lightly and entered. If she was not welcome, the door would not budge at all.

She opened the door and smelled smoke just before she heard the roar of expanding flames. Using the door as a shield, Tsarra began casting a defensive spell.

If it weren't safe, girl, I would have warned you thusly.

Tsarra stepped fully into the room, confused by finding flying spells instead of a sick bed for the injured count. He stood with his back to her, his sleeveless tunic revealing his wiry, tattooed arms as he wove another powerful spell. On the far side of the room, a wardrobe, chair, and side table smoldered with light smoke, the charred blast points on the wall suggesting one of the two wizards had unleashed something earlier.

The morning sun did not diminish the glowing shimmer at the room's center. The magical creation was new to her, and she looked to her mentor, one eyebrow cocked quizzically. He merely inclined his head back at Gamalon, who unleashed his spell into the shimmering area. The fireball exploded at its center but did not expand to its full potential. It highlighted a ring of invisible menhirs around the shimmering area, all of which absorbed the magic of his spell. Once the roar of the spell died down, Tsarra could hear the count's ragged but deep breathing.

The totally bald wizard was obviously exhausted, sweat gleaming on his scalp and running down his neck. He turned, and Tsarra smiled as she bowed to him, happy his wounds from the previous night were all healed, save a long-standing injury covered with an eye patch. He nodded to her in return, coming over to grasp both of her hands in his as a typical Tethyrian greeting.

"Well met, young lady. I regret I am not at my best." His dark face showed the strain of heartache, his eye bloodshot. Still, he attempted a slight smile, easily seen around his salt-and-peppered beard, fully regrown and neatly trimmed.

"No regrets, your excellency, save my own. I am sorry not to have been of more assistance to you last night and this morning," Tsarra said. Remembering another Tethyrian custom, she took his hands between hers, folding them together over her heart in honor of his grief.

His only response was to drop his head as tears flowed freely from his right eye. He bowed his head to hers, his voice choked with emotion. "You honor me with that mourner's prayer. Thank you." He dropped his hands and collapsed into the nearest chair, his shoulders and head slumped in grief.

Tsarra looked to Khelben for a cue as to what she should do. He walked around the glistening spell construct, his face an unreadable mask, and spoke up from across the room: "A worthy and intriguing spell, Gamalon. If not for its overlong casting, it would be a boon on the battlefield. Still, truly a spell that needs carry your name." His pacing brought him close to where Gamalon and Tsarra were, and his face relaxed into a look of compassionate concern. Speaking to neither one of them, Khelben looked at a wall and said, "Laeral, please bring the globe if it's ready." He knelt down and placed a hand on Gamalon's shoulder, and the wizard looked up.

"My anger's spent, as are my spells, Blackstaff. I'm just . . . I can't believe Mynda . . . Why didn't her necklace protect her? Why? I . . . I don't understand . . ." Gamalon began a series of wracking sobs that did not stop when Laeral entered the room.

In her hands, she held a wooden box. She went directly to a small table near Gamalon and placed the box on it, opening the latch and letting the box's hinges open to reveal its contents. Set into each of the hinged covers was a scroll tube. Inside the box on a velvet cushion rested a globe of rose quartz about two hand spans in diameter. Its surface was polished smooth save for a few sigils lightly etched into it. Laeral and Khelben both murmured the same spell, which Tsarra did not recognize, and their palms glowed as they placed their hands upon the globe, their faces a mixture of sadness and compassion.

Tsarra shuffled around the room, opening windows to let out the lingering smoke. She busied herself with the mundane tasks of tidying the bed and moving the smoldering furniture beneath the windows. Hearing Gamalon cough, Tsarra poured him a cup of water from his bedside pitcher. She sent the clay cup over to him with a minor cantrip. Gamalon looked at her and nodded.

"Aha. 'Use every occasion to sharpen your magic, even the most mundane. It is not vanity or laziness that makes a mage use his skills in all things, but to honor the gods Azuth and Mystra for their gifts and their trust in him.' That still holds true?" Gamalon asked.

Tsarra smiled in return. "It would seem Khelben's lectures remain the same across the years. You were an apprentice here, your excellency?"

Gamalon said, "Never an apprentice, but kin and a intermittent student over the years. Poorer in magic would I be, were it not for my great-grandfather."

Tsarra asked, "So you too know he's not who he claims to be?"

"Less than one per twoscore who have studied within these walls realize Khelben knows too much to only be a mage of fifty-odd winters. I always knew my paternal grandmother Kessydra was born in the Year of the Bright Sun as the daughter of Khelben the Elder and Cassandra Simtul-Arunsun. Mind you, I called him cousin for many years before I uncovered the truth. His secrets are there, but only decipherable if he trusts you enough to show you the trail that leads to them."

"Enough, Lord Idogyr," Khelben intoned from across the room. "Here is another secret, though it is pale recompense for its costs."

Gamalon turned to look at Khelben, and stood up, his face paling as he said loudly to the mages Arunsun, "A Nykkaran Mourninglobe?"

The spell's glow shifting from their hands into the globe, Laeral and Khelben pulled their hands away. Both opened their eyes, and Khelben spoke. "Yes. Laeral and I spent the night preparing this one while you healed and slept. This one is for you—for Mynda."

"Khelben," Gamalon said, "these are priceless, their secrets lost."

"Not exactly true on either account," Laeral returned. "You have four scrolls here with the mourning spell on them—enough for you and your children to mourn her within the globe."

As Laeral spoke and Gamalon sat down at the table with them, Khelben looked at Tsarra and sent to her, *You're usually better at keeping your emotions off your face, Tsarra. Your confusion is apparent.*

Well, I don't usually see this much new or old magic this quickly. I've seen more secrets in two days than I've studied in a dozen years here. I've never heard of either mourninglobes or Nykkaran before—was he the wizard who made them?

I forget my days can seem overwhelming to those unused to such tumult. You'll have to get used to this, I'm afraid. As for Nykkar, it is a place. Calimshan has always had Nykkar, a city dedicated to funerary practices and the dead. Some funeramancers of this city first created these globes back when the Shoon dominated the south.

Khelben's lecture went much faster, as Tsarra received images, memories, and knowledge relating to his topic as he sent.

A highly specific spell cast by someone touching a globe allowed one to fully mourn and remember a person recently passed, draining all their grief quickly and leaving them with a globe full of memories. *In fact, with enough people embedding their memories and impressions of the deceased into a globe, one could touch the globe later to gain a sense of meeting the departed. They fell from use for centuries when desperate wizards after the Shoon Imperium's fall enchanted them to mind-rape wizards foolish enough to touch one. The keepers of Nykkar stopped making them about the time of the Warlord Laroun, and the mourning spells have been lost to most even longer. Laeral can bring Gamalon the sole surviving copy of* Rituals for the Dead *by Harun yi Nykkar from my personal library to study today.*

She sent, *And you just happened to have one of these lying around?*

No, he replied. *I have yet one more in reserve, which may be used all too soon.*

Tsarra realized their entire mental discussion happened rapidly, and Khelben ended it just as Laeral finished speaking.

Khelben answered both her and Gamalon's lingering question. "It is as Laeral says, Excellency. I only wish it were not needed. I've only made nine of these in as many centuries, when I found myself or allies in dire need of mourning without the time to do so properly. There are two mourningglobes in the tower for two former wives. A third rests with her namesake granddaughter Cassandra at the Thann villa. Yet another lies within my first son's tomb in the City of the Dead, untouched in eleven-score years. A fifth has some notoriety, as it mirrors Lhestyn's spirit, though I know not its whereabouts, thanks to the Shadow Thieves."

Gamalon stared at Khelben, exhausted but attentive, and Tsarra wondered about the history between the two men and the women in their lives. She could not grasp the despair gripping Gamalon, as she had long avoided any chance of losing herself in relationships. She had had lovers, including three fellow apprentices, over the years. She always remained pragmatic about them, never letting them get too close. Ever since her father died, she never wanted to feel that pain of loss again. Her reverie was broken by Gamalon's icy words leveled at Khelben.

"I have made many vows to you and through you to great causes, Blackstaff. You have had my trust and allegiance much of my life. If I had known the cost of those vows, I would never have promised them. Never!" Gamalon appeared calm and quiet as he spoke, but Tsarra could feel the impacthis words had on Khelben. "You gave me my 'eye' fifty years ago, hinting it had a great destiny and warning me it could be a great burden. Did you know then *this* would happen?"

Khelben said, "I did not know the secrets of the gem might cost you so dearly, no."

Gamalon's hands trembled, though his voice remained steady. "Is there anything else with links to this lightning to strike tragedy at my family?"

"No," Khelben said. "What you bear as a kinsman and *tel'teukiira*, you bear with full knowledge of their abilities."

"Why didn't you tell me, Khelben?" Gamalon pleaded. "I've paid the price with blood—I deserve to know what that bought!" The count pounded the table as tears began to flow again from his right eye.

"Yes, you do, as does Tsarra," Khelben replied. "Unfortunately, the time for such revelations is not yet here, and I need to ask your patience."

"Promise me, Blackstaff," Gamalon said. "Reveal every secret that cost me my wife. Swear by whatever you hold holy."

"You shall know the truth, blood of my blood, and the redemption and peace that shall come from Mynda's unfortunate death." Khelben's sorrow was genuine, Tsarra felt through their link, but even Laeral was agape at Khelben's vows. "This I swear by the silver in my veins, by the Weave, and by the emerald eyes of my daughter Kessydra, your ancestor. Do you need me to pledge by the Nine who Remain, the Six Argent Guardians, or the Twelve Mysteries, among other things?"

"No. Enough. Potent vows, those." Gamalon sighed. "To

be honest, I expected equivocation, not a straight answer with vows holy enough to bind a temple elder." The count leaned on the table and exhaled. "I shall assume there is more you need of me, or else you'd have taken me directly to Tethyr."

"There is, I'm afraid," Khelben replied. "Tsarra and I must away to unavoidable errands, while Laeral shows you Harun's tome and leaves you to grieve in private. Later, she will fill you in on the preparations, but for today, rest and honor Mynda's memory. Both Tsarra and I know how devastating that lightning can be, and we'll all need to be ready for a high magic ritual on the Feast of the Moon."

Tsarra exclaimed, "High magic? Khelben?"

Gamalon said, "You have an unmatched gift for keeping allies and enemies alike guessing, Blackstaff."

"Mynda may be gone, Gamalon," Khelben said, "but her friendly spirit shall be with us two nights hence, to see a working unseen in anyone's living memory."

CHAPTER SEVENTEEN

29 Uktar, the Year of Lightning Storms
(1374 DR)

Tsarra fumed as she and Khelben waited in the antechamber outside of the private office of Lord Maskar Wands. Despite her sendings and verbal pleadings, Khelben refused to divulge any more information since they'd left the tower.

For the last time, Tsarra, it was hardly safe for me to divulge what I did inside the walls of Black-staff Tower. To utter it outside invites foolishness at the very least. Khelben's sending carried a grim resolve. *You will know everything soon enough. Mystra demands my silence for now, but I can tell you one thing. The weight of these secrets can adversely effect events in the interim, so for now they remain unsaid. Now, comport yourself a little better than your tressym. I saw him chase Olanhar's familiar into one of the outbuildings.*

The pair of them had come to the Wands villa

on Shando Street by a public carriage at Khelben's insistence, "To give the gossip-mongers something on which to chew." The manor and grounds were awhirl with activity, as the staff and family prepared for Lord Maskar Wands's one hundred and thirtieth birthday the following day. Two stewards immediately led Khelben and Tsarra to the chamber, in which they had been standing for only a short while when a spiral mosaic on the floor began to glow. Rising from the spiral as if he merely walked up a staircase, Lord Maskar Wands appeared before them. Or at least, his head and shoulders did. The magically embedded noble turned and beamed at them.

Lord Maskar's voice was a pleasant baritone that sounded far younger than his appearance. He spoke at a rapid-fire staccato pace, but Tsarra couldn't tell if he was particularly excited or if that was his normal behavior.

"A surprise, this is, Blackstaff. You're not one to advertise your comings and goings, so you startled me when your mark appeared on my glass." His voice dropped to a whisper when he asked, "A new blackstaff, Khelben?"

"Aye, 'tis new, milord Wands." Khelben replied.

Tsarra realized she had not noticed the change in his staff, nor that he had not carried one since the accident. It was not the gnarled and ragged, blackened wood staff she saw then. The polished blackstaff was shod on the ends with golden metal that entwined the staff like veins. In fact, it looked as if it were black stone with marble-like veins of gold, the metal protecting the ends of the staff.

Another secret you've neglected to share with me, Khelben? she inquired silently.

Lord Wands beckoned, his arm coming free from beneath the floor. "I want to see that, then. Come down to my workshop, will you? We won't be disturbed by servants or exasperating relatives. You remember the passwords to my study doors, of course." With that, he turned in his place and disappeared into the floor.

"Shall we astonish him yet again?" Khelben asked, mischief in his voice and eyes.

Tsarra was constantly surprised by the Blackstaff. The dour and serious man she had known for years was, like the Lord Wands, acting like a child at a game he was rarely permitted to play. Khelben touched the spiral mosaic with his right foot three times, recited a short incantation, and grasped Tsarra's hand firmly. He began walking downward, and Tsarra realized that, even though it was still a mosaic, the staircase felt as if it descended naturally after the first step. The two of them entered Maskar's workshop, where they were greeted by a hearty laugh.

"And here I thought only Olanhar and I knew the charm to use that stair! I'm going to have to unearth some of your home's secrets as well, Lord Arunsun."

Tsarra had only been to the Wands villa twice in twenty years, and neither time had she actually been introduced to Lord Wands. Khelben stood over him by nearly a foot. The man's reputation stood far taller than he did in life with his pronounced stoop and slight hunchback. She knew he was older than most humans, but unlike Khelben, he chose to keep an aged and wizened face and body. He had recently cut his beard to closely trimmed muttonchop sideburns and cut his white hair very short. His ginger-colored eyes practically laughed for him as he clasped forearms with Khelben wordlessly. Tsarra noted Khelben had set the blackstaff aside, and it stood on end, perfectly balanced and without any apparent support.

"Well met, milord Wands, and a premature wish for the happiest of birthdays to you." Khelben said. "Your staircase charm remains a close family secret, for who do you think helped your father build it, and the others?"

Maskar's bushy white eyebrows rose, and he grinned, revealing a broad row of white teeth. "Well then, you'll have to reacquaint me with one or two of them that have been lost over the years, if only to get us into forgotten cellars." Maskar smacked Khelben on the back between the shoulders and laughed. A small chime sounded on the table behind him, and Maskar stopped, his face immediately serious.

"Excuse me a moment, would you? This brew is temperamental and has to be taken almost immediately." He turned his back on them and levitated a bubbling beaker off a flame, setting the glass bottle down in an ice-filled cauldron. He counted out to thirty on his fingers then grabbed the bottle and drank down its contents. If his stamping foot and shuddering didn't communicate his dislike of the potion, the gagging sound and heavy breathing of Lord Wands told Tsarra enough.

The old man turned back to them, and Tsarra watched his hair shift from white to a dark salt-and-pepper gray. His back straightened, his hunchback disappearing, and his face bore many less wrinkles.

"If anyone ever asks, child, why wizards don't all drink life-extending potions, tell them this: Each and every one of them smells like otyugh scat and blood, tastes like rancid milk mixed with sawdust and grass trimmings, and feels like you're imbibing razors and glass shards." Before Tsarra could ask, he smiled weakly at her and continued, "So why do I drink them, you wonder? Since my fiftieth birthday, I have traditionally drunk one of these every twentieth year. I don't trust most of my heirs to do right by the family, as happened at my brothers' passing. And perhaps a little because I'm just arrogant enough to want to finish a few more spells with my name on them as legacies for my children and for this city."

"Well, you're only a third into your second century. Give it time," Khelben said.

Maskar's eyes narrowed. "You're being cavalier with your secrets today, Blackstaff."

"To be honest, it is refreshing to let down one's guard among trusted companions, a luxury none of us gets to enjoy very often and never too long," Khelben replied. "As for the taste of your potions, I've always said you were a bad cook."

Maskar's face went through contortions, both from the potion's age-reducing effects and his mixed emotions of surprise, concern, confusion, and finally amusement. The man began laughing and slapped Khelben on the back again.

Tsarra couldn't believe what she saw. Common knowledge said the Blackstaff and Lord Wands held a mutual respect, but distrust and wariness for each other. She realized that, like Khelben's personal behavior, Lord Wands apparently kept up appearances in public as well. When Lord Wands turned back to her again, she bowed deeply, aware of the awkwardness of her shouldered bow.

"I'm glad to finally meet you again, Tsarra Chaadren nee Autumnfire. Your father was a kind man and far nobler than most who carry such title. You appear much changed, girl, from our first meeting. Those tattoos are bold statements that suit you. Welcome once again to my home."

Tsarra smiled nervously.

"My apprentice wonders how you know her secrets, Lord Wands," Khelben said. "She doesn't believe anyone outside of her choice confidants knew the nickname her mother put to her."

Maskar winked at Tsarra. "You have your mother's beauty with your father's eyes and bearing. It has been many years and I meet many folk, but I shall always treasure having known Taalmuth and Malruthiia Chaadren."

"Thank you, milord. I wasn't aware we had met or that you knew my parents," Tsarra said.

"Of course you don't remember our first meeting. You were not yet three at the time. You left quite an impression on me and my daughter, at least." Maskar chuckled. "You played with Olanhar's first tressym familiar and turned him a bright purple! My daughter was just beginning her wizardly studies and was jealous of the sorcery you used when you napped with the creature. It took her a month to change his coloring back to normal. Tressyms, however, were one of the reasons I expected to meet you today."

"Sir?" Tsarra asked.

Lord Wands motioned both of them toward a wide table, its surface a smooth dark mirror. He rested his hand on the glass, and the ring he wore—a gold signet stamped with his House seal in silver—twinkled with magic. Instantly, the tabletop became an overhead view of the manor's grounds. Glowing wizard marks moved about on its surface in various colors, and Maskar whispered another command word. The illusion expanded upward, becoming a translucent model of the building and the ground beneath it. Tsarra saw Khelben's wizard mark glow gold in a deep sub-basement, alongside the mark she guessed was Lord Wands's sigil—and her own.

Maskar waved his hand to get Tsarra's attention and pointed upward. In the attic of one of the outbuildings on the grounds, Tsarra's wizard mark glowed a bluish-silver atop another steel-colored wizard mark.

"The silver sigils are familiars or anyone enspelled by a particular wizard. Gold ones are the wizards themselves. It serves to know exactly where any trained in the Art are at any time on my property." Lord Maskar stood back from the holographic illusion, his arms crossed. "Your familiar arrived about an hour ago, and Olanhar and Snowhunter recognized him immediately. While Olanhar isn't pleased by the inconvenience of his "gifts", the last litter of tressym kittens greatly excited my grandchildren. I will be as well, provided they don't shred more Phalorman tapestries." Maskar winked at her again, and Tsarra felt a blush creep up her neck as she realized Nameless's trespass.

"Speaking of gifts, Lord Wands," Khelben interrupted the old man's teasing, "this blackstaff you admired is my birthday gift to you. I regret we won't have time for you to deduce all its powers for our amusement at present."

"A blackstaff to call my own—a princely gift, Khelben, thank you." Maskar nodded to Khelben then turned to Tsarra. "You do know this is how your master hoodwinks people into doing him favors, don't you? This is only the seventh time in ninety-eight years of knowing him that Khelben has gifted me on my birthday. So what favor does he need of me now?"

"Three things, milord. First, I need to see the Weeping Blade of Rholaris Wands, and mayhaps borrow it," Khelben said.

"Easily enough done."

Maskar walked to the far side of the room. Tsarra realized she'd not even taken a look around. She fully believed people's tales of the magnetic personality of Lord Maskar Wands. Two massive bookshelves stood behind that staircase, and seven more sets of shelves continued along the left-hand wall, interrupted twice by large work tables, one covered in books and scrolls, the other with bubbling beakers, potion flasks, and component jars. The center of the room held the large table, its illusionary tracking of the wizards on Wands property still glowing. The far end of the room held a circle of over-stuffed chairs and small tables, and a few of them were turned to face the right-hand wall, which was covered with paintings and maps of Waterdeep, the Sword Coast, the Savage North, and much of the rest of Faerûn. Lord Wands motioned them toward the farther wall, on which were three doors. He approached the second one, pulled a key from his pocket, and opened it. He went through, and Khelben made sure to hold Tsarra by the arm as they stepped through the door simultaneously.

Tsarra felt a slight tingle as she was shifted spatially to Maskar's study on the third floor of the manor house. The room was more richly appointed than the lord's workshop. Rich walnut panels lined the ceiling and walls of the study. A massive duskwood table with eight formal chairs dominated one side of the room. There were two bookshelves there, both with glass-paneled doors protecting their contents. They seemed to hold only bric-a-brac and trinkets undisturbed for many years. The carpets under foot came from far-off Zakhara, and Tsarra had little doubt that at least one of them might fly if so commanded by the lord of the manor.

The trio approached the western wall, and Tsarra shielded her eyes slightly as they crossed a strong sunbeam coming through the tall windows. The wall held a display of weapons: an arc of seven swords atop a quartet of shields and a row of nine daggers.

Khelben said, "My Lord Wands, I believe we can test my

student's knowledge to find the item that we seek."

Tsarra took her time, looking the weapons over from top to bottom then she said, "It's the third sword among the seven—the silver pommel with the sapphire tang button, two more sapphires on its steel-banded scabbard."

Maskar's eyebrows rose, and he chuckled. "Very good, girl. How did you know that?"

The old man muttered a command word before he magically floated the sword off the wall and into Khelben's waiting hands.

Tsarra whirled when Khelben smacked his palm on the nearby table and cursed, "Hrast!"

Tsarra silently asked, *What is it? What's the matter? Didn't you need this sword?*

No—the scabbard was actually more important in this case, Khelben replied then spoke aloud. "Lord Maskar, when was the last time someone removed this sword from its perch?"

"My sons and nephews made use of all of those weapons to fend off Myrkul's Horde sixteen years ago. Other than that, it has stayed there. Only three of us can remove the weapons from their places."

"Well, Lord Wands, someone tampered with this regardless. I don't have time to check the sword's authenticity, but the scabbard is a forgery. Were it true, we would have seen blue sparks the moment we entered this room." Khelben fumed, smacking his fist into his other palm as he paced.

"What?" Tsarra yelled. "You risked the lightning again without warning me?"

Khelben stared out the window. "No. The lightning only occurs when three of them are within a certain proximity. Two together only spit out sparks to cue the seeker as to their connections."

Tsarra lashed out at Khelben. "I can't believe you! With all that's gone wrong, you don't even warn me?"

Khelben said, "You are more than capable, Tsarra. I also knew there was no danger of the lightning today."

"Like you knew at the tower?" Tsarra snapped. "Danthra's

dead, Khelben. Dead! Do you need the tower to collapse before you part with another secret? Are the secrets more important than people?"

Khelben's shoulders sagged then he stiffened his back and replied, "No, that was never my choice. That happened because Mystra willed Danthra's fate. Even if I had tried to prevent it, the results would have been the same for all of us, perhaps with greater costs. You must believe that, Tsarra, if nothing else."

"Why should I trust you?" Tsarra screamed, pent-up frustration fueling her rage. "How many more of us will die for your precious secrets?"

"Tsarra, that's enough. We need to move on to our next errand." Khelben said, his voice gaining an edge of exasperation.

"Tish-tosh, child," Maskar said, putting a kindly hand on her shoulder. "Khelben loves his secrets, but you must know he loves good people more, even if he hides it." His merry eyes helped Tsarra calm down, and he nodded as he moved closer to Khelben by the window. "I heard something had blown a hole through the tower. That's not happened since my father's day and the Harpstar Wars."

Taking the sword from Khelben's hands, the old man set it on the table and pressed his palm on the surface beside it. Hands morphed from the table's surface to hold the sword and scabbard fast.

Khelben said, "It's obvious someone stole the scabbard long ago—it may have happened during Epira's collusion with the Guildmasters a century back. We cannot spare the time to look for it, but we'll hope to find the remainder of the items before our foe claims the true legacy."

Tsarra sat down on a chair, clenching her fists. She tried to listen in to the archmages across the room, but the ringing in her ears made that difficult.

"Good. A second favor, milord, is to see Belkram's Fall. Using the Yawning Portal right now would draw untoward attention."

"Young lady, we'll need you over here, please," Maskar

called, and Tsarra rose from her chair. She felt slightly dizzy and no less angry, but she approached and the wizards each took one of her hands. Maskar spoke an incantation, and instantly they went from the sun-flooded study to a dark stone room with no light. Torches flared to life around them, blue flames dismissing the darkness and revealing a small chamber with a massive sealed doorway.

Khelben and Maskar had their backs to the door but dropped their hands and turned to it. They intoned together, *"Ahrakelsharith Hilathrellas Orekarla Belkrammath."*

The stone door split down its middle and opened like wardrobe doors. The scraping of stone was loud in the small chamber.

Bile rose in Tsarra's throat, as she smelled decay and death on the chilling draft of air that rushed out the doors. Khelben stepped to the edge, and Tsarra followed, more curious than invited. She looked past the doorway to see only darkness, and looking down, she perceived a massive shaft disappearing beyond the edge of the light. She heard distant sounds and saw some flickers of light far below, but she couldn't identify what they were.

Tsarra gulped, her dizziness and nausea not abating at all. "How far down does this go?"

"We've never measured it properly, dear," Maskar chuckled. "We only know we've never heard anyone hit bottom."

"Belkram's Fall is perhaps thrice the length of the City of Splendors, give or take a ward." Khelben remarked flatly. "It was once a major mining shaft for the Melairkyn dwarves when they worked the Underhalls. We're not descending, though. Merely sending a message."

"Into Undermountain?" Tsarra gasped. "Why would you want to get the attention of the Mad Mage?"

Khelben produced a small carved stone swallow from his pocket. He cast a number of spells on the bird too quickly for Tsarra to follow then tapped the bird's head three times. It woke in his palm, twittered a gleeful greeting, and took flight down the tunnel. In its wake glittered five different colors of magical sparkles, but within moments even those sparkles had vanished.

Khelben said, "Those defenses should allow it to pass through the antimagical fields that span the shaft and get my message through. As to your question, sorcerers and wizards both must attend to some courtesies, regardless of power—or perhaps because of it."

As Tsarra looked down, her dizziness increased, as did the smell of decay. The ringing in her ears became the patter of rain on stone, as the vision overwhelmed her. Tsarra collapsed, and as she pitched forward a small part of her brain wondered what would happen next.

CHAPTER EIGHTEEN

12 Kythorn, the Year of Unleashed Fears
(451 DR)

The young man looked down upon his captors. "You have left me but one avenue, my lords. Sure, are you, that you want to force this path upon me? You know not what you do."

"You have nerve, boy, I'll give you that. I expect bluster from a sword-bearer, not a boy wizard in humble woolen robes." The wizard hovered near to him and bared his fangs. "Youngling, you are the ignorant one. You wandered off the path and stepped into Silorrattor. You found us, to your despair. Reap what you sow."

"Nay, wait, Kaeth," the second said, his voice a grating of iron on stone. "This one carries the secrets of elves, does he not?" The black-skinned wizard let his gray hood fall back, pointed ears and white ponytail revealing his drow nature.

"My agents tracked him from Myth Drannor

itself and led him to us, Ahaud. More importantly, he carries secrets from the Seven as well."

Yessss . . . the third projected, a stray tentacle waving outside the edges of its cloak's hood. *Let usss ssssuck the sssecretssss from hisss mind. . . .*

"You forget, Saquarl, of our pact," the fourth figure said from the throne at the center of the tower's floor, her voice softer. She stepped off the shadowy throne's dais and into the light. "All prefects share equally of magic gained, or else we see it destroyed before others benefit from it." The woman shrugged off her umber cloak, revealing a voluptuous figure in a shimmering red gown that flattered her like a sycophant. "I have other ways of making the boy talk. Palron? Ready him for my interrogation."

"Of course, milady Xaerna. At once." The floating wizard gestured, and when his arms slashed through the air before him, the young man's robes ripped away. The young wizard was naked and still suspended from his invisible magical bonds. His rent robes and cloak fell to the floor near Saquarl, disturbing the dust.

Xaerna finished her own incantations, and black bats' wings sprouted from her shoulders. She took to the air, looping around her young prey. As she passed, her hands caressed the young mage's muscular form.

"Hm. A human in every way. Pity. I prefer my men less hairy, but your secrets won't last us long." The woman's satin gown trailed against the young mage's trunk and legs, and he shivered.

"Ha ha! Mayhaps he's aching for something other than freedom, Xaerna?" Ahaud the drow laughed. "We can extract information from this hostage of ours in so many ways, some for which you are eminently suited. Exactly how long do we have before we need to sacrifice his body?" The black-skinned elf unfurled an oily whip from his belt and lashed it out, its tip snapping dangerously close to the captive's bare feet.

Are we cccertain thissss one walked with the Sssseven? Saquarl the illithid sent to all minds. *Nothing on him indicated sssuch an allianccce.*

"Do you doubt me or my agents, mind flayer?" Palron Kaeth snapped back as he settled to the ground.

"No," a fifth figure intoned. "He merely wants confirmation from someone with a pulse."

The vampire laughed and said, "Our friendship may have spanned my death, but don't vex me, Luuthis." Far above, no one noticed the young man smile grimly.

Luuthis said, "Saquarl, My Lady sees through all lies. He is who Kaeth claims he is. Do you need me to prove Leira's powers through me are greater than your Underdark-born faculties?"

Palron moved over to the fat Northman and threw an arm over his broad shoulders.

"None of us doubts Luuthis Fharren's convictions or the powers of your goddess, Lord High Obfuscator. We need only know how long before the boy's sacrifice is of most use to the Three in Darkness we *all* serve."

The young man smiled broadly, and Xaerna giggled. "Fellows, our captive enjoys my attentions."

"Hardly," he replied. "You've told me what I needed to know. I'm ready to go, now that my mission is completed."

The only sound in the tall chamber was the sound of the vampiress's magical wings beating the air. Then evil laughter filled the chamber from its obsidian floor below to its ceiling just as far above.

Saquarl, in moving away from Luuthis, brushed against the pile of rent clothes. The fabric and leather fragments slithered and swarmed around him, wrapping tightly around his head and body so quickly that none of his comrades noticed until Xaerna screamed and clutched her head. The illithid brought her down, her defenses useless against his psionic attack.

Palron leaped to defend his vampiric mistress, while Ahaud clambered up the wall like a spider, drawing two very ornate black short swords as he ran. Only the Leiran priest watched their smiling captive as he flexed his arms and legs then clenched his grip, magical energies surging from his hands. The priest brought up his triangular holy symbol to start a spell when the mage drew his knee across his body as he pulled his left leg up. Luuthis crumpled, never seeing the flagstone smash into his head.

"Interesting maneuver, child." Ahaud remarked. "We'll have that secret as well before you free yourself." The drow touched the tips of his short swords together, and a purplish-black bolt of magic exploded toward the defenseless mage.

"Indeed?" The mage's steel-blue eyes sparkled with contempt for the drow as the blast hit him full force. The color of the magic shifted immediately to light blue, and the magic leeched into the magical webbing that spread-eagled the man in the center of the tower. Suffused in blue energy, the mage kicked his right leg out and yanked his right arm down and across his body. Two stone blocks attached to the webs hurtled toward Ahaud.

The drow disappeared with a *pop,* reappearing a few yards up the wall, still clinging to it like a spider. "You missed, boy!" he crowed. "Enjoy your freedom a few heartbeats more. . . ."

"It will last longer than your life, Ahaud of House Tanor'thal." The young mage spun in mid-air, and the three stones still attached to the spell webs that once held him scraped and rebounded against the walls below him.

"Don't count on that, wizard!" Xaerna cried, her face twisted in anger as she flew toward him. "Your death will be as miserable as that whisper of a beard on your chin."

Down below, the wizard could see Palron Kaeth hunched over the body of Saquarl, the illithid's neck obviously broken. The scraps that once possessed the illithid swarmed around the male vampire.

The young wizard pulled with his anchored left arm, which drew him into the tower's upper reaches and dislodged the stone. He floated of his own volition, but his final anchor stone crashed into Xaerna's left wing and slowed her pursuit. Ahaud continued the chase, easily running up the smooth black stone walls.

Ignoring his pursuers, the wizard began a new spell. He spun rapidly, the arcane webbing and stones it trailed all glowing. Ahaud and Xaerna avoided the stones, and they too cast spells. The fireball left her fingers a few seconds after the drow unleashed his lightning, and while the wizard reflected the bolt right back at Ahaud, the fireball exploded just above him, slamming him against a wall and burning away his hair.

"Pity the much-vaunted Seven Wizards of Myth Drannor failed to teach you better." Xaerna flew to where the naked man smoldered in one of the upper windowsills, and she began casting a paralyzing spell.

Despite the distractions, the young wizard uttered the spell's final syllables looking into Xaerna's eyes.

"Xymmaoth Piurasjk Atox!"

Wincing from the pain of burnt skin, the wizard pulled all his limbs together, tucked himself into a ball, and fell backward through the window. The magic he cast remained on the windowsill and the wall, gold and red energies leeching into the stones.

"All that effort to escape, and he wishes to fall to his death? And what is that? Ahaud, do you know this spell?" Xaerna demanded. "It's seeping into the stones, and I can't dispel it!"

"I don't know, Xaerna. I've never seen its like." Ahaud glanced out the window, scanning down then up toward the tower's peak. "The boy's atop the roof!"

The mage shivered as wind and rain lashed against his naked form, but he smiled back at Ahaud as the drow clambered out into the night and started walking up the outer tower. The silent wizard took to the air and looped swiftly once around the tower. Then he slammed into it with his shoulder, screaming in pain as he hit. Ahaud could see the human's shoulder was broken with bones jutting partly from his skin.

The drow's satisfied smile lasted only moments as he realized the tower had shuddered beneath the impact. He saw the results of the earlier spell. Red and gold magic weakened mortar and stone. With the magically enhanced impact, the tower fell inward on itself.

In a matter of moments, Silorrattor lay in a huge mound of rubble and dust. The son of Arun barely even heard the screams of his former captors over the din of grinding stone. By the time he reached the ground as well, all was silent. Arun's son groaned as even the slight jar from landing sent spasms of pain through his shattered shoulder. Still, he smiled grimly as a cloud of stone dust settled in the rain.

"They taught me enough, witch. They taught me architecture, to be sure."

      ◈ ◈ ◈ ◈ ◈

"Easy, Tsarra. I'm sorry—I thought the visions would ease on you in time." Khelben's voice penetrated her consciousness before her vision cleared.

"I don't recall your other apprentices being so inclined to faint, Blackstaff." Lord Wands chuckled as he held her on the opposite side. "Are you afraid of heights, my dear?"

Tsarra gulped as she got her bearings. They were back in Maskar's study, and she lay on a divan in one corner beneath the windows. The sun was muted and much closer to sunset. "No, Lord Wands, I'm not. I think it was the smell that triggered the vision . . . or perhaps the sound of scraping stone . . ."

Maskar asked, "What visions are those? From that *kiira* you wear?"

"She sees my past, Maskar" Khelben said. "Amazingly, even before I was Chosen."

Tsarra felt his concern and admiration, then was surprised as her master's eyes rimmed with tears.

"I'm sorry this onus fell to you, Tsarra."

Maskar had also moved closer, and he touched Tsarra on her shoulder. "My dear, are you wearing the Coronal's Beljureled Belt?"

Khelben and Tsarra noticed the belt had become exposed from beneath her leather top. Maskar stared at the glowing green gems and gold scales alone, as did Tsarra—the gems and the buckle were the only things that didn't seem to be part of her flesh! She touched it, and the gold scales shimmered, but they felt like skin.

"Yes," Khelben sighed. "I'd not told her, as I didn't want her intimidated by bearing one of Eltargrim's gifts. Do not worry—its wearer can remove it at will. The merging is just another way to hide the belt from thieves."

Tsarra smiled and ran a finger along the belt. "My mother taught me not to revere things over people, milords, and that all items are meant to be respected as tools and used, not feared or venerated."

Khelben said, "That woman continues to earn my respect long after her untimely death. Yes, Maskar, you know I would only bring that item from the shadows for one reason."

Lord Wands cleared his throat again and said, "So it's that time, Blackstaff? Rhaelnar's Legacy is to be fulfilled? *That's* the third favor? Do I need to hide a Nether Scroll for you, should a foolish treasure hunter actually reform one?"

"No, old friend," Khelben replied. "Rhaelnar's Legacy is a blind that hides a greater secret, one I'd hoped to forestall for another three-score years yet. As my hidden foe now has two components I'd never expected uncovered, an inheritance more powerful than Netheril's writings will soon rise. I need you—we shall locate the scabbard in our own way—to participate in a high magic ritual out on the High Moor on the Feast of the Moon."

"High magic?" Maskar said. "I have neither elf blood nor that kind of intimacy with the Weave, old friend."

"I have it on good authority we'll have help in that regard."

"Who can promise you that?"

The air around Khelben's head shimmered slightly, a hazy halo of stars coming into view. His eyes were rimmed with silver, and Maskar and Tsarra both gasped as Mystra's symbol manifested clearly for a breath before dissolving into the remnants of the sunbeam.

"Very well," Maskar said. "What's the task—fully restoring Myth Drannor?"

"No, though a few worthies of that realm may join us for the working. No, 'tis something older still. We need your wisdom as much as your knowledge of the Art for our ritual. Besides, you've little delight in these galas of overstuffed shirts. Join us at Malavar's Grasp, and help us tame magic that has slept for millennia."

"Getting away will take some doing, Blackstaff, especially if it needs to happen without undue notice. For me to disappear from my villa during a birthday feast in my honor will draw attention."

"You're capable of slipping away without anyone the wiser, Maskar. Besides, it has been a score of years since you reminded people you're a wizard of power with many secrets they dare not invade."

"Good point. My reputation is in need of repair, and it's been longer since I've been well and truly surprised by magic. What you're hinting at sounds too intriguing to miss. You have my promise to meet you at the Fallen One's Fingers, aye. I cannot break away earlier than daybreak on the Feast, but I shall meet you at Malavar's Grasp by moonrise, regardless of my family's wish for a three-day-revel." Lord Wands smiled as he shook both Khelben's and Tsarra's hands.

"Are you well enough, Tsarra? We need to move quickly now." Khelben helped her into a sitting position.

"I think so," Tsarra said, standing up and stretching. Her balance was restored, and she readjusted her top to cover the belt again.

"All right," Khelben said. "Many thanks, Lord Wands. It is now time we consulted with another god. I've a feeling there's much for us to learn at the feet of Oghma. Summon your tressym, Tsarra, and let us make haste for the Font of Knowledge. In the interests of both safety and propriety, we owe Sandrew the Wise a visit."

CHAPTER NINETEEN

29 Uktar, the Year of Lightning Storms
(1374 DR)

Raegar woke abruptly as the slap tore him from an exhausted slumber. What kept him conscious was the flesh-chilling cold from the lich's touch, the marble floor, and the many other pains across his body. The stunning effect had long worn off, but the beatings and lack of sleep were having a cumulative effect on him. The late afternoon sun lit the upper dome of the Stagsmere entry chamber through its shattered skylight, but the rays were intermittent as clouds still gathered overhead, as they had all through the night and morning. While Raegar enjoyed the fleeting warmth of it, the afternoon sun in his eyes had lulled him to sleep for a time.

Raegar hated feeling helpless, but he could only turn his head from left to right. The night before, the lich had summoned and morphed a trio of skeletons into a bone cage that anchored him spread-eagled on the floor. Turning his head away from the lich, he could see his broken short sword, two of his daggers, and his magical rings in a clump against one wall, tossed aside when the lich's spells overwhelmed and disarmed him. He couldn't see where the lich had taken the Diamondblade, but he was glad he didn't need to dodge any lightning because of it.

"I realize you're not genteel, Raegar, but you must stop falling unconscious when I'm talking." The creature's skull loomed close to his face, its soulless features even more disturbing up close. "You're young, but Waterdhavians were made of sterner stuff in my day."

Raegar spat a stream of invectives at the lich foul enough to make a Dock Ward sailor blanch. To his chagrin, no sound came from his throat due to a magic placed on him a few hours before. Raegar had been hurt many times by people and circumstances in the past. Never once had he ever felt so helpless. He pushed against the bone cage, but his efforts were less effective than they had been hours before. He was weak from exhaustion, but his hatred for his situation and his captor burned bright. The thief entertained methods of revenge and stored them away for more appropriate times to exact them.

"Yes, this is better . . . much easier with you incapable of interrupting me," the lich gloated. "Besides, don't you wish to learn more for those little scribes of the Font of Knowledge? Laughable, that they think themselves worthy to take for themselves the secrets wizardry has wrested from the cosmos. At least this venture has proven fruitful with a number of new pawns and Rhaelnar's Legacy itself within my grasp." The lich paced around the chamber, sprinkling an area with powders and herbs, gesturing mystically at various points, and obviously focusing on a major work of magic while simultaneously torturing the captive Raegar.

The lich had spent the past eighteen hours magically building something in this chamber and torturing Raegar for more information on Khelben and modern-day Waterdeep. The creature also lectured on the superiority of southern magic and the gentrific elegance that was the Shoon Imperium and its magical works. One thing the lich did not do was reveal his name to Raegar, which was fine. Raegar had more colorful names for him in his head.

I would gladly kill this lich simply to spare anyone else the boredom and pain, Raegar mused to himself. *At least he's taken off that skullcap and I'm able to think without him stealing my thoughts.*

The thief shuddered when he felt the lich invade his mind and mine every detail of his life, significant or otherwise. His only pleasure came when the lich discovered how many insulting swear-word-filled names Raegar had silently given him.

That rattled him enough to shout, "Boy! You will fear the Fro—No. Very good, Raegar. Very good indeed. You'd almost wheedled my name from me. No, I want Khelben to go mad wondering who brought his plans down around his ears. Not until I am assured of victory will I face the Blackstaff again."

More hours passed, and the only sounds in the chamber were the lich's incantations and the whistle of the wind in the upper chamber around the broken masonry and skylight. The lich's robes stopped directly in front of Raegar, and he continued a particularly complex incantation for a few moments. Raegar turned to look up at the creature, breathing through his mouth so as not to smell the dusty and pungent smell that came off the lich. He almost wished the wizard would reactivate that harness, if only to mask the creature's smell and horrific looks.

"Why are you smiling, Raegar?" the lich inquired. "Thinking up petty revenge? Well, you shall soon be free of my skeletrap and back in the City of Splendors. All I need do is temporarily reset my newest portal to link with Kerrigan's Gate that we used earlier. But first, a few preparations."

The undead wizard knelt by Raegar's left hand and placed

a ring on it—the one that had sparked when close to the Diamondblade. Raegar got a good look at it when the lich walked away. The crude iron ring had an intricate silver emblem—a rack of antlers framing a tiny sword with a crescent moon for the sword-haft on the hilt. Raegar could not remember where he had seen this symbol in the past. He wondered why the lich would part with such a powerful item.

The lich returned with a pair of chain-mail gloves forged from four different metals. He cast a quick spell and touched Raegar's forehead twice, then stood up. He said one odd syllable, and the bone-cage around Raegar clattered into an inanimate pile.

The thief knew better than to leap up, given how cramped and chilled his muscles were from lying on the cold marble all night and day. Raegar shook the bones off of him, never taking his eyes off the lich, and knelt while he stretched his arms and legs. The lich laughed his hollow laugh and tossed the metal-link gloves at him. Raegar let the gloves fall to his feet rather than catch them.

"Put them on, puppet," snarled the lich.

Raegar's stomach wrenched when his body obeyed without hesitation, slipping the metal gloves onto his hands. The rogue felt them clench into his skin. Raegar shot the lich a look of fury and hatred and mouthed another silent stream of invectives at him.

"Yes, yes, be angry if it helps," the lich said. "You'll still fulfill my direct instructions and be unaware of why you're doing what you're doing. The enchantment preventing your speech will also last a goodly time. Those gloves are yet another Shoon relic—the Gauntlets of the Syl-Vizar Tnarrak. They will remain linked to your hands until your death or until they hold my specified item—another Legacy artifact. Once they do, the gauntlets will come to me along with all they touch. Then you'll be your own man. Of course, more likely you'll also be dead at the hands of Khelben Arunsun."

Raegar sidled over to his equipment, taking up his daggers and pocketing his two silver rings. He cast a wary eye at the poor black boots he found with his equipment. His own magical boots were missing.

The lich stared at him and pulled his hood back around his fleshless head as he said, "You'll have to do without your boots, as I've another agent who deserves them. Now, stop delaying, Raegar, and walk across the mosaic. Oh, one thing to note—the sharn will detect magic on you from the Legacy artifacts once you use this portal. My suggestion when you arrive back in Waterdeep is to run quickly. We shall not meet again, little thief."

Raegar, standing, noticed subtle differences in the chamber. What was once a smooth marble floor had magical runes etched into it by the lich's spellcraft and powders. An intricate knotwork pattern encircled the center of the room. Inside that circle, the floor wavered with tremors of energy. Raegar didn't want to step anywhere near it but found himself a passenger in a body that stepped forward as ordered. As he felt a magical tingle crawl up his legs and the portal enveloped him, he gestured rudely toward the lich, glad to have at least managed that small act of defiance.

Raegar stepped from thin air into the tunnel near New Olamn, and his head ached as it always did from teleporting. The pain wasn't reduced by the scream of a startled horse, rearing up and away from this obstacle suddenly appearing in his path. Raegar dodged out from under the horse's flailing hooves and noticed his body was wreathed in greenish sparkles as his arms came up to guard his face.

As Raegar broke into a light jog toward Swords Street, he watched the color of the strange light shift to blue. By the time he broke into a full run, the remaining sparks glowed purple.

Raegar had ignored the oaths and yells of passersby objecting to his magical arrival, but he dared a brief look back when the screams began. The rosy color of the setting sun illuminated the tunnel's exits on both ends, but

Raegar could still see lingering footprints glowing purple where he'd stepped. The shadows along the walls and ceiling dripped together around those sparkling prints. Familiar four-clawed hands reached from the shadows. The hapless horse Raegar had startled screamed as a toothy mouth erupted from the wall and savaged its hindquarters while other claws slashed at the horse's rider.

Raegar ran as fast as he could from the tunnel and into the streets. He raced east, skirting the back of Shukar's Chandlery, the Preening Peryton Inn, and the collapsed corner of masonry and wood that used to be the Pharraoth Alchymistary. His feet seemed directed toward Zelphar's Walk until they slid out from under him, and he scraped to a halt against the outer wall of Soonymn's Finecrafts. His head screaming with pain, Raegar looked up into the hate-filled eyes of Kemarn Darkthrush of Nesmé.

Raegar tried to push himself up but found the ground beneath him more slippery than ice. I thought only Damlath used that grease spell effectively, he mused.

He grabbed a dagger from his belt and threw it hard at Kemarn. The dagger hit the man in the arm, and the action as well as his grunt of pain was enough to disrupt the new spell Kemarn had been casting.

Screams closed in behind them as well as the screeching wail Raegar had heard at the Sleeping Dragon. He used the slippery spell to his advantage, spinning on his back then kicking hard against the stone wall to slide quickly across the street and away from Kemarn. When he skidded out of range of the spell, Raegar tucked into a backward somersault and drew his dagger from its sheath, rolling onto his feet in a defensive crouch.

The mage growled at him, "I owe you pain, thief!"

Raegar barely saw the gestures before four purple pulses of energy rocketed from Kemarn's fingers. He gritted his teeth against the pain of the spell and scurried backward. Kemarn paused for a crucial second. Raegar sheathed his dagger and ran as he saw the sharn looming at the opposite end of the alley.

"Coward! The Darkthrush of Nesmé wants revenge!" Kemarn shouted, oblivious to the danger behind him. "You can't run fast en—"

Kemarn's taunting threats ended with a wet crunch and a muffled scream upon which Raegar had no wish to turn. He was too busy fighting the impulse that had his feet crossing Swords Street and mounting the stone steps leading up into the Font of Knowledge, Oghma's great Waterdhavian temple.

Raegar took the steps two at a time and vaulted through the open doors into the Hall of the Binder, the three-story-high temple entry chamber. Dominating the stone-walled chamber was a massive green marble statue of Oghma as an unclad male with exceedingly long hair and a beard. The god's muscular form was posed as if in flight, his left arm stretched out ahead of him and its fist more than twenty-five feet from the floor below it. In that fist was a golden scroll, long held by rumor to be either simple gold sheeting or some hidden secrets of the gods. Raegar remembered that Khelben the Blackstaff had donated the statue to the temple during its construction and claimed that it once blessed the grounds of the Binder's temple in Myth Drannor. Behind the statue on either side were the two-stories-tall sets of double doors leading into the Great Library of the Binder, a four-story scriptorium and library that rivaled houses of learning centuries its senior.

Raegar's mad rush into the building scared a number of yellow-robed priests and attendants, and his refusal to either stop or speak to them caused many to crowd around him, demanding explanations. Raegar felt ill as his body shoved aside pious monks he knew as friends and punched worshipers who blocked his path. He couldn't stop himself from forcefully making his way to the back of the chamber. Ahead of him were the doors leading into the Great Library, but Raegar halted at the foot of the massive statue set between the doors.

Raegar found himself clambering up the statue, shouts of "Blasphemy!" and "Shame!" rising among the faithful below him. Raegar's body knew what to do to climb the unwieldy construct, even if he didn't command it, and he was surprised that the chain mail gauntlets on his hands didn't hinder his sense of touch or his grip. He confidently grasped each handhold and foothold, clambering through Oghma's stone tresses and up his back and shoulders. He thanked Tymora for his luck that not more spellcasting priests were on hand to see him and smite him rightfully from this perch. Then the screams of terror began below.

The sharn's massive black form glided into the temple, and what few people resisted its entry paid for their actions with their lives. The sharn retained a simple teardrop shape save for two heads glistening with fangs. Purple shimmers surrounded its form, and purple energy flared on both sides of Raegar as well. He threw himself flat against the statue to avoid four flailing claws launching from the sharn's portals. Raegar climbed, hoping to dodge the sharn's attacks, but the purple shimmers kept flanking his path. Just as he reached the statue's left shoulder, he realized that blue sparks crackled around his left hand—as did the massive scroll in Oghma's left hand.

Raegar, still mute, begged forgiveness from his god for his blasphemies as he began to walk out along the stone arm toward the scroll. As he reached the elbow, the claws flashed out again from the left. From the right, a third sharn head roared through the portal, its teeth gnashing at him with savage intensity. Raegar felt his legs collapse beneath him and wondered if the lich's control included unwitting suicide. Instead, his legs looped around the arm, and his body used the momentum to swing forward and grapple the statue at its wrist with his hands. The blue sparks on his hand and the scroll grew into small, stinging lightning bolts, and Raegar wondered what would happen once the magic of the gauntlets came into play when he touched the golden scroll. The only lucky thing at that moment was that the blue energy seemed to be holding the sharn's attacks at bay.

Raegar wrapped his legs around the statue's hand. He

smiled as he noticed the hand with the Legacy ring held him in his current position, so he couldn't make an immediate grab for the scroll without falling. He clung to the underside of Oghma's wrist and tried to twist his torso forward, straining to reach for even the edge of the golden scroll, which was awash in crackles of blue lightning bolts. Unfortunately, the spot his right hand tried to reach was occupied by an angry, jet-black tressym with its claws and fangs extended. At the same time, Raegar heard a booming voice exclaim, "That's quite far enough, young man!"

CHAPTER TWENTY

29 Uktar, the Year of Lightning Storms
(1374 DR)

Raegar knew the voice of the Blackstaff without even looking. Khelben's shout boomed over all the noise, including the keening shrieks of the sharn.

One thing at a time, Raegar, the thief said to himself. Your only foe right now is the little winged tomcat. Nothing else.

The tressym growled deeply and launched toward him, all claws extended. Raegar couldn't backhand the creature aside, as that would throw his balance and grip off, causing him to fall. The black-furred creature lunged for his eyes and face, but his hand held the creature off, getting a good clutch of fur around the tressym's chest. The lich's control over him made him more brutal than Raegar might normally have been, and his right arm slammed the tressym hard against the statue. Raegar expected it to be stunned at least, but the winged cat all but roared as it slashed its wings at Raegar's face. Some feathers jabbed hard into the thief's eyes, and Raegar felt his arm fling the creature hard away from him. The tressym recovered almost instantly, even avoiding the black-robed mage floating a few feet off the floor.

The mage looked up at him, splitting his attention between Raegar and the sharn. Raegar watched Khelben's eyes dart to the thief's hands, the lightning bolts, the scroll, the tressym, back over to the sharn, and back to his eyes at long last.

"Tsarra," he said to someone out of Raegar's eyesight, "stay back, but get him off the statue. Once the lightning is quelled, we have a chance to calm this sharn down enough to talk."

Raegar heard her say, "Done," followed by the sound of a bowstring.

Pain lanced through Raegar's left arm, and he let go. A small fountain of blood gushed from his forearm onto his face, and the arrowhead jutted from where his wrist and forearm met. His legs squeezed hard, and even Raegar was surprised to find himself hanging fully upside-down, lightning crackling between his left hand and the scroll. Khelben hovered almost directly below him, but Raegar could not hear or see the tressym. Tsarra also remained out of sight behind him.

Raegar smiled ruefully as he heard her say, "Very manly and stoic, not making a sound. Guess I'll need another arrow."

Raegar liked her sense of humor, despite the circumstances.

"Tsarra! You're not a tressym playing with your prey. End this now!" Khelben growled at her then uttered a stream of arcane syllables to summon a globe around the sharn, muffling its harsh cries.

Raegar found that instead of falling or remaining still, his body rocked back and forth. He screamed, "Hrast!" without sound as he realized what his body was trying to do. His torso snapped backward hard as his legs released, and Raegar swore loud and long inside his head as he back-flipped through open air, his left hand aching toward its goal of the scroll. The thief blanched even whiter when his flip revealed the tressym's location directly behind him. Raegar wasn't sure what he felt more at that moment—stunned pride in his body for having executed such a bold move, the sharp sting as the tressym's foreclaws slashed into his neck and face, the harsh pain as one claw hit the arrow embedded in his forearm, or the shock and shudder as his hands successfully grabbed one edge of the metal scroll and red sparks of magic coruscated all over his left arm and the scroll. After the initial contact, however, Raegar lost his grip with his left hand as blood gushed from his arm and covered the glove and parts of the scroll.

The red sparks increased to a radiance that spread across the scroll and built in strength, rendering the blue lightning bolts purple within it. Raegar noticed they were arcing in a different direction—toward the woman below him, her bow drawn and ready. The blue sparks erupted around her midsection, and she said, "Khelben?" a moment too late.

The sparks grew, as did the red glow around the gloves and scroll. Tsarra threw herself backward and away from the statue, but Raegar could only grit his teeth as he felt the lightning bolts build. At the same time, he felt a different tingling around his hands from the magical gloves.

From below him, Khelben yelled, "No!" and launched himself up into the air just as the lightning bolts grew into one massive bolt focused through Raegar's left hand.

The massive bolt—the bluish magic leeched out to more brilliant white—thundered out and slammed into the Blackstaff with staggering force, blasting Khelben down to the floor. Raegar noticed that the sharn also crackled within its globe, and it keened in pain.

Raegar's attention returned to his own precarious perch. He didn't know what magic the gauntlets worked, but his left arm was totally numb, and his right hand was freezing cold as the red magic began pulsing. With the first pulse, all eyes not blinded by the earlier blast looked upward to see the red energies start to contract with each pulse. The energies also rendered the golden scroll in Oghma's marble hand smaller. The second pulse pulled the energy into both gauntlets while rendering them and the scroll translucent, almost invisible save for the red luminescence. Raegar sensed what was coming and prepared to fall as the third pulse contracted the radiance to pinpoints on his hands, and the scroll and gauntlets disappeared.

Raegar fell backward toward the cold marble. He lashed out at the last second, hoping to spin himself around so he might land better, but he only managed to kick empty air. The tressym zipped around Raegar and almost seemed to laugh at his predicament, mocking him with the very flap of its wings. Raegar struck the floor with his left shoulder, his head bounced off the marble, and he fell unconscious.

26 Mirtul, the Year of the Normiir (611 DR)

The man without a name flew fast and silent. It mattered little to him most days, but some days brought up raw emotions decades old and saw him rage at the burdens namelessness placed on a child. That day, he raged for other reasons, and his anger fueled his speed. His swiftness also came from a new spell that rendered him incorporeal while in flight to allow no winds to hinder him.

He had spent the past two days in constant flight. A recent vow to his Lady of Mysteries barred him from using gates, portals, or other methods of instantaneous travel. Flying across the North forced him to see the Everhorde's devastations firsthand. He saw the ogre war bands, the orc legions, and the giant patrols ravaging many places dear to him. His dreams and connections to her bade him press on and rein in his fury and his will to slow the Everhorde's onslaught.

Not until he approached the mountains scant miles north of Deepwater Bay did he find an unavoidable battle. The creatures sounded like orcs, attacked as orcs did, but they had scaled skin of black and red, spat fire and acid, and flew on scalloped wings. The nameless one had never seen their like before until he suffered their mid-air ambush when he flew through Peryton Gap. His spell, which prevented interference by the winds, did not protect him from their physical assault.

In his youth, the man had learned to fight in treetops and defend against foes coming from every side. As a mage, his spells placed him in many arenas stranger than the air amid a mountain pass. Magic protected him as he took their measure.

He swept a flare of silver flame, an expanding aura of fire that blasted to cinders the two who grappled him. The other four he dispatched within minutes, using spells to break or ensnare their wings and doom them to deaths by long falls.

The man let nothing hinder his mission, even though he suffered some wounds and his clothes were worse for the battle, singed or acid-burnt in various places. He wore a wool overcloak of steel blue that matched his eyes. Beneath his cloak were a simple tunic, leathern breeches, and soft doeskin boots. Due to hardships and spell battles long past, the only memento of his earlier life was the iron badge that was his mother's, worn on a chain around his neck. A botched counterspell in battle six tendays back against an undead Shoon vizar had left him with badly burnt hair. While the gifts of his goddess allowed him to alter his features at will, he deemed it too mundane a task for magic. Thus he shaved his head and trimmed his beard down to the modern Cormyrean style of a beard and moustache only covering his upper lip and chin. The look was deemed "appropriately sinister to match your moods" by acquaintances in Dolbron's Mill two night's prior. The people there had long since taken to calling him "the Nameless Chosen," "Grimspells," or "friend."

"Mystra grant me strength," the Nameless One said through gritted teeth as he soared lower toward the mountain and into the smoke coiling around its still-snowclad upper slopes, smoke he had spotted even before the ambush. The spell had an added benefit of sharpening his hearing, but the wizard worried as he heard no sounds when he alighted in the courtyard at his destination—the Pentad Retreat.

He had visited the mountain sanctuary only once early in his service to the Lady of Mysteries. Reachable only by well-hidden tunnels, a barely discernible and treacherous footpath, or by air, the monastic enclave rested within an extinct caldera and remained hidden to all but the most attentive of those who traversed that cluster of peaks. It was known to very few outsiders, as the ideas embraced by those pious folk would bring down the wrath of five religions on their collective heads. Of five modest stone temples and chapter houses, a granary, cookhouse, smithy and forge, and a common hall, only smoldering rubble lay. The dream he had two nights past had come true. He had seen the mountain and the five symbols of the gods aflame.

Only the library—the largest building and the most fortified beyond Dumathoin's Altar—remained standing. It dominated the northern side of the complex, leaving little room between itself and the outer defensive walls. Two stories tall, the building was made entirely of a silver-white stone not indigenous to the mountain range. The merlons and crenelations atop the walls were carved as open books, unrolled scrolls, and one unique symbol for the gods of the place: a circle enclosing five smaller circles which held an eight-pointed star, a partially unrolled scroll, a mountain with a gem at its heart, a pair of eyes atop a crescent moon, and an oak leaf superimposed over a sun.

Arun's Son knew the Everhorde raged everywhere across the North as it had since earlier spring when it claimed Luskan and later Mnarsvale, Suthcliff, Droversford, and countless other hamlets north of the Delimbiyr Vale. It encroached on Yarlith, and the forces of Phalorm moved to intercept it. He had hoped the monastery would remain safe, but his earlier attack showed him the horde had reached even there. The wizard also knew the orcs—even altered ones such as he fought—could never have found the place without help. He ran toward the library to discern what had happened.

Many orcs lay as if they had fallen from great heights, others killed by arrows. Of the nine bodies he found sprawled on the library's steps, four wore amulets with a sigil on them—a wizard's mark known to him.

"Palron Kaeth. Of course he would use the Everhorde to his advantage," the man mused aloud. "A reckoning will be coming soon to you and yours, Prefect. So vows the son of Arun."

The bodies were all cold, some with ash and snow settling on their graying skin, suggesting death was not recent for them. He heard a muffled clang through the closed doors of the library. The mage placed a hand flat on the door and whispered the password: *"Siilathaeraes."*

The door, which had remained firm against an onslaught of axe blows, acid bursts, and fiery blasts, opened easily to his touch. As he entered, Arun's Son whispered spells to make himself invisible and silent.

The room had a perimeter around its stone floor more akin to the naves of a church, allowing him to make a circuit of the chamber with ease. The library was one singular area, its open balconies and roof held aloft by ten fine-crafted stone pillars of lighter stone than the building itself. Carvings on the pillars depicted twice each the idealized forms and sigils of the five gods of the Pentad: Corellon Larethian, Sehanine Moonbow, Dumathoin, Mystra, and Oghma. The tables and desks in the center of the room made three rings that demarcated the divisions of labor in the library.

The wizard sighed in relief as nothing seemed disturbed or destroyed, the inkwells on the desks still open and unspilled. The secondary ring were granite slab tables numbering twenty in all, each longer than two adult humans and half again as wide. The tops, sides, edges, and legs were all replete with Dwarvish runes. The innermost ring of tables consisted of secretaries, desks with three bookshelves attached to them. Six were placed in a row, back to back with another row of six, each row facing either side of the room. The angled desks each held a tome and the shelves above the desks were all thick with massive volumes chained to them. The Nameless Chosen could also see additional secretaries, cabinets, and shelves on the balconies overhead, most with books chained in place to prevent theft.

The only place where someone could hide was the curate's office that enclosed the eastern balcony. The Nameless One approached the stone spiral staircase in the northeast corner that led directly to the office, still silent and unseen. At the foot of the stair was a golden goblet resting on its side with a bent lip. That had made the noise that alerted him, and the wizard glanced up to find the trapdoor into the office wide open.

He cast three spells on himself and one upward into the room as he slowly ascended the stairs. He could not detect any evil or any invisible creatures beside himself. His last spell was merely guaranteed to counterspell the first magic cast upon him.

The noiseless and invisible mage rose up into the curate's office. The room, like the library below, had light filtering in through theurglass skylights in the ceiling. Unlike the light below, the rectangular room glistened with refracted rainbows of colors on the wood paneled walls. The sparkles came from the eleven crystals hovering in mid-air among an arc of six tall wing-backed chairs, five of which had their backs to him. Four small gems, each about the size of his thumbnail, orbited the others with faster motions, and those were colored brown, umber, orange, and red. The other seven crystals were clear and as long and thick as the wizard's torso.

The Nameless Chosen inadvertently spoke aloud in his astonishment, "*Kiiratel'Uvaeranni . . .*"

Voices answered him from among the chairs.

"Very good, Nameless One."

"Approach us and sit."

"Be quick—our time grows short."

"Are we sure he's the one?"

"He has ties and loyalties to us all. He is the one."

The Nameless Chosen froze where he stood when an elf's hand appeared above the back of the nearest chair, beckoning him forward. Its skin was glistening and jet-black, and claws seemed to flex in and from its fingers like a stretching cat. The wizard pulled some iron, diamond dust, and an assortment of herbs from his belt pouch as he yelled out a quick spell. The magic wrapped each of the chairs in glowing chains, each link a handspan wide. Another chorus of dispassionate voices considered his actions.

"Niyadra's Chains? He knows his elven spell-lore. Pity about his human patience."

"I will not be bound." The chains on the far right chair dissolved with the sound of iron clanging on steel.

"Of the five, his power alone can keep our secrets."

"Power alone is not enough. Our sharing with the elf of Ardeep proved some cannot abide all secrets."

"Aloevan's love and trust of history shattered with our secret. This one understands the past has many layers and many truths inside shells of deceit."

"He is human, the starred one's gifts besides."

"Human born of half-breed, true, but elf blood is his. He is worthy."

During those retorts, the Nameless One maneuvered to the empty chair, the one the other five all faced. He dropped his invisibility spell as quickly as his jaw. He had recognized the voices as those of the high priests of the Pentad's temples, but they were not precisely whom he faced just then.

They each looked like the priests in basic form and profile, but a glistening black slime covered them from foot to throat. What little flesh remained uncovered had darkened considerably. High Hammer Arnathus the dwarf had claws and fangs sprouting and disappearing in his prodigious beard, its russet-brown hair black and oily. Saarvip and Mijala Oakenstaff, the elves whose marriage mirrored those of their gods, held hands, and the wizard could not see where one black form ended and the other began. Magepriest Laume of Summersreach always had the kindest eyes, and they smiled on the wizard—all seventeen of them blinking about the gnome's body and face. The Chondathan woman he knew the least. She had only recently come to the Lorebinder's service, but he knew that

Naarys the Morninglark had never before needed five hands to play a lap-harp.

All five spoke in unison but alternated among themselves, as if they all shared the same mind. The wizard sat in shock as five of the massive crystals manifested each of the Pentad's holy symbols within their cores in blue and purple energy, underscoring the acceptance of their gods in the event.

"We are in transition, Nameless Chosen, for the good of all."

"Understand we are in no harm, nor pain, nor fear."

"All your questions are answered in these crystals and our books."

"Attend them, know them, guard them, and keep them safe and secret."

"Our legacy must be kept but we guard others greater still."

"Know we are not the first to make this transition, for we join many vanished waiting to be found later."

"Among us are minds and souls of many peoples, all of us coming from realms falling."

"Many have been lost to greed, ambition, or evil, and we protect those few who cling to their dreams."

"Redemption may come for all, but neither soon nor easily."

"We enfold the lost, the missing, the dreaming, the worthy, and the bold."

"Many are we but all are one in form and purpose, e'en if we forget that for a time."

"Our guise and goal shall remain hidden until the lightning calls to us."

"Wake us not to our old selves, as that is the task of that which destroyed us all—greed and power and guile and treachery."

"All our brethren are among us, the faithful of this place, but we waited to tell thee true things."

"Thou art more than Mystra's Chosen—the Pentad Chooses thee as well."

"We ask you to remember us and keep our works and secrets."

"What you see here you may comprehend fully with study of our library and learn the secrets of lives and lores and labors long lost."

"We shall await the time when we may be singular yet united."

"We charge thee to ready the Realms for our return."

"We all take Oacenth's Vow and Dragmar's Promise to heart."

"Until we meet again, we may redeem lives and reclaim lores lost where we find them, e'en if our actions match not our intent."

"Until the world can accept our message, we remain hidden, even from ourselves."

"Dutiful one of secrets many, we honor and thank thee for thine service."

"Fare thee well, honored son of five faiths."

As they spoke, the priests seemed undisturbed as the black oil crept over their faces and into their open mouths, eyes, and noses. Once fully covered, the priests' forms began to shift and merge, regardless of initial height or breadth. Their individualities melted, and features, clothing, profiles, and limbs flowed together into shapeless jet that remained pinned to the chairs by the wizard's spell until a nimbus of purple light settled around them all. They disappeared with only the chuff of softly imploding air to mark their passage.

The Nameless Chosen sat for five days and nights without movement, pondering what he had witnessed. He read what he could from sunlight and moonlight filtering through the seven meditative lore crystals—priceless artifacts from Uvaeren, the long-fallen realm of the elves. In his ruminations and trances, he learned from the patron gods of the Pentad. The priests of the Pentad were creatures that the Nameless One learned were called shiftshades, blackclaws, simmershadows, skulkingdeaths, or the *fhaorn'quessir*, though most knew them as the sharn.

CHAPTER TWENTY-ONE

29 Uktar, the Year of Lightning Storms
(1374 DR)

Tsarra shook her head to clear her eyesight, and she realized she was sprawled on the floor of the temple between the statue and Khelben. For the first time, there was no disorientation from the vision or any headache. She knew at least the general truth about the sharn. She also awoke angry, then realized it wasn't *her* rage as much as it was that of her tressym. The avian creature darted in and out, slashing at the sharn . . . or was it?

The creature that batted away at Nameless wore the greasy black skin of the sharn and its limbs ended in the same elongated tri-arms with claws, but it stood on the four legs and body of a strong stallion and had a heavily muscled torso. It seemed more to be a silhouette of a centaur, save for its two oddly distended limbs. The creature advanced on

Khelben, and the tressym looped around its front, hissing savagely to warn it off.

She sent to the tressym, *No, wait. I don't think he means harm.* His reaction was to hiss again at the sharn and bare his claws as warning as he flew back to Tsarra.

Dangersmell, predator, darkelder wounded, helpless prey! he sent to Tsarra as she stepped forward between the sharn and Khelben.

She tried not to flinch when she saw her mentor collapsed on the marble floor. Silver flames and blood alike spilled from a large ragged hole in his robes where his left hip and torso met. Were he a normal man, Tsarra guessed he might have been either dead or, even with expert healers, hobbled for life.

Khelben? Tsarra sent to her mentor through the *kiira*. *Can you hear me? How badly are you hurt?*

Yes, apprentice, I hear you. The bolt knocked me out for a few breaths, and it obviously left me a significant wound. For now, it's more important I get a few moments to prepare a spell. Distract him for me, would you?

Tsarra stepped closer to the sharntaur and drew her scimitar, holding it point upward across her chest. "Come no farther, creature." She wasn't quite sure what to expect of it, but she knew her grandfather's blade Maornathil should do well against it, regardless of what strange magic it wielded.

"You don't need to fear us." The sharntaur's voice sounded deeper but more commonplace rather than the odd echo in what Tsarra deemed a sharn's usual tone.

"I don't." Tsarra surprised herself with her unbidden answer. She really had no fears of the creature for the first time. She understood what she faced and knew it was well within her abilities to deal with the creature. Gone were the flashes of temper, the nagging fears and doubts, and all the uncertainties of the past few days. She wondered how much of them were hers and how much were perhaps those of Danthra, her friend whose soul had come to link her with their mentor.

The sharntaur nodded at her then stamped its hooves. This action seemed to surprise it, and it rotated its head completely around twice, staring at its own form even as its actions defied its normal structure. Eyes erupted across its form, opening along its torso and lower body. Its skin shimmered as it reasserted its centaur nature, closing all eyes but two that looked at Khelben, Tsarra, and Nameless. It then distended its head around them all to look at the fallen thief.

Tsarra backed up and knelt by Khelben, resting her scimitar on the floor. She held him around the chest and under his arms so he had both his arms free to cast his spell, rather than prop himself up on one elbow. The wound's blood flow had soaked his lower robes, but the silver fire cauterized it and prevented any further blood loss. Only after she had done all that did Tsarra realize he'd not said a word. Had she read his mind?

Khelben wove subtle sigils in the air as he spoke, interspersing his statements with his spell's arcane incantations. What he spoke was apparently a dialect of Elvish that Tsarra had never heard, as she couldn't understand all that Khelben said.

"*Ye who have been* sukarat a'layr *are* sinaglar *again. Accept* nuamil *and learn of* tuul edemp *close at hand.*" Khelben completed his spell, and his hands suddenly held a crackling globe of purple and azure energies that drifted in the air toward the creature.

The sharntaur reared up on its hind legs when a chorus of yells erupted from its right hand side. A handful of wizards, bards, and spellcasting priests burst from the Great Library's doors, weapons drawn and readied. Khelben yelled, "No!" and waved them off, but two of the bards aimed arrows at the sharntaur.

With a feline snarl, Tsarra urged her tressym into action. "*Spoil their shots, now!*"

Nameless bolted toward them, spraying into the face of the first bard while clamping claws and jaws on the bow hand of the second to make him drop his weapon. For her part, Tsarra pulled up the memory of ice growing on a still pond and the smell of the frosty snap of chilling air. This spun together the magic that put an invisible shield between the archers and their target. The only hint that she had cast a spell at all were the whispered incantations only Khelben could hear.

Nameless flew past the swiftly growing group and looped up in the air for another pass when a voice from behind the archers boomed out, "Enough! Stand your ground and do not interrupt them unless they bring direct harm to you!"

Tsarra and Khelben both sighed in relief as the temple's founder pushed his way to the front of the group. Sandrew the Wise, lorekeeper high and ranking priest of Oghma here, spread his arms wide then moved toward the fallen thief while keeping an eye on the goings-on in front of him. The man's priestly calling to Oghma demanded he value knowledge and history as well as tending to the aggrieved. He seemed equally fascinated in what Khelben was up to with the sharntaur and horrified at the disturbance of his temple's peace.

Tsarra watched him as he began weaving healing spells around the man's arm and head. She thought it odd treatment for a rogue who had defiled a god's temple, but she had never met Sandrew. For all she knew, he might be among the more compassionate of high priests, unlike the callous Meleghost Starseer of the House of Wonder. Her initial impression of the Oghman priest was of strength and purpose as he rose and helped the red-shirted rogue to his feet. Sandrew was clad in white pants and shirt with a golden vest and slippers. The head of the Font of Knowledge stood relatively tall, his shoulders square and strong, unlike many lifelong scholars with stooped and bowed shoulders. Aside from a receding line of graying hair, the priest's age was not apparent. Tsarra realized with a start that the red-shirted thief was the man they'd encountered the previous morning—and the same man whose blade set off the lightning that killed Danthra.

Yes, Tsarra, he's entangled with our fates in many ways.

Tsarra returned her attention to matters in front of her, including the injured Blackstaff. *Khelben, what happened? I didn't even see the lightning strike—I lost consciousness a moment after the three artifacts reacted to each other. I was lost in your memories for a few breaths, but I learned a lot about our friend here.*

Good. There's less to explain now. As for my predicament, I intercepted the magic directly and paid the price. Khelben's response shocked Tsarra as it exceeded his typical penchant for understatement.

You caught the lightning? Weren't you the one who used to warn me about taking too many risks or asking questions too late after leaping?

Good advice, that. We should both listen to that prudent sage. It isn't exactly lightning, though.

How can you tell?

Because I'm immune to lightning, my dear. Adamar's song, I've not been hurt this badly . . .

. . . since your encounter with the Crown of Horns?

Khelben's face darkened, and his eyes blazed into hers for a moment. Through their link, Tsarra felt a roiling upsurge of rage, pain, sadness, horror, and regret. If she had not felt his emotions, she might have missed that look, as it took him less than the blink of an eye's time to restore his features to their normal unreadable state and his emotions under tight rein once again.

Sorry, Khelben. It's not easy for me either, sharing your thoughts and memories.

No apologies necessary, Tsarra. You're holding up better with this than I might have at thirty-four. I'm simply unused to having someone other than Laeral complete my thoughts so concisely. I am more angry at myself, having counted on a certain invulnerability when I should have heeded my instincts.

So why did you throw yourself into its path? You already knew it could affect you since this morning.

Khelben's chagrin and resolve were all evident in his response. *The lightning would have destroyed the support walls of the temple, collapsing it upon all of us that were within it. Lives would have been lost, as well as that statue— a legacy of Myth Drannor actually crafted by my father. I just didn't expect to take as much of the bolt, given the transfer of energies to the sharn through the globe.*

As Khelben and Tsarra silently conversed, the sharntaur slowed its rearing and pawing at the air with alternating hooves and its strange tri-arms. It settled down and stared at the globe that hovered in the air before it. Eyes again peppered the creature's surface to reflect the energies of the globe. It reached out, and its skin glowed in response as well. Its claws dissolved as it touched the globe, its tri-arm melting into a normal centaur's hand, albeit obsidian-skinned. Once both hands embraced the globe, its energy leeched into the sharntaur's skin and body, forming constellations of winking purple and blue stars among the blackness of its shape.

Tsarra found herself speaking in concert with Khelben, finally understanding the obscure Elvish dialect as the two said, "*Remember and return redeemed and readied. We shall await you at Faertelmiir.*"

Tsarra didn't quite know what she was referring to, but the certainty of it never wavered in her or Khelben's minds. She looked down at her mentor, who she helped settle onto his back, his wound still a massive hollow where his hip and side should be. The only evidence revealing his incredible pain was his shallow and rapid breathing. He smiled at her.

Don't miss this, Tsarra. Watch the sharn, not me.

The sharntaur, its silhouetted form fully centauran save for its glistening black skin, bowed to Khelben and Tsarra from its waist. It also wove a number of hand signals and gestures as it bowed in Sandrew's direction as well. The priest returned a number of the gestures and bowed. The sharntaur crouched then leaped high into the air, which elicited a chorus of screams and gasps as it appeared to leap for Sandrew and the statue. Instead, it disappeared into a nimbus of purple lights at the apogee of its leap.

Tsarra looked down at Khelben again, surprised to find tears of joy rimming both their eyes.

Khelben whispered, "You feel it, don't you? Even if you're not fully aware of it all, part of you knows what's to come and rejoices at it. Remember that when things get bleak. It will help you through harder days than this one. Now, prepare to bear the endgame that is upon us. I'm sorry I did not prepare you better—I thought I had more time. So many things undone, unsaid."

Tsarra felt a flash of warning in her head along with the loud growl of Nameless as he flew down to protect her. The tressym landed on her left shoulder as the priest and their opponent stepped close to them.

His eyes not on them, Sandrew muttered a few words in prayer, and a glow emanated from his hands. He spread his arms in arcs overhead, and the glow settled into a radiant hemisphere around the quintet.

"There," said the priest. "Oghma loves to share knowledge, but he also knows when to keep secrets from prying eyes and ears."

"Glad to see that prayer book I gave you for the founding has seen good use," Khelben said then coughed violently, expelling small amounts of blood and smoke from his mouth. Tsarra felt his embarrassment over his seeming weakness, though he seemed to have some concerns toward his continued health.

"Lord Arunsun?" Sandrew the Wise asked as he kneeled down opposite Tsarra on the other side of Khelben. "Thank you for saving my temple from destruction, milord archmage. May I heal your suffering?" Sandrew's clean-shaven face was both young and ancient at the same time, as his unwrinkled brow and umber-colored eyes seemed to hold the insight of ages.

"No, thank you, Loremaster High. It looks worse than it is. That matter is well in hand." Khelben nodded, though Tsarra noticed his face had returned to its usual stony facade, revealing no more than absolutely necessary. "The scrolls will unfurl in due time, old friend. For now, introduce us to our erstwhile foe. I believe we all have met briefly, though names were not exchanged."

Tsarra found herself unable to look away from the young man who locked eyes with her rather than submit to Khelben's interrogation. While his loose-necked crimson shirt and black leather breeches still bore the marks and stains of a few recent battles, the man himself was clean and whole, his dark brown hair pulled back in a tight ponytail. His youngish face had a close-trimmed full beard. Tsarra was distracted by his eyes—slate gray with highlights of blue, like eclipsed marble—until he averted them to look at and offer a palm toward Nameless, who had been growling loudly.

The tressym sniffed warily, his head bobbing to get a better range of scent about the man, and Tsarra felt her familiar's reactions—an odd stream of emotions from surprise, hatred, curiosity, disgust, amusement, jealousy, contempt, and confusion. Nameless began meowing loudly, which Tsarra understood as *"Stinks of longdeadnots and marsh and stone. Didn't smell that before through sparksmell and fearstink. Like his scent, and he knows not to risk scratching my ears. He still goodforyou matefriend maybe? He huntercurious but also smellfury and wantflightfight like me."*

Tsarra picked up her scimitar and said, "He says you smell of undead, and that makes me distrust you immediately. Despite your open approach toward him, my friend knows you're furious at something and really want to be elsewhere."

"Undead, you say? Thank you, Nameless, for that information." Khelben's irritation was obvious in his snapped query. "Well, boy? Can you account for your actions? Tell us for whom you work." His voice never wavered, but Tsarra could feel his strength waning, and his breathing grew labored.

The man's eyes widened, and he looked frantically at Tsarra, Khelben, and Sandrew, mouthing words mutely. He grimaced and seemed to scream, but no sound came from him other than the rustle and creak of clothing and the rush of air from his mouth.

Sandrew's hands glowed as he touched the man on the throat, but an attempt to speak after that only produced a rasp. Sandrew looked down and said, "I'm afraid we can learn precious little, Blackstaff. He has been rendered mute by the forces that turned him against his own church."

Tsarra asked, "So he's a lay worshiper of Oghma?"

"Aye, lass," Sandrew said. "This is Raegar Stoneblade. He first came to us as a stonecutter during the Font's construction, but he has since joined us as a devout worshiper as well."

Khelben asked, "Is that why he's been spying on my tower and students?"

Sandrew's eyes widened, and he spun toward Raegar. "Not by my authority, Blackstaff. Betimes the Font will have seekers pry secrets and lore from those unwilling to share openly, but you and yours have always been friends to us. It appears I have not been as diligent as I might have been over loremasters who may have approved such mischief. Is that the case, Raegar?"

Raegar nodded and gesticulated wildly, trying to pantomime his point, but Khelben began a violent coughing fit, and his shaking reopened his wound. Blood gushed over the floor, and Tsarra felt Khelben weaken, then go silent. His eyes fluttered and closed.

"Khelben?" she asked, kneeling in the blood and putting her hand to his neck to find no heartbeat beneath her hand. *Khelben!*

CHAPTER TWENTY-TWO

*29-30 Uktar, the Year of Lightning Storms
(1374 DR)*

Tsarra's heart leaped into her throat as she whispered once more, "Khelben? You can't be—"

Khelben's eyes snapped open, and his body shook with a violent spasm of coughs. More blood poured onto the floor, but silver flames flickered to life and seared the wound shut once more, an acrid stream of smoke rising from Khelben's shattered hip.

Eltargrim's Bones, this hurts. Khelben looked at Tsarra with eyes drained of energy, before he said, "Out of time. We need him and what he knows." Khelben's eyes closed for a moment, and Tsarra felt him scream angrily inside, though that emotion never made it to his face. "Tsarra, take him to the tower. Ask my wife to attend to the boy's tongue. She should mindspider him if she has to, but I hope it won't come to that."

Raegar clenched his jaw, and his knuckles

whitened but he relaxed when Nameless growled at him and drew attention to him. He nodded to Khelben and Sandrew, but Tsarra noticed his face still blanched.

"You'll not punish him, Blackstaff? I sense he has been a pawn and deserves no reprimand beyond helping right what he has wronged," Sandrew said. "I cannot openly acknowledge what he does for my church, but I can vow that his heart is a good one and his skills and actions do not overshadow that."

"Punishment is far from my mind, Sandrew," Khelben gasped, "save to let him help us visit it upon the one who wronged all of us. Now, time is short for us all. We must away."

"Are you certain you don't want healing?"

"Too many gods' magic affects me already to accept one more right now, Lorekeeper. I have my own remedies, thank you. There's no need to carry me, either of you." Khelben glared at both Tsarra and Raegar who had moved to either side of him. He sent to Tsarra, *Back away, as both of us can't use this magic and I need you to be my hands for a while. Look to your intuition for guidance, in case I don't respond for a while.*

Khelben's blue eyes lit up with silver and gold as he whispered a spell. Gold shimmered in the necklace he wore, a tiny tapered bottle. As he finished, his form dissolved into a golden mist, shrank, and seeped into the bottle. A necklace alone rested on the bloodstained marble floor. Tsarra and more than a few onlookers gasped with his disappearance.

Sandrew the Wise smiled and said, "An Anyllan's bottle. I read about these ancient elven devices, but I never thought I'd see one that still worked. Khelben should be safe to heal slowly inside there."

Tsarra stooped to pick up the necklace off the floor and place it around her own neck. She sent out tentatively, *Khelben?*

Khelben's mental voice wavered. *Need sleep to save my energy. Go to the tower, and both of you talk to Syndra.*

She knows what's to be done, and Raegar knows who is to blame. Be respectful, but hurry. Know I am sorry for this burden forced upon you. I can no longer carry it alone.

Tsarra flinched despite herself, but with the visions and what she'd learned in the past day, she knew why they had to face the undead. *Stop worrying. You've trained me well enough. Sleep and I'll do what I can in the meantime.*

"You three and Khelben brought much trouble to my temple." Sandrew the Wise looked sternly at all of them. "I trust that when we meet again that I may have a suitable explanation for this disruption—" he glanced upward toward Oghma's empty fist, deprived of its scroll—"and desecration."

On that last word, Raegar's shoulders slumped, and he knelt by the priest, bowing his head for forgiveness. Sandrew's hand hesitated but settled on the man's head in benediction.

Tsarra, Raegar, and Sandrew realized the circle of angry people had pressed close around them, just outside the glowing hemisphere set by the priest.

"Khelben insists on utmost speed, but I'm afraid your priests don't look all to willing to let us go quickly."

"What else would you expect, girl?" Sandrew said. "There are many here who wish the guards would clap you both in irons. Run now and get you away so I may cool tempers, but vow before Oghma that you will return and explain all this."

"What little I know, Lorekeeper, I'll share with you. I promise that everything you saw today leads to the betterment of the Realms."

Tsarra turned to Raegar, and said, "You are going ahead of me, and we're running at best pace to Blackstaff Tower. Try to lose me, and my familiar will be the first to correct you, followed by my spells or arrows." Tsarra jerked her thumb up at Nameless, who bared his teeth.

Raegar rolled his eyes and nodded. The three of them darted through the glowing energy. Their movement startled most from their path, and they flew or ran through the temple doors and into the streets.

Behind them, Sandrew cleared his throat and snapped his fingers both to dispel the sound-blocking hemisphere and to draw the attention of the crowd. "Oghma wills their secrets remain their own for now, brethren. Return to your lore and lives, and the Binder may or may not reveal what enigmas he sees fit." He whispered to himself, "And may what magic you work be as good as you claim. . . ."

"That should do it. What say you now, handsome rogue?" Laeral's merry eyes looked into Raegar's from beneath a heavy silver helm, its forehead adorned with three stripes of sapphires.

Raegar knew whatever that lich had done bound him no longer. He inhaled, and "Thank you" sounded in both his head and throat. He smiled broadly and stretched his arms and shoulders.

"I don't know what you did." Raegar took the heavy helm from his brow and set it on the sidetable next to him. "I don't feel anything crawling around inside my head any more. Thank you, ladies, for that."

"Enough. Under whose control were you? Answer me, Stoneblade!" Tsarra had been pacing the room and snapped her head around. Raegar watched the arc of auburn curls more than the angry look on her face.

"I never got a name," Raegar said, and Tsarra growled in anger, pacing around the chairs in which he and Laeral sat. Raegar watched her a moment then looked back at Laeral when he said, "By the gods. How anyone can get anything accomplished around so much distracting beauty is beyond me."

Raegar smiled, winking at Laeral in the opposite chair but watching Tsarra for her reactions. He had never been so close to anyone of Blackstaff Tower in either his recent missions nor in all his years in the City of Splendors. Still, he knew enough about them to expect what would happen next. For his part, he bent over in the chair to touch his toes and stretch out his torso and back.

As he anticipated, he rose from the chair to find the point of a glimmering scimitar near his throat. As he smiled and felt a rush of excitement go through him, Raegar heard a complicated growl come from the tressym, who lay nestled among a pile of books on a high shelf over the door frame. Tsarra's gaze snapped to him and she uttered a similar tangle of purrs and growls. The conversation between the woman and her familiar continued for a few moments until Raegar cleared his throat, earning a glare from Tsarra. He raised his hands slowly, smiling his most sincere smile, and tried to push the point of the blade away from his neck by his fingertips.

"Ahem. If I'm to duel, I'll need to borrow a blade, milady." Raegar wasn't sure how she would react to his teasing, but he hoped Laeral might aid him.

Laeral smirked as she set down her helm and stood. "Tsarra, please. You'll hardly get the lad to answer any questions that way. Besides, Nameless tends to be right about a great many things, whether you want to acknowledge that or not." Laeral's fingers danced and a small silverfish appeared to swim upwards through the air and into the black tom's claws.

"This is not the time for jokes, Laeral!" Tsarra snapped back at the taller woman, the point of her scimitar not moving an iota. "Khelben urged me—"

"Yes, yes, girl, but allow a moment to revel in irony aplenty." Laeral moved closer to Tsarra, easing her sword arm down and whispering to her as the two women moved away from Raegar. He wasn't sure if Laeral meant him to overhear, but his heart leaped as he caught her whispered comment. "After all, holding him at bladepoint was the first thing I did to *my* beloved when we first met."

Tsarra's reaction was a frustrated growl followed by what Raegar guessed might be a chuckle from the tressym. The auburn-haired half-elf glared at the tressym, Laeral Silverhand, and Raegar as she sheathed her scimitar. After a moment, Raegar saw her catch herself, close her eyes, take three deep breaths, and her shoulders dropped as she relaxed. When she opened her eyes again, Tsarra looked directly into Raegar's eyes, but he couldn't read anything in hers other than impatience.

"Well, stonecarver, chisel us some knowledge from that grinning stone face of yours. Who or what was behind your attack on the Font of Knowledge?" Tsarra's tone was brusque and clipped. Raegar had seen her do that with others in the street—cloak off her emotions and keep things strictly on the matter at hand, despite how she felt at the moment. He admired her a little for that.

Raegar dropped his smile, and said, "I don't know his name, but he's obviously a lich who killed my friend. I want to see him dead and buried far more than you, woman."

"I doubt that. What does it look like?"

Laeral said, "Even without their original gender characteristics after death, Tsarra, liches are never 'its.'"

"To me, they'll never be more than things that desperately need to be put back into the ground." Tsarra replied. "Well, Raegar?"

Raegar said, "Tsarra, I hate to disagree with you, but the lich was—er, is, er . . . Blast it! Is it 'is' or 'was?'"

Laeral snickered and said, "Keep to the present, Raegar. Liches still obey the identity they bore in life, so give them the benefit of present tense. You *are* sharper than some give you credit, lad."

Raegar smiled at the compliment and continued, "The lich is most definitely a man, Tsarra—sorry to disagree. You can tell by his stance and how he moves, not to mention his swaggering. He wears olive green robes embroidered with gold runes, keeping the hood up. I think that's less for show and more to hide the fact that he's only got a little skin left on his face. Just enough to hold his jaw on and a little around one eye socket."

"He could be any one of five liches from that description, three of whom are in the North," Tsarra said. "Did he wear any distinct jewelry?"

"He had a ring of cold iron, really rough workmanship except for the silver part placed on top. Its sigil was a sword with a moon for a hilt among a rack of antlers. I thought it seemed familiar but I couldn't place it."

Laeral snapped her fingers, drawing both their attentions. "Did it look like this?" she asked, and her hands wove an illusion in mid-air of a dusty shield hanging on a wall. The seal on it was a sword with a crescent moon hilt painted atop a dark stag's head on a midnight blue field. Beneath the shield was a pillow holding a dark iron ring with the silver emblem, just as Raegar had seen earlier.

"Yes, exactly. The rings seem identical. What are we looking at, milady?"

Laeral sighed and said, "If my husband could copy these items, someone else could too. How is a question for another time, though. This is Raurlor's Ring, which sits under heavy magical protections in Castle Waterdeep. Only a lord of the city can approach within five paces of it, and yet somehow it lies in another's hands. That's equally fascinating and worrisome. Khelben, our plan isn't as secure as hoped."

Raegar saw Tsarra's eyes flash with anger, and her jaw tightened, but she looked at nothing in particular. He asked, "Lady Laeral, Lord Arunsun's in that necklace. Why are you talking as if he can hear us?"

"Oh, my love could hear me if he stood in far Kozakura and I here, Raegar. Trust me. He's just having a silent chat with our lovely apprentice here." Laeral nodded toward Tsarra as she rose from her chair. "Try and tear your doting eyes off of her, young man, and follow me. We've much to do, and you don't want to find out what the tower likes to do to those without a proper escort." Laeral's fingers trailed across Tsarra's throat and shoulder as she walked by, her index finger touching the glowing necklace.

Raegar looked at Tsarra, who hardly seemed to notice what Laeral's touch meant. Her shoulders were tense, and Raegar wondered what went on inside the young half-elf's head. He noticed the emerald gem on her forehead glinting and glowing. He watched her grimace, tensing all the muscles in her jaw, neck, shoulders, and even her clenched hands were white-knuckled. Her posture changed, and she shifted her weight as he and Laeral moved past her. Tsarra fought something deep inside herself.

If I didn't know better, Raegar thought as he pursued Laeral, she's either fighting herself or she's possessed. She changes how she stands as if she's not sure who she is.

CHAPTER TWENTY-THREE

*30 Uktar, the Year of Lightning Storms
(1374 DR)*

When Laeral addressed Khelben, Tsarra felt a stirring in her mind. She paused a moment as waves of emotions and thoughts hit her simultaneously. For a moment, she felt dizzy and tasted and smelled something sour.

"Sweet Lurue," Tsarra prayed under her breath, "don't let the vision take me. Don't let me be swept away by these thoughts and emotions not my own. May your horn cleave this wave and leave me with my senses."

She concentrated and gently pushed away other thoughts and feelings, letting them flow around her rather than flood over her.

Tsarra felt more timid and her shoulders bunched up when the sending came to her. A red flare of anger came with Khelben's waking thought.

Blast it!

Don't shout, Tsarra sent to Khelben, idly fingering the necklace that held his reduced form. *It makes my ears ring, even if I'm not using them.*

Tsarra felt more than heard Khelben's mental sigh. *Tell Laeral not to check on the ring. An agent can retrieve it for later inspections.*

Khelben, when you're conscious, it's very hard to . . .

Hard to what, Tsarra?

While you were dormant, all my doubts went away. I was thinking more clearly than I have since this all began. What are you doing to me?

I'm not doing anything, apprentice. Now tell Laeral—

Gods take you, wizard, you are doing something to me! I've lived here for nearly two decades, but I've not been this apprehensive around you since my first year! My temper's not been this bad in at least ten years. What's going on?

We don't have time—

Well make time, Khelben. I'm not sure of my own self, and if you need my sorcery to be ready to fight a lich, I have to be able to focus. Right now, I'm fighting a war inside myself and I'm losing. What is happening here?

Tsarra felt Khelben's surprise, followed by a pregnant pause. Finally, Khelben sent his thoughts to her: *I stand corrected. We were affecting you without knowing we did so. Luckily, the explanation will take a fraction of real time outside the* kiira. *Close your eyes and think of the design of your tattoo.*

Tsarra imagined the image of the tattoo on her forehead, its seven whorling lines converging on or wrapping around their central green gem. The verdant light flared into flames along the lines of her mark, and filled her head with emerald energies. She saw Khelben's private library, but it was all olive-tinged and glowing. Khelben stood before her, whole, unharmed, and smiling. She gazed around, noting how everything glowed or was entirely a translucent green, and sent in a whisper, *We're inside the* kiira, *aren't we?*

Khelben nodded, and the barest hint of a smile crept

out over the silver wedge in his black beard. *I love teaching sorcerers. Your intuitive flow with the Weave is so much quicker than another intellectual lecture.*

Tsarra looked around, and aside from the color, every detail was the same as the physical world with one exception. Wisps of mists snaked throughout the chamber and clung to both her and Khelben. She gasped as she turned, looking for concentrations of mist, and found herself face to face with the ephemeral Danthra the Dreamer.

Danthra?

The ghostly girl, eyes wide and wet, reached for Tsarra and winced back when her hands dissipated into thin mist as they met the half-elf's fingers. Tsarra had only seen such despair on Danthra's face twice before—when she foresaw and predicted the death of a first-year student six years ago, and when her first lover, a Watch armar of Sea Ward, died in a tavern brawl two summers back. Her pleading eyes bored into Tsarra's and begged her release from pain.

Danthra? Dreamer? We'll help you, dear heart. You'll see. You'll see. Calm yourself. Are you in pain? Khelben, why isn't she responding?

She cannot speak or send to either of us, Tsarra. In truth, she's barely alive on any level, but we both feel her sorrows and her fears. She is the innocent victim here again, as are you. To keep focused the past few days, I unconsciously shoved the burden of bearing her soul remnants onto you. That's why you've been having her uncontrolled visions, albeit you're pulling them from me through our connections. Another result of that was your feeling her emotions and fears. When added to your own apprehensions, they overwhelmed your normal emotional balance.

Khelben approached both of them and tenderly placed hands on their cheeks, and he was careful enough not to disturb Danthra's misty face. His shoulders slumped and his face carried the burdens and guilt of nine hundred years years rather than his usual stony demeanor. *For all this, I am sorry, and I pray I may help us all through this crisis as safely as possible.*

Tsarra stood still, staring into his eyes for a long moment until tears blurred her vision. She blinked them away and reached up to hold Khelben's hand in hers. *You're not used to someone getting this close to you, are you, Blackstaff? Our emotions affect yours too. This is the first time you've actually had to feel what great sacrifices you regularly ask of your agents.*

Aye, and it's dredging up some regrets on which I've not the time to dwell. For now, I promise that I shall cradle Danthra as well as I may. You should know that she sees you as her protector more than me. She clings to you, oblivious that her own efforts to be comforted force her talents as well as her fears to the forefront in your mind.

Well, asked and answered, then. Thank you for showing me this. Can I enter the kiira *like this just by seeing my sigil in my mind?*

Yes, and with the proper meditation techniques, you can visit my memories under more controlled methods. There are many, if they knew what you now possess, who would kill you for my secrets. I'll help you keep that information away from them as best I can. For now, I believe we can hold off any more visions until our task is fulfilled.

Are you ever going to tell me what that is? Even what little I know, this plan of yours isn't falling together like you'd hoped. We've spent days calling in old favors, but for what reason I don't know. We've chased after artifacts but seem to be three steps behind a lich, not to mention one powerful enough to mindtwist a number of people into doing its dirty work. Give me more information and let me help you. For Lurue's sake, don't make me your puppet while you sit inside that necklace!

It's hardly comfortable or comforting to be there, considering. The only reason I am in there and refused Sandrew's healing is to prevent such from disrupting the links among our three souls. As for the details I've not yet found the time to share, you're right. It is time for you to learn the matter in full.

Khelben gestured and a chair grew up from the stone

floor beneath Tsarra, forcing her to sit down before him. Another conjuring motion of his wrist and green fires hovered in one palm.

Tsarra, I ask for your trust again. While we can converse and exchange information very quickly speaking like this, you need to know the full extent of these events, and if I were to tell it to you physically, it would be a lecture at least two tendays in length. With this spell and our mutual concentration, I can open my memories and thoughts to you directly, gifting you with everything you need to know and what may be yet to come in this gambit. Are you ready?

This won't harm Danthra, will it? She seems so fragile, Khelben. Are you sure we can't help her before we do this?

Resolving our tasks in the physical world will be the best help for her now. Concentrate on my eyes and my voice. Ignore the flames. They're just a manifestation of the magic and thought behind this.

Just make sure that you don't shove any spells into my head along with this plan. You wizards always make mountains from molehills to craft spells, and I don't want you mucking up my sorceries.

Khelben's mouth dropped open in surprise until Tsarra winked at him. He smiled, and his eyes danced with amusement.

You have a pleasant smile when you don't hold it back, Khelben.

So my mother used to tell me. Khelben had a brief faraway look then stiffened. His stony face returned as he cleared his throat and focused his eyes on Tsarra, muttering his incantations.

Tsarra relaxed and allowed the magic to flow around and through her. She suddenly had memories and knowledge she'd never read but had fully experienced through Khelben's senses. She gasped as the enormity of their task unfurled before her mind, and tears of joy and sadness flowed freely on both their olive-tinged faces.

Raegar paced around the round chamber, cat nervous. Nameless kept pace with him, as if he were a watchdog gliding from perch to perch around the room, never taking his eyes off the rogue. Both had followed Laeral from the chamber and back into the main entry hall of Blackstaff Tower. She went to a small cabinet near the base of the stairs, flipping its top up after muttering some words and knocking on it twice.

"Does he always stare at people like that?" Raegar asked.

"Only those he's uncertain about. Like my husband, he watches those he cannot predict, but never betrays how he feels about someone until they need to know," Laeral said. "Despite that, he's one of the most forthright tressyms I've ever met." While she talked, Laeral took out a number of oilcloth bundles from the lower cabinet, as well as a wooden box intricately carved with runes and set with gems of all colors.

"Well, I would've had a few scars from his claws, if not for the Binder's forgiveness and healing, so I know how he feels about me." Raegar rubbed his healed face and scowled at Nameless. In response, the tressym yawned, and flared and stretched his wings and back all at once.

"No, lad, I don't think you do. He's actually on your side, despite Tsarra's protests." Laeral stood up and faced Raegar.

"What's that supposed to mean? On my side about what?"

"Gods, you children complicate things so. In time, you'll know. For now, let us prepare for tomorrow's work. Can you remember anything else about the lich?"

Raegar thought a moment. Shuddering as he conjured up the memories of the past night, he said, "All of his spells were cold. Bitter, biting cold. I've not met many undead, and never any liches before him, but the air grew chilled like Auril's kiss near him."

Tsarra stepped into the room, her stride confident and quick. She said, "Of course it did. We face Priamon

Rakesk, traitor in exile and former Tower apprentice."

Laeral grimaced as she said, "The Frostrune."

"How do you both know that? Who is he and why did he kill my friend?" Raegar asked, his attention bouncing between the two women.

"Remember a few Highharvestides ago, when Undermountain vomited its creatures into the streets?" Tsarra asked. When Raegar nodded, she added, "He caused it by ripping Halaster from his home. Lord Arunsun believes he used that gambit to join a conclave of other liches in the south called the Twisted Rune."

Raegar let out a low whistle. "I've heard rumors of them, and nothing good."

Tsarra made a few odd hand gestures at Laeral, who nodded. "Laeral will tell you more," she said and dashed up the stairs into the tower, leaving Raegar alone again with the Lady Mage of Waterdeep.

"I've been meaning to learn a hand language, one of these moons," Raegar said. "They're so useful for speaking without seeming to do so."

Laeral raised an eyebrow at him and said, "Yes, well, you should expect secrets aplenty in Blackstaff Tower, lad. You can't expect us to trust a thief, even one who works in the Binder's name, do you?"

"No, but it's just rude. I expected better manners from ladies," Raegar said, and both smiled.

"The message," Laeral said as she opened a taller wardrobe by the door, "was from my husband, who speaks to Tsarra even while in that necklace she wears. It wasn't for your ears or understanding, even if you are proven trustworthy. Now here, take this and this." She held out a burgundy-colored cloak, russet-colored boots, and a silver ring set with a sapphire for him. Raegar took the items but did not put them on.

"Don't be so suspicious, Raegar Stoneblade." Laeral said. "Those will protect you from some of the cold that Frostrune might throw at you. His affectation is to use cold and ice in all his spells, hence his name."

Raegar's eyes went wide, and he slipped the boots then the ring on and donned the cloak.

"Any chance you've a spare sword around here I could use too?" he asked. "This Frostrune took both the blades I had. I've only one dagger, and I expect we'll be heading into a fight soon enough, right?"

Laeral stopped, whispered a few words to an empty corner as she turned away from Raegar, and smiled as she turned back to him. "Yes, and Khelben agrees it's appropriate."

She closed the wardrobe and tapped on its door in three places. She opened the wardrobe and brought out a short sword in a deep red leather scabbard. With a gesture from Laeral, the weapon and its scabbard flew across the room and lashed itself to Raegar's belt.

"That is Perivaernikerym. Wield her with honor and earn our trust. Know that the Blackstaff and I expect much from her wielder. The word you'll need to know is carved in her quillons."

Raegar drew the blade from its scabbard, and flames flickered to life along the blade. "No need for torches anymore." Raegar looked at the word on the quillons. "Eye . . . gan . . ."

Laeral clapped her hands sharply to grab his attention then warned him, "Don't say that word unless you mean to throw up a shield of flames, boy! That power only works once a day, so don't waste it playing. Wielding the blade makes you immune to flames, but it doesn't protect your own clothes or surroundings." Her tone lightened as she added, "She's a good blade to use against Frostrune, and she is balanced so you can throw her if you need to."

Raegar admired the delicate runic carvings along the light, thin elven blade. He swung the sword a few times, getting used to its weight and balance, and nodded his approval.

"May I look into its history and lore later, Lady Arunsun, should I prove worthy enough to keep this?"

"Ah, a true Oghman. The blade is yours, Raegar, by

Khelben's say-so, and I have seen inside your head and heart. You will wield her with honor, just as her two other wielders did long ago, the first being Khelben's mother."

"A blade wielded by Lhestyn, the Masked Lady of Waterdeep . . ." Raegar stared at the blade. "You do me too much honor, lady."

"More than you know, Raegar Stoneblade," Laeral said, as she continued to take large bundles from the wardrobe. "Learn more later, but sheathe her now and help me."

A breath later, Raegar and Laeral stopped as the tower and all its stones suddenly hummed, the tone reverberating through every stone. The edges of every block glistened with silver magic before returning to normal.

"What was that?" Raegar asked, turning in amazement.

"Khelben, no!" Laeral whispered. "It's not possible. Not now, beloved!" Tears flooded down her cheeks as she stared up the stairs.

"What's going on?" Raegar asked. "Is something wrong? What are they up to up there?"

"Shut up, fool!" Laeral snapped and yelled up the stairwell. "Khelben! Don't you ignore me! Talk to me!" She seemed not to notice the stream of students coming down the stairs, abuzz with questions and confusion.

Laeral seemed furious in her conversation with empty air. "Khelben, you owe me a far better explanation . . ." Her shoulders fell and she slumped to the floor, two teenaged students catching her as she fell.

The flood of questions overwhelmed Laeral and in a daze she said, "Return to your rooms, students, for your own safety." Amid the protests and offers of aid from older students, Laeral repeated her request, which went unheeded again. She drew herself up, and her eyes blazed. *"Parekalrath!"* she exclaimed, and the entry hall once again was empty save for herself, Nameless, and Raegar. Laeral shot a look at Raegar that seemed almost as cold as Frostrune.

"Sometimes students need to be put in their places. We have a cell downstairs for you, if you're going to argue with me as well."

Raegar swallowed hard and shook his head as she approached him.

Laeral reached into the tall wardrobe. She shoved a large parcel into Raegar's arms that was taller than he was but only two handspans around and wrapped in a woolen cloak. "Place that in the center of the room, and stand back from it."

Raegar did as instructed, and he was amazed that what seemed like a bundle of tall sticks stood upright without support.

"Step over toward me, quickly." Laeral said with some urgency as a bell began chiming up the stairs. "*Now*, Raegar!"

Raegar jumped across the room to stand next to her. She stared into the room's center and gestured, magic crackling among her fingers, and the woolen wrap snapped taut and unspooled from around the bundle as if pulled. Raegar gasped when he saw what lay beneath that covering—blackstaves!

CHAPTER TWENTY-FOUR

30 Uktar, the Year of Lightning Storms
(1374 DR)

The exposed blackstaves spun and whirled, propelled by the unfurling of the cloak, which swooped back into the wardrobe. The thin black wooden staves grated and scraped across the stones of the chamber, each moving to a different point in the room, stopping about a footstep away from Laeral and Raegar. Raegar stared, never having been close to the legendary blackstaff and in awe as he watched thirteen position themselves around the room. All seemed to be made of duskwood or some other darkened wood and were black as night. That's where their similarities ended. Some were shod in metal or had it infused in them. Others held large gems embedded in their tips or elsewhere. Still others were carved to appear as sinuous snakes or a collection of fists. Raegar was fascinated by the staves, most of which were polished to a glossy sheen, though a few were dull or apparently burnt to achieve their blackened status.

"I never knew there was more than one blackstaff," Raegar remarked.

"No reason you or any outsider would, boy," Laeral said. "Khelben rarely shares secrets unless time or expediency demands it."

Raegar, entranced by the blackstaves, only realized Laeral had moved when she spoke. He heard the door to the tower open and turned to see five figures enter silently and quickly to take their places around the room's perimeter. Raegar kept his face impassive but even he knew some of these notables of Art within the city. His mind boggled at the thought of a plan that required the Blackstaff to join forces with the arrogant and preening purple-cloaked wizard Maaril the Dragonmage. While he didn't know him well, Raegar nodded in greeting to a surprised Winter Zulth, the half-elf wizard they'd met the previous summer in Dock Ward when Damlath insisted they visit the Horizon's Sails to find some magically created navigational maps. Two other wizards—one male elf and one human woman—Raegar didn't recognize, but he certainly knew the final entrant.

The half-elf woman walked with a slight limp, her gnarled white ash staff providing her with support. The mistress of Selûne's Smile had the ample curves of humanity with the aquiline features and pointed ears of elvenkind. Her clothes, as always, were daringly tailored with ample décolletage to flatter her figure. The steel blue and dark purple of her clothes accented her floor length dark hair, which seemed to gleam with starlight save for a stripe of white along her temples. Her purple eyes beamed at the thief after she'd given a quick hug to Laeral and turned to face the room.

"Raegar, darling! Whatever are you doing here, and where is that rascal Damlath?" Kyriani Agrivar moved quickly to his side and snuggled close to Raegar.

"'Tis crowded enough here, lass. Don't wish for more, especially strangers," Maaril growled at her. Kyriani stuck her tongue out at Waterdeep's infamous Dragonmage.

Nameless, from his perch atop the wardrobe, hissed down at Maaril, who twisted his dragon-headed staff toward the tressym, its eyes glowing with malice.

A whoosh of displaced air and a twinkle of blue sparks placed a tall man in iron-gray leathers and a sky-blue cloak between Maaril and Nameless. The man's back was to Raegar as he faced Maaril, who glared then stared away and appeared to find interest in the blackstaves still spinning around the room. Two crackles of green energy and a whirlwind of gold dust heralded the arrival of others by teleport magic. Raegar tried to identify them, but Kyriani distracted him by slipping her hand inside his shirt and rubbing his chest.

"Raegar, sweetums," Kyri teased, "you're going to make me think I've lost my touch. I asked you nicely where Damlath is and you've ignored me."

"Sorry, Kyri," Raegar whispered. "Damlath's dead, and I'm going to help take out the bastard who killed him."

Kyri's playful teasing and the laughter in her eyes stopped instantly. She whispered a prayer to Selûne then kissed Raegar on the cheek before whispering, "Avenge our friend, Stoneblade. If I could help you, I would, but the Blackstaff demands other tasks of me tonight."

"What is *he* doing here, Laeral?" The tall man's voice boomed across the room as he pulled his hood back, revealing a strong, clean-shaven face and long, dark hair. "Bad enough I've had to work with—"

"Patience, Malchor," Laeral interrupted. "We all have our roles to play here, whether planned, foretold, or otherwise. He has a stake in this too, and one far more personal than yours."

"Raegar has met the foe who drives our plan forward and will face him where you won't." To Raegar's surprise, Khelben appeared on the stairs. He bore none of the wounds he'd suffered only hours before, and Tsarra was nowhere to be seen. Raegar glanced toward Laeral and cocked an eyebrow, and she shook her head. Raegar knew life among wizards could be puzzling, but he found himself distracted by the missing Tsarra Chaadren.

"Who is our foe, exactly?" Winter Zulth asked, his voice soft and barely heard among the general buzz of muttered conversations.

"Time," Khelben said, as he descended the stairs into the chamber. "Time and Priamon Rakesk."

Kyriani asked, "How can you expect Raegar to survive alone against that creature? Frostrune even managed to surprise Halaster!"

"Using the honorific that fool gave himself just feeds his arrogance." Khelben said. "That said, Raegar shall not face him alone. He and I do this together along with Tsarra Chaadren and her familiar."

Nameless sat up and promptly snapped his wings open when Khelben drew the room's attention to him.

Khelben moved to the center of the room, holding one blackstaff shod with silver caps on each end in his right hand. Another staff was slung across his back, a thick ruby set one foot down its shaft and intricate carvings crawling the length of its surface. Crooked in his left arm, he carried a large oaken box similar to the one Laeral had placed on the floor behind them. Khelben turned and nodded greetings to everyone in the room, eight visitors in all beyond himself, Laeral, and Raegar. By the time he'd finished greeting the others, he stared at Laeral and said, "Gamalon can remain secluded a bit longer, until you truly need him, dear. But where's Nain? I thought he had arrived earlier this afternoon. It's not like him to be late."

A sneeze from up the stairs heralded the arrival of Nain Keenwhistler. Coming into the light, his chalk-white hair and pasty appearance set him apart from the shadows of the stairwell. The wizard was gangly, a well-dressed scarecrow in well-appointed russet robes and shining black boots. He bore a massive tome in his hands, and his attentions were on that. He did not see the room or the persons there until he looked up. Raegar noticed the man looked sickly and wan, but Nain blanched even further when he saw the blackstaves standing at attention in the chamber. The large tome fell from his hands and tumbled down the stairs.

"Oh no," Nain whispered. "No, Khelben. Not again. You promised. Never again."

"If there were any other way, I would do it. There is no other option," replied Khelben.

"Then find another to do my part." Nain's voice quivered with tension and desperation.

"Khelben, do you really think it's . . . ?" a tiefling mage unknown to Raegar asked, but a glare from the Blackstaff stopped his inquiry cold.

"Yes, I do, Tulrun, and Master Keenwhistler knows it as well. You all know that I do not trust easily." Khelben's pause rested in a pointed stare at Maaril. "Each of you has talents, abilities, and proclivities we need for this plan to succeed. Each of you will contribute more than you even know to a work of utmost importance. So much depends on you all on this Feast of the Moon."

"I don't want to touch one of those things ever again, Khelben! Haven't I given enough? How many times can you ask me to do this?" Nain Keenwhistler sat down, his face ashen in despair.

"Only this one last time, Nain," Khelben said, placing the box in Nain's lap. "Mystra has vowed it be so, and our Lady of Mysteries smiles on those who bear their burdens with trust in her."

"Easy for you to say, Blackstaff," Nain wailed. "You haven't died *four* times in her service. Twice by *your orders*."

"True. I've only done so *seven* times, and countless others have given their lives for our plan to reach this point. Any sacrifices are worth it, and you all know it. The stakes and what we do—what we gain for the Realms—are too high to not risk all we can . . . all we must." His tone softened, and he reached out to rest a hand on Nain's shoulder, who flinched in response. "You are far stronger than you ever believed yourself to be, Nain Keenwhistler. Do not doubt, when this night shall show you what true strength and character can do. Believe in this and yourself."

Maaril snorted behind Khelben and said, "If I'd known I would be working with simperers, I would never have left my tower."

Laeral snapped back at him, "Maaril, this man needs no dragons to bulwark his power."

Maaril opened his mouth to protest but stopped as Laeral narrowed her eyes at him and continued, "In his lifetimes, Nain has faced terrors you could not without soiling your oh-so-splendid robes. Now hold your tongue, lest someone here volunteer to hold it for you."

Khelben said, "Well put, my dear. Now, we must away. Laeral, Malchor, I trust you two can ready our allies and the site." He turned on his heels, heading toward the door. "Raegar, tressym, both of you come with me, now."

Khelben moved to the door and opened it, finally turning around to face the crowd of assembled Art-wielders. He bowed from the waist, tipping his staff to his forehead in salute. "We shall all meet on the Plains of Kahyraphaal before moonrise tomorrow at Malavar's Grasp or its environs. Milady and Malchor Harpell speak for me in the meantime. Good luck, the speed of gods, the wishes of Those who Watch, and the Moon's Benison upon us all. We shall meet in the eye of the storms before dawn."

Raegar didn't understand half of Khelben's farewell, but the tone was hopeful, and most heads in the room nodded agreement. Nameless leaped off the wardrobe and settled around Khelben's shoulders, tucking one wing under the wizard's chin to stabilize his perch.

The Blackstaff's pace forced Raegar to dash after him, and the two of them left Blackstaff Tower at a fairly good clip. Raegar drew up the hood of his cloak as rain pelted down on him. He glanced up and saw lightning bolts play across the sky, thunder booming in response. Five more lightning bolts zigzagged across the clouds and struck the peak of Mount Waterdeep. The thunder rattled shutters and startled many a horse in the City of Splendors that night. Raegar wondered if the weather was an omen of worse things to come.

"Um, Lord Arunsun?" he asked, as Khelben moved far more quickly than he expected. The mage was already five paces ahead of him and marching straight down Swords Street. "Where are we going?" Raegar noticed that the rain seemed too afraid to touch the Blackstaff, as he and his clothes remained dry despite the downpour.

"To the Eightower."

"Isn't that tower haunted?"

"Indeed."

"And we're going there because . . .?" Raegar finally caught up with Khelben.

"Because its mistress has cause for revenge against Priamon, as do I."

Raegar put on a tight, toothless smile. "Good. I'd hate to be the only one."

Raegar and Khelben made their way down past Tharleon Street, and the pyramidal top of the Eightower loomed above them. It shone in the stormy night, but its light barely spread beyond the edges of the tower itself. Raegar had heard of the tower and passed it by many times. The pyramid on top was Shoon-inspired architecture that marked the building as the home of a wizard or sorcerer. He heard that anyone who crossed the threshold of the garden gate drew the attention of the spirit who haunted the grounds. Raegar's father loved telling spook stories, but all his son remembered was that the ghost was a member of House Wands. The Wands clan kept the property undisturbed, aside from having servants harvest flowers and vegetables from the gardens, in respect for their lost ancestor.

"Khelben, are you sure this will lead us to Frostrune?" Raegar asked. As they entered the archway into the garden and stepped onto the slate flagstones of the garden path, the rogue felt a slight chill.

Lightning lit up the sky in a massive triple strike of bolts into Mount Waterdeep. Just as those struck, another bolt exploded overhead as lightning erupted from the pyramid, joining its brethren in the skies. The crystal facets glowed and crackled, shimmering with energy. Khelben stared upward into the driving rain at the tower, and Raegar barely heard his reply over the wind.

"Indeed."

CHAPTER TWENTY-FIVE

30 Uktar, the Year of Lightning Storms
(1374 DR)

The three of them walked quickly to the doors of the Eightower, only to find them shimmering with an opalescent gray field of energy. Khelben frowned then looked up, shielding his eyes from the rain with his hand.

"Would you mind a spell that would allow you to climb the walls like a spider?" Khelben asked. "I'd as soon avoid wasting spells to bypass this barrier."

"Fine by me, Blackstaff. If not for that lich stealing my last pair of boots, I could do that myself."

Khelben cast the spell and Raegar jumped up, his hands and boots sticking to the stone walls like glue. "I'll assume you have some way to get us inside once we're above the main floor?" the rogue said as he started climbing the rain-slick tower.

"Yes, Stoneblade. Now hurry up." Khelben

flourished his hand and slowly rose into the air. Despite the winds, he levitated straight upward and outpaced Raegar's climb.

"Show-off," Raegar muttered under his breath. He thought he heard a strange purr come from the tressym, but the noise failed beneath the crash of lightning. Raegar tensed and waited for the thunder to end, but instead it subsided into a constant rumble. Looking up, he saw no end to the lightning bolts coming from the pyramid.

The two of them stopped at the last arrow slit beneath the pyramid. The smell of burnt air was strong, and lightning relentlessly crackled from the pyramid's top, linking the tower to the thunderheads above the City of Splendors. Smaller lightning bolts splintered off the pillar of energy and crackled toward Mount Waterdeep and the taller spires across the city.

Three brave griffon-riders swooped from the clouds toward the tower, narrowly avoiding the stray bolts.

"Lord Arunsun! Our attempts to dispel this lightning have failed. Do you have any orders?" Raegar barely heard the rain-soaked Guard captain over the wind and thunder.

Khelben yelled, "Back away, now!"

"But sir—" the captain's protest was cut short by the crackle of lightning, and the energy slammed into the griffon's wing, knocking it and its rider into a screaming spiral toward the ground.

"Blast it!" Khelben shouted as he cast a quick spell that slowed the griffon's fall.

The other guards guided their griffons down to aid their comrade just as two women flew from around the other side of the tower. Raegar had seen both of them in recent days coming in and from Blackstaff Tower—Carolyas Idogyr and Maliantor, former students of Khelben and current members of Force Gray.

"What do you need, sir?"

The redheaded half-elf was impatient, like another half-elf Raegar found himself thinking about more and more often. Where was Tsarra? The darker-skinned and black-haired Maliantor said nothing, instead casting a spell above them.

"Ah, good." Khelben looked at her and said, "Go retrieve your uncle Gamalon from my tower. His vengeance is at hand."

Carolyas's surprise was evident on her face, but she immediately flew in a straight arc toward the top of Blackstaff Tower.

Raegar had a hard time keeping an eye on the white-clad wizardess and keep his grip on the wall. Magic or not, his muscles ached from the climb and clinging to the tower. He looked at his perch, one foot in the wider well at the bottom of an arrow slit, examining the stonework. He ran his fingers along the mortar and picked at it with his fingernails until his attention was drawn away by Khelben's yell.

Khelben looked up at Maliantor and shouted, "Mali! We need you here!"

Both men watched her complete a spell, which created a pulsing ring of colored energy. Maliantor looped around the tower and zipped between Khelben and Raegar. Lightning, which once flashed perilously close, went harmlessly into the spell-ring or up into the clouds.

"An interesting spell, Maliantor All-Seeing. What do you call it?"

"It's still unnamed, but I suppose 'nyth barrier' will do for now." The black-tressed woman, Raegar noticed, was untouched by the rain, a transparent field of magic keeping all the water off of her. "What did you need, old man?"

"A passwall, if you would. I need to conserve spells for the moment."

"Sorry, Khelben. In accord with your message yestermorn, I prepared for lightning, not stone."

Khelben's jaw dropped. Raegar's and Maliantor's eyes all widened in surprise. In a heartbeat, Khelben's usual stony face returned.

Raegar cleared his throat and said, "How strong is that sword you loaned me, Blackstaff?"

"Two balors couldn't break it fighting over it," Khelben replied. "Why?"

"Just get some spell ready that can hit it with some force," Raegar shouted over a gust of wind. He shifted his perch sideways and down on the tower, drawing the sword. The orange flames came to life on the short sword and resisted the rain. Raegar looked back at the two levitating wizards and said, "Once this is set, hit the pommel with whatever force you can."

He eyed the stonework one last time before he stabbed the short sword's point into the mortar just beneath the round hole at the arrow slit's bottom. Maliantor completed a spell, and a massive hand grew from her palm, mimicking her finger movements but soon becoming as large as she was tall. She shoved her own arm forward, and the giant hand hit the sword's pommel. The sword vanished into the stone wall, and the stone blocks around it also tumbled. A few more blocks above the breach fell from place, their supporting stones gone, leaving a hole three feet wide.

Raegar looked back at them, winked, and blew a kiss toward Maliantor, then clambered in through the hole.

"Shoddy work, isn't it?" he joked as he began pulling stone blocks from the blade. "Well, you're coming, aren't you?"

Khelben stood on the air, staring at Raegar with an irritated look. "Warn all others away from here and keep us from being interrupted by outsiders," he told his apprentice. "We're tackling the problem from within." Khelben reached out with his blackstaff and pulled himself into the hole, even though Raegar could see the staff didn't hook onto anything.

Raegar held out a hand to help Khelben the rest of the way in. The Blackstaff's hand looked strong and rough, but it felt very delicate to Raegar's touch. He felt a strange sensation as he helped the wizard inside the tower's guardroom.

Khelben drew his hand away from Raegar and got up, holding his staff parallel to the floor rather than using it for support. Nameless flew into the tower, landed on the pile of rubble, and promptly shook as much water off his wings and fur as he could.

Raegar said, "Something's not right about you, Blackstaff. You're acting far more daintily than your usual stomp and swagger. And since she's also on my mind, when is your lovely apprentice joining us? You said she'd be with us, and her familiar is here, so where is she?"

"The ways of wizards always look strange. Tsarra is nearby, not that that's any of your concern right now." Khelben looked around and pressed his ear to the door. "Well, your method of getting us in was inventive but also noisy. So much for surprise. Let's prepare you."

Khelben's fingers traced a quick symbol in the air before he rested his hand on Raegar's shoulder. A shimmer of green energy flowed over Raegar's wet cloak and body, and he felt a slight tingle as the magic spread across him.

"Thank you, sir. Feels a little different than the defenses Damlath used to grant me, but every bit helps," Raegar said, swinging his sword arm and watching the telltale glimmers the motion left behind.

"You're welcome. Now, let me go ahead of you," Khelben said, as he dumped his sodden overcloak on the floor.

"Glad you don't want the man who's never been here before in the lead," Raegar snorted.

"Don't make me regret gifting you with that sword, Stoneblade. Stay sharp, now." The Blackstaff glowered back at him then turned toward the tressym and stared at it. Nameless slipped through the door as soon as Khelben opened it.

The door opened onto the tight tower stairwell. Khelben pressed a hand to the stairs overhead and furrowed his brow. Nameless stuck his head back around the bend in the stairs and growled lightly before disappearing again. Raegar noticed the ring on Khelben's hand glowed, the red gem pulsing and going dark as Khelben opened his eyes.

"I've dispelled the warning spells he put on the stairs,

but we're still going to have to be fast about this, Stone-blade. Don't be thrown by whatever you see, but wait to attack on my signal." Khelben said, staring at Raegar.

The thief nodded but shook off an odd feeling as he looked into the man's hazel eyes. The two men crept up the stairwell, catching up to the tressym. Khelben knelt for a second to touch the creature between its shoulder blades, and Raegar saw the green shimmer envelop Nameless with magical protection as well. The three of them moved quickly up the stairs into the tower's top chamber.

"Wait. One more spell each." Khelben held the tressym and Raegar back a moment. He touched the tressym first, and after his ring flared a moment, the tressym vanished from sight. Khelben reached for Raegar, who held up his hands.

"Just a minute, Blackstaff." He pulled both his daggers from their boot sheaths. He tucked one in his belt, held the other in his left hand, and drew the short sword in his right. Both men cringed as the flames flickered to life.

"*Hyarac*," Khelben whispered. "That mutes the light of the blade."

Raegar whispered, "*Hyarac*," and the blade's flames snuffed out. As he turned, Khelben's hand clapped on his shoulder. Within a breath, Raegar too was invisible.

"Thanks for waiting until I had things in hand before doing that," Raegar said, looking around at empty air.

Khelben's whisper came from behind him: "You and the tressym are far more adept at walking silently than I, which makes me the stalking horse. Slip into the upper chamber and wait for your chance. You'll know it when you see it, but don't waste the surprise until we know his defenses are weakened."

They moved forward, Raegar silently praying as he climbed the darkened stairwell toward the flickering blue-white lights up above. "Oghma, Lord of Knowledge, hear my prayer. Make my passing a whisper with your blessing. Make me a secret, so that I may share what I learn beyond this moment. Thus may I strike vengeance against one who abused your servants."

Raegar felt calm and an image flashed through his mind of Oghma's statue from the Font.

The three invisible intruders exited the stairs, all silent as tombs. Magic rasped across the air throughout the room as opaque black shards rang sharply against lime green razors of magic. The constant swirl and eddy of conflicting currents danced upon the air, and nearly distracted Raegar from the powerful sight above that—the pyramidal walls awash in blue lightning bolts, a blinding cluster of energy at the pyramid's corners and peak. Despite the fury outside unleashed by that energy, only a clash of long-held hatreds made any noise within the chamber.

The two dead persons in the room, however, were neither silent nor inactive.

"By all that's holy, I'll see you destroyed, Priamon!"

The translucent woman who stood directly in their path didn't block the view of the room. She hovered slightly off the floor, only the vaguest hints of an ochre gown and long floor-length russet hair outlining her existence. The only things solid about her existence were her spells. Raegar looked through her to scan the rest of the room.

The chamber was, by Raegar's eye, ten paces across and its octagonal walls made it nearly circular. The walls sloped in as they rose, two walls each flattening together to seat the crystalline pyramid. The room culminated in the lightning-soaked peak. Though the room was now lit by the lightning and the clashing magic, each of the eight walls of the room bore a torch. From its many tables and bookshelves Raegar assumed it was a workroom or study. All were shoved or toppled out of place, their contents scattered on the carpet-covered stone floor, apparently cleared by the spell battle in the room's center.

There was Raegar's enemy at the room's core—the lich Priamon "Frostrune" Rakesk. His green robes swirled among the fury of spells, the hood fallen back from his near-fleshless skull. The inhuman creature's spellcasting rose above the noise, and blue energy blasted at Syndra Wands, only to crystalize in the air against her shields before crumbling in sheets of frozen vapor.

Raegar moved to his left, hugging the walls and keeping his eyes glued to the lich. He ached to throw the short sword at him, followed by his two throwing daggers, but he knew to wait. Raegar smiled as Syndra wove her green magic into a flock of woodpeckers. The magical constructs settled onto an invisible barrier around Frostrune and they began poking small holes in his magical protections. Raegar had never been so close to a major spell battle; Damlath had often used magic to get them as far away from them as possible. It was fascinating, horrifying, and sobering all at once. Raegar wondered if the air always felt so pressurized during a spell battle, as if the space itself recoiled from spells or pushed against them. He noticed a few fallen books shift on the far side of the room as the invisible Blackstaff made his way around the room's perimeter.

Is he trying to get noticed? Raegar thought, then he saw Khelben slowly become visible.

Frostrune dissolved the flock of birds on his shields just as Khelben completed his casting and came fully into view. Flames coalesced into a ball of fire that bounced around the lich, setting fire to the areas all around him but leaving him untouched.

"Blackstaff, you should have struck to kill outright," the lich said. "I'll not leave you the chance to cast another ineffective spell. Say good-bye to your granddaughter a second time."

"Hardly!" Syndra yelled, and to Raegar's ears, the voices sounded as if they were underwater.

Despite the smoke from the fires at the room's center, Raegar managed to keep from coughing and giving away his position. The ghostly sorceress and the lich cast furiously fast spells, and while power built up at their fingertips in green and blue energies, both fizzled out without effect. He'd seen Damlath do enough counterspells to understand each had cancelled out the other's spell.

"Khelben," Syndra yelled, "he's got Isyllmyth's Bracer!"

Khelben stood in an odd position, his left hand holding

his blackstaff perpendicular to the floor, rather than aiming it at Frostrune. His right hand was back by his shoulder, which seemed odd to Raegar until he heard the hum of a bowstring. The air shimmered around Khelben and the illusion melted away, revealing Tsarra holding her short bow and reaching back for another arrow.

CHAPTER TWENTY-SIX

30 Uktar, the Year of Lightning Storms
(1374 DR)

As Tsarra let the arrow fly, she yelled, "Now!" and hoped both the tressym and the thief would know what to do.

Her arrow hit the lich's shields, lit up the magic, and pulled it and a successive shield beneath it in its wake, forcing the magic of the shields to twist and stab into the impact point of the arrow. Frost-rune screamed as the arrow caught him squarely in the chest, and he rocked back on his heels from the impact.

Raegar's invisibility shimmered to an end as he yelled, *"Hyarac!"* and threw his flaming short sword at the lich.

The blade stuck Rakesk squarely in his right thigh, scorching his robes. As the lich tried to pull the sword from his leg, the flames leaped up and consumed the blade. The lich growled in frustration as flames remained on his robes. Fires leaped from Raegar's palm, and the sword returned to his grasp!

Tsarra sent to Khelben, *I hope you've healed up enough to stand, old man.*

Nameless carried the Anyllan's bottle in his mouth, and he stayed invisible as he silently flew behind the lich. The ceramic bottle on the necklace shattered when Nameless reached his destination and bit down on it. A gray mist rose from it behind Rakesk.

He replied, *Fret not, Tsarra. You played my role beautifully, but we can't allow our surprise to go unexploited. Ah good, my granddaughter's quick to realize an advantage. You should learn this spell from her, should all of us survive.*

Syndra Wands screamed in pain. The spell she cast made her body grow paler and more insubstantial. Tsarra recognized the casting as very similar to a spell of hers, but this obviously had more power. Green energy lanced into the lich. He roared as his animating energies warred with that new magic. As he arced away from the sources of his pains, he realized a figure stood behind him. The red glints within the lich's eyesockets flared as he stared deep into the eyes of the Blackstaff.

Khelben's spell was nothing more than a stare, but twin streams of silver fire stabbed into the Frostrune's skull, and the lich doubled his howling. Khelben's attack stopped abruptly and he bore a surprised look.

"No," Khelben gasped, gripping the lich's robes. "You can't possibly dare to wake—"

"*Enough!*" Priamon Rakesk's anger seemed to fuel the harness on his torso. Its magical pulse shoved everyone flat against the walls with a surge of crimson power. "I dare much, *Master.*"

"Bastard!" Raegar yelled, throwing his sword at the lich again. "You killed Damlath!"

The sword whistled through the air, aimed at the lich's head, but it bounced off of a renewed protective shield with a crackle of red flames.

"You will join him soon. Our dark friends have been held

at bay long enough. Enjoy their embrace, fools. It's almost a shame you'll miss the rise of the Frostlord, master of the Twisted Rune!"

Priamon raised his arms, and a silver bracer pulsed with power on his left arm. The lich floated up into the maelstrom of energy around and on the pyramid, and both he and the pyramid disappeared.

Exposed to the sky, the room filled with wind, rain, and thunder. The air above and around them swarmed with amethyst sparkles. The night skies became darker still, as sharn after sharn materialized around the top of Syndra's tower. More and more appeared, not giving way for each other—they flowed around and into each other like water.

Almost immediately, three sharn had the stairwell exit blocked, and more than a dozen formed a ring in open air around the top of the truncated tower. Sharn dripped like thick liquid down into the chamber among the heroes.

Tsarra tried to move but found herself frozen. She also failed at speaking. *Khelben? Can you move? I'm paralyzed.* She looked in his direction to find him splayed across an overturned bookshelf.

I'm afraid Priamon's obsession with the Shoon gave him rather effective dueling items. The Harness of Choramm the Cowardly generates magic that paralyzes those with arcane energy inside them for a time, if its wearer gets grievously injured. And I'm afraid we may run out of time before the effect wears off. I wonder where he found the blasted thing. . . .

Overhead, a huge fiery hand grabbed a sharn and boiled it in its grasp. The sharn fled before its screams faded, and Maliantor moved through the space it vacated.

She hovered above them and yelled down into the chamber, "Khelben! What happened?"

Syndra replied, "Grandfather is stunned, as is his apprentice, thanks to the Frostrune. My phantom state may have shielded me from the worst of it, but I cannot seem to cast any spells right now."

Syndra floated about the room, checking on the two

paralyzed spellcasters. When she approached Tsarra, the apprentice recoiled, as she always did from undead, until she saw her eyes. Syndra's translucent face was pleasant, a dimpled chin with a beauty mark drawing yet more attention that way. She and Tsarra shared similar half-elf features, though Syndra's face was disarming by having one rounder human brown eye and an almond-shaped elf hazel eye. Tsarra had never seen kindness in the face of undeath until just then.

Syndra said to Maliantor, and to those in the room, "The handsome one in red seems mostly unharmed, so he may be of some help to you. I need to go secure the relic of utmost importance right now." With that, the ghostly Wands woman seeped into the stone wall of the tower.

Nameless hissed loudly, and Raegar yelled, "Look out! Behind you!"

Maliantor screamed and a flurry of claws rendered her white robes crimson. The wizardess fell from the air, and Raegar managed to catch her before she slammed into the stone floor.

Tsarra was surprised at how happy she felt when Raegar approached and looked down at her. He carefully laid Maliantor down next to her then stood over them.

"I don't know if this will help any, but I'm not leaving. He drew his sword and said, *"Iganris!"* Flames flared up and jetted from the blade, forming a small semicircular field of flames. The sharn nearest them reared back, and Raegar kept waving the fiery shield back and forth. "Khelben . . . anyone . . . do something!"

Tsarra coaxed the tressym with her feelings, since she could barely speak, let alone in the creature's native tongue. She urged him to flee. She couldn't see him, but she felt the tressym's concern for her and his reply was right near by.

"No leave mistressfriend alone. Mousesize, weflyaway?"

Tsarra half laughed and half cried inside. She couldn't shrink herself to fly away from her friends any more than the winged cat could abandon her.

Nameless yowled a defiant response, *"I stayfight night-fangdrippypointears with horsehead firesword."*

The tressym's brave defense of her made her proud, but she wondered about his name for Raegar until she saw the rogue's ponytail swing like a horse's tail as he darted back and forth.

Khelben said to them both through the mental link, *Loyal, isn't he? I haven't missed my owl Nighthunter in centuries until I felt the bond you share with Nameless. Nevertheless, bold tressym, you cannot follow where your mistress and I soon go.*

The sharn arrived more and more quickly. The space within the sundered chamber began to fill up. Raegar was backed up against the wall with the two women and the tressym. The only open space left in the chamber was between the wall and his fiery shield. Tsarra had a sense of what was to come, and she tried to utter some words of comfort, but she was still frozen. She looked up to see the stars, but all she saw was the mass of sharn overhead losing cohesion and falling toward them like an oily black wall of water.

CHAPTER TWENTY-SEVEN

30 Uktar-Feast of the Moon,
the Year of Lightning Storms (1374 DR)

Tsarra closed her eyes as the sharn multitude descended, bracing herself for what she assumed would be a cold, oily, and painful embrace. After a moment, she opened her eyes to see that the sharn were not advancing. The mass of sharn above them remained airborne, only dripping slight bits of blackness into what had come to fill more than two-thirds of the open chamber.

Tsarra could move slightly, and the paralysis around her throat relaxed. She touched Raegar on the leg, making him jump.

The rogue looked down at her and said, "Hey—you can move? Great, let's get you up. I don't know how long before they either attack or just flow over us."

"Your fire shield was a good idea, Raegar, but you can drop it. Don't worry about the sharn. It's only attacking those who attack it. And while the help's appreciated," Tsarra said, "you need to leave and take my tressym with you. You and he will not be able to survive where Khelben and I are going." Purring, she repeated her plea to the tressym. He was even less pleased than the thief, and the pair of them had a long moment's hissing and growling between them.

"I'm not abandoning you or Maliantor, Tsarra." Raegar knelt down by her, and for the first time, she looked deep into his eyes. She never expected to see nobility and earnestness, and it touched her.

Her eyes teared up, but she steeled herself and snapped at him, "Listen, Stoneblade—Khelben and I know what we're doing! We have to collect all the remnants of the Legacy while you, Syndra, Nameless, and Gamalon have to stop the lich. Now give me a moment and I'll give you a location." She cringed at the hurt look that crossed his face, but she had to get them both to focus.

Tsarra slipped into a quick trance, summoning the smells and calm of a wooded glade. She let the sense surround her, and she caught a whiff of decay—that was her prey. She opened her eyes and looked at the world with different eyes.

Tsarra saw Raegar, the sharn multitude, Nameless, and Maliantor plain as day. Superimposed over and suffused through them was the Weave. To her eyes, it was a pulsing green sward filled with life and energy. Concentrations of magic appeared as trees of varying height, and other living things as random plants. Maliantor was a slender willow tree, damaged, but still alive and in need of care. She glanced Khelben's way and saw him as a silver dusk-wood tree of massive size and strength, though one with its limbs bare for winter and many axe blows to the bark and wood at its base. The sharn were unlike any beings she'd ever seen. Rather than the growing wall of black amorphous flesh, she saw over a score of elves, centaurs, dwarves, gnomes, and humans assembled before her, all peaceful and smiling. All were naked forms outlined in purple stars, and she also saw them as Weavewood images of lush conifers.

Tsarra focused and used her skills as a tracker to scan the Weavewood. Unlike the few other times she'd cast her "weavetrack," Tsarra saw the Weave smoldering from the lightning strikes. Lightning crackled in the skies overhead. Other disturbances—a bent sapling here, rotting leaves there, and footprints sprinkled with ash and rot—filled the vision. Tsarra looked at how far apart and in which direction the tracks led.

She couldn't find a second set of prints, so she said to Raegar, "I still can't move much. Can you pick me up and turn me to face south? Mind where you put the hands."

He laughed nervously as he knelt and picked her up, cradling her in his arms and turning her south. Tsarra could see a greater forest in the Weave, dozens of tall trees and hundreds of smaller ones dotting the cityscape below. She looked hard, tracking her prey, and finally spotted a second set of prints over the City of the Dead.

Then came the tricky part of the casting, as she let her mind take flight to scan the horizon beyond where she could physically see and continue to track. She tapped into how Nameless felt during a pleasurable flight and found herself flying along the Weavewood to spot additional tracks over the northern reaches of Ardeep Forest. She looked at a trail of smoke and tracked the lightning strikes. Tsarra's eyes followed the lightning bolts across the skies to where the smoke was the thickest. It covered the northeastern quadrant of the High Moor. She felt the spell starting to waver, so she pulled her focus back toward Waterdeep. Her eyes paused a moment over the view of Ardeep, curious about another silver tree there. It had fallen but was still alive with silver energy.

Poor Aloevan. Would that I could help her, Khelben sent, snapping Tsarra's concentration. Her vision of the Weave as a woodland nearly ended. *This spell is utterly fascinating, my dear. You described it to me before, but being able to see it through your eyes is an experience I'm glad I got to share.*

Tsarra shook off Khelben's words. She stared into the Weavewood, gauging the distances between each track marked on the Weave.

Khelben interrupted her again. *Of course. Seeing how far between each step he leaves on the Weave gives you an idea of how far he's teleported. The direction shows you toward where he teleported. Brilliant. Have you uncovered where the fool has gone to ground?*

Tsarra yelled, "Ow!" and Nameless growled low at Raegar, who glared back and said, "Hey—it wasn't me!"

"Not all of us can analyze and talk while casting spells, Blackstaff!" Tsarra snapped out loud. "It feels like Lurue's horn stabbed through my brain!"

Khelben's only response was to glare at her, and she glanced down at his wounds, then softened her tone. "Raegar," she said, turning to the man who held her, "thank you. You can put me down, now. You need to go to—"

"Wait," Khelben said, staring not at them but at the pulsing and shimmering wall of sharnstuff that enclosed all but where they stood.

"Why?" Tsarra asked, though she realized Raegar had not put her down. His eyes remained locked on hers, and she could see his concern. She felt her stomach flip a little but she turned back to Khelben to steady herself. "We need to tell our allies more. They're just as likely to mess up the situation as I might have until you confided in me at the tower."

"I agree. Now, boy, are you—ah. Reinforcements have arrived," Khelben said as twin rainbows of colors flashed across the night sky, tearing into the sharn floating above the tower. Behind their attacks flew Carolyas and Gamalon Idogyr. The bald mage wore a Tethyrian battle-robe, a forest green cape, and white tabard that left his arms exposed and free for movement. Elaborate sigil tattoos covered his arms from hands to shoulders and crept onto his back and chest, all of them glimmering with jade magic.

The sharn surrounded them with a forest of claws and teeth through their unique teleportals. Apparently,

Gamalon came prepared, as every sharn attack proved useless against the shields he wove around himself and his niece. He cast another spell, while Carol drew a rod from her belt.

Over the storm, the thunder, the screaming of the sharn, and the noises of the crowds below came a bellow. "Stop blasting!" Khelben roared, startling both Idogyrs into submission.

His roar drew everyone's attention to him, and even the sharn recoiled from their slow advance toward him. Khelben had emerged from the Anyllan's bottle unhealed. He leaned heavily on his blackstaff for support. His robes were rent and burned, and his left leg was a stump. It no longer bled or burned with silver fire, but it was an angry wound surrounded by blackened flesh. What worried Tsarra the most was his sickly pallor, but she took her cue from Khelben's emotions and kept a guarded face.

"Sacred Alram's Tears, Blackstaff!" Gamalon gasped.

Khelben said, "Gamalon, I've endured far worse in our Lady's service. Your faith tells you she demands as much as she grants. Now, tell me of those assembled at Blackstaff Tower."

Gamalon flew closer and hovered next to Khelben, while Carolyas zipped over to Maliantor, drawing a vial from her belt as she flew. Tsarra watched Carolyas ease a healing draught down Maliantor's throat, though she couldn't tell if rain or tears fell from her face onto her friend's. All the while, she listened to Gamalon.

"Nain still wavers on his role, but Laeral and Kyriani see to him. The three of them await the few stragglers, while nine others have gone on to prepare the Highstar Plains." Gamalon wavered a moment then continued, "Are you entirely sure we'll be able to trust some of these allies of ours?"

"They may not know all our plans," Khelben replied, "but what they understand keeps them on the same path as us at least through the Feast of the Moon. Laeral still holds the gnarled staff?"

As Gamalon nodded, Carolyas chimed in, "The fact that you've been seen with more than three different blackstaves in as many days has people buzzing, allies and others alike. Even if they know nothing, the streets chatter that their archmage is up to something big."

"Indeed," Khelben said with a weak smile. "Stick to our plans, Gamalon. All will turn out for the best, *e'e'a'sum*. I swear it. Take the boy and the tressym with you and meet us when you can at Malavar's Grasp. Take Syndra, as we'll need her to wield Isyllmyth's Bracer for the second circle after we recover it. Trust me, your excellency. You shall see your wife's vengeance fall from the sky." Khelben's eyes glanced at Gamalon's staff—an elaborate quarterstaff of polished white beech carved with a gap for his hand to fit inside the staff as a grip. At its top, the staff had a small lanternlike cage, inside of which whirled a large, free-floating green gem sparkling with magic. "That staff shall strike best, methinks," Khelben said then shifted his attention to Carolyas and Maliantor. "Carol, fly Mali to Rivuryn's Mark by the Seaseyes Tower and say *'Maldiglas.'* We shall lose no lives today without need."

"What are you talking about?" Carolyas snapped back, her eyes angry with tears. "Who was Rivuryn?"

Raegar stepped near and said, "Open Lord Baeron's dog. There's a marker just south of the trees and set at the base of the western wall."

Khelben nodded and said, "Take Maliantor, child, and she will be healed at the Refuge. Now go, before another death is on my head from this storm alone."

Gamalon moved to her side and helped her cradle Maliantor into her arms. He kissed Carolyas on the forehead, and said, "Our Lady's blessings will see you safe, niece. I'm sorry we can't tell you more right now, but understand we all do her work tonight. See yourselves safe and back to Blackstaff Tower. Methinks you'll need to help the apprentices keep order from the notables pounding on the door for answers."

Carolyas smiled. "Doubtful. Jardwim and others already

occupy the courtyard. Harshnag's on the gate, and I've yet to see anyone stare him down. Best of luck, uncle, and stay alive."

"From your lips to Mystra's ears, child," Gamalon sighed. "It must be so, as I look forward to the winter for us to catch up on our stories."

Gamalon waved her off as she took to the air once again, shuddering as the sharn parted to let her by. Once she flew past, the sharn closed ranks and began once again to drip or simply fall into the massed sharn on the tower. With the sharn slowly expanding to fill the chamber, Raegar scrambled atop the masonry wall, still holding Tsarra in his arms.

Khelben stood his ground, not seeming to notice that the sharnstuff touched his right shoulder. He snapped at Raegar, "Leave her, you lovesick fool. She and I move with the sharn. You and Nameless need to stay with the count."

Khelben didn't move, but the sharn continued expanding, and half his right cheek melted into the undulating black sharnstuff. The Blackstaff's voice seemed more hushed and far away

"It's all right, Raegar. Put me down. I'll be fine," Tsarra said, as she started to flex and finally moved her legs and arms easily. "You and his excellency have to get to Malavar's Grasp on the High Moor." When Nameless hissed at her, she said, "Sorry. Both their excellencies." Nameless, satisfied, now flew over to bat at the top of Gamalon's staff, trying to get at the spinning gem therein.

"What are you two talking about?" Raegar yelled. "We're about to be eaten by monsters, and you two act like it's not even a danger! Not to mention you've got us going a long way on a hunch. How do you know that's where that undead bastard went?"

Tsarra muttered, "Strong and dumb. Just how I like 'em." She smiled at Raegar then kissed him impulsively. "You really do need to put me down, please."

Khelben sighed, "Strike up a romance later, girl. Raegar,

follow the count's orders and we may yet see each other in this lifetime. We are in no danger from the sharn, nor have we been since our encounter at the Font of Knowledge. Tsarra and I will work with them to regain the remainder of the Legacy items. We shall meet again by highsun on the Moor. Apologize to Syndra for me for once again not saying my farewells."

With that, Khelben's face and most of his body melted into the sharn, and the rest of him slid in as if he sank into a pool.

A black-sheened hand reached out a moment later, and Tsarra took it, smiling at Gamalon and Raegar. "Never a dull moment around the Blackstaff, is there?"

With a final purr and smile at Nameless, Tsarra stepped forward into the sharn without a ripple. In less than a breath, the sharn above and around the tower glowed dark blue, sent forth a shower of purple sparks, and vanished with a whisper.

CHAPTER TWENTY-EIGHT

Feast of the Moon, the Year of
Lightning Storms (1374 DR)

Raegar, Gamalon, and the tressym stood silent. The only noises around them were the wind, pattering rain, and the occasional crack of lightning and thunder. Nameless crept between Raegar's feet in an effort to put something between the rain and him, and Raegar looked down at him.

"Five tendays of watching the tower and little beyond the norm happens," Raegar sighed. "The past two days, on the other hand, have had more activity than I've seen in a year. Is this normal?" Raegar directed his question at the creature at his feet, whose response was simply a bored yawn and what might have been a chuckle, if Raegar knew more about tressym.

"Did that blasted mage leave again without tellin' me?"

All three males whirled around at the woman's

yell, but they didn't see Syndra. A duskwood rod set with a row of diamonds and sheathed at head and foot in bright-steel floated in the air at the top of the stairs. It swung itself forcefully, dislodging a few loose bricks from where the pyramid had been torn off the tower. Nearby also hovered an intricately carved silver bracer covered in metallic holly with rubies for berries.

"Hrast! We need to—"

"—keep our heads, yes, I agree," Gamalon finished her sentence. "On that note, could you become visible?"

A copper-colored mist congealed around the rod and solidified into Syndra Wands, the silver bracer on her right forearm. Her face was still stolid but she was a striking half-elf woman with floor-length russet hair, a form-fitting ochre gown flattering her every ample curve. Raegar found himself wondering how Tsarra would look in a gown like that, as Syndra and she were very much alike aside from the arrow-straight hair on the woman before him.

"Your stare flatters, lad, but it's not me ye're seein', is it? It's that livin' girl with the Blackstaff you're lustin' after." Syndra laughed, floating around the red-shirted man. "Oh, for a solid body for just an evenin' with ye . . ."

She leaned in and kissed him, running her hands along his body. Every point of contact felt as if Raegar were rubbing against ice-cold silk. Stranger still, a trail of mist led from her to the rod. Nameless sniffed it and ruffled his feathers in response.

"Oh, I know ye don't like its smell, cat. I've just never cleaned it off. Vowed when I first joined with it that I'd only wipe that blood off on the Frostrunt's corpse." Syndra smacked one fist into her palm, and the rod mimicked a swing in response.

"So you're in this for revenge alone? What manner of undead are you?" Gamalon asked.

She raised an eyebrow, placed her hands on her hips and squared her shoulders in front of him.

"His Excellency the Count of Spellshire and he's not rememberin' an ally? For shame. That injury must've scrambled your wits. We've met, ye and I." Syndra winked at the one-eyed wizard whose look of astonishment forced Raegar to bite back a snicker. She paced around him, nodding, and said, "A right smart robe, though not for Waterdeep in winter—ah. Loved those rings of warmth when I had need of them. Ye're in better shape than when last we worked together. Khelben loaned me to that centaur friend of yours when we spent a few tendays occupyin' that wee hamlet of Trailstone against the Amnian troops."

"Forgive me, milady. Well met again." Gamalon bowed his head and shoulders to her, spreading his arms wide.

"Apology accepted."

"Forgive me, Syndra, but where did that bracer come from? I thought you mentioned the Frostrune claimed Isyllmyth's Bracer."

"And after he'd killed me once to get at it, ye think we'd be daft enow to let him find it so easily again? The Frostrunt's got a forgery, which is good, seein' as he's done the same with a few other artifacts we thought safe. Nay, he'll be able to do some of what he plans, but he'll hardly be able to do what he hopes. Even without it, the pyramid gives him enough power to be a right menace."

Gamalon said, "All right, then. We need to be off at best speed to the High Moor—an area I know not well enough to teleport into. You?"

The apparition shook her head and said, "Not my style. All right—chat later. If Khelben was right about you and yer staff there, one-eye, you can handle the transportation, then?"

Gamalon nodded and added, "Provided you'll not mind the wear and tear on your home."

Syndra shrugged and said, "Served me well a long time, but we both saw this coming. If this does what I think, it'll be worth it to relocate." She turned and gestured to Raegar. "Come on, tight-pants. Ye've got to help me prep the tower while the count gets us movin'."

Raegar stared at her a moment then turned back to see Gamalon cast a shimmering dome over the exposed top of the tower, waves of magic pulsing from the end of his staff. The older man gripped the staff with both hands and slammed the foot of the staff hard onto the stone floor. Magic leached into the stones and began to spread.

"Hey!"

Raegar was shoved from behind, and he turned to see the floating rod gesture menacingly. Syndra's voice came from both the rod and behind him as it said, "Let's get movin', friend!" Raegar put his hands up and began walking toward the phantom Syndra and the stairs. The tressym shook his coat and wings and meowed happily to Gamalon for keeping the rain off of them.

"What is he doing, exactly?" Raegar asked, as Syndra led him down two levels and into a library. It was a small room, fitting the tower's compact nature, but it was neatly packed with books on every available space. The lore-seeker in Raegar started scanning the books, but Syndra said, "Carefully move each shelf out from the wall and toward the center of the room. Don't knock any books off."

As Raegar fell to it, Syndra's spirit floated over the large square rug at the center of the room. Arcane symbols on the rug glowed when she moved over them. After she finished one circuit around the pattern, the whole rug glowed, and with a slight smell of burning sage, burned itself and its symbols into the floor. She gestured him forward, and Raegar shoved the first shelf onto the pattern. She gestured for Raegar to step back and said, *"Sheivah-nom!"* The shelf sank into the floor quickly and easily, and she cocked her head at the other bookshelves while smiling at Raegar.

"Again, please."

Raegar put his shoulder into the next, larger shelf. "So are you ever going to answer my question?" he asked, then grunted as he finally shoved the shelf onto the pattern.

Syndra repeated her command word to send the shelf wherever she was sending it. "Not until we're properly introduced, lad. I am the all-too-incorporeal Lady Syndra Wands, servant of Mystra and most hated foe of Priamon Rakesk. What are ye called?"

Raegar moved another shelf onto the pattern before wiping his brow on his sleeve and bowing. "Raegar Stoneblade, at your service, apparently. I'm in this for revenge, too. That tluiner killed my best friend."

"Pleased to meet ye, and know that he'll do more than that if ye let him, lad. Vengeful prat, that one," Syndra said, curtseying before him. "Of course, ye're not in it for revenge. I've seen the looks ye shot at the other redheaded half-elf. Pretty, but those curls must drive her insane."

Raegar stopped dead in his tracks and it dawned on him. "No. Just me. More the fool that I let her go."

"Oh, *let* her, my spells! That one does what she needs do, not what some swaggering male 'lets' her do," Syndra scolded Raegar. "Still, now that ye've untangled some of why ye're on this adventure again, mayhap ye'll make some better choices."

Raegar kept quiet and moved what Syndra pointed at. After a while, as he pulled two large trunks onto the pattern, he asked, "Why are we doing this right now? Where is this stuff going?"

"Portable transdimensional room. Didn't want to lose all of my books or things if it gets ugly. Now be careful with that looking glass—it's been in my family for four hundred years without a scratch . . ." Syndra started gesturing smaller, lighter objects onto the pattern to send them on their way.

Raegar shook his head. The more questions he asked of wizards and sorcerers, the more riddles he got. A few more minutes and they had cleared that room. Syndra said, *"Prieem,"* and the pattern became a carpet again, which rolled itself up. She looked at Raegar, the carpet, then Raegar again.

"I'd be glad to, milady," Raegar sighed, and he hefted the carpet onto his shoulder. "Where do we want it?"

As Raegar shifted his balance for the load, the tower itself rumbled, groaned, and sounded like stone grated on stone. Raegar dropped the carpet and fell over as the tower lurched hard—upward.

"Seems like One-Eye's gotten us moving. Bring that up top, in case we have to jump with it," Syndra said, and she floated into the ceiling while the rod moved as if it walked up the stairs.

Raegar grabbed the carpet again and carried it up the stairs. Rhythmic booming shook the tower and the steps, so he took his time. He tossed the carpet to one side of the stairs, and dust exploded from the carpet into his eyes.

Across the room, Syndra said, "Good thing I made this tower immune to lightning over the years."

Cursing at the dust, Raegar blinked his eyes clear again. He saw Gamalon holding the staff firmly on the floor, a silvery dome overhead providing cover. Syndra smiled at him as well, and said, "Oh, c'mon One-Eye. Let's have the real view. Neither of us gets out of Waterdeep enough."

Gamalon's voice sounded far away when he replied, "Of course."

The silvery dome overhead shimmered and became perfectly clear—and lightning bolts crackled and boomed all around them. The sky was filled with nothing but gray fog and lightning.

Raegar threw himself down on the floor as he saw a lightning bolt crackling directly toward them. He yelled, "Duck!"

After a few breaths, he opened his eyes to stare directly into the tressym's face. Nameless rolled his eyes upward and seemed to chuckle.

"Good reflexes on that one," Syndra giggled. "Pity he's just gotten himself dirty. Can I take him down and shower him off?"

"Sorry, Raegar. We should be through this . . . just . . . about . . . now," Gamalon said, and Raegar sat up to see the clouds part and the sky above fill with more stars than he'd ever seen in his life. He rose and moved to where Gamalon stood, not taking his eyes off the stars all around them.

Syndra chortled. "I'm not easily impressed, but this is one great view, Idogyr."

"You've—er," Raegar stammered, and both the tressym and Syndra sighed, while Gamalon smiled.

Raegar shook his head, almost in total disbelief. He'd seen a lot of strange things while he worked with Damlath . . . but this . . . "We're flying a stone tower?"

"No, you're riding in one, son," Gamalon joked. "I'm flying it."

"But—how? Why?" Raegar noticed the clouds retreating away from them. He couldn't tell how fast they were going as he had nothing to look at for comparison. "Why?"

"The *how* is the magic in my staff and myself that allow me to . . . well, I won't bore you with those details. The *why* is simply speed and expedience. We need to get to the High Moor as quickly as we can, and none of us could teleport there. I'm just taking us up toward the Tears then back down atop the High Moor. We should be able to easily spot Frostrune's lightning pyramid to pinpoint him."

Raegar leaned against one of the walls, staring out and down at the Realms. "I'm in a stone tower flying high over the weather . . . how are we still breathing air?"

"Air travels with us, though if we had planned a longer trip, we'd need something to replace the air we breathe. This is just a short jaunt."

Raegar started asking another question when he noticed the skies above Gamalon. "The Tears of Selûne . . . they're just huge rocks? That's disappointing. All these years, I rather liked the legend that they're massive gems or dragons' eggs."

"Aye," Syndra commisserated. "I was let down too the first time I saw them. But look behind you."

Raegar turned, looked back at the Realms, and gasped. They were high enough up that the curve of the planet was now visible. He whispered to himself, "They always said, but it was so hard to believe. The world isn't flat after all."

Even with Syndra's ribbing and ribald jokes, he remained quiet for a long time.

CHAPTER TWENTY-NINE

*Feast of the Moon, the Year of
Lightning Storms (1374 DR)*

Hours later, they were no longer climbing, and Raegar watched the Realms far beneath them. The entire Sword Coast and much of the interior was shrouded in storm clouds. When he thumbed in the clouds' direction and started to say something, Gamalon replied with an annoyed grunt of exasperation.

"No, we can't see, because those magical lightning bolts appear to have created a massive stormfront that's engulfed a lot of Faerûn with lightning storms like we saw in Waterdeep." Gamalon sighed, furrowing his brow, and said, "One of the main reasons I took this route was to minimize the delays of flying through bad weather, but now I'm trying to find the shortest way to our foe through the storms."

Raegar's curiousity got the better of him. "Well,

Khelben mentioned Malavar's Grasp a few times. If you know where that is, head for it. I've never heard of it, but then I avoided the High Moor for reasons most sane folk do as well. You know what it's all about?"

As soon as he asked, Raegar regretted it. He was still in way over his head in wizardly intrigues, and everyone else—even the tressym—seemed to know more about what was going on than he did. Unfortunately, Gamalon had a far-away look in his eye, something Raegar recognized from far too many Oghman clerics about to lecture him. Despite Raegar being on his blind side, Gamalon looked over at him and laughed.

"Don't worry, boy! My stories aren't nearly as long as Oghma's services."

Gamalon concentrated a moment, and Raegar felt the tower shift slightly and start to descend. The wizard began talking again.

"Khelben has woven so many lies around this gambit, even I have a hard time keeping track of it all. I say this as a 'renowned historian' myself. Malavar's Hand, down on the High Moor, is a false legend—a cautionary tale told to wizards who seek to abuse magic. Different places have different versions, but in most tales, Malavar sought to wield the might of the great sorcerous powers of the past, be they the Shoon, the Netherese, the Imaskari, or even older powers like the Ilythiiri. For his hubris, his spells to make himself a colossus failed, and his twisted body fell through the crust of the High Moor under its massive weight. All that remains above ground are the fingertips of his right hand, and these stand as tall stone menhirs on a blasted plain west of Highstar Lake."

Gamalon cleared his throat and continued, "I don't know which legends Priamon has read, but given his obsessions over the Shoon, I'll assume he's followed three or four more accessible historical texts. There are three Malavars who are real people in historical records. The most recent is an insignificant tradesman of Athalantar and another was a notorious pirate, slaver, and early member of the Rundeen.

The eldest Malavar is the one allegedly buried in the High Moor. A second-generation Asrami, Malavar of the Three Hands, was a sorcerer who fled Asram about forty years before the Standing Stone rose among the Dales. He arrived in Tethyr in time to become a key vizar for the Shoon Qysar Amahl Shoon III."

Raegar snorted and said, "Malavar of the Three Hands? Did a barmaid give him that name, or is it a tale that's going to reinforce my belief that wizards are all as well-balanced as a fomorian on ice?"

Gamalon laughed and continued, "Malavar gained his third hand by slaying Akhir, the second son of Amahl III, who tried to assassinate his father and become the second Shoon emperor. The boy had sorcerous powers, rather than the typical wizardry, and Malavar made a decades-long study of his corpse and his confiscated books on magic. Amahl's third son rose to power as Shoon I by the time Malavar crafted the mummified Hand of Akhir into a powerful relic. Accurate accounts as to the hand's full powers have been lost for centuries. All we know for certain is that the Hand of Akhir allowed Malavar to remain a power in the court of the Shoon for more than fifty years and remain young well past three times that many winters."

"This Malavar wore a mummified hand?" Raegar laughed, "How do you people think these things up? If I want something powerful, I'll go track down a nice clean magical sword, thanks."

"Don't mock, boy," Gamalon said. "There is more power in the severed hand of a sorcerer than in some countries, strange as it may seem. I could tell you of a hand down in Chult that, should you light candles upon its fingertips, bends tomorrow into yesterday. But I digress. Here is the truth—Malavar existed, along with Akhir's Hand, and they were both powerful, but not powerful enough to stand against two whole clans of wizards. He was exiled from Shoon lands in the Year of the Moor Birds. For two years, he then was chased all across the Sword Coast by dozens of mercenary wizards hoping to even old scores or claim even a piece of his powers.

"He finally made his stand at Highstar Lake against five archmages. Depending on which sources you read, Malavar attempted magic unseen in centuries and lost control of it. He and most of his foes perished and were buried in the High Moor's blasted crust. All that remained to mark the battle were the five curved stone slabs that Maildak of Westgate first coined as Malavar's Grasp in *Things I Believe and Have Seen* over seven centuries ago."

"So what's the truth? What was this fellow after, and does it tell us what Frostrune's looking for?" Raegar asked.

"Thanks to Khelben and his friends—myself included—there are more than fourteen different accounts as to exactly what Malavar was doing and how he died, as well as twice the number of references and legends that reinforce each one." Gamalon chuckled. "At this point, it's likely only Oghma, Mystra, and Malavar himself know the truth. Khelben would try to hoodwink you into believing he's got all the knowledge. Most of it, true, but just enough is missing that he can be blindsided."

"Wait a breath—you're telling me wizards have made up false accounts and passed them off to us as history?" Raegar rose and paced angrily. "Bad enough to hide secrets for themselves, but to actively confuse and distract honest historians from—"

"Oh, ye'd think someone told ye Leira had mists in her shift, the way ye're goin' on." Syndra became visible again as she rose through the stone floor. "Of *course* there's false histories out there. If ye actually believe there's only one or two sides to any story, ye've not been payin' attention, lad. Now, I agree that some of Khelben's more creative 'histories' may have done as much harm as good, but the truth is still the truth, and for those who need to learn it, they do, despite any obfuscatin'."

"But . . . well . . ." Raegar sputtered. He caught himself and took a deep breath. "All right. Setting that aside for now, haven't his secrets and changed histories brought a lot of danger down on folks? If he hadn't hidden so many secrets in so many lies, wouldn't your wife still be alive? Or you?"

Gamalon and Syndra both paled then turned scarlet with anger. While Gamalon kept a white-knuckled grip on his staff, Syndra's hand began to crackle . . . until Nameless flew up among them and snarled loudly. Raegar took a step back, hands up, and whispered, "I'm sorry. I'm sorry." The quartet remained deathly quiet for a few moments, as they drew closer to the clouds over Faerûn.

Gamalon cleared his throat and said softly, "Regrets and sorrows are for another time. Know this, young scholar-thief. Had such secrets not been buried—a mystery inside an enigma inside a puzzle—they would have been uncovered centuries before the Realms was ready for them. 'Mystery cloaks the walk of the Lady, for in her wake are secrets to be earned, not granted.'"

"Spare us the sermon, temple-goer," Syndra growled. "Listen up, boy. I paid for this with my life more than a century ago. I was angry. I was bitter. I was dead. I hated Khelben for more years than ye've been alive, and here I am workin' his will and hers. Why? *Surprise!* Mystra'll have her sacrifices, just like any other bloody god. And no matter what the cost, the ultimate goal that's hidden for so long makes it worth it for *everyone.*"

Raegar stomped around the open room. "Then what's the goal, if it's worth setting fire to Waterdeep and killing innocent people and covering the land with lightning storms?"

"Magic and unity," Syndra whispered. "Magic untouched in millennia to stave off the darkness growin' all around us. For once, it will be magic for many races, not just elves or humans. Isn't that a goal worth any cost?"

"No," Gamalon croaked, "but the Lady of Mysteries deemed it so, and my faith demands I accept until I too believe it."

"I just want to know why Damlath had to die," Raegar said. "Why, if Khelben knew about the power of those items, didn't he hold them all himself? Or better yet, if it's to bring some great magic to life, why didn't he do so before the Godsfall and save Mystra herself and so many others who died then?"

"Boy, ye're asking the right questions. Gods know, I've asked them of him too." Syndra sighed and continued, "What ye find is that Khelben's never parted with secrets until he's forced to. I respect that, if only because I don't want his responsibilities. After all, half the reasons the man's so exasperatin' is because he's workin' angles that take centuries to complete. The other reasons involve visions from Mystra herself, and she can be a vague bitch sometimes . . ."

"Blasphemer!" Gamalon barked, then turned his head up with his eyes closed in prayer. "We walk beneath your stars and eyes, accepting in your wisdom, Lady. Forgive those who sully the Path." Gamalon halted the progress of the tower, and calmed himself. "I take my faith seriously. I take my studies and my work equally so. All you need to know is that all things have happened as they needed to—to give us all the motivation and drive to do what we must."

Syndra stalked away, the rod and the bracer swinging wildly to express her frustrations.

Raegar said, "Well, I have to live with my part in your wife's death and I can never apologize enough for it. I never harmed anyone who didn't deserve it, and that's one of many reasons I need to see that lich in the ground."

"I've prayed, and I've cast spells to understand everything that happened that night, Raegar. Mystra herself forgives you, and I forgive you. If not for your actions, everyone in that inn would have died, rather than the five who died."

The silence on the tower was interrupted by the booming thunder in the clouds below. No one said a thing as they moved closer and closer to thunderheads that loomed higher than any others.

"Of course," Raegar muttered aloud. "The most lightning bolts—with that pyramid of his—would have the greatest storms over head."

"The magic we're fighting toward, Raegar? And how

Priamon seemingly amassed power so easily?" Gamalon said. "We needed him too. I hardly believe Priamon knows the truth behind Malavar; he simply wants to claim the Hand of Akhir or other relics to conquer the cabal of liches of which he is a part. Priamon thinks to use the lightning to awaken Malavar, but he awakens a vastly older magic. Malavar's Grasp is not the petrified remains of a Shoon wizard. So, Priamon is doomed to fail in his quest."

"Well, what is it then? It's obviously important and dangerous, or else Khelben wouldn't be pulling together all those high-powered wizards." Raegar paced around Gamalon, his feet matching the pace of his thoughts. "What sort of magic are you facing?"

"Heard of killin' storms, kid?" Syndra materialized directly in front of him, and Raegar stumbled right through her. A wave of cold passed through him, and he shivered while Syndra snickered.

"They're impossible. Those were lost when the High Moor was formed, weren't they?"

"No," Gamalon said, "despite many efforts. Every few centuries, someone cobbles together a similar magic that's not quite the same, but enough that elf assassins find and destroy mage and magic."

"Wait a minute—are you telling me these are killing storms?" Raegar recoiled from the wall.

"No again." Gamalon sighed, his face looking exhausted. "The lightning storms fulfill Alaundo's predictions for the year, but they're only a byproduct of Priamon's collection of artifacts. When he brings the pyramid into proximity with the five menhirs, that will accumulate enough power to release and reactivate the killing storm magic that was trapped in the land more than twelve millennia ago. *That* is why Khelben manipulated him into this."

"So it's a *good* thing that the lich can unleash a true killing storm? I don't believe you—"

"I'm not *finished*, boy. The killing storm is a magic so ancient, that the only way to undo its effects is to let it loose and change its magic with a group casting. There are mysteries tied to the killing storm that only get answered when it is unleashed again and tamed at long last. We have assembled the forces for the past twelve millennia and the time to see it through is tonight."

The full moon glowed brightly, and a solid beam of moonlight arced beneath them, parting the clouds and lighting a path ahead.

"There is our sign, thanks be to the Moonbow," said Gamalon. "Five gods have watched and waited—both ours and three more. All we need to do now is let Priamon do his part before we take our revenge."

With that, Gamalon urged the tower into motion, and the shattered Eightower slipped into the stormy clouds. Raegar gritted his teeth and reached up to scratch Nameless behind the ears.

He whispered, "I hope your mistress is doing better than we are."

CHAPTER THIRTY

*Feast of the Moon, the Year of
Lightning Storms (1374 DR)*

Tsarra found it odd that she was smiling as she faced
the shimmering wall of black sharnforms.

*Before I forget, Khelben, that face you made at
Priamon was priceless,* Tsarra sent to Khelben as
he slipped beneath the surface of the sharn.

*It wasn't too much? Laeral accuses me of being
a ham at times.*

*It was a little over the top, but he took the bait.
As long as he keeps moving in the direction we
need him to go. . . .*

*Indeed. You've learned more than I realized
in your short time with us. Now, step forward
and learn more about magic than you previously
dreamed. We shall need this insight with the sharn
for what we do next.*

Tsarra looked back once at Nameless and
Raegar, and she yearned to stay. Still, what she

knew moved her forward. She smiled at them, turned, and stepped forward into infinity.

Tsarra's first impression was that it felt equally like slipping into an overly warm bath, the empathic embrace of her familiar's bond, and the chaotic stomach-tumble of falling in love. She felt herself move around, willing her arms and legs to move, but she also sensed that they had temporarily ceased to exist. She felt the air moving around her, but it was and wasn't her skin across which the breeze flowed. In fact, she felt as if clothes no longer impeded the breeze. She sniffed, and her usually sharp senses could not isolate scents beyond the strongest—wood smoke, cinnamon, and the bitter coppery smell of spilled blood.

Where is all this coming from? she asked herself.

Tsarra blinked and felt dizzy—she looked out on more than nine different scenes all at once. She recognized a few features of Waterdeep through one eye, while another watched the sun rising on the shores of a small island, and more scenes than Tsarra could process. More and more eyes opened until she shut hers, or so she thought. She looked upon dozens and dozens of sights both sunlit and dark, beneath storms or clear skies, in deep tombs and atop mountains . . . and the images kept coming. . . .

Tsarra!

The shout drew her back to herself. Once again, Khelben drew her out of madness.

Lass, you dive in too easily. This isn't mere sorcery or wizardry, so you need to be careful. Focus on my voice again. I'll stay with you. Khelben's voice rang strong in her mind, but thundering behind it was a cacophony of voices. Khelben's face appeared near her, the white wedge of his beard shimmering with purple light as blue sparks revealed his face separate from the darkness.

Remember who you are, Tsarra. Don't drift or meld too far into the sharnmind. Just listen to it and watch. See through its eyes, but only as much as you can handle. Know you are a part of all this. Neither give in to it or fight it—just be with it, and it will teach us all we need to know. Thanks to the past few days, you've become adept at bearing more than one soul. Now, get in touch with being both one singular form and many forms.

That was the strangest sensation—like dreaming and feeling your body but not . . . but still seeing and moving and feeling something, Tsarra sent to Khelben. *Are we sharn now? You said earlier it was a way to more quickly move to where we needed to go.*

It is, yes, Khelben replied, *but it is also an experience you'll need in order to help me do what I foresaw nine hundred and ten years ago this night when I was Chosen.*

You've been waiting for this to happen for nearly a thousand years? You saw us melding with sharn? Is that why you've kept me in the tower for so long? Waiting for this?

Aye—that and more. Know that they who are with us, around us, within us, have waited far longer than that.

The noise surrounding her moved closer, and she recognized it as both a sea of random voices talking amongst themselves and the collective droning of a repetetive phrase: *n'fhaorn . . . avael . . . avaess . . . n'quel . . . n'sukarat'layr.*

Tsarra knew she wasn't blind, but she wasn't seeing physical forms. The overall gloom seemed almost empty until magical sparkles winked into existence near her, as Khelben appeared. When a form arrived near her like that, its voice stood out from the overall din. Each form was little more than a hint, purple and blue sparkles outlining muscles and features of an unclad but ideal creature: gnome, human, elf, centaur, or others. Their outer and inner forms had not matched in ages, and many of them stared at their sparkling outlines in wonder, as if waking from a long dream. Tsarra knew without asking that all of them comprised the sharn collectively, not individually, and they had all chosen their form and their fate.

Very good, child.

The voice came from "behind" Tsarra, who shifted her attention to that area and found herself staring into an eye larger than her head. Despite the softness of the sending, Tsarra's instinctive reaction was fear. As the eye narrowed and the dragon's outline morphed down into a beautiful elf woman, Tsarra saw three dazzling points of light—far brighter than all the others—approaching both of them.

What or who is that? Tsarra sent and asked aloud, though both became mental impressions of her question, rather than anything audible.

They wish to meet you, as did we all. The elf woman who was a dragon carressed Tsarra's face, her touch both warm and cool in this maelstrom of sensations.

Khelben's face and form shimmered near, and she saw that like the others Khelben's outline was stripped of any clothing. Tsarra looked down at her own form, realizing that she too stood exposed and vulnerable, right down to the birthmarks on her left hip—three dots of purple sparks. The oddest difference between Khelben and all others was the scars he bore on his image—random scars on his face, arms, and legs, and the massive hand-wide scar slashing across his torso. His left leg went missing here as well, and he bled silver sparkles from the stump and around his hip.

Khelben? What aren't you telling me? And why am I so afraid of those three lights? Tsarra sent to her mentor.

Fear is healthy when one faces fundamental changes. What you learn now is how to navigate a sea of thoughts and intentions and sensations and magic. What they may teach you, even I do not know. They are the Three Watchers. The last person they spoke to in any direct manner was Oacenth, coronal and grand mage of Jhyrennstar. Khelben's sending felt reverent and totally in awe of whom he spoke.

At last, Arun's Son. You
Are welcome among us,
Tsarra Autumnfire, and we
Honor you as
Our hands.

Tsarra bowed to them, but asked, *Your hands? I don't understand.*

You have borne three souls in part and thrived. The laughing elf woman appeared before her as if a reflection on a still pool. Tsarra liked her face with its deep dimples and broad smile. The image scattered, only to be replaced by another, as if a breeze blew through the sharn and disturbed its surface.

The male's voice matched the seriousness of his tone. *Greater still is your burden to come. Know you are of our blood, thin though it may be.*

The bald woman's visage shimmered into Tsarra's sight, and she leaned forward to kiss her on both cheeks. *So open and closed all at once. She knows and ignores both heart and head. Half an elf, half a woman, but always stronger than you believe yourself, like so many. Your strength shall carry us all this day. You only need unlearn your limitations.*

And here I thought Khelben was cryptic, Tsarra mused to herself.

I heard that. Khelben's voice whispered from her other side, and it felt like he took her right arm as the bald elf woman had taken up her left. *There is no difference here between thought and voice, Tsarra. Now, for all our sakes, listen to them. Hear them.*

Tsarra felt her neck get hot, which it always did when her temper rose. *I'm willing to play my part, but someone had better ask soon, rather than assume I'm able and willing to do what you need me to.*

Good. The gravel-voiced elf became the bearer on her left. *Stop tamping down emotions. Emotions are the heart of magic. We should not have to tell a sorcerer that.*

His face shimmered into the rounder-faced woman who looked up into her eyes and asked, *Autumnfire, what would you know? The answers are within you and all of us. Let them in, rather than fight. We awaken to individuality for the first time in millennia. We need ask of you no more than you ask of us, for we are all one. Do not fight this as you do your heart. Let us in, and we shall all understand.*

Hamra is right, Tsarra. I'll be here to help you, if you need me. Khelben's voice reassured her and grounded her.

Tsarra's heart felt like it was bursting and she seemed to be breathing very fitfully, but she realized it was simply fear.

They are magic too, in their own ways, but rarely for the

good. Fear is ignorance and anger. Unlike most half-breeds,
you do not fear one side or the other. You are whole, for you
were not raised by fear but love. Humandelf. No division.

Tsarra remembered both her parents repeatedly telling her, "You are not a half-anything. You're our daughter,
you're whole, you're loved, and that's all you ever need to
know." She smiled and relaxed as he sent, *Learn what we
understand* . . .

Tsarra remembered both her parents repeatedly telling her, "You are not a half-anything. You're our daughter,
you're whole, you're loved, and that's all you ever need to
know." She smiled and relaxed as he sent, *Learn what we
understand.*

Tsarra knew the gravel voice was T'karon, Cor'Selu'-
Taar'Miyeritar. The awareness came to her like an awakening.
Despite his gruff exterior and voice, T'karon had a kind heart.
She understood his simplest pleasure was walking barefoot
in dew-covered grass. She found herself remembering things
that were dust five thousand years before her grandfathers
were born. Her eyes welled with tears as she watched the
olive-dark stormclouds sting and sear the Syavaeor Fields.
She saw the fires choke and sunder the shimmering citadel
of Kraanfhaor. She screamed as she felt the sting of the acid
rains falling on her—his—her—his skin, and she howled as
the whirlwinds shredded stone, wood, and flesh. She felt the
fall of cities and armies and fell to her knees beneath the
weight of all that tragedy. She sobbed over the corpses of loved
ones and beat her breast in memoriam of those fallen at Myth
Akherynnar and shaved her head bald to mourn imprisoned
far from home and among her enemies. . . .

Too Much! Khelben's voice shattered through a thousand
memories and feelings to reach her. *Grand Mages T'karon,
Hamra, and Alunor,* Stop*!*

Khelben's voice fell away again, as Tsarra was caught
once more in the undertow of wave upon wave of memory,
emotion, and more power than she'd ever known. She
smelled the rewaran blooms beneath a full moon, when
Chearel finally proposed, the scent of a healing draught,

the sandalwood-and-sawdust scent of his love's hair, the smell of burnt air in a spellduel . . . She felt the hot embrace of lovers, the cool stone and the smell of dust and metal as it shaped by his will, the merry drumbeat of her hooves beneath her at full gallop, chasing after Karnoth in the Courting Herd. . . . More than a thousand minds pressed upon her, but Tsarra focused on one thing she knew very well—Khelben's voice.

This place is nigh-timeless, but to force her to relive a thousand lifetimes to understand is too much.

Tsarra had never before heard Khelben plead. Only in his own memories did he defer to anyone's authority. Her senses were awash with hundreds of smells, tastes, touches, and voices, but she clung to his words.

Do not sacrifice who she is for what you need! It is within your power to overwhelm her, possess her, and have her act out your will as a puppet. Do so and you do not realize your dreams or those of your protégé Oacenth. You only repeat the sins you fled from. Do not become Vyshannti!

What scared Tsarra the most was the immediate stillness. No memories, no senses, nothing. She saw the three *selu'kiira* of the grand mages hovering nearby, the faces and bodies of their bearers hidden from her. She sensed their shame, their anger, and their fears, knowing everything hinged on what happened next. She needed to learn what was expected of her, what they all needed . . . but to ask them for information was too overwhelming.

Tsarra smiled as she realized the solution. *Khelben? I need you to help me speak with Danthra. If everyone can focus on her and send her energy, we can guide her visions toward what we need to know. Is that possible*

More than possible, and an ingenious solution that had escaped me. Khelben beamed broadly, and the sparkling crowd returned as the mood lightened. Khelben faced her and the three kiira floated down to form a straight line between Tsarra's kiira and Khelben's forehead. Smaller lights glistened off the gems and Tsarra heard the three speaking all around her.

Apologies, Autumnfire. We have been of singular mind
Longer than an age. We have forgotten that not
All minds are ours to use at our will and for our
Purposes. Let us make amends and work together
As friends, not as subjects.
Friendship, too, is a magic and one we needs foster
Anew. Let us speak with the Dreamer and see
What she sees, and from there, we shall seek
The final remnants of our realm—
the seeds of our future.
The seeds of everyone's future.

CHAPTER THIRTY-ONE

*Feast of the Moon, the Year of
Lightning Storms (1374 DR)*

Tsarra smiled as she hugged the sparkling form of
Danthra the Dreamer, who kissed her cheek and
promptly dissipated into the sparkling void of the
sharnform.

Why can't she stay with us, Khelben?

*She'll only distract you now and pull your
attention away from where it needs be. She will
be there when you need her, as will all here. Now,
all fears allayed?*

Tsarra smiled. *All the old ones, aye. It's the new
ones that are crowding in now.*

*As with all things—you reach the end of your
climb to understanding and you find yourself at the
bottom of an entirely new slope invisible from below.
One of my mentors said it's the tree you can never stop
climbing. The fall would kill you once you'd climbed
high enough, so it's best to focus on going farther.*

So let's keep climbing, then. How long has it been since we left the Eightower?

Not even a half-bell. Remember that we communicate far more swiftly enmind than we do in mundane ways. Now, the sharn have their abilities to slip through the ethereal and broach nearly any protections or barriers. Focus on watching the Gathering, Tsarra, and participate where you can. Every chance to work cooperatively will help you in the working to come in a few hours. I need to converse more with the grand mages. With that, Khelben's presence drifted away.

Tsarra turned her attentions outward, again trying to see through the multitude of eyes of the sharn. She realized that the sharn had always been one form that budded off a seemingly separate form that remained part of the collective group mind. She saw through three different forms at once and marveled at how much more vast it was to see through seven or more eyes at once to take in each scene. She settled into hunting mode, and a number of centauran minds and a few dwarves sparkled in around her, all of them focused on the gathering of other hidden remnants of Miyeritar. She smiled, understanding all of them enjoyed the hunt. Tsarra opened her eyes and let her sharnsenses scan the Realms.

Tsarra understood that, like the items and relics they had collected thus far, there were shards and pieces of Miyeritar all across Faerûn, hidden away by accident or design. Very few were whole items, and fewer still held enchantments from that time. What she did know is that the sharn were awake to their true purpose. The last time the sharn acted with such focus of purpose was to construct the Sharnwall around the Phaerimm of Anauroch. Most often, magical fields or internal conflicts among their groupmind made the sharn act unpredictably or madly. The sharn tracked by scent and by magic, and everything they sought had a shared scent

Every single thing exposed to the Killing Storm brought down on Miyeritar by the Vyshaanti of Aryvandaar was touched by a singular magic unused since then. Thus, everything held a scent, even after all these millennia and even if forged or changed anew. All those touched by that magic reacted to the storms engulfing the Sword Coast and much of the rest of Faerûn. Depending on its location, items rattled or hummed or vibrated or sparked in relation to the storms and the rising magic involved within them.

A belt buckle here that was once an ore-laden rock on the High Moor hummed curiously, its Sembian wearer thought, though he fainted dead away when the sharn stuck its head and arms through its portals to claim its prize. Tsarra felt the cold as a sharn materialized in an ice cave far to the northeast to snatch a small broken dagger from the ribcage of its victim, who lay embedded in the glacial ice. Tsarra actually felt the sting of many magical missiles when a sharn infiltrated a meeting of the Arcane Brotherhood, smashing its meeting table to bits to claim the carved wood tile at the table's heart. She heard the snores and smelled the peaty breath of a green dragon as a sharn quietly pulled fifteen seemingly random coins out of a rather proud treasure hoard.

Each time a sharn reclaimed an item, it was drawn into the sharnform, but then Tsarra felt a shifting and the item was almost immediately dropped out onto a wet and storm-blasted heath she had never seen, save in Danthra's vision. Each item, with or without any power of its own, needed to be in place for the rituals to come. Luckily, none of them were dropped near the vicinity of any of the others, so no additional lightning bolts crackled to life to reveal the items' existence there. Every time Tsarra tried to focus on the pattern they were putting in place, the collective's attention moved on to the next item.

Only once did Tsarra pull the collective sharn's attention toward the storms overhead, and they all saw their enemy. The Frostrune flew standing atop the base of his pyramid, the point blasting the ground below with eldritch lightning and power. The four corners of the pyramid also connected to the storms by four constant streams of lightning linking to the clouds. She ached to lash out at him, using her new connections to the sharn to attack, but calmer voices prevailed around her.

Soon. Soon. He still has one last role to play here.

Tsarra accepted that and shifted her focus to an even darker place—a web-covered crypt, where their sharn encountered resistance. A vampire held fast to a metal-shod tome, blasting the sharn back with effective spells of black fire. Stranger still, she recognized him—Asraf yn Malik el Kahaman yi Manshaka. She asked the collective for help, and she willed two of the sharn hands to trace glowing sigils in the air. Once she completed the star-enclosed scroll mark of the *tel'teukiira*, the vampire stopped and stared.

Tsarra spoke and her words came out in the hollow voice of the sharn, "The Blackstaff has need of that, but you have his gratitude for being an able guardian. A reward shall be forthcoming."

She reached out, snatched the tome with three claws, and pulled the book into the sharn as it dematerialized and returned to the central form. Tsarra helped reclaim more than a dozen items in this manner, everything from a vambrace off a suit of armor in Dhedluk to a dungsweeper's shovel from Arabel, until they finally encountered two places even the sharns' magic could not penetrate.

Khelben? Grand Mages? Tsarra and a number of her fellow hunters asked to the collective. *We've found most of the remnants and delivered them into place. Priamon is nearly at Malavar's Grasp. There are only two things that are not in place—and when we push against the magic screening these places, the mark of the Blackstaff flickers to life in silver flames.*

Ah. Tsarra, it is our time to leave the collective then. Hopefully, this was enough of an education to guide you through the working we have later today.

That's the one thing I don't understand. I saw myself at the center of a great working, but I didn't see you. Why didn't I see you there?

Khelben's eyes grew sad, and his visage turned away for a moment. *All in good time, my dear. Now, simply push yourself at—no, not that one, the other barrier. Push yourself against it and will your* kiira *to rest on the sigil.*

Tsarra concentrated on moving forward and focused her attention on her forehead. She saw her own magical mark in her mind, aglow from the *kiira*'s energies, and when she touched the flaming sigil, the barrier bent and flexed around her, snapping behind her like the string of a bow. She fell hard onto a stone floor and coughed as a thick layer of dust erupted into a cloud around her. Lights whirled around her, and Tsarra coughed more when she realized the lights were shaped to be muscular men no more than a few fingers' length tall with birds' wings.

"There you are." Tsarra's head snapped up and she had her scimitar half-drawn before she saw the woman who spoke. Tsarra had never met her, but she'd seen enough paintings and likenesses for sale in the Market to know the woman anywhere.

Tsarra sheathed her weapon and remained on her knees as she greeted, "Lady Alustriel, forgive our intrusion."

The silver-haired woman sat atop the flat bier at the center of a dust-choked and webbed crypt, her purple linen gown immaculate despite the mess around her. Her feet were clad in fine wine-colored slippers. Her eyes danced and her smile was infectious. Over her heart was a pearl brooch of a unicorn's head, its horn and mane shining in polished silver. She appeared every inch the queen she was, though Tsarra was distracted at how similar she and her sister Laeral were in appearance. Even so, each one's bearing and carriage made a totally unique impression on those they met.

The crypt, aside from being small and dust-choked, was nondescript. One spiral stair of stones led down into it in the far corner, and there was only the one large sarcophagus in the center of the room. There was room for two men to walk around it, but nothing else seemed to be in the tomb. Tsarra read the inscriptions on the bier and realized it was a husband and wife buried together:

Halver Gehrin
844 – 956 DR
Honored Father, Mage, Mentor

Lyia Moonwhisper
844 – 879 DR
Treasured Mother, Mage, Mate

"Don't be silly, my dear. Stand up. 'Tis no intrusion, as this isn't a place of mine. I'd make a comment on how awful a housekeeper my brother-in-law is, but I suppose one need not keep a tomb tidy."

"I've never found it necessary to do so, dear sister." Khelben's voice sounded before he appeared, stepping from a wall. "After all, why clean if you only intend to visit once every two centuries? Now, I realize we are in your city, but how did you know we would be here?"

"Mystra," she said. "We should know by now that the only times I fall asleep without meaning to are when she needs to send a message via our dreams. You're to give me something, and I'll assume it has to do with our Moor working? I've a council quite irate with me for postponing two meetings and a city disappointed I shan't be on hand for any of the fetes tonight."

"Not so loud, milady." Khelben barked. "There might be prying ears and eyes around."

"Unlikely. I cleared the Chapel of the First Magister earlier this morning and my Spellguard keeps watch outside. Besides, we're two cellars beneath it as well. Who's likely to overhear?" Alustriel floated over then giggled, and hugged Khelben and kissed him on the cheek.

"Wh-what are you about, woman?" Khelben sputtered.

"It's been years since I've been either mother or aunt, so let me be a little excited in private, you grump," the Lady Hope chided. "Even if Laeral had kept it secret, our Mother did not. Your mate bears the children of two Chosen. Blessings, indeed, and happiness deserved."

Khelben's face betrayed nothing, but Tsarra felt him pass

through a maelstrom of emotions—pride, love, happiness, gratitude, wistfulness, sadness, grief, and resignation—in the space of a breath. All Alustriel knew was that her brother-in-law gruffly shrugged her off and hobbled around the bier. His, "Thank you, sister," was barely audible at all.

"Khelben! You're wounded!" Alustriel gasped.

While their clothes had been restored when they exited the sharn, Khelben's wounds had only been cloaked by his robes.

"Let me help you."

Alustriel's arms lit with silver fire, and she knelt by Khelben's missing left leg. Her hands dripped with silver fire, and Tsarra felt a rush of life, power, and warmth, but it did not linger. From Khelben, she felt only felt his sadness, as his wounds did not heal. Alustriel looked up at him, puzzled, and he rested a hand on her shoulder.

Khelben said, "My thanks, but things are as they must be. Save your strength for the working."

Khelben hobbled around the bier, and his hand trailed briefly over Halver's and Lyia's names both. He cleared his throat and said, "Saproath Khar," as he touched an empty torch sconce on the far wall. The sconce flipped forward off the wall, exposing a small recess behind it. Khelben reached in and pulled out a dusty, web-choked box. He blew off the worst of the dust and handed the box to Alustriel.

The ruler of Silverymoon opened the thin box after motioning for Tsarra to join her. Inside, atop a bed of velvet, lay a white ash wand with a scarlet gem set into its top. The glow alone attracted the attentions of Alustriel's malelights, who flocked atop the box's open side. The gem was flat on one side and perfectly rounded on the other, as if it were cut for another purpose.

Alustriel looked up at Khelben. "Hosskar's Blinding Baton?" she asked.

"Yes, but what it's been constructed from is more important—that gem is a *selu'kiira* of a grand mage of Miyeritaar. You, the Aumar, and Alvaerele shall bear them in the first circle, even though our foe unwittingly holds the third of the three. Given Laeral's condition, I dare not allow her a *kiira*'s touch."

Alustriel nodded and closed the box, much to the mute complaints of her lights. "Very well. You need to visit this chapel more often or at least make a donation. It's only Master Paral, his relatives, and a few loyalists. Most prefer the larger temples to Azuth and Mystra at the university grounds."

Khelben moved to another part of the wall and tapped another hidden panel open with the head of his staff. A shelf slid from the recess, holding four dusty black leather-bound books. He handed them one at a time to Tsarra and Alustriel.

"So far as I am aware, this is the only complete four-volume set of these prayerbooks, penned when Azuth's faith was less than two centuries old," said the Blackstaff. "They can go to Master Paral after your scribes make four copies over this winter—one for the Vault of the Sages, one for my Silverstars, another for Gamalon to take to Tethyr, and one copy for Candlekeep. After that, the originals remain here among Mystra's and Azuth's faithful. The *Codici Magistiri* should draw in a few zealots and many mages, once word gets around. Fair enough?"

"And they say the Blackstaff knows naught about quiet statecraft," Alustriel teased, winking at Khelben. "Shall we be off then? Are we to worldwalk to the moor?"

"No. We take the—what did Dove call this? Ah—'Dead Man's Walk.'"

"Dove always did have a sick sense of humor," Alustriel observed, "but never as sick as your wife's."

Khelben nodded, and both of them chuckled.

Khelben, what's this Dead Man's Walk you're talking about? Tsarra sent silently, rather than disturb the two Chosen's banter.

Simple. We just travel across the Realms using portals at my graves.

"What?" Tsarra yelled. "Tell me you're joking!"

"Oh, he doesn't joke, girl," Alustriel teased. "You know that."

Khelben's sigh was felt as well as heard by Tsarra. *None of them are truly my grave, as would be obvious. They are simply where I chose to mark the passing of previous identities. I also set portals at the graves of my aliases to allow me secure hiding places for things. Only a senior Harper, Moonstar, or a Chosen of Mystra who knows the names of my aliases can use these portals. This makes them easily but little used. We use this as we have yet one more item and two agents to retrieve.*

Khelben moved quickly to her side, grabbing her arm and pinning a badge on her tunic beneath her cloak. Alustriel took his other arm, and the three of them walked them toward the stone wall. Khelben said, "Acris," and instantly they were awash in sunshine.

Tsarra blinked and held her hand up to shield it from the sun, and Khelben swore under his breath.

Tsarra asked, "Khelben, where—" She looked out over a small, overgrown graveyard on a hillside overlooking the sea. Waves crashed far below at the bottom of a cliff.

"Wrightsvale. A village a slow day's walk northwest of Starmantle. No time to visit, as we're already running out of time, if I read that sun right." Khelben tightened his grip on Tsarra's and Alustriel's arms, backed them both up a few steps before walking toward a split and ruined gravestone, and said, "Seamar."

The trio arrived in an outdoor mausoleum. Unlike the previous tomb, it held recessed biers in all four walls and a large sarcophagus in the center. Tsarra scanned the names of those buried there—Seamar Ruthyl, Adaram Ruthyl, Caras Ruthyl, and Wyrick and Nura Ruthyl—and recognized not a one, nor did any dates adorn the biers.

Alustriel noticed Tsarra's investigations and explained. "Impilturans rarely date their graves, Tsarra. They count on historians to track all that, either royal or family scribes. It has something to do with keeping demons from taking on old shapes and forms, but I've never made a study of it."

The sun beamed through the tiny windows at the top of the walls, their directions suggesting it was near highsun where they were. Swearing as he floated upward, Khelben traced a complex sigil over two walls and the ceiling in the upper corner. The sigil flashed a green color, and Khelben tapped it twice with his blackstaff. Beside her, Tsarra felt the central sarcophagus of Wyrick and Nura slide backward without a sound. Looking down, she found a stairwell leading down into a chamber that was growing with light.

Alustriel asked, "So who are we supposed to meet here? You never mentioned there was a chamber beneath this before, but I've only ever used Adaram's coffin to dispose of more problematic things."

Tsarra asked, "Why there?"

Alustriel smiled and replied, "Khelben built this mausoleum for himself as a hiding place and a way to dispose of evil artifacts he dredged from Serôs—the Inner Sea. Adaram's bier was specifically built around a stable dead magic zone, making it perfect for that purpose. He's buried standing up on one end of that, which is why his bier is longer than the others." Alustriel strode forward toward the stairs, but Khelben's blackstaff whipped around to block her.

"It's not safe yet. I'll call you down," he snapped. Khelben walked down the stairs, using the wall and his staff for support. He stopped in front of a torch burning with silver flames, looked back up at Tsarra, and said, "I'm sorry, lass." He shoved his left hand into the torch's flame to set his own hand alight with silver fire.

Tsarra fell to her knees, clutching her left hand and gasping from the sudden pain. She could feel the magical fires burning both of them, until he gripped the unlit torch at the bottom of the stairs and lit it, placing the silver flames on the torch. Once that torch flickered to life, Tsarra's pain ended, and she and Alustriel watched five different fields of magic dissipate. Khelben motioned them down, and he moved into the chamber.

Tsarra and Alustriel descended the stairs to face two stone biers, atop which were two forms. On the left hand side was an ancient sun elf, bald, with delicate Elvish sigils tattooed around his temples and down his neck. An orange gem glinted on his forehead. Khelben finished a complex casting and waved his hand over the man's face.

"*Rejhar amreh tolaer,*" Khelben chanted, and the gold elf's eyes flickered and opened. He stared up into the Blackstaff's eyes without saying a word, but his gem flared with amber fires. His eyes spat the same color flames directly up into Khelben's eyes, and within a moment, the Blackstaff's back stiffened, his gaze darting to Tsarra then to the shelves at the back of the room.

After a moment, Khelben helped the old elf sit up as he introduced him. "Alustriel, Tsarra, meet Ualair the Silent, keeper of Uvaeren's Secrets and master of the N'Vaelahr of Myth Drannor. Beside us is his protégé and an unsung hero of Myth Drannor, Rhymallos the Hidden Eye."

Khelben pulled the covering off the adjacent bier to reveal the insectoid form of a demonic mezzoloth. Khelben and Ualair held up their hands for peace as Alustriel and Tsarra stepped back.

The orange gem flared on Ualair's brow, and Tsarra heard a soft voice in her head. The ancient elf's expressions matched the sendings his *selu'kiira* projected. *Peace and light laughter to you beautiful girls. Rhymallos took this form to infiltrate the Army of Darkness, and he has slept here alongside me for many centuries as we awaited the last stage of the Pentad's plans. He deserves to be restored and remembered. I merely do my part to help undo my failures of the past.*

Tsarra knew of the legends surrounding the great mute Grand Mage of Myth Drannor, and she fell to one knee. "You do me too much honor, *teless*. I am unworthy to hear you speak."

Tsarra realized the power and dangers involved in Khelben's work, if such were the people he was gathering for a ritual.

Ualair's kind voice came in a sending and a touch to her shoulder. *Rise, child, and fret not. My silence is merely physical and one of necessity.* His wrinkled hand raised her chin to look at him, and she saw the jagged white scar across his throat that robbed him of his voice. He had one last comment for her, and he sent, *Do not believe yourself unworthy, girl. Your role in this is vastly more important than mine, and mayhap people shall speak as highly of you in days to come as they seem to speak of my meager contributions to the Art.* Ualair's smile brought tears to Tsarra's eyes, as he reminded her of her long-gone grandfather.

"What about your friend, Rhymallos? Why doesn't he move?"

He is under different enchantments that allow him peaceful and painless slumber yet. He shall be awakened only when we truly need him to be. That time is not yet. Look now to him who was Nameless. He needs you now.

Ualair looked toward Khelben, then back at Tsarra, and finally over to Alustriel. While his gem kept flashing, Ualair's attention was on Alustriel alone.

Khelben hovered over a table in the back of the room, casting spells onto something. He sent to her, *I have a gift here for you, Tsarra. It has been a long time in coming.*

Tsarra approached, and Khelben brought out a jet-black recurved short bow and placed it in her hands.

Tsarra sent, *Thank you, Master. Does it have a name?* She could feel tremendous power in the duskwood bow and in what appeared to be a silver bowstring.

Not as such. I made it about two hundred years ago, but it's never been drawn. It's a simple thing—it allows any arrow fired from it to penetrate magical shields as if the arrows were blackstaves.

That will prove useful against our foe to come, for certain. Still, why give this to me now? I know that ritual is later today, but what's your sudden hurry?

I've added a few spells to the bow that should help in the coming day. Ualair is connected to this plan on many levels, as he's one of its architects, along with a number of my tutors—the ones they now call the Seven Wizards of Myth Drannor.

Yes, and?

Five others sleep as he did, though more openly and in disguise. The Five who Sleep are integral to the Pentad's plan to restore the high mages' city of Faertelmiir.

Tsarra finally understood Khelben's haste and anger as she said aloud, "The Five who Sleep are Malavar's Grasp?"

"Yes, and in his ignorance, Priamon Rakesk may well kill them . . . and doom everyone on the Sword Coast!"

CHAPTER THIRTY-TWO

Feast of the Moon, the Year of
Lightning Storms (1374 DR)

Tsarra threw off her cloak and adjusted how her quiver lay across her back. She took up the new bow and slung it around her shoulder. She opened her hand to take the three blue and one green crystalline arrows Khelben handed to her.

She asked, "These are arrows like those you gave me at the tower?"

"No," Khelben said, as he threw open cabinets and growled in frustration. "Those were new spells I was testing. These are designed to damage undead more than the living. Your bow should help you penetrate Priamon's defenses. And remember—that green-glass arrow you save until I expressly tell you to use it."

Tsarra added the arrows to her quiver alongside her regular arrows. Khelben spent a few moments grunting as he opened and closed boxes, searching for something. Finally, he pulled open a drawer and sighed with relief as he pulled out a small black bottle. He uncorked it and a slight flash of silver magic shimmered on the stopper as he put that down and motioned her closer.

He began to tip the bottle and said, "All right, Tsarra—we're going to jump through this portal." He poured the black liquid in a circle on the floor. "We'll travel through the sharn to the focal point of our problem. You'll have to distract and fight Priamon for a short time while I get the Five awake and to relative safety. I'll fire two spells to help you, but you'll be on your own after that. Ready?"

"Ready." Tsarra turned back to bid Alustriel and Ualair good-bye, but they were deep in conversation over the still-prone body of Rhymallos. Tsarra looked back at Khelben, who had continued pouring black liquid into the circle while chanting. The entire circle was jet black, and as the final drop fell from the bottle and Khelben's chant ended, familiar purple sparks erupted in its depths. Khelben joined hands with Tsarra, and the two of them leaped into the circle and jumped out into a dark, rainy environment filled with ear-shattering thunder.

Khelben, Tsarra, the undead one activates the Mormhaor'sykerylor! The pain returns! You must stop him! a voice boomed through the darkness.

All around them were the blasted plains of the High Moor, here and there dotted with pools of blackness that could either be dark water or sharnstuff, as was the black puddle from which they had emerged.

In the distance, Priamon stood silhouetted between them and the lightning-wrapped pyramid. The pyramid hovered point down just above the top of the five stone plinths. Lightning crackled and blasted away at the plinths and the heath beneath them. Meanwhile, Frostrune spun other spells that focused the lightning bolts, keeping the worst fury of the storms focused within Malavar's Grasp. The wind commiserated with the pain of the ground and rock. Overhead, the sky crawled with lightning burrowing through the clouds and lancing both up and down from ground and sky.

Tsarra looked for cover, only to be disappointed at the stunted scrub that counted as foliage in the High Moor. Khelben tapped her on the shoulder and motioned her forward. Tsarra soon realized the rain was doing more than just getting them wet. Her leathers were starting to steam, as if the rain were acid.

Strange that it doesn't have the same effect on flesh, she thought.

They moved quickly across the moor, Tsarra and Khelben both readying spells. The only benefit of the storms was in covering their approach. Once they were within fifty paces, Khelben summoned a massive energy hand into being around Priamon, and it squeezed, shattering magical fields and defenses around him.

The hand shimmered and disappeared, and Khelben said, "Now!"

Tsarra summoned up a spell that used all her anger and hatred toward undead and focused it with precision. It always left the odd taste of pickles in her mouth when she cast it. Five pulses of white light exploded from her right hand and quickly arced toward the lich. Two of them glanced off the large metal plate and harness the creature wore, but the remainder struck him in the head, arm, and leg. Priamon's howls of anger and pain told them they'd made an impact. He lashed back with a massive fireball of cold energies, but Khelben cancelled its effects.

As Tsarra dashed in an arc around Priamon, she saw Khelben fire a green bolt of energy that struck Priamon squarely in the face but did no damage. The lich started a new spell, but she fired an arrow at him. That too struck him squarely, and he seemed surprised to find an arrow lodged in his chest. Had his heart mattered to him, that shot would have killed him.

"Bothersome gnats!" Priamon howled at them. "The powers I awaken here shall destroy all who stand in my path. I'll collect enough magic from your corpses to train upon the Rune. Those who don't stand with me shall fall. And first among them is you, Blackstaff!" Rather than attack, the lich wove a new defensive spell around himself.

Tsarra, I need to stop that pyramid for now. Do what you can to buy me time, but don't throw your life away!

Khelben flew off toward Malavar's Grasp, and Tsarra quickly thought of eating dewmelons and spitting out the seeds. In response, green pulses spat from her fingers and zipped at Frostrune, only to bounce ineffectively against his shields.

"Little girl," Frostrune mocked, "never dare to fight your betters."

The lich's claws blasted a shuddering beam of cold, arcane energy, and Tsarra could feel the air around her freeze. She dived to one side, avoiding the worst of it, but she landed hard on frost-rimed ground and ice-covered puddles. The glass arrow she had nocked and readied shattered when she fell forward. *At least I didn't break the bow,* she thought.

Tsarra jumped up and ran in an arc, from the frozen area and away from Khelben. Luckily, she'd irritated the lich enough that he kept his attention on her.

Khelben! Any chance now *is the time to use that green arrow? Or even to tell me what good it will do?*

No, it's not the time! It can strike more effectively later, not now.

I hope I'm alive and warm enough to use it by then.

Tsarra fired off one quick arrow to dispel Priamon's new defense and followed it up by summoning more white energy. The arrow dispelled his defensive spell, and her bolt of living energy wrung another howl from the lich.

"Bothersome wench! Those lifebolts irritate, but they do not distract." Priamon raised his arms and blasted a beam of cold energy at Khelben, who managed to counterspell it and reflect the energies right back atop of the lich. Surrounded by frozen ground and ice-covered ground shrubs, Priamon turned his back on Tsarra and refocused on Khelben.

Perfect.

Tsarra wasn't sure if the idea came from Khelben or her time within the sharn, but she realized a new way to manipulate her environment. Imagining that short stab of shocking cold upon the first winter's breath, she redirected that shock toward Frostrune. The ice all around him crackled together into a solid lance and speared him squarely in the back. The attack took him by surprise, and though she knew he was immune to the cold of the spell, Tsarra knew he took a solid hit.

Khelben stood on empty air, his cloak slapping wildly in the wind and rain. It too steamed and burned in the acidic rain, but the Blackstaff seemed not to notice. He was lost in his spellcasting.

"Blackstaff, the girl grows tiresome, but you're still my primary threat."

Priamon cast his spell, and Khelben's flying form glowed blue. His cloak stiffened with ice, and his hair froze across his paling face. Khelben groaned as all the heat drained from his body.

Khelben! Tsarra sent when she felt him grow cold and frozen, but he still had life in him.

Now! Fire the green arrow at his feet! Despite the pain from the spell, Khelben seemed to be willing himself to fly out of the lich's range.

Tsarra drew the arrow and fired, shattering the green glass right beneath the lich at his feet. A flash heralded the eagle-head buckle's arrival on the spot. Tsarra was glad it wasn't on the belt as it crackled with blue energy, and two massive bolts of lightning forked off the pyramid, slamming into Frostrune.

Khelben? Are you all right?

Tsarra felt the stabbing cold through their link, and she found herself weeping and angry. She wanted to help her mentor, but she couldn't . . . except by destroying the lich. She ran forward, drawing Maornathil. The scimitar gleamed sapphire blue with an inner light, and Tsarra knew she could end it. She let her temper take her and Frostrune became her sole focus.

Tsarra—no! That's what he wants you to do!

Khelben's warning came too late. Tsarra charged across the frozen moor to engage her foe, and the Frostrune gestured and floated the sparkling belt buckle toward Khelben. Tsarra swung her scimitar to knock it from its path, but it dodged and arced right into Khelben's right palm.

Tsarra wasn't sure what was louder in her ears—the lightning strike, Khelben's scream, the cackle of the lich at her feet, or the blood rushing through her ears. She didn't look at Khelben at all. She stared with unabiding hatred at the loathsome creature on the ground. His right leg had been shattered, so he sat on the ground to cast a spell at her. She knew in a heartbeat it was too complex for her to counterspell, even if she could concentrate. She prayed to Lurue, to Mystra, to any gods watching that she struck before he finished.

Blue energies crackled on the lich's bony fingers, and Tsarra leaped, somersaulting over the lich and dodging his spell, which lanced into the growing dawn. Tsarra landed hard on the heath behind the lich and stabbed backward with her scimitar. The point of the blade crackled through Priamon's left shoulder blade and collarbone, nearly severing his left arm. The blue energies of the blade arced throughout his exposed skeleton, and the lich spasmed in agony. Tsarra smiled grimly, her prey at her mercy.

Tsarra! You're too close!

Khelben's sending snapped her from her rage. She took a step away, but the lich threw himself backward and grabbed her leg. Piercing cold chilled her to the bone, and Tsarra stood paralyzed and at her foe's mercy.

"Accursed girl! Holy scimitars? Spell-laden arrows? Troublesome but not insurmountable, girl. Undeath always wins in the end." The lich's gloat dropped to a whisper as the partially shattered figure clambered up Tsarra's paralyzed form. "Still, you've done me more harm than any have done in a century. As your reward, I think I'll take your body in exchange."

Tsarra watched helplessly as the glow within the lich's eyesockets grew and its jaws parted, wrapping her head and torso in a clammy mist that stank of the grave. A lone tear trailed from her eye, only to freeze upon her cheek.

❀ ❀ ❀ ❀ ❀

"I don't think she's done with that body yet, bastard!" Raegar suddenly appeared behind her and pulled her from Frostrune's embrace. He yelled, *"Iganthris!"* and a fiery shield flared to life between them and the Frostrune.

The lich, off-balance and surprised, stumbled backward and a mighty roar preceded something large and powerful slamming its claws into it.

Priamon "Frostrune" Rakesk flew an impressive distance and landed in a blackened pool. He rolled over to face a black tressym the size of a mountain lion. The lich tried to raise a hand to blast the creature, only to find his limbs held fast. Black sharn-claws pulled on him, and he fought himself free at the cost of his spell.

Raegar whistled to get his attention, and Priamon turned toward the rogue.

"I wanted you to see this coming."

Raegar threw the flaming short sword, and Priamon Rakesk watched with dread as the blade spun end over end before slamming into his ribcage, breaking more bones and setting his robes alight. Raegar laughed hollowly, scooped Tsarra up into his arms, and jumped onto the giant tressym's back. The trio flew away, and the flames flared in Raegar's hand again, returning his sword to him.

Raegar brushed Tsarra's hair from her face. He smiled at her and said, "Two dashing and fearless rescuers at your service. Nameless and I make good rescuers, don't we?"

Nameless looped higher into the sky. Raegar noticed Tsarra was shaking and her eyes were terrified.

She managed to whisper, ". . . too far . . . Khelben. . . ."

Silver flames erupted from Khelben. Nameless tried to dodge them, but the fires were things alive, dancing all around them for a breath before they focused on Tsarra and swirled into the gem on her forehead.

"By the gods above," Khelben's voice croaked from Tsarra's throat. "My allies will be the death of me yet. "

Raegar saw Tsarra's hazel eyes flicker to blue when Khelben spoke, and they returned to hazel as her face grew frantic.

Tsarra asked, "Frostrune?"

Raegar said, "He's about to be Frost-ruined."

He looked up, holding Tsarra's head to see the remains of the Eightower hurtling from the sky. Raegar whooped and Nameless roared as they heard the desperate screams of the lich, who saw his fate coming fast. Three stories of masonry and rock crumbled into rubble atop him. The shock of the impact was felt even dozens of feet up in the air, and Nameless flew them all through the erupting dust cloud to land between the impact site and Malavar's Grasp.

Khelben's voice croaked from Tsarra again, "You had better pray to Oghma that you did not destroy him, Raegar, or you may have killed everyone on the Sword Coast."

CHAPTER THIRTY-THREE

Feast of the Moon, the Year of Lightning Storms (1374 DR)

"Are you crazed?" Raegar yelled as he slid off the back of the tressym. "You want a lich to survive *that?*" Raegar spread his arms to take in the whole scene of the tower rubble, many stones still rolling and settling amid the dust.

"That's because we—don't—" Khelben's voice snapped, but Tsarra's face lost the Blackstaff's stony stare.

Her face and eyes shifted through a number of expressions and colors before settling back to normal, and she said, "Thank you for stopping Frostrune, but we still need the lich's remains and the last remnants of him as well."

"And destruction shall come upon the dawn . . ." Gamalon's voice drifted down as slowly as he did in the storm. Wind and rain whipped his robes about, but the Tethyrian floated down gently, holding on to his staff with one hand and bearing Syndra's rolled-up carpet with his other arm. "He's been extinguished, as he rightfully deserves."

"Stop quoting Alaundo," Khelben's voice snapped from Tsarra, "and tell me where Syndra is, Gamalon." Tsarra's eyes fluctuated in color again between blue and brown as she wrestled for control of her body. Nameless jogged toward her, his growl deep and low in his chest. Surprisingly, the growl remained almost as loud even though his size dwindled back to normal.

Gamalon asked, "What's going on? How did Khelben throw his voice in her?"

"Well, the rest of him's in there, too, it seems . . . and not in agreement with his hostess." Syndra's voice came from the duskwood rod hovering in mid-air. "Saw his body get shattered by that lightning strike and his fires go into her gem there. Guess I'd better finish what he started, eh?"

Syndra's ghostly form appeared atop the rod as she flew upward again. She cast a complicated spell Raegar had never seen before, but the noise level dropped considerably as a pearly globe of force completely encircled the lightning-wrapped pyramid. Within moments, the rain stopped. Breaks in the clouds revealed the full moon in the western sky and dawn reddening the clouds' undersides to the east.

Tsarra growled in tune with Nameless, and she frantically cast a spell that produced the image of Khelben from thin air. Her *kiira* flashed and an identical gem appeared on Khelben's image.

She hissed at him, "Here! Speak for yourself, Blackstaff. And don't *ever* try to possess me again."

Khelben looked himself up and down, finding this illusory form acceptable. *Your carelessness in battle forced us into this situation.*

And your carelessness was what started all this three days ago. Or have you forgotten?

Khelben looked embarrassed for a moment and turned

to comment on Syndra's spell. "Erm. Good, Syndra. Thank you. My spells were disrupted."

For her part, Tsarra huffed in anger and stalked toward the pile of rubble. She muttered a quick incantation and scanned the pile, her eyes covered with a fine gray mist conjured by her spell.

"Fine," she said. "Rakesk or some undead of similar power is still under there."

Khelben slid next to her and said, "That bow I gave you earlier can act as a blackstaff. Say the word *barkalrhael* when he frees himself."

"This is a pre-set spell? And what if he just teleports away?"

"I anchored him here against his will. Spell battles are not times to stop being observant, my dear."

The air between them and Raegar seemed to twist and wring itself until Laeral stepped sideways from the fold in space.

"Husband," she chided, "apologize. Tsarra's done far more for you in three days than other apprentices ever have, myself excluded." Laeral hugged Tsarra then tried to kiss Khelben but found him an illusion. She drew back a moment, but Raegar couldn't see her face or hear her voice.

"Where are Nain and Kyriani?" Khelben barked.

"Apologies and better moods first," Laeral said.

Khelben growled furiously at his wife, who leveled an equally stern look at him. Moments later, Khelben and Tsarra locked eyes and a thin stream of energy spanned the air between the gems on their foreheads.

"Guess we don't get to hear that conversation," Raegar joked.

"Most suffer for overhearing one of my conversations, Raegar Stoneblade," Khelben said. "Consider how fortunate you are to keep your Oghman-blessed wits. Now, stay with Tsarra while the rest of us confer."

Khelben motioned to Gamalon, Syndra, and Laeral, and the quartet moved off a bit, leaving Raegar with Tsarra. All he heard as they walked away was Khelben's growl and

Laeral's reply of, "Well, *I* think it did a world of good. He needed to relax."

Raegar turned toward Tsarra and smiled as he realized his feelings toward her had grown.

Tsarra looked at him then nervously glanced away. "Why are you staring at me like that?"

"Well, you're the most beautiful thing to look at here, so suffer," he teased. "That and apparently five gods have something to do with us constantly falling into each other's arms. At last—a destiny I've no problem embracing."

"You will if you try it without my approval, Stoneblade," Tsarra said. "Still, you do know how to impress with that arrival. Now, what exactly did you people do to my tressym? No growth spells I know can increase a creature by more than three times its size."

"Weirdest thing, that," Raegar said, scratching his head as the pair of them watched Nameless step into a puddle to clean his plumage. "We saw the battle as we descended, and I wanted to help. Syndra cast a spell on Nameless to grow him, and the spell seemed to get away from her. He went solid silver for one instant, and the next thing we knew, he was the size of a cliffcat! By the way, it was *his* idea for me to ride him to your rescue. He can really snap those wings when he wants to make a point." Raegar rubbed one shoulder and grimaced from the aches.

Tsarra knelt by the tressym, and she purred at him. He looked at her, and she yelled, "Khelben, look!"

Everyone turned to the tressym. His eyes were no longer a mismatched blue and green—both were the steel blue of Khelben's eyes. His sable fur was also broken by a silver-white wedge that ornamented his chin.

Tsarra asked her familiar in his own purring speech, *"What happened? Are you all right? Why did this change happen?"* The only response Raegar saw was a wide yawn and stretch by the winged cat.

In her mind, Tsarra heard him respond more clearly than ever before, *Only magic, and it helps. I stronger. Want to go hunt more not-right-cold-prey? You need nap, calm yourself. Ah—food!* Nameless launched himself into the air, arcing across the heath to nab a ground quail, which he tore apart and consumed.

Tsarra shrugged when she turned back to the others. "He's content and feels stronger, but he's either not sharing any details or he doesn't know any. I don't understand. He's never had this kind of reaction before to magic."

Khelben said, "Then again, his mistress has never been quite so tethered to Mystra's raw Weave either. Perhaps the silver fire and my body's destruction carried some effects through our link."

Tsarra heard a yowl at the same time she felt anger from the tressym. His howls were fast and frantic, but she understood his rage—someone teleported in atop his tail. As she and Raegar ran around the rubble, she felt the tressym's satisfaction as he attacked the robes and feet of the offender. She found Nameless, his jaws being pried loose from the ankle of Elminster. The old mage held the hissing, furious tressym by the scruff, seeming more surprised than injured.

"I'm sorry! I'm sorry! Don't hurt him, please, sir!" Tsarra felt embarrassed, but she also felt the outrage coming from Nameless.

"Now, why would I go and do something as silly as that, my dear? Granted, he's insulted me more in the past breath than most do in a tenday, but I *did* tread on his tail. For that, you have my apologies, Nameless." Elminster smiled as he let the tressym go.

"How did you know that?" she asked. "Laeral calls him that, and I've not met anyone who could read another's familiar."

"So little time for questions, my dear." Elminster kissed her hand. "I'm afraid Laeral learned her sense of humor from me. Given your tressym's appearance and temper, I can't think of a more suitable name." As if on cue, the tressym looked up and cocked his head to one side, a pitch-perfect impression of a curious Khelben with the white wedge within black-as-night whiskers. Elminster chuckled, "Don't you think it sad that more don't learn to speak Tressym? Such an expressive language beyond the usual Avian or Feline—in nine hundred years, I've never been called a 'haggard food-carrier who smells like a burnt dungheap' before."

Tsarra opened her mouth to apologize but started laughing instead. "I'm sorry, milord, but I—"

Elminster's smile disarmed her, the mirth in him spread through his eyes and the face behind his wintry bramble of beard. "Fret not, lass, and belay the lordship I never took up. I've heard tell of your past few days. It is you who honor us and Our Lady, and I know we can expect greater things of thee in times yet to come." Elminster bowed deeply from the waist, causing Tsarra to blush.

Khelben's image shimmered between them and he said, "If you're done trying to seduce my apprentice, Graybeard, it's time to begin."

Elminster took Tsarra by the arm, winking at her while addressing her mentor. "Serenity, Khelben. Remember, 'Waken darkness in lightning's strike; Waken Sleepers when dawn breaks night; only then may the Gathering attend the Feast of Five Gods.'" Elminster nudged Tsarra in the ribs and said, "I penned that little something into a poetry chapbook in Myth Drannor. Some fools think it has something to do with Bane." He shrugged and returned his attention to Khelben, who tapped his illusory foot impatiently. "A few stars need to fall into place before our work begins, but we must assemble. Are all in attendance, then?"

"Imagine my astonishment that you're an early arrival for the first time in centuries."

Elminster waved his hand in dismissal. "You never know to enjoy a situation when it comes, son of Arun." The old wizard squeezed Tsarra's arm and whispered, "Remember this if things get rough. Think of the sun-dappled happiness of the woods, child, and that shall carry ye through. I'm off to see how Malchor and the others have fared preparing the lakebed. See you in a trice!" With that, Elminster of

Shadowdale's form popped like a soap bubble.

While Tsarra had more questions, she found her attention snapping to the rubble pile along with Nameless. Rocks tumbled out of the way, and Priamon Rakesk flew from the mound of broken masonry as if it weren't there!

Raegar drew and threw the flaming short sword, but its flame trail missed all but the tatters of his black and green cape and robes.

Luckily, the blur that was Syndra's rod zipped in to intercept the flying lich. The duskwood rod slammed onto the lich's head and shoulder mercilessly. The weapon reared back in the hands of its invisible wielder a third time, eager to lunge as the Frostrune fell back toward the ground, but Khelben yelled, "No, Syndra! Don't disrupt this spell!"

Tsarra yelled *"Barkalrhael!"* while pointing her bow at him, and a dark emerald ribbon of energy launched from it. The energies gelled over the lich's hands and his one remaining foot, the ribbon snaking around his limbs and his mouth. The spheres pulled the lich's arms and legs apart, leaving him spread-eagled and hovering over the rubble.

"Intriguing spell you created, Priamon," Khelben said. "I look forward to studying it more, now that your compatriots saw fit to send it to me as insurance that I would save them the trouble of dealing with you."

Raegar watched the lich struggle, and tiny lightning bolts crackled across Priamon's spasming body whenever he pulled his limbs closer togther. His soulless stare said enough for Khelben.

"Of *course* they knew you betrayed them by setting up backdoor portals into their sanctums. I took your spellbooks, and Sapphiraktar and I agreed to turn a blind eye to each other's activities for a time."

Khelben turned his back on the bound lich, and asked Tsarra, "Could you and Raegar guide him over Malavar's Grasp? Just push him forward. Tsarra, we need to awaken the Sleepers before dawn fully breaks over the Graypeaks, and it's better Priamon is in place for his part in this ritual before the Gathering occurs."

Tsarra and Khelben moved toward the stone plinths, the sky rosy in the east. She grumbled, "This Gathering is all those we've met the past three days? Everyone is here to work some magic?"

"All of them and more. Raegar, move him a little more south so he rests beneath Syndra's sphere of force. Good—right there."

"I'm still furious at you for trying to force me into submission earlier," Tsarra grumbled, "but we're stuck this way for now. It's obvious you're needed more than I am to command this crowd, so. . . ." Tsarra cast a spell, and her form shifted to become Khelben the Blackstaff.

Gamalon and Khelben both said, "Mystra sees and Mystra knows, every trouble found in her work, an oblation on the altar of stars."

"Myaaklyr's Fourth Sermon from Myrjala to the Arathenes, eh? Who's preparing to do something rash and life-threatening?" His voice preceded him as Elminster popped back in. He turned to look up at Frostrune and puffed a cloud of smoke from his pipe. "Honestly, Khelben. The Moor is forbidding enough without ugly decorations."

"Tsarra," Khelben said softly, ignoring Elminster for the moment, "forever and always, we are tied together. Never easily does the Blackstaff incur life debts to anyone, but I owe you much more than one life can repay." With that, Khelben's illusory self stepped forward and merged with Tsarra, his corporeal double. The only clue that he was not the typical Blackstaff was the green *kiira* glinting on his forehead.

"And there it is. 'Ye hearken, the three-souled-one shall lead them and the blasted heath shall impart wonders.' Myrjala's Prophecy fulfilled." Elminster puffed out a smoke replica of Mystra's symbol. "My congratulations, Blackstaff. What your strategies have brought together is a much sounder plan than you had at the Silversgate." Elminster's tone had not changed but his face was grim.

Khelben said, "That's a mistake I'll not repeat. Temper is useful only for scolding oneself, not leading a charge."

Tsarra got a flash of Khelben's memory through the *kiira*, but concentrated and did not lose consciousness. She felt something powerful grasping her right arm and both of her legs, pulling them in opposite directions. Tsarra realized she saw through Khelben's eyes and felt his memories of his success and failure during the Fall of Myth Drannor. He had driven a battalion of creatures from the fabled city and battled them in the mountains east of Silverymoon. While he slew many and was proud to fight back to back with Elminster Aumar, the Nameless Chosen lost track of Colonel Cvor the Whipmaster. When he found his foe again, the mezzoloth had used Alayris's Harness to grow to giant-size and seize him.

Tsarra saw a snow-dappled mountain pass from that dizzying perspective—held aloft by the powerful arms of a giant demon as it tore him or her apart. She gasped and fell to her knees as she felt herself ripped nearly in half, blood and fire exploding from the wound.

CHAPTER THIRTY-FOUR

*Feast of the Moon, the Year of
Lightning Storms (1374 DR)*

Tsarra fought against a scream and channeled the pain into ending the vision. She found herself on her knees in the illusory library Khelben had established earlier. Khelben's image remained there, standing by the fireplace. Once she'd steadied herself, Tsarra stood up and said, *I don't know what felt worse—what Cvor did to you or the despair you were feeling about Myth Drannor's fall. Now I know how you got that massive scar across your chest.*

Forgive me, Tsarra. Some of my memories are too powerful to block entirely. Likewise, some magic, as you've felt already.

Tsarra rose, ignoring a gentlemanly hand from Khelben, but fell back onto a chair as she saw a tapestry depicting Nameless. *Khelben! This possession—will it harm my tressym?*

Hmph. Intriguing. I don't believe so. He can be a part of the ceremony through your links, or he can be an observer. Your choice. In the physical world, Khelben reached down and scratched Nameless behind the ears, eliciting a loud purr.

No. The choice is his alone. I'll not force anything upon him against his nature. That's why I wait for him to tell me what he wishes to be called. He's listened to all of this, and if he wishes to participate, I'll be happy he's with us. If not, I'll be glad he's safe.

Nameless looked up at Khelben's face and narrowed his eyes. *Thinktoomuch, goodfriend. Call me Nameless, if that pleases. Strong name for mystery, and suits me, like smellybeardwhitewizard says. Makes silverlaugher happy too. We all same pride, stand together.*

Khelben said, "He wishes to stay. Would he mind helping Raegar keep watch?"

Elminster said, "Aye. He can't stay with us here. Were they near the first two circles, both would be cinders within moments."

"So, should Nameless and I start walking now?" Raegar jested, though all could see how nervous the last comment made him.

"Nay, lad," Laeral chimed in. "You two will stand with a friend soon. He will keep you safe to observe much of what occurs here on this Feast of the Moon."

So what's to protect me, or at least my body? Tsarra found it odd to be watching the conversation through a massive mirror in the *kiira*-library. Staying more inside the *kiira* allowed Khelben to focus his concentration more.

I am, and those who watch us now from the Grasp. Khelben's sendings still came from the simulacrum that sat with her in the *kiira*-library. *Forgive me, my dear, but I must move our body and give it my full concentration to perform these preparations.*

Khelben walked around the five plinths, finally laying both hands flat against the third stone and intoned, "First Sleeper, awaken to your task. *Ivaakh!*"

A surge of silver permeated the stone beneath his hands. Once the silver reached the ground, black sharnstuff began flowing over the plinth, filling in the handprints last of all.

Khelben approached each plinth in turn, repeated his actions, and intoned the same summoning, altering only the number of the Sleeper. After the fifth time, he turned to a figure stepping from the first plinth. The hooded man looked at his hands, body, then up at Khelben. Both men laughed and embraced each other.

Khelben? Who is this? Tsarra concentrated, hoping she might slip the names from Khelben's memory. Her efforts created a large tome open in her lap. The page showed the man's face, Khelben's script beneath it identifying him as Mentor Wintercloak.

The two men broke their embrace, and as Mentor turned to embrace Elminster with equal strength, Tsarra watched Khelben's reunion with the other four Sleepers: white-haired Orjalun of Silverymoon, the elf wizards Darcassan of Windsong Tower and Shalantha Omberdawn, and the seemingly young human Jhesiyra Kestellharp.

Sweet Mystra's stars, Tsarra muttered to herself, all of them mystics of note who disappeared under mysterious circumstances over the centuries and all assembled here. Has there ever been such a collection of power in one place for one working?

Bells sounded within the plinths, and the ten assembled beings turned toward them. The first two plinths manifested the marks of Corellon Larethian and Sehanine Moonbow. Mystra's eyes appeared next with her seven stars, then the mountain of Dumathoin on the next plinth, and the last showed the rolled scroll of Oghma the Binder. Once all the sigils were in place, three figures stepped from the black-ened plinths as well, each wearing the high priest's regalia of their respective churches.

Tsarra willed the names and faces to remain in her tome, to have a record of the day's events. Pages ruffled forward to continue recording names and faces of the attendants, though few were known to her.

Raegar recognized the all-too-surprised face of Sandrew the Wise, who returned his grin. Twenty-five people soon filled the space within Malavar's Grasp, but aside from brief nods among those familiar with each other, not a word was spoken for long moments.

"Are we too late? Nain and I found more friends for our party," a woman's voice broke the silence, and a hole seemed to draw itself in space.

Kyriani laughed as she stepped through, a floating disk bearing a large chest behind her. As she looked around at the faces of the assembled personages, even the ebullient mistress of Selûne's Smile fell silent. Her right hand trailed behind her to lead Nain Keenwhistler, who held a blackstaff gingerly in his other hand. He stopped and stared agog at that aggregate of the powerful until the people behind him cleared their throats. Two hooded figures exited the open circle in the air, though only the female bore another blackstaff.

Lathander's dawn streaked across the High Moor as the sun finally rose over the Gray Peaks. Khelben cleared his throat and said loudly to all assembled, "Gentles, we have waited centuries for this, and the time is upon us at last. If you would, step outside of Malavar's Grasp so we may start our working."

All but the three Chosen moved beyond the stone plinths, while the new arrival stepped forward with her blackstaff. Raegar and Nameless moved with Sandrew.

Inside the *kiira*, Tsarra saw a sketch appear of a lovely half-elf blonde woman with short-cropped hair before the woman let her hood drop open in the world beyond. Her name flashed on the tome's right-hand page—Alvaerele Tasundrym.

The Silent Chosen? When was the last time four Chosen assembled for any working of the Art? Tsarra wondered.

Khelben's scrawl wrote on the page beneath her image: *When we sealed Hellgate Keep. Today we shall see five.*

Khelben, Laeral, and Alvaerele levitated their blackstaves into place, bridging the gaps between the tops of the plinths and creating archways. Elminster blew a smoky hand, which drew a blackstaff from his cloak and settled it into place. A fifth blackstaff shimmered atop the plinths, turning Malavar's Grasp into five curved archways. In like fashion, a shimmer of silver rain brought three figures into the palm of the Grasp. The silver rain coalesced into Alustriel Silverhand, Ualair the Silent, and a hulking mezzoloth.

Tsarra's tome showed a pleasant gnome's face in front of the mezzoloth's chitinous insectoid head. He was identified as both Rhymallos and Parthar the Valiant.

Spells erupted from the crowd directly toward the mezzoloth, but a flare of energy from the orange gem on Ualair's brow absorbed them all as Khelben yelled, "Stop!"

Arguments and murmurs rose and fell among the crowd, but Khelben continued, "I stand with a tragic hero of Myth Drannor and know that all who stand here today do so with purpose and warrant. Our brethren of the Pentad's faith can certainly attest to that. Now, our final compatriots will arrive momentarily, and the Gathering will commence."

CHAPTER THIRTY-FIVE

*Feast of the Moon, the Year of
Lightning Storms (1374 DR)*

Beams of sunlight streaked out across the moor, reddening the still-thick clouds overhead and gilding the plinths and staves. Curtains of magic shimmered from the staves, and elves, humans, centaurs, and others walked into the building crowd, each face as astonished as the next. Friend greeted friend, and foes locked eyes but held their spells in check. The most hushed receptions came for the devil-cursed Tulrun of the Tent, the white-caped Mistmaster and his consort Azure, the sneering Sememmon and his lady Ashemmi, and the elf woman who transformed into the gold dragon Tlanchass as she exited the gateways. She sniffed loudly with disdain as her gaze fell upon Maaril, and she made a point to fly to the opposite side of the Grasp from him.

Whether previously instructed or simply patient, all attendees held their tongues after initial grumbles and turned to look at Khelben. He stared at the archways, each still producing participants in the great working. Tsarra gasped as the roster of those assembled grew to more than seventy major and minor wielders of the Art from all across the Realms. As expected, many of the elves sequestered themselves together and away from most of the others. What struck Tsarra as strangest was that few gave any pause or attention to the struggling Frostrune, who remained bound and floating above them all, along with the sphere of force binding the lightning pyramid.

Once the golden glow diminished from all the staves and the plinths, Khelben cleared his throat.

"Welcome, one and all. Our time is short, but all will be revealed soon. Many of you know only fragments of why you are here, while others understand our true purpose. Some are here by power of the Art. Others are here by secrets within their blood—powers hidden in your ancestry. Still more attend by their gods' faith in them. Know this—regardless of races or pasts or beliefs, we all do divine Art today. This work spans twelve millennia of plans and sacrifice. Today, we all work together to cleanse this place and these peoples and ready it for the Art they will unveil."

A murmur rose among the crowds, especially among the elves who realized upon what desecrated ground they stood.

"What peoples, Blackstaff? Which of us?" The voice came from a black cat, which morphed into a slim, black-haired woman, much to the surprise of the man who had picked up the small feline earlier.

"Elsura Dauniir and all ye gentles of the Art, meet our hosts, allies, and soon to be restored friends. We stand among *quessir'Miyeritaari*."

Khelben gestured outward, and everyone found the plains around them were dotted with dark figures in the recognizable shapes of dwarves, gnomes, centaurs, and elves. Randomly interspersed among them were the teardrop shapes of the sharn as well. The blackness that clung to the plinths slid off into a black moat completely encircling Malavar's Grasp and leaving the Chosen, Ualair, and Rhymallos separated from the crowd.

The sharn also flowed over the chests Kyriani and Nain bore and dissipated them in a flurry of purple sparks. The morning sun glinted off dozens of golden rings, bracers, and circlets floating on the air. They hovered for a short time before they all drifted down toward the black moat. The items sank beneath the surface quickly until no more gold was visible.

"Each of you will take up one of those items. Those items link you to the working and take you to your appointed task. This working has three central circles and nine smaller circles comprising the fourth perimeter. Some circles span so large a space that you may seem to be alone, but know you are not. Each role is crucial, no matter where you make your contribution. Many have sacrificed much to reach this point. The Gathering will be complete once all are in their places, and our hosts will attend to that."

The assembled sharn dissolved into liquid, forming hundreds of black pools and streams all over the High Moor. One tri-headed creature remained, hovering above the black moat around the Grasp. It reached into itself and pulled out a dagger apparently carved from a single ruby. It cut its own finger and let some blood drops fall to the surface of the moat.

"Very well. Our task is before us. If you would approach and do as it does, blood chooses our roles."

With much formality, the mezzoloth within the Grasp lumbered forward and cracked its own shell open on a claw. A breath after one blood drop hit the black surface, a shimmering bracer floated up to the surface. He picked it up, clamped it into place on his tail, since his forearms were too large, and blinked away to his designated spot.

With similar ceremony, sixty wizards, mages, sorcerers, and notables of the Art stepped toward the black moat and dripped their blood into it. Each time, a golden item bobbed to the surface of the moat and each took up the linking item that would bind them to the working. Most nodded to Khelben as they donned rings, circlets, or bracers, and Tsarra was able to spot more famous faces and names as each joined the working: Malchor Harpell, Phaerl Hawksong, Maskar Wands, Fourth Reader Shaynara Tullastar of Candlekeep, Luvon Greencloak, and a bronze dragon of near venerable years named Essioanawrath the Elder. Tsarra sent a fervent wish of good luck to Raegar and Nameless, as they glittered away with a circlet-clad Sandrew.

By the time the sun cleared the Gray Peaks and tucked its blazing glory beneath the blanket of heavy clouds, all those assembled had shed their blood and taken their places. All, that is, save some of the elves, including those who bore their family's moonblade with them. Tsarra happily noted that Yaereene Ilbaereth had been among the first to take her place in the working, so she was not one who questioned the rightness of it all.

The tallest elf said to Khelben, "It is not your place to command this working, Blackstaff. None of you, even as Mystra's Chosen, should usurp the honor that is the elves' alone. Let that venerable elf help us restore this place to right and we shall be his first two circles." The elf acknowledged Ualair the Silent, but it was obvious he knew him not. "You and your fellow *n'tel'quess* can serve as our bulwarks in the lesser circles. Spare us the insult of having half-breeds, horse-men, and demons within our rituals."

Khelben glared at all the elves.

"Gods, what an arrogant cuss . . ." Laeral muttered.

Alustriel rolled her eyes, Elminster inscrutably puffed on his pipe, and Alvaerele laughed in response.

"You're banishing half-breeds now, Araermal Phyallandar? Care to know how many of your by-blows exceeded your accomplishments, half-breeds or no? They spread far beyond your home in Shilmista."

Araermal glared at the half-elf woman, who only tapped one finger on the massive volume hovering near her.

Ualair walked over to the black moat's edge, nicked his finger with a dagger, and let a blood drop fall into the pool.

The ripples shimmered with many-colored magic, and a bracer bubbled up to the surface. The ancient elf gestured, and the bracer flew up onto his arms. As his form dissolved into purple sparks, one final magic erupted from his *kiira*, and a flaming Espruarn sigil declared, "Shame."

"Apparently, you have failed to sway Myth Drannor's grand mage, Araermal. The mentor of my mentor has taken up the role five gods and the *fhaorn'quessir* would have him shoulder," Khelben said solemnly.

"This is how you dishonor elvenkind, Blackstaff?" Teharissa Ulongyr howled, tears streaming down her face. "For small slights that stung in your youth but tempered you into becoming the archmage you are now? You demand we sacrifice priceless moonblades to this working and you insult us by having us work beneath you? This is high magic, and there is no elf within the center circles. We share history, last Maerdrym, but you do not share the true nature of the elves necessary for this work."

"For all we know," Araermal sneered, "you Chosen have enchanted all these linking items to favor your own agents and gods over ours."

Khelben glowered at Araermal. "Given our history, Araermal, you should choose your words more carefully. Were it not for the specific need of your bloodline, I would not ask you to cast a fishing line."

His eyes turned and locked on the Lady Ulongyr's and his words stung the air. "My dear, I spent five and a half centuries trying my all to be the best elf I could imagine. All I learned was my grandsire's and my House's approval would never be mine. I also learned something crucial about the blood I share with more than a few here. Elves are quite good at planning, thinking, and philosophizing, but they stubbornly resist any change. Humanity, on the other hand, is all about action and transformation. For this, I accepted my mother's heritage over that of my father. While the legacy we awaken here is elf by birth, it should well be apparent that Rhymanthiin will be something far more extraordinary than all of us combined."

The elves blanched or grew red-faced at Khelben's reproof until calmer heads looked skyward. From the clouds came a multitude of fireflies, which swirled around them all but more around Khelben. Murmurs of, "a sign from Oacenth!" and, "Corellon allows a message from Arvandor!" swept through the elves. Even Ualair's sigil dissipated into fireflies as well.

Slowly, with resentment or resignation, the elves approached the moat and repeated Ualair's actions. Each drop of blood elicited a golden ring bobbing to the surface of the pool, and each elf knelt and put on the ring presented. Within moments, only the two objectors remained as they stared at the two circlets floating on the black liquid.

A cleared throat and a light cough drew everyone's attention. "Few are those among us," Elminster intoned, "who remember what Eltargrim's laugh sounded like. Please, think of that as we work and the friendship that laugh held for all. Bitter words and resentment are not the foundation on which to restore what many have forgotten."

With tears streaming down their faces, the two elves donned their circlets and disappeared, teleporting to their rightful places in the great working.

"Carrots and sticks, Blackstaff," Elminster said, chuckling. "I know you loathe carrots, but you wield far too much stick to foster friendships where they are needed."

Khelben said, "Enough jokes and delays. The Gathering is complete. It's time to raise the hope of the Realms by reviving its worst nightmares. We must unleash the Killing Storms."

CHAPTER THIRTY-SIX

*Feast of the Moon, the Year of
Lightning Storms (1374 DR)*

Tsarra paced around the *kiira*-library, and she
jumped when Khelben suddenly appeared by the
fireplace. She followed him to the case that held
the jagged blackstaff with the wolf's head axe at its
top. Khelben placed a flat palm against the glass,
and it popped like a soap bubble. He reached in
and grabbed the rough staff.

Tsarra felt the rush of emotions and a flood of
memories go through him as he performed that
simple action. She braced herself and focused,
not allowing the flow of recollection to drag her
under. What she saw nearly did anyway. She saw
Khelben's sacrifice in Anauroch, the blade point
even closer to her eye in Stornanter, a shattering
door giving way beneath a flurry of troll claws, the
trident of an archdevil stabbing him through her
midsection—and she screamed in pain as she felt,

as he did, the pain of a dozen deaths all at once.

I'm so sorry, Tsarra. Sorry for it all. Sorry for the burden the fates have put on your shoulders. His voice was heavy with nine hundred years of suffering in it. Tsarra wasn't sure what frightened her more—the fleeting memory of so much death, or the smell of death permeating the illusory chamber as Khelben held the one true Blackstaff out for her.

I thought you said this was what made you the Blackstaff.

And so shall it make you, Tsarra Autumfire Chaadren.

Tsarra felt resolve coming from her mentor, but she also felt despair and his resignation to this fate. *You expect to die today? Why are you giving up now, Khelben? Don't you want your children to know you?*

You and Laeral can teach them of me. What we must do today—now—is to preserve as many lives as possible. That only happens with my sacrifice.

She wanted to argue, but her own understanding wouldn't let her do so. Her hand reached out for the blackstaff, but she drew back before touching it.

Let me sacrifice myself to the working. You're too important to too many, she sent.

Khelben reached out and cupped her face, his eyes sad but firm. *No, my dear. You can't, or else I'd have no body in which to do this. Remember this always—the blackstaff is important, but its bearer less so. And it must be me, or else the ritual will claim the lives of my wife and children or other Chosen. The only way this ritual works is by giving up all my silver fire and my life to keep the Killing Storm from destroying those tempering its fury.*

Does Laeral know this is happening? That you'll die today?

She suspects, but I dared not confirm it for her. She would lose the focus she needs to do her part in this ritual.

Tsarra wracked her brain for other options, to argue against Khelben's cold logic. *There are five gods here! Can't they do something?*

Two of them have saved me from death before, so they

act by my returning their gift. No, they attend to watch only. Their involvement stopped at choosing their priests and changing Nameless earlier to save your life.

Is what we're doing truly worth giving up your life, Khelben?

Aye, lass, ten times that cost, but I can't do that without your help. You have a role to play, even in here. Now relieve me of one burden at least. Become the Blackstaff.

Tsarra's hand closed around the rough staff, and the silver metal along the staff crackled with magic. She had a sense of Blackstaff Tower in Waterdeep, the location of every student within it, and more. So many secrets lay open before her from Khelben's memories and the powers tied to that staff. . . .

I never realized . . .

You'll have decades in which to learn more about the powers and responsibilities that have been forced on you today. Truthfully, I expected this burden to fall to Malchor and groomed him thusly. Alas, the fates had other plans. Khelben suddenly seemed older and weaker than before, and he stumbled as he let go of the staff. *After tonight, the* tel'teukiira *are yours to command. Many of them are in attendance here.*

Tsarra felt a tingling, and beneath her cloak she found a dull metal badge of a scroll surrounded by seven stars.

You should make one of those for Raegar as well. There's much promise in that boy, don't you agree?

Indeed. Tsarra mocked Khelben's normally grave tone and favored phrase, but neither had the energy to laugh. Tsarra helped Khelben over to a chair and sat across from him before asking, *Why didn't you stop the Frostrune, if you knew what he set in motion?*

Don't call him that, for the last time. I regret what was lost while we gave him free rein to collect his power. We had to leave the Legacy items in play and allow him access to such levels of magic. The Killing Storm's binding into the High Moor could only be undone by one not seeking to activate it but having the power to do so. The magic necessary is also inherently evil, and none of us could bring the items together and cast what needed to be done. Now that Priamon has primed the area for us—I hate to admit, ingeniously— with that pyramid and the lightning bolts, we can now take the activated magic and transform it.

Why not Sememmon or Ashemmi? Don't tell me they aren't evil enough to have done that!

Truthfully, they are not. Ruthless and self-absorbed, to be certain, but wholly and indisputably evil? Nay, lass. They are destined for more than this gambit with the tel'teukiira. *Besides, with the Legacy as a lure over time, its false leads exposed more than a score of would-be world conquerors who trouble the Realms no longer, including Priamon. You know all this now, Tsarra; it's in the Blackstaff. You also know what you must do in concert with what I do in the physical world.*

But why unleash the Killing Storm? Won't this cause more harm than good?

Magic, like all natural forces, likes synchronicities. One of the many keys to unlocking this great secret was the need for this level of magic, power, and the specific forces found only in the Killing Storm. Until the crusted barrens we call the High Moor are cleansed, the secret remains buried. By cleansing the land, we shall reveal the great secret of the sharn. What has been called Malavar's Hand is the top of the highest tor of Miyeritar's city of high magic, once called Faertelmiir.

Khelben had paused a moment, his eyes closed as he conferred with Tsarra inside the *kiira*. He focused his intentions and concentration to the magic ahead of them. After a breath or three, he exhaled, stretched, and approached Laeral. He kissed her deeply on the lips, placed one hand over her abdomen, and gave her some of his silver fire for her protection. When she started to ask him a question, he put a hand to her mouth and backed away. He bowed before her, arms outstretched. She reached into her robes and pulled the gnarled, tangled blackstaff of Miyeritar from its extradimensional pocket. Blue sparks crackled among the tangle of roots on its apex. Laeral laid the staff across Khelben's palms.

Khelben centered himself at the dead reckoning of the Grasp. Raising the staff as high as he could, he drove it a foot into the rocky heath.

Inside the *kiira*, Tsarra did the same with the blackstaff, thrusting it into the stones of the library, seeing her place in the work.

Silver lightning bolts and flames erupted around the staff's impact, but Khelben maintained his grip on the staff, though the flames claimed robes, clothes, hair, and even the flesh on his hands. The blast shattered the sphere of force above their heads, and lightning bolts quintupled in intensity and number around them. The staff drew the lightning bolts from the pyramid, and the air over the structure thickened even more with clouds and storms.

Inside the *kiira*, the plume of silver-green energy lanced upward from the blackstaff. Tsarra realized that action unleashed most of the silver fires Khelben had previously stored in the tower in Waterdeep. The silver magic danced into the clouds as lightning, but she could feel it subtly changing the storms. The City of Splendors would be spared any harm, though much would be said of the night Blackstaff Tower crackled lightning-white till dawn. A fleeting glimpse outside the tower also showed Tsarra that the magic had rebuilt the Eightower anew.

Tsarra pulled her focus back from the blackstaff and felt all the magic in play on the High Moor. Khelben harnessed the lightning bolts on the High Moor and changed them to pulses of silver fire that flickered to the four Chosen and the five curved menhirs behind them. As the fire drew them into the magical effect, Tsarra could feel their minds and souls within reach, just like Khelben's. She could see the structure of the Working within their minds and hearts.

She and Khelben were the central casters along with

Danthra, making them the three-souled one. Elminster mused about a prophecy of the Three becoming a Reunion of Many. . . . Alvaerele thought about all the sixteen blood-lines of power represented among the workers in the first three circles, blood that stretched as far back as Uvaeren in five of them and to Miyreritar in three people. . . . Alustriel carried Silverymoon foremost in her thoughts and its unity and friendship, focusing her hopes into exceeding that spirit herein. . . . Laeral worried about Khelben most of all and the lightning-wracked Sword Coast. No matter what else, each also had in mind a tiny gem.

Each Chosen reached into extradimensional pockets and withdrew gems pulsing with power in red, orange, black, and brown hues. They let the gems float in the air. A ring of lightning crackled among them, which blasted the blackstaff at the center of the pyre too. That stoked the fires, and the flames engulfed the First Circle and Malavar's Grasp. The flames leaped higher, and the central bolt of power shattered the crystalline pyramid overhead. The five legacy items at the points of the pyramid whirled into the fires. A greasy cloud of flies, dust, and corruption rose to infest the bound and floating corpse of the Frostrune.

With the pyre lit and burning, the five Chosen urged the *selu'kiira* they unleashed to find their bearers. One zoomed over to Khelben's forehead and began orbiting a tight circle over the existing *kiira* already there, both *kiira* pulsing with energy. The three other gems flew no farther than the black moat surrounding the flaming Grasp. A massive three-headed sharn rose, and the three gems affixed themselves to its heads. The sharn erupted, fires consuming its oily black form and producing three separate bodies, each as tall as Elminster. The two women and one man still kept the blackened skin of the sharn, but their forms were those of nude elves who easily joined the five Chosen within the pyre. The trio formed a ring hovering over Khelben and around the core plume of energy pulsing from the blackstaff.

The three elves manifested briefly in Tsarra's *kiira*-

library, and each kissed her, leaving her with their silent sendings:

You have awakened us to our purpose and our pleasure.

Know you always shall have the gratitude of the cor'sel-u'maraar'Miyeritaari.

May your sacrifices be few and your rewards many.

CHAPTER THIRTY-SEVEN

*Feast of the Moon, the Year of
Lightning Storms (1374 DR)*

The Chosen of the First Circle, having found the grand mages for the greater Working, harnessed their wills and sent the energy of the pyre out in a wide pulse to link their minds, wills, and hearts to those of the Second Circle. Those who claimed bracers from the sharn stood in the Second Circle. The bracers added their hands and strength to the working, focusing its energies to their highest purpose. The silver flames crackled across the plains and hit every member of the circle simultaneously. The fires held at that circle for a time, as the wielders intuited what they needed to do.

The Central Caster sparks the flame. The First Circle lights the pyre. The Second Circle uses that flame to restore wwarmth and light.

Once that message was received, the twelve of

the Second Circle blasted the fires into the heath, scoring the ground among them for the city soon-to-rise.

Four hundred strides separated Tlanchass across the circle from Mentor and the others. She wept openly, knowing that she stood for her fallen love as a student of the Seven Wizards of Myth Drannor. She worked the magic in his name, though her long-bound tears flowed freely due to the embrace and condolences of Mentor Wintercloak. She also bristled at working with corrupt and evil people, but Mentor reminded her they all shared a purpose and a need to be there, even if all was not shared with them.

Tlanchass returned to her normal gold dragon form as the fires engulfed the Second Circle. She felt the mind-touch of the eleven other souls within the circle—the dragons Essioanawrath and the Argentalon, Jhesiyra Kestellharp, High Mage Orjalun, Mentor Wintercloak, Darcassan, Shalantha Omberdawn, Syndra Wands, Ualair the Silent, Maskar Wands, and Rhymallos. They all raised their bracer-clad limbs in unison, but Syndra Wands raised both her ghostly arms. Isylmyth's Bracer gleamed on her other arm and the two bracers glimmered in sympathetic magic. Each created a massive stream of magical energy, and all twelve blasted away the soil and rock. The energies penetrated the High Moor and traveled away from the Second Circle in magical manifestations of ground fires, unicorns, giant ants, bulettes, or even small dragons that scored the heath with golden claws and fire.

From their actions, the dirt released its poisons and the magic of the Killing Storms. To some, the fell magic looked like greasy fog, to others virulent plagues of flies, and still others saw nishruu of a slate-gray color. All of this magic they released and directed back toward the center of the working. Tlanchass did as the magic directed her. Her energies and her illusory drakes cultivated health back into the blasted heath she had ever known as the High Moor. She only hoped the strength of her comrades would last, engulfed as they all were in the miasmic fog that killed the people of Miyeritar.

Tsarra marveled at the linking of the minds and perceptions of nineteen souls. She wondered just how much she could handle as three souls in one body. She had already gained much knowledge and power by taking up the mantle of Blackstaff. Still, she ached to fully understand the magic around her. The three grand mages cast another spell of their own above the Chosen—a high magic working within their own ritual. Tsarra tried to focus on what they did, but she went deaf and blind.

A chorus of voices sent to her, *These are Arts you cannot know. Mystra's fires may keep you safe from the* akhelben's *working, but to espy on high magic would destroy you utterly. You shall feel its touch soon, child, which shall be gift enow.*

Tsarra sat back, deflated. Khelben's working still sang all around her, but she prayed she could find a way to stave off what he deemed inevitable. It was then she heard the murmuring in Elvish, "Assemble . . . Assemble . . . Assemble . . ."

She tried to isolate the voice, but it circled the library. Each orbit, its call pulsed through the *kiira:* "Assemble . . . Assemble . . . Assemble . . ."

Tsarra followed the whisper around the room, and she spotted the *selu'kiira* floating about her own brow in the mirror. Within a moment of that realization, another *selu'kiira* arrived in a nimbus of red brilliance, and it too took up both the sending chant and an orbit around Tsarra's own gem. Tsarra stared at the two gems orbiting her own *kiira*, fascinated.

It was nearly highsun, but the sky remained storm-wrapped. Mentor coughed violently, much to his surprise. The bracer and the magic he controlled teased nutrients from the Weave and into the soil around him. The clouds and gray detritus of the life-poisons rose more swiftly, and the gray-green hue of the heath slowly became healthy soil for the first time in twelve thousand years.

Unfortunately, the poisons took their tolls on the casters within it, and Mentor found blood on his sleeve when he wiped his mouth and nose.

So be it, if that is our cost, he thought to himself.

He sensed that the toxins surrounding them weakened some fellow casters. Maskar, Jhesiyra, Orjalun, and Ualair nearly succumbed, faltering and lying prone but still manipulating magic as the masters they were. All had reserves of power that defied age and infirmity, but the work sorely taxed their abilities to fight off death.

Despite that, Mentor marveled at how well the plan had come together, that working he and his six comrades had inherited back in the Incanistaeum. Much had been rumored about the Seven Wizards of Myth Drannor, but their greatest secret had lain unguessed for centuries. Mentor was proud of his former student, the proud non-elf of elf's blood who had made quite a few names for himself since the Wintercloak had called him "Nameless." They had inherited the secret from others, who had carried it before them. The seven had believed they guarded the secrets of Uvaeren. It took Khelben to piece it all together and show even his own teachers that secrets within secrets provide a fertile loam in which much magic and mystery can grow. Unfortunately, the deeper they all dug and tilled the soil, the more virulent the venoms they unleashed into the storms.

Mentor and the eleven others of the Second Circle moved into the second stage of their working. They took their cues from Syndra Wands, who taught them the magic within Isyllmyth's Bracer. They all cast simultaneous spells, and they became pillars of lightning and flame. The twelve pillars struck the clouds overhead, energies crackling in the ominous clouds. More lightning bolts erupted swiftly from the full-fledged Killing Storm, scoring the earth for miles around. Each strike left silvery flames in its wake, and the Second Circle also released its contained fires, allowing the High Moor to become awash in silver brushfires. They sent their glad tidings, best wishes, and magical thoughts with the fires, which merged with the others and built as the ground flames surged slowly across the heath.

Inside the pillars, the twelve sighed in relief as the magic kept them safe from the poisons that threatened their lives. Each soul hoped such cures might be forthcoming for those who might fall into the Killing Storm's path before they could tame it.

Ualair lived up to his name, keeping even his mind partially silent from the link among the Second Circle. He sensed what most others could not—the building of high magic at the center of the working. He knew the costs that would be asked of them soon, and he prepared to pay them without a second's thought.

CHAPTER THIRTY-EIGHT

*Feast of the Moon, the Year of
Lightning Storms (1374 DR)*

Sandrew the Wise still could hardly believe his eyes
and ears. All around him, the ground steamed and
smoked, unleashing belches of olive-green smoke
and ground fog. At various times, lightning bolts
scored the ground and set it alight, though there
was little heat from the flames.

Sandrew had been praying for understanding of
the previous day's encounters with Khelben when
light filled his private chapel. Oghma's glowing
scroll appeared before him, its fore-edge shaped like
a stairwell. Without hesitation, Sandrew answered
the call of the Lorebinder and stepped boldly onto
the scroll. Within him, Oghma left a simple message: *You are called. Be my hands to mold old magic
and lore into a new future.*

Sandrew continued his ascent and found himself
joined on the stairs by Shaynara Tullaster of

Candlekeep and Loremaster Cadathlyn of the House of Many Tomes, two other high-ranking priests among the Binder's faithful. Once all three greeted each other, they reached the end of their journey.

Sandrew the Wise stepped onto the High Moor from the curving menhirs of Malavar's Grasp. Foremost among the people before him were the Blackstaff—restored and whole, though oddly wearing the green gem he had given his apprentice—and Raegar Stoneblade. Soon after, Sandrew accepted a golden circlet and donned it, fervently wishing his friend could accompany him. When he arrived atop a small rise, he looked around to find Raegar and the black tressym—which resembled Khelben, strangely—clambering or flying up the hill toward him.

"Good to have you near, Raegar," Sandrew called. "Oghma wishes witnesses to this historic event."

As he spoke, a lightning bolt struck the ground very near the three of them. An explosion of choking, poisonous smoke engulfed Raegar and the tressym, knocking them down. Sandrew slid down the gravel embankment and pulled them away from a vent of noxious gas. Neither seemed to be breathing and both had a sickly olive pallor to them, their eyes a blackish-green.

"Lorebinder, allow these beings to learn more yet. Do not close their books. Erase their names from the scrolls of the dying." Sandrew prayed earnestly, pouring healing energies into both of them at once.

Their eyes returned to normal, as did their skin, and both revived, only to spend their waking moments vomiting black and green bile from their lungs and throats. Nameless thanked Sandrew by rubbing his head into his palm, while Raegar clapped his hands on the priest's shoulders in thanks.

"I don't know if I'm worthy of this much of the Binder's attentions and energies within one tenday, sir." Raegar demurred, but Sandrew dismissed that notion by responding, "You may yet find your service increasing in the church, young Stoneblade."

The trio climbed back atop the hillock, only to find the landscape around them filling with the horrid stench and deadly gases. All around, poisons cloaked the High Moor as the Killing Storms rose from slumber.

"I thought we had it bad, but it looks worse at the center there." Raegar pointed at Malavar's Grasp, over a mile away and only visible as a tall pillar of flame and lightning brighter than the other flames and lightning bolts around it.

The Second Circle had just become twelve pillars of lightning, and their storm ignited the ground scrub near them. They saw the gold flames of the Second Circle engulf the areas and grow outward, like a wildfire across the hills.

"I hope Tsarra's all right in there," Raegar muttered.

Nameless trilled in agreement, with just enough doubt to make the rogue worry.

Sandrew said, "His hand is in this, as well as other gods, and we may have some amendments to the Coda soon, Lorebinder willing."

Nameless swooped near one of the small silver ground fires and landed. He sniffed at them, purred curiously then leaped into the flames. Raegar and Sandrew leaped forward too late to stop him, and he barreled into them, his fur wreathed in fire. Despite Raegar's efforts to keep him at bay, the tressym batted both men with his wings. He tagged Raegar's head and the small of his back, leaving small silver flames burning on the man. As Nameless batted at Sandrew's robes as well, the flames coalesced into an aura of light flames around Raegar and eventually Sandrew. The priest gasped as the fire partly brought him into the links among the central circles.

"It's all right, Raegar. The golden fires unleash the poisons, while the silver fires protect us from them. The toxins are drawn to the center." Sandrew spoke aloud, as he doubted Raegar could hear the magical voices without his circlet. "They make of the lich a forbidden binding—a repository for all things foul, vile, and corrupted." Sandrew marveled at the ideas and thoughts in his head, shared from those already in the working. "Just as we might have once bound a corrupt man in with his own lies or books of evil intent and set it afire . . . The Frostrune will be forced to take on the blight that was the Killing Storm and the venoms it left behind."

"Fascinating, but what am I supposed to do?" Raegar asked, while Nameless enjoyed setting small bushes aflame and fanning the flames yet higher with his wings. "Or him, for that matter?"

"I think your role here is to bear witness," Sandrew replied. "It's too early for me to say. When the full flames reach us, I should know more. The circlet lets me communicate with the score and three others of the Third Circle. They know through us of the healing silver fires."

It took just under two bells' time by Raegar's guess before the flames had reached Sandrew and his fellows of the Third Circle. As the flames roared over and past them, the circlets they all bore linked them mind to mind and shared with them the visions and intents of the core Circles.

The Central Caster sparks the flame. The First Circle lights the pyre. The Second Circle uses that flame to restore warmth and light. The Third Circle uses the flame to awaken understanding.

Sandrew found himself more fully linked in mind with others, sensing they stood in a vast circle around Malavar's Grasp. All steeled themselves to be worthy of the work and the Art, and all of them heard the words when they rang in their ears.

Your knowledge educates the restored. What you know shall help all within the risen land discover a world they long left behind. Share with us your wisdom, and learn ye will so much more in the process. Children we all are before the Weave, but share with the Weave and we shall be siblings all.

For unknown hours every member of the Third Circle stood, their circlets glowing white with magic.

From the surrounding flames, Raegar got a reassuring feeling that all was working as planned and that the flames were restoring the moor to its original state, pumping life across the High Moor and burning off the venoms long dormant in it. He had never been exposed to so much magic before, but he barely felt a thing. In fact, he realized that the pounding headaches teleporting usually gave him were gone. He even watched as an old scar across his knuckles began to fade.

Nameless settled to the ground. He purred and moved his head as if Tsarra were there stroking his neck. Raegar couldn't understand him, but the tressym certainly sounded happy.

Yaereene stood alone and ill at ease atop a tall spindle of rock. In a deep trench below and around her were a large number of sharn that hewed away at the rock. Miles to the west, she saw the plumes of energy rising into the sky—the central casting.

"So I am to be of the Fourth Circles . . . what shall our tasks be?"

Behind her was the vast Highstar Lake, a sight she'd not seen in over a century. She clutched the gold seal given to her by Khelben as she looked at the golden ring on her finger. She knew this was a ring for an acolyte of Windsong Tower in fabled Myth Drannor. Were the secrets in play once held by that fabled school of magic? Her reverie ended as three others glinted into view around her, forming a circle.

The chalk-pale Nain Keenwhistler she knew, and she nodded at him, raising an eyebrow at the blackstaff he carried. Of course she recognized her cousin Kroloth Ilbaereth, who bore her family's dead moonblade at his right hip, and her adolescent maiden niece Ynshael Ilbaereth, whose talents for magic outstripped her own.

"So this is how it is to be—each family and its sacrifice standing with an agent and a seal of the Blackstaff's making? All this in a minor circle leagues away from the center? I smell deception," Kroloth grumbled.

Nain, his voice never more than a loud whisper, replied,

"You sense it from yourself, young Ilbaereth. Would you trust this if Malchor Harpell stood here rather than me?"

"I would," Kroloth said, "for he is a friend of Neverwinter's elves. He and I have spilt blood together and shared honors. I trust him, yet I know not you. I am here as honor demands and at my cousin's request. You shall pay for that slight, pallid—"

Yaereene interrupted him. "No he shall not, Kroloth. He plays a role just as we do, and he too has reason to mistrust the Blackstaff. Yet there he stands, ready as called. *Tel'quessir* dare do no less." As she spoke, light sparks rose between the seal she carried and the rings on everyone's fingers.

"Place the seal at the center of our stone pedestal here, *osu'nys,*" Ynshael said. "I think I see the pattern that is to come, both from my studies and from the ring . . . and this." She stooped and picked up a rusted and shattered sword, its pommel gone as was much of the blade's point. It too crackled with energy due to the proximity with the rings.

"Are you sure we're not supposed to wait for those fires to reach us?" Nain asked. "Khelben's workings tend to be rather stingy where it comes to bending the rules."

The three elves all said simultaneously, "Magic happens in its own time, and it is never anything but the right time."

They smiled, and Yaereene placed the thick gold seal on the ground. A light shimmer made each of their rings glow and chime, sending shivers down everyone's spines. Ideas lit inside their eyes, and they relaxed into their individual work.

Ynshael and Nain surprised each other by saying, "The staff goes next . . ."

Nain raised the blackstaff and stabbed it down hard upon the gold seal. The staff suffused with light and energy, and magical power lanced upward.

"Now, the blade," he whispered.

Kroloth unhooked the moonblade—still scabbarded—and

looked at his cousins. "For the People." Nain, Yaereene, and Ynshael corrected him, "For *all* people."

For the first time in nearly two thousand years, an Ilbaereth drew the family's moonblade from its scabbard, its dead blade cracked instead of rune-marked. Kroloth swung the sword toward the glowing blackstaff, but energy erupted when his blade hit the surrounding light. The sword and the scabbard were wrenched from his grasp, and both hit the blackstaff from the top, shattering it into four long pieces. Each piece fell as a shower of energy and engulfed each of the four assembled there. The blade seated itself in the scabbard magically, and both buried themselves hilt deep into the center of the stone pillar on which they stood.

Magic corruscated from the entire circle, and Ynshael yelled above the roar of ancient power, "Once I add this to the pillar, we must all grasp hands!"

Ynshael picked up the rusty shard, kissed it once, and tossed it into the conflagration. She grabbed for Nain's and Kroloth's hands as thunder slammed into them all and the powers boomed both above and below. The power among them was contained by their hands, and they all watched as some magic rose from the shards of the blackstaff and focused into a tiny gem. The gem swirled about in the maelstrom of magic then quickly flew off to the west, faster than a rage of dragons. The casters knew that gem had something to do with the central casting, but their rings told them to concentrate on the pommel of the blade.

As they focused on the embedded sword, the earth shifted beneath them. They kept their balance, as where they stood was stable and rising. All four knew the legends of Cormanthor and recognized it as a variant ritual to summon a tower beneath them. They were only barely aware that the shift had dislodged the stone walls that made their location a peninsula. The waters of the lake were no longer held back, and it began flooding the trenches carved around the pillar where the quartet stood.

Nain smiled as Highstar Lake swelled into a new lakebed. Earlier, he had asked Malchor what work Khelben had him doing with Sememmon and Ashemmi, and the elder wizard grumbled, "I've had to build a lake bed without letting a lake into it. Hard enough working with that former Zhent, no matter what Khelben says, but harder still as he and his mistress challenge each other with creative uses for earthquake spells . . ."

Nain saw their work at hand as his vantage point rose. He guessed that by the time they were done with the tor and the waters setteled, Highstar Lake would be at least a mile wider and longer, a tower in its midst left inaccessible by land.

The magic merged with the casters as the tor grew. They drew apart as the tower grew wider, but stony duplicates of their own forms linked hands with them as the width of their circle grew. By the time they stopped rising, twenty figures linked hands atop the tor. The merlons and crenelations looked like five duplicates of each caster forming the upper battlements here.

Kroloth had a personal vision. He knew that his destiny would be to command this outpost that rose with them. In his mind, he saw the moonblade purified into a crystalline broadsword. He knew it and its eight brethren sacrificed at the other eight Sentinel Tor sites would be called hopeblades. Kroloth beamed—it was his duty to wield the hopeblade of Tor Arsuor as its commander.

Ynshael had never before left the safety of Neverwinter Woods. She responded to Yaereene's call when it intertwined with a vision from the Moonbow herself. She gasped as she realized the mate for whom she had prayed to Sehanine stood near. He was a human and had shining dark hair long past his shoulders, and hair on his face and chest. His build was elfin—whip-strong and wiry, but not as muscular as some humans. Ynshael realized that she had seen his eyes—a pale green like the snow lettuce growing in her garden—and she found those same eyes in Nain Keenwhistler.

Stranger still, Ynshael saw what Nain didn't seem to notice—his restoration. His hair grew within the fiery magic, darkening to a chestnut brown and becoming more lustrous. Nain's scraggly beard thickened and lengthened down to his chest, and all that darkened as well. The only white hair he kept were twin stripes of white along his temples and in his beard where sideburns would be in a clean-shaven man. Ynshael smiled and gripped his hand harder. Her patron goddess had shown her a path, and while she never expected to live beyond Neverwinter's boughs, she believed her home to be with that man. The both of them, often underestimated by themselves and others, would come together to fulfill destinies they dared never dream of before.

CHAPTER THIRTY-NINE

*Feast of the Moon, the Year of
Lightning Storms (1374 DR)*

Tsarra heard four whispers whirling about her library, each chanting, *"Assemble . . ."*

Ghostly elves entered her sanctum and summoned thrones for themselves around her. They studied her mutely, some with open disdain. The sendings grew one by one, and so did those assembled before her. She tried to talk with the elves, but she only ever got a one word sending: *Patience.* Tsarra hated the mystery, and grew frustrated when even her tome would not or could not identify the figures invading her sanctum.

She examined the library and found that every book in Khelben's true collection had a simulacrum there as well. She looked for books discussing high magic, in hopes of understanding those rituals, both the one with Khelben at the center and the second one under the direction of the grand mages of Miyeritar. Khelben's working was incredibly powerful, but it wasn't high magic. It cleansed and prepared the High Moor for the return of its people, destroyed that last taints of the Killing Storms, and raised the city's defensive towers as they were twelve thousand years ago.

After hours of the droning chant, Tsarra jumped as the elves suddenly stopped. Magic crackled around the sanctum. Nine additional thrones rose swiftly, and within a few moments, elves appeared in them. All smiled broadly. Tsarra felt suddenly powerful, and she approached the mirror. Thirteen gems swirled and circled around Tsarra's head, leaving trails of arcane fire behind themselves and lighting up her own *kiira* and tattoos. The fires and the gem's pulses suggested the hints of a crown around her head, and Tsarra recognized it—and the degree of power in the working.

At the same time, all thirteen elves stood as one. The first to arrive drew Tsarra into the center of both circles and embraced her. He gestured, snapped his fingers, and Khelben's image joined them in the library as well. He too was embraced. The thirteen bowed their heads and their collective sending went out with a pulse of power: *The Highfire Crown is worn once more, and we bless the Weave and the People as one!*

A sending rang through the head of everyone bearing a golden item for the Gathering. Later, people would remark that the voice sounded like a mixture of Tsarra, Khelben, Danthra the Dreamer, and sixteen other elves of various tones and timbres.

Hearken ye, and hear the People's thanks. Nine tors rise without, our guards and our sentinels. Our home rises within, our symbol and our hope. All your actions and sacrifices shall be rewarded. Remain united yet retain your differences. Be brethren in intent, if not in blood. Honor knowledge and ability without judgement. These are the hallmarks of Oacenth's Vow, of the Promise of Cormanthor, of every hope for unity from Silverymoon to this place.

The Central Caster sparked the flame. The First Circle lit the pyre. The Second Circle restored warmth and light. The Third Circle awakened understanding. The Fourth Circles raised awareness and vigilance. Your work is done. The land is risen and restored.

All Circles now join in fire and friendship. All Circles shall see Miyeritaar restored in Rhymanthiin, the Hidden City. The city and its denizens, its secrets-keepers, its loyalists, and ye, its saviors all—ye shall be restored to health and happiness, if that be your wish. Now begins the Rejuvenation.

Tsarra found herself seeing and feeling a flurry of images and sensations as ninety-five souls felt the play of magic that used the links of the first ritual intertwined into another more primal, more powerful ritual. She felt the magical connection she and Khelben had with the sharn, and she realized it was the trio of grand mages at work. She readied herself to add her spirit to theirs, but the elves surrounding her in the sanctum shook their heads.

Watch and learn. Your strength is needed next.

She realized the thirteen were the high mages of Myth Drannor manifested as the Highfire Crown. She and Khelben both turned to the mirror to watch the other participants who gave their spirit and magic to the ritual.

Gamalon felt a tingling in his left eyesocket but bowed his head and sent a prayer to Mystra, "Let me honor Mynda's sacrifice by bearing that scar."

When he opened his eyes, he realized his Lady had answered his prayer with a new gift. His left eye showed him a green world awash in magic, just as he had seen with his magical gem-eye for more than forty winters.

Rhmallos cried tears of joy as the chitinous armor fell around him in pieces, and he stood a gnome once more. To feel soft loam and grass beneath his bare feet and the rush of breeze and magic across his skin was a blessing after seven hundred years as a demon. His role to infiltrate the armies fighting Myth Drannor was long over, and he danced gleefully to have a life again in a place of new hope as Cormanthor was in its day.

Numerous cries of joy echoed through the links as those who had long lived under curses or enchantments found their burdens gone. Tulrun laughed his deep, booming laugh at his restored youth and humanity. Ashemmi wept as the foul contortions Manshoon had once placed on her soul were shattered, and she found her love unchanged for Sememmon, knowing he struggled toward the light of his own will. Many chose to drink in youth and vigor from the ritual, the energy freely given by the grand mages.

Hundreds of sharn sloughed off their shimmering black skins, and many Faertelmin stepped from the darkness to reclaim lives as elves, humans, dwarves, centaurs, and others. Their skins slid across the smoldering plains, slithering toward the central pyre or a closer sentinel tower.

All the beings caught up in the eldritch flames heard a new sending as they marveled at the magic at play: *Know there are yet sharn in the Realms. There are those of Miyeritar who would become dhaerow with the Corellon's Descent, should they become n'fhaorn'quessir. They choose to remain as Rhymanthiin's defenders as well as defenders against corrupt magic across the Realms.*

Tsarra and others wept for their sacrifice.

His imprisoned form hovering near yet conspicuously untouched by the flames, Frostrune struggled, but not even his hatred could break the bonds his own magecraft built. How could the Rune have betrayed him so, sharing his greatest spell with his worst enemy? How did they dare defy his obvious superiority?

Frostrune's self-absorption kept him from noticing the buzzing flies and hazy brown air that rose from the High Moor toward him. The ochre- and olive-drab rain and poisons also rose on the winds whipped up by the Second and Third Circles. It wasn't until the poisonous matter was heavy enough to fill out the lich's form for the first time in more than a hundred years that he realized what was happening. The magic pulled the poisons and infestations and killing magic from the soil, the sharn, the plants, and the air. Worse yet, they imprisoned those poisons in his own form, and they proved virulent enough to eat away further at his form and the energies that bound his soul to it.

As the sun crawled toward dusk, all that remained of Priamon "Frostrune" Rakesk was a partial skull without a jawbone and a few spinal bones. The Killing Storm had rotted his form and also undid much of the necromantic magic that kept him active. Still, while he had feared he would be destroyed, he knew his phylactery was safe. He had contingencies in place, and he would have laughed if he could speak. He had but to wait patiently, a skill natural to liches.

When the swarming fireflies obscured his sight, Priamon felt a subtle shift. He had been teleported away from his enemies. Priamon found his head being turned around by someone holding it. His eyesockets aligned with darting and twitching eyes set in a wrinkled bald face. Priamon discovered that even the blackest of hearts can be broken by the unexpected.

"Khelben was right," the Mad Mage of Undermountain gloated. "I owe you a grievance, Priamon Rakesk, for pains ye visited upon me five years agone."

In his other hand, Halaster Blackcloak idly toyed with a rod of Shoon trade rings, a collection of seventeen gold coins looped onto a platinum rod—Priamon's phylactery.

Screams echo unceasingly in the halls of Undermountain. The same can be said within the minds of those without hope.

CHAPTER FORTY

*Feast of the Moon, the Year of
Lightning Storms (1374 DR)*

Tsarra heard the sending meant only for Khelben's
ears, which by necessity were hers at present:
*Khelben, hear me. I've known since yesterday, dar-
ling. Khelben, you never say good-bye when you
die. Khelben, let the fires heal your body again.
Khelben, do not leave me, leave your children.
Khelben! Not so soon. Not now . . . not now. . . .*

It shocked Tsarra to hear Laeral beg, and the
despair in her sending tore at Tsarra's heart. It
shocked her even more to see Khelben. He was
just as distraught, but he did not respond at all.
He slumped forward in his chair, his face hidden,
his body wracked with sobs. Tsarra understood,
but it tore at her, the two archmages whose love
outshone their power, and both trapped by fates
beyond them. She reached toward Khelben,
hoping to comfort him . . . and Ualair's image

appeared in her way within the *kiira*-library.

Ualair embraced Khelben, and the two images merged together. Ualair turned, and Tsarra saw he had traits of both wizards in his face and form. *Tsarra, Khelben is in both of us now, as he must be for this final ritual. We shall ensure you survive this, even though Khelben and I cannot. It is the toll exacted to restore the City of Hope to the Realms.*

Can't I be the sacrifice in his place?

No. This world needs its Blackstaff for reasons you shall learn in time. For now, that Blackstaff is you. Now come, and be the first half-elf ever to be a central caster in a High Magic Ritual of Myriad.

Ualair leaned forward, and rested his hands on Tsarra's shoulders. She did the same, and when they brought their *kiira* together, a flash of blinding magic escaped and flashed from the pyre. The pyre wove itself in a pattern of fire, creating the massive Highfire Crown among the stories-tall flames.

❧ ❧ ❧ ❧ ❧

Out on the High Moor, wizards, sorcerers, and priests stopped as the golden objects they wore began trembling and glowing brightly. Through them, they heard a strange voice—an amalgam of voices speaking as one.

The trinkets you wear are now sacrifices to bind the powers at work here, to restore a world's faith in brotherhood. The akhelben *and many others made these sacrifices so that ye might aid a high magic without the cost of all your lives. Now, with these oblations, surrender yourselves into the high magic and help us build hope anew. The restored* fhaorn'quessir *ask our aid with their city. Lend them and us your thoughts and hopes and magic to help build a city that shall not fall to treachery again.*

One reward for every soul is the knowledge that this city exists at all. For now, you shall be the only souls on this plane who can find your way here to the City of Hope. This city shall be a dream of unity to draw people together. Those who truly embrace the brotherhood in Oacenth's Vow may be brought here or may find their own ways. The city shall accept only those worthy of her, and those with malice in their hearts shall not find their way here. For your courage and your aid, homes are being built here for every participant throughout the city, where you may better get to know our brethren in years to come. Now attend us with your hopes and dreams and magic.

As the sending ended, every golden item borne by those of the Second, Third, and Fourth Circles dissolved into golden fireflies and buzzed around their former wielders. Magic filled every breath, every step, every moment of the waning day into the night. The Highfire Crown animated the pyre and above it, the once-sharn grand mages concluded their ritual. The grand mages of two realms guided the magic and drew on the emotional and magical support of everyone within the working.

Tsarra's body stood immobile, still cloaked in the illusion of Khelben's form, even though his essence resided with Ualair. The ancient grand mage maintained a stream of energy between his *selu'kiira* and Tsarra's *kiira'n'vaelhar*. She could feel the magic, even if she was still blocked from hearing the rituals or truly participating. What she was free to do was to cast about with magical senses everywhere the ritual touched. Tsarra used the enhanced senses of her tressym and the sharn, and they could find no corruption or darker magic that had tainted the land for so many millennia.

Tsarra touched the lingering connections of the first ritual working, and she flitted from one participant's eyes to the next, seeing the effects of the third ritual from all angles. The loam, rock, and scrub wood of the High Moor folded and twisted itself into new forms. Magic permeated everything, and those who had been sharn worked to build their city as a unified vision in the craftsmanship of elf, dwarf, gnome, centaur, and human equally. All of them wielded magic and brought their wills to bear on the landscape.

While much of the building material came from the Moor itself, Tsarra watched some sharn shed their oily black skins as they returned to their original forms, the nude Art-workers weaving their former skins into their new city. Thus, much of the architecture took on a variety of darkened hues, though it lacked any malevolence in its demeanor despite that.

The first to emerge complete and intact were the streets and outer walls, very dwarflike and orderly with clean lines and heavy block constructions. These would last untold generations, and they laid out the city in the shape of a circular wheel. The central court plaza surrounded the Counciltor, atop which the pyre would eternally burn. From that point, nine major trade roads split the city like spokes, each directly aligned with the nine sentinel towers twenty-five miles distant in each direction. Five broad roads provided a circumference for the city just inside the walls and each equidistant from the others down to the smallest of the ring roads that encircled the Court Plaza. The streets and defensive walls kept the black-as-pitch hue of the sharn, and Tsarra knew that any malefactors on those streets would face the three-mawed avengers that could form from any wall or street.

The full moon shone brightly over Rhymanthiin as it grew in the night. More than ninety minds and souls lent their energy to the high magic, while many hundreds more labored directly and under the mystical direction of their own ruling grand mages. Tsarra stared in amazement as buildings of various styles and shapes and sizes grew along the skeleton of the major and minor roadways. She laughed as perfect duplicates of the Eightower, Blackstaff Tower, and the Dragontower rose from the loam in various places throughout the circled city. The magic continued into the night until Highmoon and the end of the Feast of the Moon.

To those attuned to it, the City of Hope was a marvel.

Tsarra reined in her senses as she felt the ritual wane. She returned to her body at the center of the pyre, more than fifty feet above the ground and atop the Counciltor of Rhymanthiin. As she returned, she saw the only participants still attending the high magic ritual—Elminster, Alvaerele, Alustriel, Laeral, and the three grand mages of Rhymanthiin stood in a circle around the silver and green flames. Tsarra willed herself back into her body, and the pain and sorrow hit her all over again. She couldn't feel Khelben's presence in her gem at all. She barely felt the touch of Ualair on her shoulders, as he seemed almost entirely mystic flame, rather than flesh.

The thirteen *selu'kiira* still formed the Highfire Crown on her brow, and she pleaded once more with them before the power left her. *Please, noble ones, is there no way to save him? There's no other way?*

Only if you would sacrifice all you have built. The chorus of voices was cold, impassive, and without emotion.

Khelben's voice snapped Tsarra from her sorrow. *Tsarra, let me go. Ualair and I must close the ritual in the only way possible.*

You once told me death is not a viable solution to a conundrum, damn you! Tsarra yelled at Khelben, but she lacked the will to stay angry. *Do you realize how painful this is for the rest of us?*

Yes. I've seen death from both sides, and it's nothing to fear, only to endure and learn from. What is more painful is a world losing its hope. Let us go. Ualair and I both can feel Arvandor's call, and our work is complete, but you hold us here.

I'm not ready, Khelben! How can I be the Blackstaff? The minute your enemies realize you're—

You shall have my counsel always. If you truly need me, I'll be there in spirit. Everything I could teach you is within you already. The blackstaves and the tower are yours. I have no body, and my soul aches for rest. Please, Tsarra, save your love for the one with whom you'll make your life whole.

Ualair's voice also came into her head. *Child, you feel*

magic rather than think it, and your emotions binds us to you. We have become our final spell, and we must be cast. Be the Blackstaff and do what you must.

Tsarra opened her physical eyes and realized she stood alone among the flames. The *selu'kiira* of the Highfire Crown remained with her, but she knew they remained only to cement the final magic in place. She reached out with her powers and her emotions, unifying her will and her heart to this action. With one word, she cast her mentor's final wish with a whispered, "Indeed."

Tsarra never saw the fountain of silver light erupt from the pyre. She didn't see thirteen gems spiral around the city, trailing fireflies of magic. She certainly didn't see the constellations above winking in agreement and sympathy with the spells permeating Rhymanthiin. All she saw were her own tears and those of Laeral, as she walked from the flames and into her arms.

❖ ❖ ❖ ❖ ❖

The procession wound through the streets of the new city and every soul wished to pay his or her respects. Elminster and Alvaerele stood before the gates, a rose-quartz globe floating between them in mid-air. More than a thousand souls touched it, leaving their memories and thanks to he who was the Blackstaff, Khelben Arunsun. Even while the city was vibrant with new life, it too paid homage to the one whose sacrifice made their lives again possible. Many of the mourners looked around to console his widow, to no avail.

She stood alone, apart from them all, looking down from the balcony of the blackest tower in Rhymanthiin. This solitary spire lacked the green marbling and ivy that scrawled across all other buildings. Its forebidding starkness once suited its builder, and he built it once more before he passed from life. She planned to keep N'Vaerymanth as Khelben would have. Without him there, Blackstaff Tower could never be home, Laeral told herself. The City of Hope would be her home for the near future.

His children should be born here in his other legacy to the Realms. He would like that, indeed.

Well past midnight, Raegar wandered up the Third Ring, gazing in awe at the glistening black and green stonework and carvings that he had watched grow from the High Moor itself. Blue-and-white fireflies floated in the air above him, lighting the streets in a flickering soft glow. Raegar had left Sandrew at the Hightome Tor, Oghma's temple within Rhymanthiin. While he felt a tugging leading him toward a small, inobtrusive building near the temple, he found himself looking intently for Tsarra. Finally, he realized he had a way to find her.

"Nameless, think you can help me find your mistress?"

The tressym took off like a shot, and even with Raegar running behind him, Nameless had to loop back and growl at him for falling behind.

The city was nearly the size of Waterdeep, but what was strange was the relative lack of people. There were people wandering the streets—gnomes and centaurs, dwarves and elves alike, everyone beaming and obviously overjoyed at their restored lives. Some remained nude, while others had found or formed clothes to their liking. Raegar never studied clothing in his historical readings, but he recognized some styles of formal robes on the elves he had only seen on tapestries or in carvings. Many waved to him, a few stopped and kissed him, wishing him to linger a while. He thanked them and moved on, Nameless leading him into a street off the Second Ring.

Raegar was almost relieved that the street seemed empty, and he stopped to take a closer look at an archway of two rearing centaurs, their hooves meeting at the keystone. Or where a keystone would be, if it weren't a solid piece of stonework. What amazed him more was the lack of a single chiselmark on the stone carvings. He hadn't even noticed that Nameless had left his side until he heard a happy purr come from him in the distance. Raegar turned and raced after him.

"Where are you, you thrice-damned cat?" Raegar growled after him, and Nameless trilled at him from atop a low archway carved to resemble a rearing centaur.

Raegar was fairly certain he was being mocked, but he didn't care. The courtyard into which he walked held a broad and apparently deep pool, a small fountain set into one end coming from the horns of nude male and female sea elves. A balcony encircled the courtyard, and golden lights lit a broad chamber at the far end of it. The lights silhouetted Tsarra, but even in the darkness, Raegar couldn't believe how beautiful she looked.

Tsarra called down to him, "I've yet to thank you for saving my life, Raegar. I've been waiting for you to find me. Some spy you are."

Raegar feined being wounded, and Tsarra gave him a wink. "Welcome to my home. Come up, after you've cleaned up first."

Raegar dived into the pool, happy to rinse off the grime from the High Moor. He resurfaced and stripped off his shirt.

"I'm glad to see you finally apart from Khelben," he said. "I was wondering if I'd ever get you away from the Blackstaff."

He didn't hear her whisper, "No, you won't."

Raegar clambered out, leaving his sodden shirt and boots alongside the pool. Then he climbed the stairs two at a time.

"Aren't you tired, after all the chaos of the past three days?"

He couldn't read the look on her face, but he suddenly felt very unsure how to approach her. She solved that problem by rushing forward and kissing him fiercely.

"Life's too short. Tomorrow, we'll see your chambers and explore the city. I'll fill you in on other things. Tonight, I just want to feel alive," Tsarra said, leading him inside by the hand.

"Indeed," he said with a grin.

THE YEAR OF ROGUE DRAGONS

By Richard Lee Byers

Dragons across Faerûn begin to slip into madness,
bringing all of the world to the edge of cataclysm.
The Year of Rogue Dragons has come.

THE RAGE

Renegade dragon hunter Dorn has devoted his entire life to killing
dragons. As every dragon across Faerûn begins to slip into madness,
civilization's only hope may lie in the last alliance Dorn and his
fellow hunters would ever accept.

THE RITE

Rampaging dragons appear in more places every day. But all the
dragons have to do to avoid the madness is trade their
immortal souls for an eternity of undeath.

THE RUIN

The increasingly desperate struggle for survival leads to a
starling conclusion on the frozen ice fields of the Great Glacier.

For more information visit **www.wizards.com**

THE WATERCOURSE TRILOGY

THE NEW YORK TIMES *BEST-SELLING AUTHOR*
PHILIP ATHANS

A MAN CONSUMED BY OBSESSION...
DRIVEN BY AN OVERWHELMING VISION OF
WHAT MIGHT BE.

THE WIZARD
Pledged to the Red Wizards of Thay from boyhood, he will do anything
for anyone who can give him more power.

THE SENATOR
A genasi, he has fought his way up from the gutter and will never go back.

THE MAN
A master builder, he walks the coast of Faerûn, and the waves whisper to
him of a mighty work, a task worthy of his talents.

WHISPER OF WAVES
November 2005

LIES OF LIGHT
September 2006

SCREAM OF STONE
June 2007

For more information visit **www.wizards.com**